THE TRUTH OF VALOUR

THE TRUTH OF VALOUR

A CONFEDERATION NOVEL

TITAN BOOKS

The Truth of Valour
Print edition ISBN: 9781781169742
E-book edition ISBN: 9781781169759

Published by Titan Books
A division of Titan Publishing Group Ltd
144 Southwark Street, London SE1 0UP

First edition: June 2014
1 3 5 7 9 10 8 6 4 2

A CIP catalogue record for this title is available from the British Library.

Printed and bound in Great Britain by CPI Group Ltd.

DID YOU ENJOY THIS BOOK?
reade   hear from our readers. Please email us a   dback
                       or write to us at Reader   address.

To receiv   , and exc   sive offers
      on   on our we   bsite.

                       www.th   un

ONE

Emerging back into sunlight after 5K of trails through old growth forest, Torin eyed the forty-five degree incline up to the top of the bluff and knew she'd been spending too much time in space and too little time paying attention to her training. In spite of having been dirtside for the last tenday, she could feel the effect of the run in both legs and lungs.

There was a time, back before she joined the Corps, when she'd end her 20K run with a six-meter dive into the lake and swim a good fifteen, twenty meters underwater before having to surface to breathe. Diving straight into the lake today would be stupid bordering on suicidal. The gravity here on Paradise, Torin's birth world, was 1.14 oldEarth norm while ships and stations both maintained artificial systems at .98—a small difference but telling after a few years.

Although, Torin admitted, throwing everything she had left into the last 100 meters, *it could be the mileage.* The distance between nineteen and thirty-six was one hell of a lot farther than the distance between Paradise and the OutSector station where Sh'quo Company had been based.

The top of the bluff hadn't changed; a silver-gray cap of limestone curved out over Lake Serella, worn smooth by wind and rain. Her older brother, Mohan, and his friends used to hunt for fossils in these rocks; spiral-shelled creatures from an ancient sea trapped in time. She wondered if he ever brought his kids out here and tried to teach them the names the Human colonists had given some of the oldest of Paradise's original inhabitants.

The narrow fissure that ran across the rock at the two-thirds point marked the exact end of the 20K. Torin crossed it and stumbled less than gracefully to a stop, the stiffer soles on her trail shoes sliding a little on the rock's smooth surface. Regaining her balance, she walked over to the edge and stared out at the view while she caught her breath.

The lake gleamed more green than blue in the sunlight, a little chop whipped up by the morning breeze. It looked cold and, being spring fed, probably was. Only the hottest of summers made any noticeable difference in the lake's temperature, and if this past summer had been unusually warm, no one had mentioned it to her. A small flock of Barnard's ducks paddled about in one of the quiet coves and a pair of blue-footed hawks swooped around each other overhead. Strictly speaking, they were neither ducks nor hawks, but the colonists had reused the names they'd brought from home. That familiarity hadn't been quite so necessary on planets settled later, Torin knew, but Paradise had been the first, gifted to oldEarth after they'd not only agreed to join but to protect the Confederation.

"Come on out," the Elder Races had said. *"We'll give you advanced technology and brand-new planets to live on. We just need you to do one small thing for us. It seems we're in the middle of this war we can't solve diplomatically and, well, funny thing, we don't actually fight, so we need you to do it for us."*

"Seems like a fair trade," Humans had replied. Later, the Taykan and the Krai had said the same.

Essentially.

Maybe it had been a fair trade. With no idea of what life had been like on oldEarth so many years ago, Torin couldn't judge. She'd been a career Marine and a damned good one until she'd discovered that the entire war had been a social experiment by sentient, polynumerous molecular polyhydroxide alcoholydes, so it was definitely 20/20 hindsight that made her think her ancestors should have locked the doors and told the Confederation to go fuk themselves.

Better than being screwed over by hyper-intelligent shape-shifting plastic.

From the top of the bluff, Torin could see past the edge of the forest to where the land flattened out and green changed to the gold of harvested grain. The family's flock of hah-hahs had been turned loose into the field for gleaning although they were too small for her to spot them from here. If she'd had a helmet with her, she'd have been able to pick out individual feathers and, with one of the KC-7 sniper scopes, make an easy kill. Not that she would. No matter how obnoxious the damned birds could be.

Leaning out a little, she could just make out the hill that covered her parents' farmhouse. They'd be finished with morning chores by now, sitting down to breakfast. Her mother would have her slate propped up on her coffee mug, and her father would be slipping bits of bacon to the cats as soon as the early news feed caught enough of her mother's attention.

When she finally heard footsteps approaching on the trail, she sat down, legs dangling above the water. Years of experience at putting Marines through their paces kept her from looking as though she'd ever been concerned. He was walking, not running, but he wasn't breathing as hard as he had when they'd first landed. Craig Ryder might have been born on Canaberra, but he'd lived most of his life in space. Civilian salvage operators had little reason to go dirtside when the bulk of their salvage came from Naval battles between the Confederation and the Others—no, the *Primacy* now; Torin, of all people should remember that—and their markets were all on stations. Paradise hadn't been easy on him.

Her family, on the other hand, had adored him.

But then, he could be a charming son of a bitch when he wanted to. It was one of the first things she'd noticed about him, back when the last thing on her mind had been taking him home to meet her family.

"Ace view." He dropped to sit beside her, nudging her with a sweaty shoulder.

"Strategically important," Torin pointed out. "Controlling the high ground gives us the edge."

"While we sit here jawing, those ducks are probably planning a doomed assault."

She grinned. "If they get into the air, that'll give them the advantage."

"Should I be worried?"

"I can take them."

"Good." Bracing his right arm behind him, Craig twisted around to rub his left thumb along the top of her cheeks. "Your father's right; you're picking up some pink."

She wrapped her fingers around his wrist and tugged his hand down between them. "My father worries too much. Don't you start." Torin had inherited her mother's brown hair and eyes, but her less than generous portion of melanin came directly from her father. Both her brothers had a significantly higher natural tolerance for UV radiation and were obnoxiously smug about it.

A barred loon called from the far end of the lake.

"Easy to see why you love it here," Craig murmured, leaning in and kissing her softly. "And," he added, pulling away, "easy to see why you left. This place is so fukking bucolic, I keep wanting to punch something."

Torin leaned forward and caught his mouth with hers, fingers of her free hand threading through the long, sweaty spikes of his hair. This kiss was messy and carnal and stole away most of the ability to breathe he'd regained after his run. "Oh, thank the fukking gods," she said after a minute, resting her forehead against his. "I was afraid all the damned pie had convinced you to stay longer."

Blue eyes crinkled at the corners when he smiled. "Not a chance. If we shoot out before dawn and break a few speed limits, odds are we can trade in our tickets and catch tomorrow's shuttle up to the station. Sleep on the *Promise* tomorrow night." The smile slipped. "You really are pinking up, Torin."

"Then I guess I need to cool down."

Craig's shoulders and arms were heavily muscled enough to pull his torso out of proportion to his legs, even at 1.9 meters tall, but he didn't have much leverage and Torin had maintained her grip on his wrist.

Also, she believed in doing what was necessary in order to

win, up to and including fighting dirty. She didn't so much throw him off the bluff as take him off with her.

The water was as cold as it looked.

"Net's away, Captain!"

Leaning back in his command chair, Mackenzie Cho, scrapped a thumbnail over his stubble, the soft *shup shup shup* adding to the background noise, and listened to Huirre counting down the distance until contact.

"Twenty kilometers. Fifteen kilometers."

"*Firebreather*'s Susumi engines have come on-line, Captain!" Di'Berinango Dysun half turned from her station, eyes darkened to a burnt orange, hair flipping around her head in a tangerine aurora.

The three di'Taykan on the crew had been running from trouble on their home world before signing on, but given the differences in Human and Taykan aging, they were still little more than kids out looking for thrills. Dysun was a natural in the control room, though—followed orders like she'd been trained to it—and both her *thytrins* had skills he could use.

When Cho jerked a thumb toward Dysun's board, she whirled back around, adding, "They must've seen the net."

"Not your job to speculate," he growled.

"Five kilometers," Huirre announced.

It was possible, Cho allowed, that the civilian salvage operator at the controls of the *Firebreather* had been feeding data into their Susumi equations since leaving the debris field, cargo pen bulging with salvage. It was possible the Susumi engines coming on-line had nothing to do with the approaching net. And if the Susumi drive didn't kick in before the net covered the final three kilometers, it wouldn't matter.

"Two, one... we have contact! Anchor lines have caught the pen, net is spreading."

"Power up the buoys."

Huirre slapped his board. "Aye, aye, Captain!"

"Susumi engines are powering down." This time, Dysun kept her eyes on the data.

Of course the engines were powering down. Only a suicidal

fool would fold into Susumi space when their equations had just been fukked beyond correction. Galaxy-class battle cruisers with a full complement of Susumi engineers had slammed out of Susumi space into unforgiving solid objects because of a missed decimal, so a seat-of-the-pants pilot and a cheap computer had no chance with the random pulsing from the buoys making an accurate equation the next thing to impossible.

Some might say actually impossible.

Cho didn't believe in the impossible. There was always a way. Case in point: in spite of a dishonorable discharge from the Confederation Navy designed to force him into jobs well below his skill level and ambition, he'd still gotten his captain's ticket. Even if he'd had to take it by force.

The days when some idiot with a bit of braid, a fool who'd got his rank from luck rather than skill, could order him around were over. Long over.

"Captain, the *Firebreather* is coming around."

"Interesting." Straightening, he stared up at the large screen he'd had installed to give the illusion of an external view in spite of the bridge having been buried deep in the bowels of the ship for safety. Most CSOs cut their losses at this point, dumped their pens, engaged their default equations, and left the victor the spoils. Against all odds, the *Firebreather* was coming around. "I wonder if they've forgotten what happens to ships that challenge us?" he said thoughtfully.

Huirre snorted. "No one's challenged for a while, have they?"

An excellent point, Cho admitted silently. Memory being what it was, it was past time to remind the salvage operators that resistance was useless. Get them talking again about the *Heart of Stone* and her merciless captain.

"Captain." Dysun's hair had flattened against her head. "I'm picking up a strange energy signal."

"Define strange?"

"Like a…"

The bridge shuddered as the *Heart of Stone* took a hit.

"Like a weapon?" Cho asked quietly.

Her shoulders rose a little at the threat in his voice. "Yes, sir."

Confederation law put all weapons in the hands of the military.

CSOs were supposed to run crying for help while the Navy—buzzing around with their collective heads up their collective asses because the war had turned out to be a big fukking joke—did sweet fuk all about the big, bad pirates. Seemed like this fool hadn't got the memo.

"Huirre."

"Captain?"

"Don't damage the pen."

The Krai grinned. On a species able to not only eat, but digest pretty much any organic matter in known space, the baring of teeth gained an added significance Cho appreciated. Huirre danced the fingers of both hands and the long, prehensile toes of one foot across his board.

An instant later, the bow of the *Firebreather* exploded, creating a miniature starburst of debris.

"Two bodies, Captain."

One of the things Cho liked best about Dysun, about all three di'Taykan, was their lack of concern when people died. People always ended up dying in his business.

"No life signs," she added.

"Damage?"

"Uh…" Confused, Dysun waved at the screen. "The shot probably killed them, but they might have decompressed…"

"He means damage to the *Heart*, you *serley* idiot," Huirre muttered. "We took some outer hull damage by the cargo bay, got one of our sensor arrays completely fukking fried, and I'm betting…" He nodded toward the flashing lights on the comm panel. "…Krisk wants to know what the fuk is going on."

"Take us in alongside the pen," Cho ordered, then opened the channel to engineering, cutting Krisk off in mid rave with a terse, "Shut up. If there's no breach and no chance of a breach, that salvage remains our first concern. Make sure the hatch to the cargo bay hasn't been compromised. I'm on my way down."

The *Heart of Stone* had been designed as a scout ship for the Navy. When Cho'd taken it over, he'd doubled her firepower and added a cargo bay. Fortunately, vacuum didn't care about aerodynamics. In his line of work, he couldn't waste time reworking Susumi equations for every piece of crap they picked up—space was big, sure, but there was always a chance the Navy could accidentally stumble over them while they were sitting around dividing by the cube root of who the fuk cares. Cargo had to fit inside the ship's set parameters.

When he arrived in the extension, delayed a few minutes by a sparking panel near the air lock that joined the old and new, the outer hatch was open and Dysun's *thytrins* were working the grapples, plucking the salvage out of the *Firebreather*'s pen.

"Pen's too big to fit inside," Almon explained before Cho could ask what the hell they were doing. Eyes locked on the screen, he had so many light receptors open very little of the pale yellow remained. "Don't know what this guy found, Captain, but he found one fuk of a lot of it."

The deck plates quivered as something big came under the influence of the artificial gravity on the other side of the inner hatch.

"Sorry, Captain." Nadayki, the youngest of the three di'Taykan, flashed him a nervous smile, lime-green hair jerking back and forth in a nervous arc.

Cho smiled back. Nadayki's trouble with the law had been the reason the three had initially gone on the run. The Taykan were stupid when it came to family loyalties. "You dent my ship and I'll space you."

"He will, too. Space you soon as look at you. Mackenzie Cho's the meanest son of a bitch in this end of the galaxy."

"How many times do I have to tell you to stop calling my mother names?" Cho said quietly as Nat Forester moved up to stand just behind his left shoulder, slate in hand.

"At least once more, Cap. Krisk says he needs condenser parts and Doc says if you pitch another field kitchen, he's going to throw six kinds of fit."

"That kitchen had been slagged."

Nat shrugged. "He says he could have fixed it. And he likes the food."

"The food is crap."

"Not arguing, but Doc likes it and there's always a market for kitchens. You're letting your prejudices cut into profits."

"It's not prejudice. I *know* the food they turn out is crap."

"And I know," his quartermaster grunted, "that these two'd

probably work faster if you weren't peering over their shoulders."

"Sucks to be them."

In spite of the captain's presence, or maybe because of it, the two di'Taykan worked full out for almost two hours, creating a complex three-dimensional jigsaw of captured salvage in order to fit it into the available space. Finally, Almon sighed and said, "Cargo's locked and loaded, Captain."

"Noted." Cho raised his voice slightly; the comm pickups in the extension could be temperamental. "Huirre."

"Captain."

"Turn us toward home." They'd kick on the Susumi drive after he and Nat had the cargo sorted, separated the crap from the cream, and ditched the crap.

"Aye, sir. Home it is." The subtext—*about fukking time*—came through loud and clear, but they'd been roaming for a while, looking for a prize worth the trip, so he let it go.

"Cap and I going to fit in there?" Nat wondered, peering past Almon at his screen.

"No. Too tight." Almon turned just far enough to wink at her, a Human gesture the di'Taykan had wholeheartedly adopted. "Tight's good."

Nat winked back. "Not arguing, kid."

The di'Taykan were known as the most sexually indiscriminating species in known space, but tossing innuendo at Nat Forester put them above and beyond. Cho trusted Nat with his life, but he'd fuk Huirre first. And given that Huirre had been involved with a cartel that provided Human body parts to Krai kitchens, that was saying something.

"That's not so much tight as wall to fukking wall," Nat snorted, transferring her attention from Almon's screen to her own. "Crowded enough we'll have to use the eye for first sort." She called up the controls on her slate one-handed, then ran the hand back through short gray hair. "Eye gives me fukking vertigo. Let's just hope I don't puke."

"Don't," Cho told her, his own slate ready.

"Yes, sir, Cap. Because my stomach always does what you tell it."

It was a good prize, Cho acknowledged as he guided the

remote camera around and through what were clearly parts retrieved from a single destroyed battle cruiser. Looked like they'd scored some of the Marine package, too, he realized as the eye picked out the crest of the Corps on a...

"Holy fukking shit."

"Cap?"

He fed her slate the coordinates without speaking.

"Holy fukking shit," she agreed a moment later. "Now that's worth puking over."

They'd scored a Marine armory. An undamaged Marine Corps armory. A small fortune in weapons if he decided to sell them. A way to change the future if he didn't.

The seals were solid and...

...had been oversealed by one of the dead CSOs.

If he wanted to get the armory open without blowing it and everything around it to hell and gone, he needed another CSO. Alive this time.

"*Promise*, you are cleared at vector twenty-four point seven for two hundred kilometers. Returning computer control in three, two, one."

"Return acknowledged, Paradise Station." Craig ran both hands along the edge of his board, the movement not quite a caress. While he understood why the station controlled all approaches and departures—the unforgiving nature of vacuum made accidents usually fatal and always expensive—it wasn't required that he actually like being forced to sit as a passenger in his own ship. So he didn't. But he sure as hell liked getting his lady back.

"All right, you said you'd tell me when we were in space." His poor old pilot's chair dipped as Torin settled enough weight to make a point across the top. "We're in space. Spill."

Torin hadn't been happy about being kept in the dark, but she hadn't done anything about it either, and Craig knew that represented a huge leap in trust for them. Torin didn't like not knowing things.

"We've seen your family," he told her, leaning back and

looking up. "I figured that now we could lob in and see mine."

She frowned. "Your parents died thirteen years ago, and you haven't seen your cousin Joe for nearly six."

"You fossicked through my records, then."

Torin spun the chair around and straddled his lap. The chair complained again, and Craig told it silently to shut up as he slid his hands up the curve of her hips to settle around her waist. At 1.8 meters with a fighter's muscle, Torin wasn't light, but he knew for a fact the chair could hold them both... while moving a lot more vigorously.

"I checked after I joined you here, on the *Promise*," she said. "Not before."

So her research had no influence on her joining him. He appreciated that she'd decided with her heart and not her head. "You could have asked."

"You never spoke of them and, just in case..." She waved a hand, the gesture taking in the bunk, the half-circle table, the two chairs, and closed hatch to the head. "...we don't have a lot of room for touchy subjects."

"'S truth. But unless we make one hell of a find— working tech say—even adding another three square meters'll cost more than we can afford this year." They'd used a chunk of Torin's final payment from the Corps to put in a new converter. As long as they could find ice—and if they couldn't find ice, he was in the wrong business—they could replenish both water and oxygen significantly faster than two people could use it. That and the upgraded CO_2 scrubbers went a long way toward removing any residual dread of sharing the limited resources of a small ship with another person.

With Torin anyway.

"We were talking about your family." She rocked her hips forward, and his eyes rolled back. Torin had relaxed the moment the air lock telltales had gone red and they were clear of Paradise and *her* family. When she got like this, it was hard to remember she knew twenty-five ways to kill a man with her bare hands. "Where are we going?"

"Salvage station."

She stopped moving. Craig made an inarticulate protest.

"They actually exist?"

"Seventy-two-hour fold and we'll rock up. You can see for yourself."

"And they're safe?"

He laughed at that. The myths about salvage stations usually included the word deathtrap in the description. "For fuksake, Torin, you were a Marine!"

"And contrary to popular opinion, gunnery sergeants can't breathe vacuum."

"Trust me, if there's one thing a salvage operator understands, given how much time we spend suited up, it's not breathing vacuum. Now then," reaching up, he cupped the back of her head and pulled her mouth down to his, "you could keep working on that twenty-sixth way to kill a man. Seems I'm not dead yet."

"It does not look cobbled together," Craig muttered. "It looks…"

Torin waited while Craig frowned out at the station they were approaching, obviously searching for the right response to her initial reaction. Which had been, all things considered, relatively mild.

"All right, fine," he surrendered, "you win. It looks cobbled together. But give it a fair go. People are raising families in there."

"Families?" Torin leaned forward and took another look at the tangled mass of habitats referred to as Salvage Station 24. "In that?" It was hard to pick out details given the glare off the hectares of deployed solar sails, but she was certain she could see one of the H'san's ceramic pods cozied up next to a piece of a decommissioned Navy cruiser, as well as half a dozen Marine packages. Tucked up against it, in no discernible pattern, she could see a dozen ships the *Promise*'s size or a very little larger. Apparently, salvage operators didn't believe in docking arms on their stations.

A direct hit by the enemy would turn ninety percent of this particular station back into the scrap it had started as.

Not at war, she reminded herself. *Not anymore.* Then she added aloud, "Shouldn't you let them know we're on our way in?"

"They know."

Eyes narrowed, Torin studied the board. There'd never been any question that Craig would teach her to both fly and repair the ship—she'd spent most of her previous career working to keep the Marines under her alive and now all that training and experience had been refocused on the *Promise* and her captain—but she'd been infantry and that meant starting essentially from scratch.

"Give me a large group of heavily armed people and I'll make it do whatever you want, but this…" Blowing out a deep breath, she'd shaken her head as she tried to make sense of the display. *"I'm neither a pilot nor an engineer."*

"You'll dux it out. This is easier than dealing with a large group of people."

"Maybe for you."

Definitely for him. Torin sectioned the board but still couldn't find a data stream that suggested the *Promise* was in communication with the station. "I don't see it," she admitted at last.

"They pinged us 100 kliks out and got the codes."

She stopped staring at the board and turned to stare at him. "That's it?"

"That's it."

"And docking?"

"I'll bring her in alongside a free nipple and we'll grapple in. Use the universal hookup if there's no match."

"Well, that's very…" Torin considered and discarded a few words. "…independent."

Craig grinned at her. "You're swearing inside, aren't you?"

"Not at all. Watch where you're going." She sat back and rested her hands on her thighs, watching so that her fingers didn't curl into fists. "I spent my entire career being carted around by the Navy, depending on their engineers to do the math right. This is just a difference in scale."

Craig's brows rose as he micro-fired a forward thruster.

"A big difference," Torin admitted.

They rose a bit higher.

"Fine. I'm swearing a little. There's a reason docking computers are the default."

"No worries, I can do anything my computer can. Although

in some cases it may take me a little longer," he added quickly as Torin opened her mouth.

As she hadn't decided if she appreciated or was appalled by the sentiment, Torin let that stand. "So who's in charge here?"

The corner of his mouth that she could see twitched. "Group consensus as needed."

"So, essentially, no one. Shoot me now." After watching mismatched pieces go by for a while, and watching Craig's brows dip closer to the bridge of his nose, she asked, "What happens if there isn't a free lock?"

"There's always a free lock," he muttered. *Promise* twitched as he gave the upper aft thrusters a bit of juice. "But it looks like we'll have to hook in a little far from where I usually dock."

"And that means? Other than the obvious?"

"We're going to need a native guide once we get inside."

"Craig! *Hombre! Empezabamos a pensar que no quisiste que los de mas te ven con nosotros*, you son of a bitch!"

Torin moved back half a step as a tall man with four-centimeter dreads and three white stars tattooed on his left cheek swept Craig up into a hug that looked painful. She didn't recognize the language—although it sounded Human—and she didn't know their relationship—although since no one had started throwing punches, she assumed they were at least friends. It seemed safest to give herself some maneuvering room.

"Pedro!" Craig locked his arms around the other man and lifted him off his feet. "Too long, mate! Too long!"

"Had to let the bruises fade," Pedro snickered as they released each other at exactly the same time. He leaned out around Craig's shoulders. "And you must be Torin."

She nodded, expression neutral. He'd had to have spent the last year without a comm hookup of any kind not to recognize her face. The vid Presit a Tur durValintrisy had shot of her conversation with the polynumerous, shape-shifting, organic plastic alien hive mind who'd been responsible for a war that had taken millions, if not hundreds of millions of lives, had been played 28/10 on some stations.

Pedro grinned at her. "All that publicity and you couldn't do any better than this asshole?"

Craig dodged the punch aimed at his arm. "Torin Kerr, meet Pedro Buckner. Best mate I ever made."

He wanted them to like each other; she could hear it in his voice. That meant he wasn't bothering to hide it since he had one of the most unreadable poker faces/voices she'd ever played against. Which meant it was important to him. Torin locked eyes with Pedro and held out her hand. "Pleased to meet you."

To her surprise—because he in no way telegraphed the move—he grabbed it and pulled her into a hug. "I, too, have spent time locked into a small ship with that man. You have my sympathy, *chica*."

Torin had no real problem with physical greetings from vetted sources, so she hugged him back and only barely stopped herself from turning it into a pissing contest like the one he'd had with Craig.

Who was smiling when they parted like he'd known how close it had come.

And, of course, he had.

She was weighing a couple of responses when the communications implant in her jaw pinged and she tongued it without thinking.

Salvage Station 24 requests access codes.

"You can tell it to piss up a rope," Pedro told her, as she frowned. He'd probably recognized the common expression of someone listening to a voice in their head. "But if we lose hull integrity, responses are faster if the OS can coordinate the implanted beyond the emergency frequency." He tapped his jaw.

According to Craig, many CSOs got basic implants the moment they could afford it. Torin had assumed it was to remain in contact with their ships while loading cargo but, as all Hazardous Environment suits had comm units, it now seemed more likely it was for the times they were unsuited. When she glanced over at him, Craig nodded. Since Craig had refused to allow the *Berganitan* access to either his implant or his ship while on the Navy battleship, that said something.

Mostly about Craig.

Torin tongued in her codes. It bothered her more to be unconnected. Being able to instantly reach the station sysop could mean the difference between trying to breathe vacuum and not. The construction of this particular station only reinforced that belief.

The inside of the station was as much of a rabbit warren as it looked to be from the outside. No point in actually making that observation aloud, though; the odds were good neither man knew what a rabbit was. Falling into step behind Pedro, Torin could see wear—everything from scuff marks to hard use—but no oxidizations. She was encouraged by the lack of actual decay but would have liked to have the scuff marks dealt with. Polishing made an excellent punishment for minor disciplinary…

Shaking her head, she dragged her finger in and out of a dent. Not her problem anymore. Sometimes, she forgot.

Creating a mental map of the path back to the *Promise* missed being the most difficult bit of orienteering she'd ever done only because no one was shooting at her.

The familiar smell of a few too many people for the air scrubbers ghosted along beside them, seasoned by something enough like curry to make her stomach growl. Their path seemed to be leading them toward the center of the station and although she could hear people—Krai and Human definitely, di'Taykan and Katrien probably—they didn't actually run into anyone.

Given the number of ships attached to the station, that seemed strange.

"What's up with the ghost ship effect?" Apparently Craig thought so too.

"Jan and Sirin were supposed to be in four days ago," Pedro explained, ducking as he stepped through an interior hatch. "Got cut off in the middle of a transmission. Brian Larson—you remember him, damn near lost his fukking arm when a tangle blew—he's heading out to check their last coordinates. Chloe Badawi's checking out the other end of their intended Susumi fold, and most folk are sticking pretty close to home until word comes in."

"Cut off in the middle of a transmission," Craig repeated, touching the tips of his fingers to the gray plastic hatch numbers as he followed. "Mechanical problems?"

Pedro snorted. "On Jan's ship? I don't think so. Jan considered her ship a part of her body." He tossed the information in Torin's direction. "No way it would have the kind of mechanical problems that'd keep them from getting a message out for four days. Wouldn't happen. Just, no. And," he added darkly, "Sirin said they'd picked up a maker."

"The kind of salvage that'll make you," Craig explained.

Torin nodded and filed the slang away as she also touched the hatch numbers. It was a habit they'd both picked up since discovering a marker left in their brains sometimes caused the plastic aliens to spontaneously react to their touch. Sometimes. But it was all they had. When the hatch numbers remained inert, she turned her attention back to the matter at hand. If the salvage ship had been military, she'd assume they'd been attacked.

"You think they were attacked?" Craig asked Pedro as though he'd been following Torin's train of thought.

"Don't like to think it, but…" Pedro spread his hands and shrugged.

It was unlikely but possible, Torin acknowledged silently, that a CSO could get caught up and destroyed in a naval battle. Sometimes they came in a little close.

"Fukking pirates!"

She grabbed Craig's arm and pulled him to a stop. "Pirates?"

He nodded. "They net your pen with buoys to keep you from folding to Susumi. Most people dump the pen at that point, give it up. Sirin wouldn't."

"Wait." Torin shook her head, trying to settle the thought. "There are actually people in ships—criminals in ships—stealing lawfully acquired salvage?"

"You didn't know?"

"There was a war on, I was busy." The concept of criminal activity on the scale of bad vid programming was a little hard to absorb. This wasn't an episode of *SpaceCops*; real people, people Craig knew, were being attacked. "What's being done about it? Are the Wardens involved?" The Wardens dealt with crime outside the jurisdiction of planets—or systems depending on local resources—and answered directly to Parliament, specifically the Justice Minister.

"Wardens don't do shit. They're supposed to send the Navy out to chase them down, but..." Pedro shrugged again. "... there's a war on. They're busy."

"War's over." Although, given the scale of the conflict and the geography of space, not to mention pure bloody-mindedness of some participants, battles continued to be fought.

"And I'm sure they'll get around to us eventually." Pedro's tone had moved past dry to desiccated.

Torin's hand dropped to her slate at the same time Craig wrapped callused fingers around her wrist. She was impressed he knew her that well.

"Okay, your first instinct is to fix it, I get that," he said quietly, "but who are you going to tell who doesn't already know?"

"Presit."

She tried not to laugh as Craig opened his mouth and closed it a few times.

"Presit?" he managed at last. "Are you shitting me? You never liked her."

"Liking her has nothing to do with it." Presit a Tur durValintrisy had been a furry little pain in Torin's ass from the moment she'd appeared on the alien ship, Big Yellow, determined to get the story in spite of its highly classified nature. While true that the reporter had far too high an opinion of her own importance, Torin had come to realize that media could be used as a powerful weapon, and pointing powerful weapons had made up a large part of her previous career.

"The pirates are going after salvage operators now because you're... we're," she corrected when Craig's grip tightened, "in small ships working independently. If they get away with it unopposed long enough, they'll up their game and start going after more lucrative targets. Ore carriers, say."

"There's a rumor unmanned ore carriers are going missing in statistically relevant numbers," Pedro interrupted.

"There you go. Presit tells the story, the mining cartels see the danger, they put pressure on their representatives in Parliament, Parliament pressures the Navy, and the Navy finally gets its head out of its ass."

"Just like that?" Pedro's brows had risen nearly to his hairline.

"It's a fairly simple cascade of cause and effect." Torin shrugged. "No guarantee, but we won't hit anything if we don't pull the trigger."

Pedro raised both hands in surrender. "I bow to your superior knowledge of violent responses."

When she shot him a pointed glance, Craig released her wrist.

"Presit's a big-shot celebrity now," he reminded her as she touched the screen of her slate. "You think she'll even answer your call?"

"Probably not. That's why I'm using your account. Presit *likes* him," she added to Pedro who grinned wide and white at the emphasis. "If he'd been shorter and furrier, I'd have had a fight on my hands."

Craig's protests carried them the rest of the way into the center of the station and the large, open area Pedro called the market.

Torin had seen variations on every station she'd ever been on. Social species liked to congregate, to see and be seen, to take comfort in knowing they weren't alone. This particular market had clearly once been the shuttle bay of a large transport. The four individual bays across the narrow, inboard end had been turned into two sizable shops bracketing what looked like a popular bar.

Torin exchanged a speaking glance with Craig about the amount of visible plastic, then stepped out of the way as half a dozen shouting kids—Human and Krai— charged past. The dominant scent seemed to be fried egg, and she wondered where the chickens were. Chickens had adapted remarkably well to space, and eggs provided a protein source that not even those Elder Races who professed to be appalled by the taking of life for food could get all more-evolved-than-thou about.

Small kiosks, selling what looked like everything from body parts to engine parts, dotted the actual docking area although very few people seemed interested in the merchandise on display. The twenty or so people Torin could see stood around in small groups. The di'Taykan's hair lay flat, and everyone's body language shouted waiting for the other shoe to drop.

Waiting to see if one of theirs had been attacked by pirates.

No. Waiting to see if one of *hers* had been attacked by pirates.

Because these were her people now.

Given that, Torin took another look around. Used to be, she could pick her people out of a mixed group because they were part of a whole. Marines, for all the physical differences inherent in three separate species, had a similarity of movement written on bone and muscle by training and experience. Even in a crowd of civilians, they were aware of each other and could be pulled into a unit with a word.

Their decision to take up the responsibility of defending the vast bulk of Confederation space and the nonaggressive species that lived there kept them a people apart.

These new people had decided to live apart, their only connection that decision.

As she followed Pedro across the docking area, she noted that Craig had been identified as one of them. A few greeted him by name, but as they were moving purposefully toward a destination, no one tried to pull him out of formation. In contrast, she had been identified as "other." All of the children and most of the adults in the market stared openly at her. Most of the stares were speculative, those who recognized her passing the news on to those who didn't. Some of the adults seemed openly hostile. Until they were in a position to open fire, Torin didn't give a H'san's ass about hostile. No one ever bled out as the result of a pissy expression.

Conversations ebbed and flowed as they passed and, in their wake, she could hear movement from group to group picking up.

Civilian salvage operators self-identified as individuals, accepted only the minimal government authority necessary for them to operate. Their obsessive need to be *unique* was what gave them their group identity, and the single word that would pull her Marines together would scatter this lot like a fragmentation round.

These new people she could identify because of their desire *not* to be part of a whole.

It was... different.

She heard her name, Silsviss, Big Yellow, Crucible, the di'Taykan phrase that meant progenitor, and the familiar sound of speculation.

Same old, same old.

As "individuals," they were clearly not averse to gossip.

Pedro and his family lived in an old cargo ship built into the structure of the station. Torin followed Craig into the cargo bay and stared around at the piles of... salvage, she assumed, although junk would be as accurate. Seconds after they'd stepped through the hatch, half a dozen kids—ranging in age from early teens to just past toddler—threw themselves at Craig. As he didn't seem to be in any danger, Torin turned her attention to the three adults descending the metal stairs from the living quarters on the upper levels.

"Torin, these are my wives, Alia and Jenn, and my husband, Kevin. The horde is ours collectively. There's an air lock there," Pedro continued, nodding at the control panel Torin had already noticed on the far side of the bay, "and another one off the kitchen. We've got a ship a little bigger than the *Promise* locked in up there and another about twice as large down here. If the klaxon goes, don't worry about which one you end up in. Closest adult grabs the kids, singly or collectively, then sings out so everyone knows where they are. We'll shuffle around once we're clear."

It was the first time Torin had ever been given emergency evacuation protocols mixed in with introductions, but what the hell.

"So you're the one sucking back half of Craig's precious oxygen." Alia extended a hand. "Never thought I'd see the day."

She was missing the top joint of her second finger. It looked like an old injury, long since healed. Torin had never known anyone—and she'd seen a lot of injuries—who'd refused the medical advances the Confederation offered.

Alia noticed Torin staring. "No regen tanks here," she explained, "and I just couldn't be arsed to get to a government station. By the time I had time, didn't see any point in regrowing something I didn't miss."

"I see." It was the tone Torin'd used on officers when they were being enthusiastic about something particularly stupid. Polite interest; no noticeable approval.

Jenn and Kevin were huggers. They were both packing serviceable muscle.

"I was going to be a Marine." The child tugging at her jacket was somewhere between five and ten, gender indeterminate, with Pedro's rich, dark skin and Jenn's green eyes. "But Da says the war is over. Are you going to have to stop killing people now?"

Torin thought about it long enough that Craig turned from his conversation with Kevin and asked the question again, silently.

"As things stand right now," she said at last. On the way up the stairs, she dragged two fingers along the gray plastic handrail.

Later, after an amazing meal, where everyone present provided her with enough potential blackmail material to even out the stories her family had told to Craig, Pedro sat down beside her on the sofa and said, "He really loves you."

"Is this the *if you hurt him, I'll do you* speech?" Torin wondered, watching Craig racing with Helena, the fourteen-year-old, on the room's bigger vid screen. He was working his slate one-handed and using the other to poke Helena and make her fall off her hoverboard into the snow. Helena knew some words Torin hadn't learned until she got to the Corps.

Pedro snorted. "Yeah. Pretty much."

"Noted."

"He's still not talking, Cap."

Cho's fingers curled into fists, and he carefully uncurled them. "Have you tried convincing him?"

"I have. I even sent the di'Taykan in without their maskers." Nat snickered. "Thought maybe all that sexual frustration might loosen his lips."

The di'Taykan exuded pheromones that crossed species boundaries—and if there was a species outside the Methane Alliance that was immune, Cho'd never heard of them. Without the maskers they wore, arousal levels were at best irritating and at worst painful. "And?"

"Well, he started talking all right. Old bugger was downright inventive. Almon got pretty pissed when I hauled their multicolored asses out of there before they could follow through." She dug her fingernails in through the short bristles of her hair and brought them away bloody after a vigorous scratch. "Oh, fuk it. I knew that damned cream of Doc's wouldn't work."

Cho stared down at the image of the armory on his slate. Rogelio Page had been working the same scattered debris field for years. A crazy old loner, even by CSO standards, he'd never salvaged anything Cho would consider worth taking from him, but he was easy to find and easy to grapple right off the side of his pen. Almon had deftly set the hooks in the old man's HE suit and reeled him in, kicking and swearing the whole way. Checking the meager contents of Page's pen while Nat took care of getting his codes, Cho had no idea how the old man managed to find enough salable salvage to stay alive, but he supposed if staying alive was all a man cared about, it didn't take much.

Cho wanted more. A lot more. To begin with, he wanted that fukking armory open.

"Let Doc talk to him."

Nat paused in mid scratch. "You serious, Cap? Page is a stubborn old bastard, and Doc's not exactly subtle."

He took a deep breath and let it out slowly through his nose. "I want those codes."

Nat recognized the tone. "Aye, Cap."

"Tell Doc I'm going in with him."

The old man grinned as Cho led Doc into the room. His teeth were bloody, bruises were rising on pale, loose skin, and he was still half erect in spite of the air scrubbers. "So you're the fly in charge of this shit pile." He spat, the mouthful of bloody saliva spattering over the toe of Cho's left boot. "Looks like we can finally get this show on the road."

Cho raised a hand, holding Doc in place. "Give me your codes and I'll put you back on your ship."

To his surprise, Page laughed. The laughter turned into coughing. "Liar," Page gasped, and spat again. "Only one reason scum like you wants government codes. You got something big—something big enough to compensate for the size of your dick and that's one fuk of a lot of compensating, so I'm thinking weapons. One really big one or lots of little ones, don't matter. You're not getting my fukking codes."

"Give me your codes," Cho told him, barely managing to keep his voice level, "and I'll kill you quickly."

"The fuk you will," Page snorted. "You'll have your trained ape kill me quick." He narrowed the eye that still worked, looked past Cho, and locked his gaze on Doc's face. "I've seen your type before, boy. You wanted Recon or Ranger, but you were too crazy even for those crazy fukkers."

Doc showed no reaction to Page's accusation. Less than no reaction.

"No one tried to convince you too hard to stay, after your first contract ran out, did they, boy? No, it was, 'So long, Private, have a nice life. Hell, have a shitty life, just have it away from us.'" Taking a deep breath, Page straightened as much as age and the earlier beatings allowed. "Sergeant Rogelio Page, 3rd Division, 1st Re'carta, 4th Battalion, Serra Company, Confederation Marine Corps. Do your worst."

Dropping his hand, Cho stepped to one side. "You heard the man."

He was, he admitted nearly an hour later, impressed with how long Doc had kept Page alive and more or less coherent. Sure there'd been screaming and moaning, but there'd been actual words as well. The ending, however, came as no surprise.

During the questioning, Doc's hair had come loose and the strands hanging around his face were stiff with blood, drawing lines of red against his bare shoulders as he turned, blue eyes looking even bluer within the crimson splatters. "Sorry, Captain. He's gone. Heart gave out. If you want my opinion, he wasn't going to talk anyway."

"I don't want your opinion," Cho growled. So close, so fukking close! With the weapons in that locker, things would be different. He'd get… no, he'd take what he deserved. No more just accepting the shit the universe threw at him. He needed that locker *open*!

"Goddamned fukking stubborn old fool!" Pivoting on one foot, he spun around and slammed his fist into the bulkhead.

Even over the sound of the impact, he heard his knuckle crack.

The pain hit a moment later.

"Let me look at it, Captain." Doc's fingers were sticky, but his touch was sure. "Yeah, you broke it. Come on, let's get to sick bay and I'll shoot you full of blockers. You won't feel a thing when I bond it."

Hand cradled against his chest, Cho shook his head. It was never smart to access the two halves of Doc's personality too close together. "I'll meet you up there after I get us moving. No point in lingering out here any longer."

Doc nodded, his hair dripping red as he tied it back. "If you take too long, I'll come looking for you."

Cho waited until the other man left the room, then crossed to Page's body. "Just to set the record straight," he growled, "Doc was a medical officer, CMO on the *Seraphim*. You remember the *Seraphim*. Two hundred and thirteen survivors from a crew of five thousand. Doc, he's a walking, talking fukking casualty of war. Huirre!"

"*Aye, Captain?*"

"Best time to Vrijheid."

He could feel how badly Huirre wanted to ask if Doc had been successful but, after a long moment, the Krai erred on the side of self-preservation and said only, "Aye, aye, Captain!"

Torin woke the next morning to an incoming message from the station OS. Brian Larson had found the missing *Firebreather*, her hull breached and her pen abandoned. He'd salvaged the debris and had begun scanning the immediate area for bodies.

"Bodies." Craig scratched the matted hair on his chest and padded across the cabin to start the coffee, shaking his head. "Why the hell would they put up a fight?"

"You don't usually?"

He blinked, visibly replayed both lines of dialogue in his head, then backtracked so far he'd have been outside the ship had he been actually moving. "With what? Confederation law specifically states, all weapons are to remain in the hands of the military. What?" he demanded when Torin raised a brow.

"While we circled the station looking for a lock, I saw at

least seven ships armed with salvaged weapons. They weren't obvious, but they were unmistakable if you know what to look for. These ships wouldn't be able to sell back to the military or any reputable recycling yard without being brought up on charges, but I'm betting someone on this station, on any salvage station, is willing to act as a middleman, providing legal tags for a price and buying the tagged salvage back."

"Torin…"

"You wondered *why* the *Firebreather* put up a fight, so you knew they were armed."

He stared at her for a long moment then he smiled. "I keep forgetting you're no drongo. Smarter than you look."

"You keep forgetting," she told him levelly, not responding to the smile, "that we're in this together now."

"I'm sorry." Craig drew in a deep breath and exhaled quickly. "We're big on minding our own bizzo, us."

She thought back to crossing the station's market, the clear division between us and them. Between us and her.

"I'm part of that *we* now."

"I know. Old habits."

"Get over them."

This was an entirely different smile. "Yes, Gunnery Sergeant."

What the hell. She could stay mad, or she could recognize she'd be sharing a small space with this person—that she *wanted* to share a small space with this person—for the foreseeable future. "What did I tell you about calling me that out of bed?"

He laughed then, a little relieved, a little turned on, and got the mugs out of storage. "So I guess the question is, what the fuk did they find that was worth dying for?"

Torin stretched out on the bunk and ran possible scenarios in her head.

"Torin?"

She glanced up at him. "What the fuk did they find that was worth keeping away from pirates?"

Craig poured both mugs of coffee before asking, "Isn't that the same question?"

"Not quite."

TWO

Torin had assumed they'd stay to honor the dead. She'd seen enough death over the years to know the importance of celebrating lives lived. She'd seen enough death *recently*—her entire company, most of her GCT, and a prison planet of Marines she'd all but promised to free—that the Corps psychologists had come to the conclusion she had to be repressing at extreme levels in order to even function. In turn, she'd come to a few conclusions about the Corps psychologists, and they'd parted on terms of mutual dislike.

Holding onto the living rather than the dead was not repressing. Binti Mashona and Ressk were all that had survived of Sh'quo Company, Miransha Kichar and Werst all that had survived of their recon unit. Kichar had stayed in, the other three had left the Corps around the same time Torin had. Kyster, di'Hern Darlys and di'Ameliten Wataru—the other Krai and the two di'Taykan who'd escaped the prison planet with them— had taken medical discharges and disappeared into the population of their respective home planets. Torin kept an eye out for Kyster, but, as Darlys had been the instigator of Torin as a progenitor, she'd let the di'Taykan go.

Torin'd served with Staff Sergeant Daniel Johnston, Kichar's senior NCO, and he'd already sent one detailed message about the young Marine's progress. And how crazy she was driving him. And how far she'd likely go if she could just dial it back a little. Torin found it comforting to know Kichar hadn't been changed by knowledge of the plastic aliens. Torin hadn't spent any civilian time with Mashona, Ressk, and Werst, but she knew where they were and they knew where she was and that fell somewhere between comforting and necessary.

Torin hadn't known Jan and Sirin, hadn't even met them; they were additions to Craig's dead, not hers.

Craig had Pedro help him set up training exercises, teaching Torin to deploy the *Promise*'s pen, load various types of "salvage," and then check that the correct variable had been entered into the computer's Susumi equation. When that paled, she spent time running pilot simulation programs—maneuvering around debris fields, finding the best position for most efficient grappling of salvageable pieces. It was necessary training, and Torin gave it the same attention she'd given the training that had allowed her to stay alive while doing her old job but, at the same time, it was clear that they were actually *waiting*.

Jan and Sirin hadn't been wearing HE suits when attacked, so it took Brian four days to find them, sweeping the area around the remains of the *Firebreather* with his scanners tuned to pick up DNA. It was a function the CSOs used to scan battle debris for residual tissue and many a military family owed them for whatever closure they'd been able to achieve.

When he had both bodies finally on board, Brian's message to the station was short and to the point. *"Got them. Coming home."*

With people free to mourn, the mood around the station changed. Now, they knew what they were waiting for.

"What do you mean, the attack hasn't been reported to the Wardens?"

Craig pushed a hand back through his hair and sighed. "What's the point, Torin? The Wardens can't bring Jan and Sirin back to life."

"No, but they can catch the bastards who killed them."

"How?"

"How?" Torin repeated. She paced the length of the cabin, seven strides and back again. "Isn't it what they do?"

"Do they?" Craig dropped his feet off the edge of the control panel. The chair protested as he spun it to face her. "They haven't hauled ass to send in the Navy, have they?"

No, they hadn't. And Presit hadn't gotten back to her. Torin spread her arms. "It isn't right that the people who killed Jan and Sirin will get away with it."

"You lost Marines all the time. How often did you get to take out the people responsible?"

Oh, he did not just go there. "We were fighting a war," Torin snarled. "And don't tell me that you're in a war with the pirates because war means fighting back. And you're not." The *Promise* was suddenly too small. "You're doing sweet fuk all for the people you lost!" she said, stepping into the air lock.

"We're remembering them!" he shouted as the outer door closed.

No one spoke to her as she wandered around the station. A few people moved out of her way.

Someone had set up an exercise wheel in an old ore carrier and since no one was around, and the surface of the inner curve was both smooth and solid, Torin stripped off her boots and ran. When her implant chimed *fifteen kilometers*, she started to slow; although it took another kilometer before the rotations had dropped to the point where it was safe to use the brakes.

Breathing deeply, the taste of the recycled air almost comforting, she stared down past her toes at the curve of plastic—resolutely remaining plastic—and thought, *Fuk it.*

When Torin got back to the ship, the only light in the cabin was the spill from the control panel. Craig was in the bunk, not asleep but not talking either. She stripped down, and settled in beside him.

"I thought when I left the Corps, that I'd stop losing people."

"I know." He shifted to wrap an arm around her. "And I know you want to fix things, but, Torin, we take care of our own."

Maybe. But their definition of "take care of" wasn't one she understood.

In Torin's experience, memorial services included a chaplain droning on about duty while the listeners thought about the part of the ceremony that would have been most relevant to the dead Marines—getting out of their Class As and to the beer. Salvage Station 24 had skipped the memorial and gone straight to the party, complete with musicians on a stage set up by the old shuttle bay doors. At the other end of the market, the pub entrance had been blocked by a pair of tables and two kegs. Craig had warned her that the beer was watered, but that didn't seem to matter to the constant stream of people stuffing mugs under the spouts. Overheard conversations reminded Torin of conversations heard in every Mess where they honored the dead at the end of a deployment. Subtle differences, sure—no one seemed especially relieved or guilty that they were still alive when the dead were dead, and it was strange not to hear the words *"Goddamn fukking brass has no goddamn fukking idea of what we do out there!"* repeated at a volume that rose in direct proportion to the amount of alcohol consumed.

The biggest difference between the way the Corps and the salvage operators did things was that Jan and Sirin's bodies had been set up on a raised platform in the center of the market, the kiosks cleared off the floor for the duration. In the field, the Corps bagged and reduced their dead into a few grams of ash that fit into cylinders that fit in turn into measured spaces in the senior NCO's combat vest. One way or another, the Corps left no one behind. Even Marines who died while serving in less chaotic theaters were bagged and reduced before being sent home unless their religious beliefs required a different treatment.

Bodies lying around were bodies that needed to be tended to.

"Is this sanitary?" Torin murmured against Craig's ear as they worked their way through the crowds to Pedro and his family. "Decomposing bodies in a closed environment?"

Craig stiffened, turned toward her and visibly relaxed, shaking his head. It took Torin a moment to analyze his reaction. Then she realized that her right hand rested against the place her dead would have been had she still been wearing a vest. "They won't be here long," he told her quietly. "And the station's scrubbers are up to the job. Jan built them."

Torin had never asked how well he'd known the two dead women. He hadn't spoken of them since their fight and barely spoke of them before, although he'd exchanged a couple of memories with Pedro during the wait. That suggested they were *his* in the broader sense rather than the specific. She hadn't acknowledged that and she needed to, but to say she was sorry for his loss would imply this wasn't her loss as well. Closing her hand around his forearm, she stuck with a basic truth. "The death of any of us diminishes us all."

He looked a little surprised.

Jan Garrett-Wong was Human. Standing, the top of her head might have reached Torin's shoulder. All things considered, she didn't look that bad, but then she'd lived a significant percentage of her life surrounded by vacuum and had no doubt known enough to close her eyes tightly and empty her lungs when her ship had been breached. Most of the damage caused by prolonged exposure to vacuum would be internal—pulmonary embolisms were tidy killers. Both her cheeks were stippled with burst capillaries, but nothing said they hadn't been there before the attack.

The lilac hair of di'Akusi Sirin lay limp and unmoving. The color reminded Torin of Lieutenant di'Ka Jarret, and her hand moved back to touch nonexistent cylinders. They'd never found his body, or even any evidence of where it was in the melted surface of ST7/45T2. If his family had held a memorial service, nothing of the lieutenant would have attended.

Given the differences in respiratory systems, Sirin had probably lived a little longer after the *Firebreather* was destroyed. Long enough to see Jan die. All di'Taykan eyes collapsed in vacuum; given the concave curve of her lids, Torin suspected that someone, at some point before the bodies had been laid out for viewing, had sealed the lids shut over the empty sockets.

It was unusual for a di'Taykan to choose a single Human as a *vantru*, a primary sexual partner. Not only were the Taykan a communal species, but any relationships formed while in the di' phase ended when they switched to quo and became breeders. Plus, a single Human would be hard pressed to keep up with a di'Taykan's sexual appetite. From what Torin could overhear, more than one person in the crowd had been as impressed by Jan's ability in that regard as by her skill as a mechanic. Easier when both parties were females, granted, but still.

Tables of food had been set up around the biers; platters of the ubiquitous processed protein patties in a wide variety of flavors as well as a surprising amount of fresh vegetables and small fruits—the station's greenhouses seemed to be producing bumper crops. Bowls filled with the paste sat next to sun-dried potato, sweet potato, and *hujin* chips clearly intended for dipping. Torin stayed well away from the *hujin* chips. Humans tended to consider them further proof that the Krai could and would eat *anything* organic.

The edge of Jan's shroud had a smear of paste on it, as though the corpse had stretched out her right hand and done some snacking while waiting for things to start. That was definitely unsanitary, no matter what Craig said.

Torin touched the edge of a plastic bowl—which remained a plastic bowl—then picked up a handful of sweet potato chips.

Warm bodies packed the market elbow to elbow and, while the dominant language was Federate, Torin could hear Taykan, Krai, at least two oldEarth languages, and the distinctive screaming cat fight sound of a conversation in Katrien. Every one of the many air locks accessing the station was in use and, according to Alia coming off a shift in ops, they'd extended mooring tethers from the last three free—crews of late arrivals suiting up rather than locking in. It seemed as though every salvage operator who could get there, had.

"Torin!"

She looked down to see Jeremy, the youngest of Pedro's children, holding tightly to the edge of her tunic, none of his parents in sight. "What can I do for you, Jer?"

"Mama made mushroom caps."

"Did she?"

"Yes. I want some."

Craig leaned in close enough to be heard, his breath warm against her cheek. "I can take charge of the ankle biter if you like."

"I can get an entire platoon moving in the same direction while under artillery fire, I expect I can handle a four-year-old." When his smile softened, she shook her head and sighed. "Don't get broody on me."

Jeremy seemed like a solid kid, but when she settled him on her hip, he weighed less than she expected and he was small enough not to affect her ability to maneuver through the crowd to the food. The mushroom caps he wanted were about four centimeters across and filled with yeast paste wrapped around something chewy. It wasn't unpleasant tasting and, over the years, Torin had learned that within species parameters it was usually safer not to ask for specifics.

Both hands holding his food, trusting Torin to hold him, Jeremy chewed and stared at the bodies. Torin had no idea if children this young were usually exposed to bodies. Her idea of *young* started at around nineteen for Humans.

"Dead means not coming back."

Jeremy wasn't asking, but Torin answered him anyway. "Yes, it does."

"Where did they go?" he wondered.

Torin chewed and thought about it for a moment. Each of the Younger Races seemed to have at least half a dozen belief systems dealing primarily with death.

Even the Elder Races held a few, although for the most part they were wise enough to keep them to themselves. Torin believed in keeping people alive. "I honestly don't know," she said at last.

Jeremy made a noncommittal noise and went to wipe his hand on her tunic. Unable to spot anything set out for that purpose, Torin redirected him to his own clothing.

"I know you."

The speaker was Human, male, close to 200 centimeters tall, compensating for the lack of hair on his head with the ugliest ginger mustache Torin had ever seen.

"I know you," he said again. "You're that Marine who says plastic aliens are the enemy, not those murdering, fukking *Others*. It wasn't fukking plastic aliens who killed my sister, now was it?"

Most of the people packed in around them had abandoned personal conversations and were waiting, with him, for Torin to answer.

"Where did your sister die?" she asked.

He blinked pale eyes. "What?"

Torin repeated the question. "Where did your sister die?"

"On Barnin Four. Those bastards wiped out the whole colony."

"Then she was likely killed by the low-orbit bombardment." The colony had been small, agrarian, with no offensive capabilities. There'd been no reason for the Primacy to attack as the entire Barnin system had been well within the Confederation's borders, but since discovering the war had been designed as a laboratory to study the species involved, Torin had come to realize that many decisions on both sides had been less than rational all along. "There's no way of knowing what species was directly responsible."

He folded his arms. "Well, it wasn't fukking plastic aliens, I know that."

"How?"

"What?"

"How do you know it wasn't the plastic aliens?"

Ginger brows drew in to nearly touch over his nose. "Fuk you!"

He aimed a shove at her unoccupied shoulder and, without moving her feet, she twisted just far enough around for it to miss.

Reaching out, Jeremy wiped greasy fingers on the sleeve of his jacket.

When he snarled and tried a second shove, Torin caught his hand, folded his thumb back, and dropped him to his knees. Face screwed up in pain, he shifted his weight back, the fingers of his free hand curling into a fist. Torin locked her eyes on his and growled, "Don't." Against all odds, he turned out to be smart enough to listen. "You want to take out your grief on me," she told him quietly, "I'm willing to beat the shit out of you any time I'm not holding a four-year-old. Jeremy, are you related to this man?"

Jeremy took a long look. "No."

"Then you don't get to wipe your hands on him. Apologize."

"But..." When Torin raised a brow, he sighed dramatically and leaned forward far enough to peer down at the kneeling man. "Sorry I wiped my hands on you, okay?"

Torin waited a moment then applied a little more pressure to the man's thumb until he choked out a reasonably sincere, "Okay."

"The plastic aliens started the war that killed your sister," she said, releasing him. Plastic alien was simplistic, but it was a lot easier to say than polynumerous molecular species or polyhydroxide hive mind. "Don't forget that, because they'll be back."

Then she turned to get Jeremy another mushroom, keeping most of her attention on the man rising to his feet. Muttering under his breath, he pushed his way through the crowd who, in spite of having been avidly watching the confrontation, were all maintaining a strict *none of my business* air about them. She wondered what would have happened had there actually been a fight. Would the crowd's individuality at all costs have held or would it have turned into a mob as she became an outsider beating one of their own?

How close to death would Ginger Mustache have to be to bring the salvage operators together?

Or did only the dead get parties?

Spotting Jenn over by a group of Krai who were probably complaining about the waste of food—they ate their dead, and saw no real reason why they couldn't eat everyone's even if the articles drawn up when they joined the Confederaton expressly forbade it—Torin caught her eye and nodded toward Jeremy, silently asking if she wanted him back.

When it appeared she didn't, Torin allowed the child to drag her over toward the stage where a band named *Toyboat*—two Humans, a di'Taykan and a Niln on the beatbox—were doing a power chord cover of H'san opera. She could honestly say she'd never heard a better version of *O'gra Morf Dennab*. And she'd definitely had worse dancing partners.

By 2100, most of the kids had gone and the serious drinking had started. Craig knew of three stills, which meant there had to be at least half a dozen more on the station he didn't know about, all supplying alcohol for the funeral—and that wasn't even counting perfectly innocent food and drink that got a lot less innocent when it crossed species lines. Personally, Craig was sticking with the *fernim* made by the Katrien collective; sweet and dark, about 80 proof and the best fukking thing ever to put in coffee. If there was anything resembling justice left in the universe, he'd be taking a bottle or two away with him. The Katrien collective hadn't been part of the station last time he'd been by. For the sake of the *fernim* alone, he hoped like hell they stayed.

From where Craig was sitting, he could see Torin deep in discussion with a couple of di'Taykan. Kiku had served one contract in the Corps as a comm tech and Meryn had been Navy, so the odds were high they were rehashing old battles. Or at least the di'Taykan were. It wasn't something he'd ever heard Torin do. He supposed, as career Corps, she'd seen enough battles the novelty had worn off. If the di'Taykan were trying to impress her, well, they didn't stand a hope in hell. Any hell. Pick one.

If he were a betting man—and he was—he'd bet the conversation had started with a proposition, even given that Torin had been named a progenitor and every Taykan in the Confederation seemed to know it. Still, it wasn't like she was planning to start a Taykan family line. Or, given the differences in biology, a Human line on Taykan. Or that anything much kept a di'Taykan from suggesting sex. They'd never discussed where they stood with the di'Taykan, Torin and him. Although it was pretty much a consistent belief across known space that sex with a di'Taykan didn't count, he found he was pleased Torin hadn't gone with them. If that made him unevolved—he took another swallow of coffee and *fernim*—he didn't fukking care.

"So *pendejo*…" Pedro dropped down on one side of him, Alia on the other. "…you are serious about this woman, yes?"

Craig toasted Pedro with his mug. "Would I have exposed her to your ugly-ass self if I wasn't?"

"You might have been trying to scare her off," Alia said thoughtfully, crossing her legs at the ankles. At some point during the evening, she'd had the H'san symbol for life hennaed onto the tops of both bare feet. "Tossing her into the deep end. Seeing if she'll swim."

"She swims fine. Threw me in a freezing, fukking lake on Paradise."

Alia snickered. "You suck at metaphor when you're drinking."

Craig toasted her, too.

And nearly coughed the mouthful back up when Pedro jabbed a bony elbow into his side. "Your woman, she's used to ordering a lot of people around. You sure you going to be enough for her?"

Yeah, it wasn't like he hadn't wondered about that. He shrugged. "She chose to come with me."

"Never doubted it."

"Never thought for a minute you could make that one do anything she didn't want to," Alia snorted.

" 'S truth." Craig nodded. "Or she didn't feel she had to."

He could hear the frown in Alia's voice although he kept his attention on the last swallow of his coffee. "Isn't that the same thing?"

Pedro leaned across him, reaching for her mug. "How much of that have you had?"

"Not enough." She easily evaded his grab and got to her feet, graceful in spite of the swaying. Or maybe swaying gracefully, Craig wasn't entirely sure. "You two behave," she added as she left.

"I love that woman. *¡Te amo, mujer!*" Pedro shouted at her back.

Alia flipped him off without turning.

"She loves me, too."

"She married your ugly ass, she must."

"So are you and…"

"Don't know. We haven't talked about it."

"She took you home to meet her family."

Craig shrugged, unwilling to read any more into that than there'd been. "I'd already met her father. Back when she was dead." Fukking mug was empty. He pulled Pedro's from lax fingers and swallowed a mouthful of… "What the fuk is this?" he gasped, eyes welling up.

"Something Kevin's been fermenting in the greenhouse." Pedro took his mug back and drank. "Good degreaser, too."

He could almost feel his tongue again. "No doubt."

"So, how long you planning to stay this…"

A howl from over by the empty stage cut him off as Newton Winkler ripped off his overalls, screaming obscenities. Looked like he'd gotten a couple of new tats since Craig had seen him last.

"Fukking Winkler's been into the *sah* again," Pedro sighed, hauling himself slowly to his feet.

Craig stood with him. For the Krai, *sah* had an effect about equal to a cup of coffee. To Humans, the mild stimulant caused—as well as a host of nasty physical reactions—delusions, paranoia, and an inability to feel pain. Craig had learned the hard way that last bit was the kicker. Hopped up on *sah*, the restraints self-interest put on violence were gone, and Winkler would keep fighting long after the damage he'd taken should have forced him to quit.

"Oh, fuk it, Jurr's trying to talk him down."

Jurr probably hadn't intended to get his ass thrown across the room. Fortunately, Krai bones were hard enough he bounced. Also, fortunately, the cluster of people he bounced off of were drunk enough they probably suffered nothing more than minor bruising.

Then Torin's left arm went around Winkler's throat, her right hand wrapped around her left wrist forcing the hold tight. Face growing darker in the crock of her elbow, Winkler clawed at her arm, blunt nails sliding off her sleeve. His bare feet paddled against the stage, then slowed, then stopped. Torin eased him down, studied him for a moment through narrowed eyes, then straightened. "He won't be out for long," she snapped. "Tie him or trank him."

Craig grinned as a couple of Krai he didn't know moved quickly in and carried Winkler away. Their *sah*, their responsibility. Allowing a Human to get his hands on the liquid could mean charges laid if anyone on the station wanted to push the matter.

"She could kick your ass from here to the edge," Pedro murmured, draping an arm over Craig's shoulders.

"Not news."

"Bet she's *realmente bueno* in the rack."

"Not telling."

"You're in love."

Craig watched as every Krai still in the room dropped their eyes rather than meet Torin's gaze. Even those far enough away she couldn't possibly see their expressions, stared at the floor.

Pedro hadn't actually asked a question, but Craig answered anyway. "Yeah," he said as Torin glanced his way. "I am."

"...so try to stay away until we've forgotten what your ugly face looks like. Torin can come around any time, though. What?" One of the family said something just out of range of the comm unit. *"Jeremy says he's going to marry Torin when he grows up,"* Pedro translated.

"I'll consider that fair warning. Stay safe, asshole."

"And you, pendejo."

It was, Torin thought as Craig maneuvered the *Promise* out past a long line of the polyvoltaic cells that helped power the station, one of the strangest clearances she'd ever heard. The station OS had been involved only in the resealing of the access lock.

"So..." Craig sounded amused. "Something you're not telling me?"

"About?"

"You and Jeremy."

"He's a cute kid."

"I never knew you liked kids."

She shrugged. "I find I'm liking them more now I don't have to watch them die." Not that she'd ever actually *watched* them die; she'd fought like hell to keep them from dying. "Jeremy's young enough, he'll never get mixed up in this mess."

"Fifteen, sixteen years; you think the fighting will stop by then?"

"I think the war will have stopped by then. Fighting? In general?" The Elder Races of the Confederation believed that an interstellar presence could be achieved only by those species that had evolved beyond the desire to blow themselves—and others—into extinction. This caused them a problem when the Primacy, who clearly did not share this belief, attacked. And continued to attack, diplomacy be damned. When it came down to fight or die, the Confederation bent the rules enough to allow Humans, Krai, and di'Taykan to join their club even though none of the three had managed to do much more than break out of their own gravity well. As it turned out, it was entirely possible that the "plastic aliens" had juiced the Primacy, but that wasn't the point. The point was, there were three aggressive species buzzing around Confederation space, and no matter what Parliament seemed to think, they weren't all likely to put down the weapons they'd been using.

"Torin?"

"Do I think the fighting will stop?" She thought of saying *Ask Jan and Sirin,* but he was asking her. "No."

"Pessimist."

Folding her arms along the top of his control chair, she rested her chin on his head. "Realist."

"You're thinking of the pirates."

"Not specifically." Pirates. Actual pirates. That was going to take some getting used to.

"So," he said again after a moment, still sounding amused, "you made an impression."

"On a four-year-old."

"Winkler was over aces, and you kept him from hurting anyone."

"Okay, I made an impression on a four-year-old and a *sah* addict. Winkler needs help."

"He needs to stay off the *sah.*"

Torin sighed. The Corps would have slapped him into a program before the charge of self-inflicted damage had even hit his slate and then would have gone after the Krai who'd allowed him access to the beverage. Much the same thing would have happened on Paradise and on any station that maintained a government presence. Any hint of Humans getting their hands on *sah* and the Wardens would move in, attempting to limit the damage. Salvage operators, though, they refused to interfere in the man's *personal choice.*

Individually, they were smart, tough, and adaptable. Working together, as a unit...

Would they work together as a unit, though; that was the question. Would they? Could they? What would it take?

Torin was just as glad to be leaving them behind. Individuality at the expense of the group went against everything she'd believed her entire adult life.

* * *

Once Vrijheid had been just another government station, but the mining operations it had been intended to support had been destroyed in the war, and the cartels had cut their losses rather than rebuild. When William Ponner arrived, the station had been stripped to bare-bones personnel, waiting to be moved off its L5 point and folded through Susumi space to a new location. Rumor said he'd barely been there a tenday when he'd hacked a database and convinced the powers-that-be the station's orbit had decayed due to damage taken during the attack. That it had crashed into the planet, all hands lost.

Apparently, he'd even implanted records of the Navy's investigation.

Cho figured hacking the Navy took balls the size of small moons and only doing it once took more brains than were usually evident in the Human species as a whole.

William Ponner—Big Bill to his friends, and everyone who used the station was either his friend or about to become a statistic supporting the dangers of living in space—had used balls and brains to create his own personal fiefdom. If a captain had cargo to sell, it could be sold at Vrijheid, no questions asked, fifteen percent to Big Bill. If a captain wanted to outfit his ship so that picking up new cargoes became a little easier, he could do that at Vrijheid. Fifteen percent to Big Bill. If a crew wanted to spend their share of the money, they could do that, too. Sex, drugs, alcohol, high tech, low tech, and useless pretties that sparkled and shone. Fifteen percent to Big Bill. If a person with skills wanted to sell them to the highest bidder, no questions asked, they could sell those skills at Vrijheid. Fifteen percent to Big Bill.

He'd created a sanctuary for those who were tired of a Confederation designed to support the belief that the Elder Races' shit didn't stink. Humans, Krai, and di'Taykan almost exclusively—the so-called Younger Races who were treated by the government like they were too stupid or too unstable to be anything but cannon fodder—although every now and then, another race found a niche and filled it.

Cho gave the Ciptran standing by the entrance to the bar as

much room as possible—the big bug made his skin crawl. Once inside, he crossed to join Nat and Doc at a table against the far wall. Although all races drank in the Sleepless Goat, the staff was predominantly Human, albeit Humans the universe had chewed up and spat out. No one ended up slinging drinks in a place like the Goat if they had options. Every server in the place showed the signs of one or more addictions, but Cho preferred it to any of the other dozen or so bars on the station. When he wanted a drink, he wanted a drink. Period. Not a proposition. Not meat pies that might have once had a name.

"Tyra's dead," he grunted, dropping into a chair. "Crazy old woman took a walk in vacuum about six tendays ago."

Doc drained his glass and held up three fingers to the server. "Her codes were so old, they probably wouldn't have worked anyway."

"We'll never know now."

Drinks arrived with a promptness that suggested the word had been passed on to new staff and the servers were keeping bloodshot eyes locked on Doc. No one wanted to be the one to tip him over. Not if the stories were true.

Most of them were.

"We need to take another fukking salvage operator alive," Nat growled, fingers curled and heading for her scalp. She scowled at Doc as he wrapped his fingers around her wrist and pulled her hand back down to the table. "What?"

"It won't heal if you keep scratching it."

"It itches!"

They did need to take another salvage operator alive. Nat's declaration had been stupidly obvious, but accurate for all of that. Cho took a long drink of his beer, then sat staring into the foam. Trouble was, most CSOs ditched their pens and ran the moment they figured out what they were facing, and oblivious idiots like Rogelio Page were few and far between. Not likely they'd get that lucky again.

"Cap."

Cho lifted his head slowly, acknowledging Nat's warning but not reacting to it. Half of the bar's clientele could literally smell fear, and all of them would take advantage of it.

Big Bill and the Grr brothers were heading toward the back of the bar. Once his destination became obvious, the noise level rose as the other patrons played *nothing to do with me*.

"Mackenzie Cho, as I live and breathe." Big Bill smiled widely, showing a lot of teeth. Given that his closest associates were Krai, teeth weren't exactly reassuring. He pulled the fourth chair out from the table, and sat, not caring that his back was to the room. Given that the Grr brothers were at his back, that wasn't even a little surprising.

Grr was not their actual name. Nor were they necessarily brothers. Both the Krai and di'Taykan in Cho's crew agreed they were male—the subtle differences in scalp mottling that made up Krai secondary sexual characteristics confused the hell out of Humans. More importantly, they were two of the nastiest sons of bitches in known space. Cho had once seen them eat a man's feet, totally ignoring the screaming.

That they barely came up to Big Bill's shoulders when he was sitting down didn't matter in the slightest. Even Huirre, who'd eaten a body part or two in his day, gave them a wide berth.

"Thanks, sweetheart." A beer and a shot appeared in front of Big Bill almost before he sat down. He smiled up at the server, tossed the shot back, set the glass back down on the table with an audible click, and smiled again. "We need to talk, Cho. People you're selling to are talking about how you're holding back, and today I find out that you've been asking after Tyra, bless her withered heart. What did you find out there between the stars?"

And why are you trying to keep it from me?

People who tried to keep things—or at least fifteen percent of things—from Big Bill on Vrijheid didn't live long.

The Grr brothers smiled.

Nat dug at her scalp again, and Doc tapped the edge of one thumb against the table. Cho felt a drop of sweat run down his back. He took a deep breath and reminded himself that he hadn't kept anything from anyone. Things were being kept from him. "I can't talk about it here."

Let this lot of degenerates find out he had a Marine armory on board, and the fukking losers would be fighting over who got to try for it first.

Big Bill made a noncommittal noise that still managed to sound like a threat.

Dragging his tongue over dry lips, Cho added, "Let me show it to you."

Big Bill maneuvered the eye deftly around the armory in absolute silence, fingers ghosting over the surface of his slate. When he reached the CSO seal, he snorted. "Given what you told me of your captive's unfortunate death, I see why you were looking for Tyra. Not the sort of lock you can plug your slate into and have it run down the combination; salvage operators write in some bugfuk crazy layers. That said, you do realize Tyra's codes would have been too old to open this?"

"Her codes would have been a starting point for hacking the lock."

"Tricky." Big Bill nodded slowly. "But possible if you have someone sufficiently skilled."

"I have someone." Depending, of course, Cho qualified silently, on how much his *thytrins* had exaggerated young Nadayki's talents.

"Good." With the eye at full magnification, Big Bill examined every millimeter of the lock, then—after snapping his slate back onto his belt—turned and swept a critical gaze over Cho and his two companions. "If you actually manage to get that open, do you know what you have?"

"A cargo we can sell for one fuk of a lot of money," Nat told him.

"No."

"No?" she repeated, eyes wide.

"What you have," Big Bill said quietly before she could continue her protest, "is a means to an end. With those weapons in the hands of free merchants…"

Doc turned a snicker into a cough.

Big Bill ignored him. "…you, *we* could take what we wanted."

"We take what we want now," Nat pointed out, wiping bloody fingertips on her overalls.

"No." Cho answered before Big Bill could. "We take what we can. There's a difference."

The big man nodded again. "That's what I like about you, Mackenzie Cho. You see the whole picture. The information about how the little gray aliens played puppet master across known space and beyond has the Confederation teetering on the edge," he continued. "We apply pressure at the right point and we can keep everything we can take." Reaching back, he pressed one hand against the cargo bay hatch. "With what's in here, we can take enough to make a difference."

"The Navy will try and stop us," Doc said slowly. Folding his arms over his chest, he frowned and added, "Advantage always goes to the side that doesn't play by the rules."

It was like both halves of his personality had made their own point.

"With this..." Big Bill smacked his palm against the hatch, the sudden impact loud enough Nat jumped and swore. "...we can make our own rules. Now then..." His smile was genial as he leaned back and folded his arms, smile broadening when Doc scowled and unfolded his. "...let's go over our options. I could purchase this from you, as is. You'd make less than you would if you sold the contents piece by piece, but opening the armory would be my concern. You would, of course, no longer have first choice of the weapons for your own personal use, nor would you be at the forefront of the revolution."

Cho could feel Doc and Nat staring at the back of his head. "No deal." This was his chance. The way Vrijheid had been William Ponner's.

"I thought that would be your answer." He nodded his approval. "The second option involves you returning with a new and preferably less broken CSO and, once you have the codes, I do the hack myself."

And Cho remembered how Big Bill had acquired the station.

"There's two reasons I don't like that plan," Big Bill continued. "First, the Corps objects to outsiders getting their hands on their toys, and they make that objection with extreme prejudice."

"I thought it'd just blow up," Nat muttered.

"Exactly." Big Bill beamed at her. "And I do not risk blowing myself up for anything less than one hundred percent of the profits. Second, I can't be associated with something that might not work. Bad for business. Option three begins the same way as option two, but you hook up to the old ore docks—there's an old explosives storage pod there that should protect the station should things go wrong. Once that lock is off, I get fifteen percent of the contents for the use of my secure space, and you can sell whatever you don't personally want after you and I discuss distribution."

"You and I?" Cho asked, his voice level even as he fought the urge to sneer. "You'll get your fifteen percent off the top, sure." He didn't want the *Heart* blown to shit any more than Big Bill wanted his station damaged. "But I have a Marine armory full of weapons. Why will I need your to help get rid of them?"

One of the Grr brothers growled.

Big Bill, however, seemed pleased to have been asked. "Weapons change everything. I know where they should go to both get you top price and have the most advantageous effect. But, more importantly, before it even comes to that, you're going to want my help because I can see that you capture a working salvage operator."

"How?"

"Captain Firrg has a small outstanding debt she'll be happy to clear."

Two ships would make it a lot easier, turning the nearly impossible to even odds. Cho nodded. "She follows my orders." Mackenzie Cho, Captain of the *Heart of Stone*, took orders from no one.

"Of course. I'll set up the meeting. Say, 1600 at the Golden Griose?"

Cho glanced over at Nat, who shrugged. "Schedule's clear, Cap."

"Good. We've got some lovely potential for change building here, Captain Cho." Big Bill's expression suggested he was moments away from rubbing his hands together. "Get me some *actual* and we'll talk again. Try to grab a Human," he threw back over his shoulder, heading for the air lock. "I've always felt we have the strongest, not to mention least ethical attachment to self-preservation."

Falling into step behind him, the Grr brothers laughed.

* * *

Cho took Huirre with him to the meeting at the Griose. Firrg's crew was completely Krai, and he had no idea how good her Federate was. Good enough to function, definitely, but he wanted no confusion on either side.

"I hear she's out here because of lost love," Huirre said as they made their way across the Hub to the Griose. "The one she wanted, wanted another, and it blackened her heart." He ducked a shoe thrown out of the pushing match over by the falafel cart, paused, and frowned. "Or that might've been on a vid I picked up at Cully's when I was in for those gloves."

"Keep up," Cho growled. "And I don't give a H'san's ass why she's out here," he added as Huirre fell back in beside him. "She follows my orders, no questions asked. And she doesn't fukking need to know what we're carrying, understood?"

"Aye, Captain. But if she asks?"

"I do the talking."

"Aye, aye Capt… *gunin yer chrick!*"

Edible was the highest compliment in the Krai language. As far as Cho could see, Captain Firrg didn't look significantly different from Huirre—a bit bigger maybe, about a meter high, greenish-gray mottled scalp, lightly bristled, three sets of paired nose ridges—currently expanded as though she were smelling something nasty as they made their way toward her.

"I don't like this," she growled before Cho could actually sit. "And when I say this, I mean Humans. Don't like them, never have. Only reason I'm in on this is because Big Bill says you're taking down a Human."

"And because you're into him for a new set of air scrubbers," Cho reminded her, sitting down. Anything could be bought on Vrijheid, including information. Firrg's Federate was better than he'd expected—fluent and without so much as an accent. He could have brought Nat instead of Huirre, who sat staring at the other captain with hunger. With the Krai, hunger covered a number of options.

"*Serley* son of a bitch wants his pound of flesh," Firrg snarled. Smart people didn't assume they could tell what another species was thinking but the hatred in her eyes was unmistakable. Cho wondered if Big Bill knew. Or cared if he did. "I have no choice," she continued, "the *Dargonar* is by your side..."

"And under my command."

"And under your *serley* command," she agreed through clenched teeth, shifting a little of that hatred toward him. "But that's it. Everything goes through me. I don't want your kind having any contact with my crew, and I don't want any part in what you and Big Bill are up to."

"Are you that certain without knowing what it is?"

"I'm that certain. One job together and I go back to not giving a shit about what you or this *cark* sucker gets up to." Holding up her slate, she nodded toward his. "I've got a set of temporary codes you can use to contact me."

She had a jagged scar across her forehead, Cho realized as the codes transferred, the angles too regular to be accidental. When she saw him staring, she drew her lips back off her teeth, and Huirre whimpered. Cho curled his own lip in response. He'd been hated before; it didn't bother him much. During his court-martial, the hatred coming off the families of the dead sailors had been so virulent the Navy'd had to remove them from the courtroom in order to get anything done. "Any suggestions where we can pick up a Human CSO fast and easy?"

Her nose ridges snapped shut. "Fuk you; I'm support during takedown. That's it. You can do your own *serley* research."

He wouldn't have trusted her information anyway. "I'll be taking the *Heart of Stone* out in about fifty-six hours. Be ready."

"If you can't give me an exact time now, I want a four-hour heads-up," she told him flatly.

"Deal." In the interest of keeping his fingers, Cho didn't hold out his hand. He watched Huirre watch her leave the Groise. "You know why she hates Humans?"

Huirre snorted. "Why does anyone hate Humans? Pity she won't be part of the revolution. I'd love a chance to sink my teeth into that one. What a pair of *amalork*."

Only the Krai could get hot about jaw muscles. "She'd have you for breakfast."

"I'd die happy."

Cho rolled his eyes and waved a server over. Krai bar or not, if he left now, it would look like Firrg commanded his movement, and he wasn't having that. "Just as well she doesn't want in on the buy. I wouldn't trust the psychotic bitch not to turn on me the moment she was armed."

"That, Captain..." Huirre reached across the table and drained Firrg's abandoned glass. "...is because you're a very smart man."

"You sure you're okay with this?"

Torin glanced up from her slate, more than happy to be pulled away from studying government regs defining legal salvage. "With working?"

"Yeah, because you used to lay about on your arse." Spinning the control chair around, Craig lifted his legs and dropped his heels on the scuff mark at the edge of the panel. "You've called CSOs carrion crows in the past."

"Never to you."

He shrugged. "You were tanked for quite a while after Crucible, and Sergeant Jiir has both a low tolerance for alcohol and a touching belief in the fairness of the universe."

"He'll draw to an inside straight?"

"Every damned time."

Torin thought about asking how *many* times but decided Jiir was an adult and a sergeant, and if the first time he'd played cards with Craig hadn't taught him to back away slowly, well, that wasn't her problem anymore. As for tales told under the influence...

She set her slate down on the small table. "I didn't like you—collectively you—making money off the dead. Which..." She held up her hand to cut off his protest. "...was pretty fukking hypocritical considering how I made my living. I know. But these were my dead, and..."

"And I wasn't in the club."

"Yeah." It sounded petty and arrogant put like that, but Torin had long since learned to own her shit. "Then there was you, personally..." She rolled her eyes as he flexed."...and by the time I woke up in that tank, it was clear you and me, we weren't an every now and then kind of thing, so I did a little thinking. When they gave me back my slate in rehab, I did some research. Do you know how many families of military personnel Civilian Salvage Operators have given closure to?"

Craig shook his head. "Nine out of ten times, it's scrap, Torin. Maybe some retrievable tech."

"And that tenth time has added up to three hundred and seventy-one thousand, two hundred and twenty brought home. And counting."

"That's..." He blinked. Frowned. Swung his feet down to the deck and leaned forward, elbows braced against his thighs. "That's a lot."

"Those little gray plastic bastards have kept us at war for a long time. And that number doesn't include the DNA evidence from the Primacy on record. As soon as the politicians stop talking out of their asses, they can go home, too."

Torin watched his mouth move as he repeated the number silently to himself. "That's what changed your mind about salvage operators?" he said at last.

"That's what changed my mind."

"Made it all right for you to throw in with me?" They didn't talk about what they had between them, so she shrugged. "It didn't hurt that the sex was amazing."

"Was?"

"It's been a few hours, I don't like to apply old intell to new condi—"

She could have stopped him from toppling her off the chair and onto the deck, but as that had been the reaction she'd been trying to evoke, she'd have just been shooting herself in the foot.

A little over two hours later, the alarm went off.

"Ten minutes and we're out of Susumi space." Craig kissed her bare shoulder and sat up. "You should take the controls."

"I should? Why?"

"Because either things are good and there's nothing you can screw up. Or," he continued getting to his feet, "things'll be fukked and we'll die instantly, so there's still nothing you can screw up."

"Or we enter regular space next to a big yellow alien ship

that turns out to be the mastermind—masterminds— behind centuries of intergalactic bloodshed."

"Yeah, right," he snorted holding out his hand. "Like that'll happen. Again. Come on."

Scooping her shirt off the floor as she stood, Torin tossed it onto the pilot's chair before she sat down. She checked the runout on the Susumi equation, then she posed her hands over the thruster controls in case they needed to avoid the unexpected.

Promise counted down from ten, then the stars reappeared in the small front port.

"Another trip where we didn't come a gutser," Craig patted the bulkhead. "I count that a win."

"Navigation says we're right where we're supposed to be," Torin told him as the forward thrusters came on and they began to brake. Half her attention on their speed, she asked, "So where are we?"

"Just on the edge of an old debris field. It's big but well picked over. There's definitely nothing left here but chunks of metal and plastic for the recyclers. No tech. No DNA. I figured it'd be best for your first time out." Out of the corner of her eye, she could see him skimming back into his shorts. "Of course, that was before we had our talk. Maybe you'd rather…"

"Scrap for a first time out is fine."

He reached over Torin's shoulder, and activated the long-range sensors. "There should be another ship out here. Old guy named Rogelio Page has been working this patch for years."

"He won't mind that we're here?"

"The debris field is big enough for two tags. He has first tag but second tag is open. He'll appreciate the company, tell us what sector we can clear, and be backup if something goes wrong. And it'll give me a chance to check on him. He doesn't come in much."

"Oh, yeah. Rugged individualists," Torin muttered. "Alone and independent."

"What was that?"

"Nothing. I just…" A sudden alarm from her implant cut her off. She tongued the volume down and frowned. "Strange. I've picked up another implant."

"Picked up?"

"Turns out the upgrade the techs put in when they rebuilt my jaw has a finder in it." The techs never left a scar. Torin rubbed at her jaw anyway. "Nice of them to tell me."

"You didn't read the documentation?"

"No one ever reads the documentation." An alert from an implant shot down Craig's belief only scrap remained out here. "I can link with *Promise*, give her the coordinates."

"So what are you waiting for?"

She worked best under a hierarchy, knowing where to push and knowing where it was best to give in. This equal partners thing took some getting used to.

As *Promise* brought them up to the new coordinates, Torin expected to find a piece of jaw, overlooked in the vastness and emptiness of space, not an entire naked body, cartwheeling slowly against a backdrop of stars.

Even before bringing the body on board, two things were obvious.

The Marine hadn't been dead long.

And he'd been tortured.

THREE

Torin knelt by the body of the dead Marine, cataloguing his visible injuries. Had she been able to download the stored medical data on his implant as well as receive the BFFM beacon, she'd have been able to list internal damages as well. As it was, she could record only what she could see. That was enough. All the bones in his hands and feet had been broken, the cartilage in his nose had been removed, and one eye had been punctured multiple times. No point in destroying both eyes—that would have kept him from seeing what was coming.

His torturer had known how to use fear.

His kneecaps had been twisted to the side. His genitals had been both bruised and burned. Given the purple-and-green discoloration covering his torso, the odds were good ribs had been cracked and then pressure had been applied to the damage.

Over the years, Torin had seen a lot of injuries—limbs lost, guts literally spilled—but nothing that provided evidence in flesh and bone of such deliberate brutality.

He had a crest tattooed on the bicep of his left arm: 3rd Division, 1st Re'carta, 4th Battalion, Sierra Company.

"Did you know him, then?"

Torin took a final recording, shifted her weight back, and stood. "He has a sergeant's implant. Given his apparent age, I assume he's been retired for more than a few years." Which wasn't exactly what Craig had asked. She hadn't served with him, but she knew him. Had stood beside him on the yellow line that first day at Ventris Station. Had sat beside him on a VTA dropping for dirt. Had lain beside him in the mud, hands steady on her KC-7 as he bitched about the weather. Torin sent a copy of the file to *Promise*'s data storage. Just in case. "He didn't tell them what they wanted to know."

Craig rubbed at the reddened dent the plumbing hook-in from the HE suit had left on his hip. "You know that because...?"

"There's nothing here that would have killed him outright." She gestured with the slate. "He died of the cumulative effect of his injuries, so his death was unintentional. Also, they didn't destroy his ability to talk— his lips are split, but they didn't go after his teeth or his tongue, although he's bitten through his tongue himself."

"Doesn't look like he carked it that long ago either." When Torin shifted her attention off her slate and onto Craig, he shrugged. "If he'd been in vacuum any length of time, he'd have dehydrated more."

"So, not left over from the battle."

"Battle?"

"The one that created the debris field."

"Fuk, no," he snorted. "That battle happened back before you enlisted."

A lifetime ago. "Where's the nearest Warden's office?"

"Torin..."

One hand on the sergeant's shoulder, she met Craig's gaze. "This one's mine."

"They won't..."

"Craig."

"Nearest Warden's office is on Sulun Station—Sulun's a recent di'Taykan expansion planet." He rattled off the coordinates, but when Torin raised a brow at him, he added, "It's a short fold."

"How short?"

"About a day and a half in Susumi." Craig gestured at the body and added in a tone so neutral it had to be deliberate. "He'll have to be secured in the pen."

Torin thought about Jan and Sirin, laid out for viewing in the market. "You say that like you think I might object."

"He's a Marine."

"He's a dead Marine. I don't get sentimental about the dead."

Craig stared at her for a long moment. "You get angry," he said at last.

"Sometimes," she admitted.

He nodded, although she wasn't entirely certain what he was acknowledging. "Well, the sergeant here's not going to get any fresher. Throw out one segment while I suit up again, would you."

With a last look at the body, Torin moved to the pilot's chair and called up the screen that deployed the salvage pen. She'd ridden in it—with the survivors of the recon team sent to Big Yellow—and even if the sergeant had still been in a position to care, he'd likely had rougher rides over the years.

"So who do you think dumped the poor bastard out here?" Craig asked. She could hear the creak of his HE suit going back on.

"I'm hoping pirates."

"Hoping?"

"I don't like the alternative." She didn't need to voice the alternative; Craig had been there for the reveal. If the gray plastic aliens had maintained an interstellar war for generations in order to use it as a social laboratory then they could easily torture a few individuals in order to provide more *context*. "The sergeant's spent a lot of the last few years in space. His feet have no calluses and there's a scar on his hip where a suit's rubbed." Glancing up as the segment began unfolding, Torin muttered, "They can come up with broccoli in a tube and yet they still can't design a plumbing hook-in that doesn't leave a mark."

Her fingers drummed against the inert trim of the control panel. One more unnecessary mark on the sergeant's body. This one placed by bad design rather than cruelty, but still.

Then she realized the only sounds she could hear, other than her fingers, were the distant booms and scrapes of the pen moving into position against the hull. "Craig?"

Half into his suit, he stood and stared down at the body like he was seeing it for the first time. Then he stepped over the sergeant's splayed legs, the suit's bright-orange arms flapping around his waist, and reached past Torin to tap the control panel. His lips were pressed into a thin line, and a muscle jumped in his jaw.

Torin breathed shallowly through her mouth—the insides of HE suits worn as often as CSOs wore theirs emitted a distinctly pungent aroma—and waited. Ships the size of the *Promise* were too small for secrets. He'd tell her in time.

When Craig straightened, a man's face filled one of the screens. The image had light-brown eyes, a broad nose, salt-and-pepper stubble, and an expression that suggested he didn't think much of having his image recorded. "Is this him?"

"Is this who?" Torin asked.

"The dead Marine."

She twisted and stared down at the body on the deck.

The chin, at least, was the same. "Probably. Who is he?"

"Rogelio Page."

They found Page's ship, *Fortune's Fancy*, drifting by the far edge of the debris field, two sections of pen deployed, both half filled with scrap. Plastics in one, metal in the other.

Craig zoomed in on the trailing safety line. "They took him while he was securing the load. That line's been cut."

Torin could think of no good reason why a man might cut his own line although a few bad ones occurred to her. "Pirates?"

"Pirates would take the pen."

"Whoever took him didn't want what he had, they wanted something he knew."

Page's ship was smaller even than the *Promise*.

"If we tighten his salvage into one pen, power *Fancy* down, and deploy all our panels..." Craig's fingers danced over the screen; the complex mathematics of maneuvering unique parameters beyond Torin's current skill set, "...we can take ship, salvage, and Page to the Warden at Sulun. Dying's one thing," he said in answer to Torin's silent question. "What Page went through, that's not part of the accepted risk package. And you're right. Dealing with this kind of shit is what the Wardens do."

"So to sum up..." One Who Maintains Order at the Edge rested long, golden-furred forearms on her desk and laced gleaming claws together, "...you believe that two Civilian Salvage Operators—Jan Garrett-Wong and di'Akusi Sirin—were killed for salvage they had gained possession of and another—Civilian Salvage Operator ex-Sergeant Rogelio Page—was tortured in order to elicit information and although you do not know if Civilian Salvage Operator ex-Sergeant Page had been in contact with either Civilian Salvage Operator GarrettWong or Civilian Salvage Operator Sirin..."

Craig shifted, and Torin closed her hand on his arm, shaking her head when he glanced her way. Experience had taught her that the Dornagain could not be hurried. Would not be hurried. Their obsessive attention to detail and insistence on considering every possible variable before coming to a decision made them the perfect civil servant. At least from the government's point of view.

"...you postulate that these terrible crimes were somehow connected." Highlights rippled slowly across her fur as she shook her head. "Your service in the Confederation's defense has perhaps made you paranoid, ex-Gunnery Sergeant Kerr."

To the Dornagain, titles and names were one and the same. Torin gritted her teeth and let it stand. Besides, being paranoid had been part of her job.

"Civilian Salvage Operator ex-Sergeant Page clearly had a falling out with someone, of that we can agree."

All Dornagain sounded vaguely patronizing. Torin reminded herself not to take it personally.

"But to extrapolate his unfortunate fate into something larger is distinctly premature. We do not yet have his post mortem..."

Page had been so lovingly brutalized the odds were good his torturer had left DNA behind.

"...or any forensic evidence from his ship or salvage that might connect this to the previous incident—which, I must remind you, did not occur in my jurisdiction."

It would have only muddied the waters to admit that the other murders hadn't been reported. Given the distances, it would take some time before the Wardens could compare notes across sectors.

"We are able to recognize coincidence," One Who Maintains

Order at the Edge continued. "But I assure you, we will conduct a full investigation once all the evidence is in. Thank you for bringing this to the attention of the Wardens' office." Unlacing her claws, she tapped out a fast sequence against an active screen on her desk. "If you provide the pertinent data to my assistant, you will, of course, be compensated for the fold."

"Feel free to say I told you so."

Craig turned far enough to see Torin's profile. She didn't look particularly angry. If he had to say, she looked weary. "What about?"

Her snort had no force backing it. "The Wardens."

"I told you so."

"Fuk you." There wasn't a lot of force behind her laugh either, but at least she was laughing.

Leaning out over the railing, Craig swept a critical gaze over the station's central hub. He could smell chilies cooking although he couldn't nail where the smell came from. Not that it mattered; most Taykan food was hot enough to fry Human taste buds—ghost peppers had been an early Taykan import—and he'd be willing to bet he could get decent tucker anywhere on the station. "We've got a hookup paid for by the government until tomorrow, might as well eat out."

"Can we afford it?"

"We can. There's a card game in maintenance with my name on it and it's bangers to bust that someone's going to put their faith in trip nines." Torin was a competent player; if she joined the game, he had faith in her ability to break even. When he turned to face her, she was staring off into the middle distance, one finger tapping on a plastic plug cover. "Beer and *tomagoras*." He nudged her shoulder with his. "Maybe go crazy and have a little *armee* on the side. What do you say?"

She frowned. "Can you hack *Fancy's* system?"

Not what he'd expected her to say, that was for damned sure. "You want to use Page's credits?" When Torin turned to face him, Craig raised both hands and took a step back, fairly certain she wouldn't take a swing at him but not one hundred percent positive and definitely not willing to find out. "Hey, I talk about replacing what we spend on food in a card game and you ask if I can hack his ship. I jumped to the logical conclusion. Now I've had a chance to think about it, what I should have asked was: What the fuk are you talking about?"

Torin narrowed her eyes but stopped looking like she wanted to disembowel him. "The Dornagain don't work quickly."

"No shit."

"Jan and Sirin died defending their cargo from pirates. Pirates tortured Page but ignored his salvage. Two exceptions to the rules could mean the rules are changing. If the pirates are changing the rules, they're going to be moving a lot faster than One Who Maintains. I want to know if Page was in contact with the *Firebreather*. If so, they could have passed on the information that got him tortured to death."

"Why?"

"Why?" she repeated.

He hadn't been shot that look since the early days when, he suspected, she'd considered him a distinct species. Not a Marine, therefore nothing to do with her. "I know you're angry about this, Torin, hell, I'm angry about this, but a tenday ago you didn't even know pirates existed."

"And?"

"And now suddenly it's your responsibility to stop them." He scratched at the spot on his jaw where the depilatory wore off first. "Look, I get that your first inclination is to fix shit, but this shit, you can't fix. We've brought it to the Wardens, who will take their time doing sweet fuk all, and now we get on with things."

"You done?"

Worse than the look was the tone. Craig hated that tone. That gunnery sergeant tone. Both tone and look had been way too close to the surface since they'd found Page. "No, I'm not," he growled. "We risked our necks to bring this to the attention of the authorities—and don't look at me like you don't understand what I'm talking about. A ship in a pen doesn't make for an easy Susumi equation. You and me, we're not living in a cheesy vid; it's not our job to illuminate the dark between the systems with the light of justice." It was a *SpaceCops* quote. He'd never seen the show before he'd hooked up with Torin, but she loved it. When Torin folded her arms, waiting for him to go on, he sighed. "Okay, now I'm done."

"We work and live in the dark between the systems," she pointed out. Unnecessarily, considering how she'd just started the job and he'd been doing it for over a decade. "This isn't about the light of justice, it's motivated self-interest."

And about the undeniable fact that ex-Gunnery Sergeant Torin Kerr was incapable of walking away from a fight.

"All right, fine." It wasn't like he hadn't known that about her from the beginning. He could get into the *Fancy*; he'd done it once already to power her down before the jump. The ship had known Page had been out too long for his air supply, so emergency protocols had gotten him in. Whether he could access her data stores though, that was another question. If Page had locked his board down before he went out, the odds weren't high he could crack it before they attracted attention. CSO codes were idiosyncratic at best, and his codes would only take him so far. "Say I *can* hack Page's ship. First I have to get to it. What happens if the Wardens have put a guard on it?"

Torin snorted. "We're on a Taykan station. They're not that hard to distract."

Page's ship wasn't guarded. No reason why it should have been, Torin supposed. One Who Maintains wouldn't consider it part of an ongoing investigation until she had, as she'd said, a lot more evidence. They walked unchallenged into the repair bay and across the deck, footsteps echoing. Without the added bulk of her pen segments—they'd been tethered outside—*Fancy* looked dwarfed by her surroundings. Someone had run a ramp up to her air lock, but the outer door remained closed and the telltales were red.

"Let's hope they haven't recoded the lock," Craig muttered, fingers on the pad. On cue, the telltales turned green, and both outer and inner doors opened.

Torin followed Craig into the tiny air lock. He paused at the inner door and when she put one hand flat against him to steady herself, she realized that the muscles of his back had twisted into knots under his shirt. He'd only just learned to tolerate having another person on the *Promise* with him, using his resources, and *Fancy* was smaller. From what she could see over Craig's shoulder as the inner door opened, depressingly smaller. The toilet and sink folded up into the bulkhead and Page had left the toilet folded down before his last trip out. It smelled like he'd forgot to hit reclamation when he finished. Or maybe he was just a lousy shot.

He'd decorated by attaching old-fashioned, two-dimensional, Human-centric porn to every vertical surface. The closest piece proved just how flexible a bipedal species could be. Not something Torin would want to look at every day, out in deep space, *alone*, but it took all kinds.

"I'll wait out here."

Craig turned just far enough to glare. "I'm fine."

"I know." Since her hand was already on his back, she traced the valley of his spine with her thumb, fingers trailing over the heavy muscle to either side. "But you don't need me hanging over your shoulder, and if I go in there with you, there won't be any other option."

His gaze swept around the cabin, then back to her. It didn't take long. "Good point," he said.

As she took her hand away, she felt him begin to relax.

Back at the bottom of the ramp, habit dropped her into an easy parade rest. If it turned out Page knew what Jan and Sirin had salvaged, knew what they'd died trying to protect, that connection might be enough to light a fire under One Who Maintains' enormous, furry ass. If it didn't, it was still information they could take to a military station in order to direct the Navy patrols. The patrols responsible for hunting down and removing the pirates.

Pirates.

She still had trouble believing it.

There wasn't enough organized violence around? People had to freelance?

Maybe the Elder Races were right. Maybe a species shouldn't achieve interstellar capability until they'd learned to manage their aggression. Not that it mattered, after a couple hundred years of war, that ship had well and truly folded and there could be no going back. She wondered how the Primacy, made up entirely of young aggressive species, was managing without the focus the gray plastic aliens had provided. Odds were about even they'd started pounding on each other.

In much less time than Torin had expected, the sound of Craig's boots ringing against the ramp pulled her around to face him.

He shook his head as he walked toward her. "Not locked, not that it mattered. There's no record of contact between Page and *Firebreather*, but," he added before Torin could respond, "he had been messaging someone fairly frequently on the Two-four. No idea who, but I uploaded their codes so we can find out. A mate of Alia's is maintaining a database—who uses what codes when. Not that I'm saying some might use more than one set of codes," he added, seeing her expression. "If Jan or Sirin happened to have been talking to the same person Page was…"

"Long shot," Torin acknowledged, falling into step beside him as he stepped off onto the deck. Even a tenuous connection would be better than nothing but it wouldn't get One Who Maintains or the Navy moving against the pirates.

"We'll bog in first, I'm starving." Craig threw an arm around her shoulders. "Then we go make Rogelio Page proud by taking a group of hardworking engineers for every credit they have."

"That would make him proud?"

"It'd make me happy."

When it came right down to it, the living *had* to be more important than the dead. "Good enough."

Torin finished checking the Susumi equation and glanced up at Craig, who backed away and tried to look as though he hadn't been checking it over with her. Given that mistakes were usually fatal, she didn't mind. "So, tell me why we're returning to the same debris field?"

"We have first tag on it, now Page is dead." Craig scowled at the empty coffeepot, then took it into the head to fill it, raising his voice over the sound of running water. "Not to mention, if we chuck back to our previous coordinates, the government will pay for the fold. It's a little ghoulish, but it's practical since the reason we were headed there originally still stands—we know there's no surprises in the salvage to mess up a rookie run."

"Except for the pirates."

He froze halfway back through the hatch and stared at her. "Shit."

Seeing how long she could let him hang wasn't really an option; maintaining a relationship took roughly the same care as training a green second lieutenant, leaving little room for error between teasing and making him look like a fool. "If the pirates had planned on staying in that area, they'd have sent both the body and the ship into the nearest star. I expect they're long gone."

"So you gave me the gobful about it because… ?"

She frowned. "Seemed like you'd forgotten them. I don't think we should."

Craig made a noncommittal noise as he crossed back to the coffeemaker. She watched him set the coffee to brew, wondering what the noise had meant. He stood, back toward her, until his mug filled, then he turned and said, "You sure you're not looking for a new enemy?"

"Why would I want a new enemy?"

"You've always had one."

"Habit?"

"Purpose."

Torin opened her mouth to deny it, then closed it again. She wasn't one hundred percent sure he was wrong. From what she could see of his expression behind the mug, he knew it.

"We just got a yabber from Alia. No connection between Firebreather *and* Fortune's Favor. *She doesn't know who Page was messaging, but she does know Jan and Sirin weren't. Weren't messaging the same person. At all. Ever."*

Torin swore softly as she cinched a tie-cable tight and checked that it was reading the mass of the salvage. "No chance of yanking the Wardens' thumbs out of their collective asses, then."

"Not for what looks to be a shitty coincidence. Torin, that piece with the electronics in it…"

Grinning, Torin silently mouthed the rest of the sentence along with him.

"…has to go in the pen closest to the ship so we can hook it up and make sure there's nothing that might go active when we fold."

"I'm on it." There weren't enough "electronics" on the piece to go active even if they hooked it directly to the engines.

"I'd mentioned that?"

"Couple of times." Considering he'd spent almost as long working alone as she had in the Corps, he wasn't doing too badly in his supervisory position. The small clump of tagged debris she was securing didn't need two people suited up, and she needed the practice. It hadn't taken her more than fifteen minutes to convince him of that. Had he been a green lieutenant, she could have done it faster. There were days she definitely missed her old life.

Demagnetizing her boots, she tightened up her safety line and used it to gain enough momentum to flip out of the pen, magging up again to drop down just forward of where she'd racked the "gun" used to attach the tags to the salvage. Fine motor skills suffered in an HE suit, so the trigger mechanism was oversized but familiar. There were a limited number of ways *aim and pull* could be interpreted mechanically.

Twisting to the left, she lined up the next piece of salvage in the crosshairs, and fired, careful to brace herself against the minor momentum. It would take a lot more than one shot to actually move her anywhere, and one shot was all she needed.

"No surprise you're good at that."

It would have been more surprising if she'd missed it, given the size.

"Your tax dollars at work," she muttered as she locked her suit on the tag, released her boots, and pushed off. Her jet swiveled to eighteen degrees almost immediately and fired a micro burst, lining her up more precisely. There were automated systems that would do all this from the control panel of the ship, but every piece of equipment added cost, and salvage operators never had the kind of margin that allowed them to ignore the brains and bodies they could wrap in an HE suit and use for free. Torin suspected Craig, on his own, had seldom bothered with either the jets or the 100 meters of safety line spooling out behind her.

She only wore the jets on Craig's insistence since jets and an unbreakable safety line was a fair definition of redundant.

"So…" Torin could hear him drumming his fingers against the edge of the control panel. Knew he was searching for things to say that didn't involve the suggestion that she come on in and he take it from there. *"…you're not arguing the shitty coincidence theory?"*

"Did you want me to?"

"Didn't figure you as believing in coincidence."

"I believe in it," Torin told him. "I don't trust it. Was Pedro able to add anything to Page's background?"

"Haven't heard from him yet. Alia says he took the smaller ship out to do some second tagging at 772ST4."

Still only halfway to the new salvage, Torin had time to run over the CSO's debris field designations. "The *Kertack* and the *Cameroonian*?"

"That's the one."

The two Confederation battleships as well as three cruisers and nearly equal representation from the Primacy had faced off about eighteen months ago. Torin had been tanked at the time but heard about it when she got out because one of her physical therapists had a *thytrin* on the cruiser that had been blown with all hands. The other ships had taken twenty-five to thirty percent casualties. Torin didn't know what the Primacy's loses had been, but they'd definitely contributed to the debris. More importantly… "That's almost to the edge."

"Yeah, but there's an ace chance of pulling in pieces of enemy tech."

"There's a good chance of attracting enemy attention."

"War's over."

She sighed and flipped around to begin decelerating. "He's got kids."

"To provide for."

"Yeah, I get that." And she did. But when she thought of Pedro out on the edge, she couldn't stop herself from thinking of Jeremy without one of his fathers.

* * *

"*Dargonar* had her engines on, Captain." Huirre transferred his slate to his right foot so he could spread both hands in a *fukked if I know* gesture. "But there's no way of knowing if Captain Firrg used the equations I sent her until we're out of Susumi space and she's either there or she isn't."

"She'll be there," Cho growled. "I don't trust her as far as you could spit a spleen, but she screws us over and she screws over Big Bill."

"She could turn on us on the other side. Lie to Big Bill about it."

"Why would she do that?" Dysun asked, most of her attention on shutting down the communications board.

"Firrg hates Humans." Huirre's nose ridges flared. "Captain's Human. So're Nat and Doc."

Dysun shrugged, hair rising and falling in time with her shoulders—both the Taykan and Krai had adopted the gesture, but only the Taykan had really mastered it. "So's Big Bill."

"Doesn't count."

She looked up at that. "Why doesn't…"

"Enough!" Cho snapped. Huirre had made the only relevant point—the *Dargonar* would be there when they emerged or she wouldn't; they couldn't do shit about it either way, and he was sick to death of the constant speculation. "Go fuk your *thytrins* or something."

"Aye, aye, Captain!" As the last of the board locked down, Dysun tossed off an enthusiastic salute and ran from the control room.

"Like there was a chance of *or something*. You'd think she hadn't got any for a tenday instead of a couple of hours," Huirre snorted. Then he snapped his teeth together and added, "*Serley* di'Taykan."

"So join them," Cho sighed, sliding down in his chair until his spine barely maintained contact. Inside Susumi space, the ship didn't require a captain and, as long as the crew managed to keep from killing each other, he didn't give a shit what they got up to.

"It's not…"

He could read the reason for Huirre's recent ill humor in the pause. "Firrg wouldn't have you if you were the last Krai in known space. You've been contaminated by contact with Humans. You want to go crawling to her and beg her to take you on so you can be horny and frustrated in her presence, be my guest."

"That's harsh, Captain." His nose ridges opened and closed a couple of times. "You'd just let me go?"

"Better than you being horny and frustrated on my boat. Go or get over her."

He shifted his slate from foot to hand and back to foot again. "Not too many female Krai out here, Captain."

"That's why the universe gave us the di'Taykan."

"It'd make me feel better if I got to *dispose* of the next CSO we pick up."

"No." Cho didn't care how fukking frustrated his helmsman got, the last thing he wanted, given what had sent Huirre out into the deep, was to indulge the Krai's taste for Human flesh. Sure, running Page through Huirre's gut would have removed any evidence of the way he'd died, but it wasn't like the Wardens would stumble over the CSO's body anytime soon. OutSector Wardens were about as much of a threat as a pouched H'san.

"So, Captain…" Huirre's nose ridges began opening and closing slowly. Cho figured he was breathing himself into a better mood. "…seems like this equation's going to take us pretty damned close to the edge."

"We need a younger salvage operator. The young take chances. The edge is all about taking chances. We've got a line on a single ship, and I don't want a repeat of Page."

"Ah." Huirre nodded. "Suppose it doesn't hurt that the Wardens never get out that far."

"No," Cho agreed in a tone that said the conversation was over, "it doesn't."

The *Dargonar* had come out of Susumi space three seconds before the *Heart of Stone*, having made no changes in the equations Huirre had sent. Cho chose to take that as a good sign.

"Move in at one eighty to our zero." Cho frowned down at the ship locked into his long-range scanners. "Don't worry about being seen, just tag the pen. When they dump, they'll hit their aft thrusters." Fukking predictable. The first thing a CSO did after dumping their pen was hit the aft thrusters every damned time. Surged straight ahead until they could fold into Susumi space. It was like every one of them forgot normal space had three dimensions. "We'll be waiting to grapple the ship in. Make sure the operator is in the ship before you tag."

"Gre ta ejough geyko. *You just do your job and leave us to do ours. We keep what's in the pen. Firrg out. "*

Cho glared at the back of Huirre's head. "Translation."

"Roughly, sit on it and rotate." Huirre kept his gaze locked on his board. "She's moving out."

"Take us into position."

"We can't just let her have the pen, Captain!" Dysun protested.

"We can if I say we can," Cho told her shortly. Let Firrg have the pen. He had a Marine armory with all the promise of a great and glorious future it contained, and the Krai captain didn't have a hope in hell of scoring anything that even came close to matching it.

As Huirre maneuvered the *Heart of Stone* into position, her signature masked by the static emitted by a pair of lopsided rings circling an equally lopsided planetoid, he split his attention between the salvage ship and the empty space beyond it, waiting for Firrg to appear.

"Captain, the salvage ship's engines have come online." Dysun transferred the information to Cho's screen. "I think they're getting ready to move out."

"No one asked for your opinion," Huirre growled, hands and feet ready over his board.

The di'Taykan's hair flipped up on the side closest to the Krai. "Who tied your *kayt* in a knot?"

"Gren sa talamec!"

"If someone stuffed it up yours, you'd be in a better mood," she snorted.

"Shut up. Both of you." Fingers digging into the edge of his screen, Cho willed Firrg to make her move.

"Nets are away, Captain!"

"I don't see them."

"We're not picking them up on visuals, but there's a ripple in the data." Hair flicking quickly back and forth, Dysun bent over her board. I'm boosting magnification. Give them a minute or two to show… There!"

"I see them."

She drummed her fingers on the inert edging. "If that ship starts to move before the nets…"

"We know," Huirre interrupted. "For *horon's* sake, we *all* know."

Twenty kilometers.

Fifteen kilometers.

Five.

Contact.

"Anchor lines have caught. *Dargonar* has powered the buoys. They've dumped their pen, Captain! They're moving!"

"Get them, Huirre."

"Aye, aye, Captain."

Huirre moved the *Heart of Stone* out of concealment directly toward the fleeing ship.

Suddenly faced with another ship, the salvage operator did the unexpected and went straight up the Y-axis.

"Son of a fukking bitch!" Cho shifted forward on his seat as though the movement would bring them into alignment. Huirre had them perfectly positioned had the other ship been where it was supposed to be. It just figured that today, when it meant so much, he'd run into the one original thinker in the entire fukking salvage fleet. "Almon!"

"Captain?"

"Get the grapples into that ship!"

"It's not…"

"I know it's not! Huirre, bring the aft end around!" In spite of the inertial dampeners, his stomach lurched as Huirre flipped the *Heart* vertically. "Almon, do it!"

"But…"

"Now!" He was not letting this salvage operator get away. Not when he was so close to getting that armory open.

"Aye, aye, Captain. Grapples away!"

Cho watched the signals from the grapple ends close in on the smaller ship, willing them to make contact and dig in. He'd haul that CSO's ass inboard so fast it would… Contact! "Huirre!"

"Aye, Captain." Eyes locked on his own screens, Huirre worked the lateral thrusters with both hands. "Adjusting angles."

"Shit!"

"Talk to me, Almon."

"Looks like the Susumi drive's punctured!"

The silence in the control room was so complete Cho could have sworn he heard half the light receptors in Dysun's eyes snap closed. "Looks like?" he growled. "Be sure!"

"I tried to warn…"

"Cover your own ass, why don't you," Huirre muttered.

"Captain! Energy leakage." Dysun's voice had risen half an octave. "There's a puncture for sure."

A punctured Susumi drive meant they were, at best, moments away from being caught in a blast wave of Susumi energy. At worst, they'd go up with the other ship.

"Release grapples!"

"Released! But it'll take twenty-seven seconds to bring them in!"

"Huirre! Get us out of here!"

"Captain! The grapples!"

"Fuk the grapples! Let them swing!" Being smacked about by their own lines was the least of their worries. Susumi explosions twisted space. "Huirre, get us back behind that rock!" The planetoid that had hidden them earlier offered their best chance of survival; its bulk would deflect most of the Susumi wave.

Huirre burned everything they had. They were still too close.

"What the fuk is going on up there?" Krisk had bypassed the comm protocols again.

Before Cho could answer, Huirre snarled a fast sentence in Krai at the engineer, who growled back, "Not on my watch."

The *Heart of Stone* surged forward. Swearing, Huirre worked his board with all four extremities, fighting to maintain course while riding the unexpected burst of power. They'd just passed the planetoid's rings and were rounding the horizon when the salvage ship blew. In the 2.73 seconds it took for the blast wave to hit, Huirre managed to get most of the *Heart* to safety. Cho made a mental note to give him a really big gun when they got the armory open.

If they survived.

The blast hit the aft end just behind the cargo hold, flinging the *Heart* end over end. Huirre danced both hands and feet across his board, firing microsecond bursts on one thruster after another to keep them clear of the rings. Rock slammed into the hull. The lights flared and went out. Dysun swore and threw herself backward as her board sparked, left hand cradling her right.

Then it was over, the control room lit only by the telltales on the boards.

"Nat!"

"Aye, Cap. Checking cargo integrity."

"Fuk cargo integrity." Krisk sounded furious. *"We've got two small hull breaches, and we're at half thrusters until someone gets out there and looks at the damage the right fukking grapple did."*

"The hull breaches…"

"I sent Lime-boy out to do interior patches…" Krisk had never bothered to learn the di'Taykan's names. *"…but at least one is going to need exterior work. Easy fix. No idea about the rest until I see on real time."*

"Could be worse," Huirre muttered, still working his board.

"I'm fried." Still holding one hand against her chest, Dysun danced the fingers of the other over a blank screen. "Scanners are out. Internal communications are using the captain's station as their primary. It'll only take a moment to reroute external comms."

"One-handed?"

She glanced down at her hand, seemed to see the reddened curl of her fingers for the first time, and whimpered, her hair flattening tight against her skull.

"Get down to Doc. Have him fix it, then get your ass back here." Pain had shut her eyes down so far there was almost no black among the orange. Given the lack of light, he wondered how she could even see.

"The comm…"

"You think I'm fukking useless, is that it?" As her eyes darkened slightly, he dove into the guts of the operating system. Theoretically, the entire ship could be flown from the captain's board, but the defaults had to be overwritten first. Thank the Navy for making sure every idiot who joined could slap together a patch. When he looked up, she was still staring at him. "Go!"

"Captain?"

He looked up from his board to find Huirre watching him. It was too dark to see the Krai's expression. Hell, it was almost too dark, given the lack of hair, to be positive he was starring at Huirre's face. "What?"

"If we want lights back, I'd better help Krisk."

"How stable is our orbit?"

"Doesn't need watching if that's what you're asking." Given Huirre's careful tone, Cho figured he must smell like he was fukking furious. Good call, given that he was. "Go. Tell Krisk I said you were to concentrate on the lights. If he gives you any shit, I'll deal with him."

"Aye, Captain."

They needed the scanners and weapons back on-line. Dysun would need the lights to repair her board. "Oh, and Huirre." He heard the helmsman pause by the hatch. "You saved our asses. Good work."

"I was mostly concerned with saving my own ass, Captain."

"I don't give a flying fuk what your motivation was." He could hear Huirre grin. "Aye, Captain."

The ship's original OS had been sliced and diced when safeties had been removed and new programming added, so it took him longer than he liked to get the external comm patched through. The system was barely up and running when it grabbed an incoming repeat from the *Dargonar*.

Cho considered ignoring it. Didn't.

"So you're not dead," Firrg sounded disappointed. *"Your salvage operator is."*

Somehow, Cho managed to hold his temper. No point in starting something he couldn't finish with Dysun's board out. "We'll find another. They're like cockroaches."

"You'll find another, not me. Not my problem if you're incompetent. I did what I said I'd do, and that clears me with Big Bill. You say otherwise, I'll hunt you down and eat your liver."

It sounded more like a statement of fact than a threat.

* * *

"Good news is the armory took no damage." Nat snorted. "Of course, that's a little obvious since we're not a smoking hole in space. Marines are hard on their toys, so the Corps builds those fukkers to last." She swept her thumb over her slate and scowled down at the data. "Fact is, Cap, the cargo hold came through aces. The galley, not so much. The Susumi energy changed all of the protein strings. Won't kill us right away, but cumulative effects would be unpleasant. Doc says we should space anything with the new markers. Not even let Huirre and Krisk eat it."

"And that'll leave us with what?" Cho demanded.

She shook her head. "Not a lot. We can stay out maybe a tenday with supplements, but we're going to be hungry after a couple of days, very hungry by the end of the tenday, and sharing a ship with very hungry Krai, specially given why those two are out here—well, frankly, Cap, that doesn't appeal."

Krisk had been a Navy engineer. Accelerated promotion to petty officer and moving up fast. Then, during a battle, he'd eaten his lieutenant. Eating her had meant Krisk could stay at his post and make the repairs that saved the ship. It might have been ignored— heat of the battle, circumstances needs must— except that there had been other organics Krisk could have eaten instead. Not to mention that the review board hadn't been entirely convinced it had been the enemy that killed her.

Cho glared down at his screen. Krisk had advised against bringing the Susumi engines on-line until he checked them out.

"Shielding could've held. They might be fine. 'Course, we're toasted if they're not. Take me some time to make sure."

"How much time?"

"If you trust Lemon-and-Lime-boy to do the external patching, I can run basic tests in three. Results'll tell me how much longer."

"You've got two." Cho indicated that Almon should suit up and join Nadayki outside.

"Well, that's fukking great. My jernil always said there'd be no one to eat me after I'm gone."

Two days minimum before they could get the Susumi drive back on-line. Five and a half days folded into Susumi space to get back to Vrijheid Station. Seven and a half days with food for two. Even if the Humans and di'Taykan went on short rations to keep the Krai fed, that was dangerous bordering on covering each other in steak sauce.

"Keep rations as short as you can," he told Nat finally. "Use the supplements. How are we for water?"

"We've got water up the wazoo, Cap."

"If a wazoo is what I think it is…" Almon grinned, pausing half into his HE suit,"…there's this place where you can…"

Cho glared Almon to silence and bent over his slate, searching for a closer station where they could resupply without attracting the attention of the sector's Wardens.

Torin checked the balance on her slate one more time as they walked away from the quartermaster's office. "You're certain people make a living doing this job?"

"Some of us do." Craig bumped against her, his shoulder warm and solid. "MidSector stations pay more, but they need less and they charge more for docking and respiration. OutSector stations need the materials, so they'll take everything you have, but they haven't the lolly. It's a balancing act." His gesture took in the minimal distractions offered in the station's commercial pier, where there was one bar and an undersupplied store. "And how could you refuse these hardworking people the pleasure of our company?"

Torin shook her head. "Let me guess. Bored people are more willing to play cards with you even though the last time you were through, you cleaned them out."

He grinned. "I may have won a couple of hands."

"Unfortunately, Lurell, at least for you, full house, tens over threes, beats three nebulas." Craig scooped in the pot as Lurell ruffled her feathers and made quiet hooting noises.

Lurell's pale-blue crest hadn't entirely grown in making her just barely adult by Rakva standards. Old enough to be in the bar, therefore old enough to play. Although Torin knew better than to extrapolate an emotional state from the facial expressions of a nonmammalian species, she felt safe assuming that, like most kids her age, Lurell believed her luck would change if she just kept playing long enough. Technically true, given that continued play would teach her luck had less to do with winning than learning when to fold. From the way her feathers kept ruffling up along the back of her neck, Torin suspected she'd already lost more than she should have—in spite of the credit chits still in front of her.

Lifting her head, Torin frowned past Lurell's shoulder and across the bar toward the windows—Craig liked the potential for a quick escape an outside seat represented, Torin preferred a wall at her back. "Lurell, you know a big male Rakva with a dark-blue crest?"

Lurell jumped and only just managed to keep from looking over her shoulder. "This one has a brother with a dark-blue crest," she admitted, with studied nonchalance. "Why does one ask?"

Torin shrugged. "He just went by outside on the concourse. He didn't look happy."

"How could one tell?"

"Could have been the way his crest was up," Torin told her, blandly. "Or could have been because people were hauling ass out of his way."

"Ah. And he is…?"

Taking a long swallow of beer, Torin put the bottle down before answering. "He's gone now."

"Ah."

Cards shuffled, Kensu, the scarlet-haired di'Taykan dealing, paused as Lurell pushed her chits around on the table "You in, baby bird?"

"Yes… No."

His eyes lightened. "Which is it?"

Crest flattened, she scooped up her chits and stood.

"This one remembers this one has things to do. This one…" She opened and closed her beak a couple of times, then ruffled her feathers—the Rakva equivalent of a blush—and headed for the door. Where she paused and turned. "This one wonders which way…"

"That way." Torin pointed.

Lurell nodded. Left the bar. Went the other way.

"Not that I'm objecting…" Kensu dropped a red nebulae in

front of her on his first circuit of the table. "...but why make up stories to scare the baby bird away?"

"I don't like taking money from children." Torin checked her cards again. They hadn't changed into something she could use.

"No brother?" Craig asked, brow up. He hadn't been able to see the window. Kensu had.

"No brother." The quartermaster had been a Rakva with Lurell's coloring. Pictures of his fledglings had been scattered around the office. The blue feathers in the crests were fairly distinctive, so she'd played the odds.

"How's she going to learn if you mollycoddle her?" Surrivna Pen, one of the two Niln at the table wondered. "Kid needs to learn the world'll shit on her if it can."

"She doesn't need to learn it from me," Torin said.

The Niln snorted something that sounded very much like, "*Soft.*"

Rolling her shoulders, Torin considered responding to the deliberate provocation and decided against it. A fight would end the game, and given what they'd made for the salvage, Craig's skill at the table had taken on a new relevance.

"Done dealing," Kensu pointed out. "Ante up, people."

Torin sighed and turned her facing cards down. Time to call it a night. "Try not to lose the ship," she murmured, gripping Craig's shoulder as she passed.

He grinned. "Have I ever?"

"Not so far."

Heading out the door, she passed an older Human woman with short gray hair hurrying in on a direct line to the poker table. With her was a Human male, moving a little slower, paying more attention to his surroundings. There was nothing about him that attracted attention, but Torin figured it was a surer thing than her last hand that his outer calm covered an inner twitchiness. No mistaking the tension that pleated the soft skin around his eyes. Ex-military—the tells were obvious to anyone who'd spent as much time in uniform as Torin had—with the look of someone who'd seen too much and not been able to let any of it go. He was the first person she'd met since getting out that she wasn't entirely positive she could beat if it came to a fight. He'd nodded in her direction as they passed, an acknowledgment that carried the hint of a warning.

Torin had no intention of sharing war stories. She let the warning stand.

"So." Craig watched the Human woman lay her money on the table and grinned, "Who are you when you're home, then, mate?"

"None of your damned business who I am at home." But she smiled as she said it. When making an effort to be charming, Craig knew he was hard to ignore. "I'm Nat when I'm here, though."

"You're not local."

"You psychic?"

"These fine folk are local…" He indicated the other four players,"…and they don't know you from a H'san's ass either. That tells me you're docked here. Like me. Salvage."

"Do tell." She grinned and scratched at her head. "Cargo."

Nearly an hour later, Craig watched a small pot move across the table to Surrivna Pen, who flicked her nictating membranes across her eyes twice when she got a good hand. Unlike Yavenit Tay, the other Niln at the table, who tapped his tail. With everyone's tells identified, he could start winning.

"So…" He turned to Nat, who *stopped* scratching when the cards went her way. "What're you hauling?"

"Bad luck," Nat snorted, beckoning the server over. "Had a hinky fold that wasted a galley's worth of food. Had to resupply."

The *Heart of Stone* had been at the other end of the docking arm for seventy-two hours. The story had spread. "So that's you, then."

She shrugged, aware that kind of luck would get talked about.

"And you…" Kensu nodded at Craig, hair flicking out and back. "…sold a double pen of scrap to the quartermaster for recycling. Now we've established strangers get talked about, it's your deal, Ryder." He tapped a long finger against his pile of chits. "Or am I playing with myself here?"

Nat glanced under the table. "Oh, sure, get my hopes up."

Concentrating on the worn cards—this late in the game they were a bit sticky, and he sure as shit didn't want play called for perceived cheating, not now, not with the groundwork done—Craig missed Kensu's response. Not that it mattered. Given the comment, any response by a di'Taykan would merely be variation on a theme.

A couple of hands later, in the pause while refills arrived, Nat turned to him, much the way he'd turned to her earlier, Human to Human, and asked, "So where you heading after?"

He shrugged. "Not a hundred percent sure."

"Well, before we got fukked by that Susumi wave, we might've stumbled over a tech field out by the edge; not more than a day's fold away."

Everyone always knew where the treasure was.

"Math makes it a debris drift from where those bastards took out the *Norrington* and the *M'rcgunn* and the *Silvaus*? The *Salanos*? Fuk it, the other ship that was with them." She topped up her new glass with the dregs of the old and handed the empty to the server. "Cap even thought about checking it out. Didn't." When she smiled broadly, her face folded into pleats that gave some indication of her actual age. "Or I wouldn't be mentioning it. Us having no tags and all. Anyway, I'm not sure anyone's tagged it yet and even if they have, it's the kind of field that a second tag or even a third tag could make some haul on."

A tech field, Craig admitted silently, even on third tag, could very well net them enough credit they'd be able to add another three square to the *Promise* sooner rather than later. He'd expected Torin to have trouble rubbing elbows 28/10 on a one-man ship, but her years in the Corps had trained her to share limited space— accepting or ignoring other bodies as required. He, however, had been used to working alone—being alone—and regular sex could only compensate for so much.

Sooner, rather than later, sounded damned good to him.

"Any chance you remember the coordinates?" he asked, checking his cards.

Nat snorted. "I might have them on me."

"How much?"

Her eyes narrowed as she studied the chits in front of him. "We'll talk when the game's over. Time to play now."

"Dangerous on the edge," Kensu pointed out absently, frowning at the pair of threes he'd just been dealt.

Craig had a nine and a seven showing, an eight and a six down. "Danger is my middle name."

"And the female you travel with?" Yavenit asked, tail still.

He laughed. "Danger is her *first* name."

"She looks familiar," Surrivna said thoughtfully, dealing out the final round.

So far, only the quartermaster had recognized Torin as the gunnery sergeant who'd blown the lid off the little gray aliens' power-behind-the-war gig. Unavoidable, given that he'd had her codes on the docket. Without the uniform, without the expectation of seeing her in a half-built OutSector station, she'd gone unnoted by everyone else. Although his economic reasons were valid, that anonymity had been a deciding factor when Craig had chosen where they'd empty their pens. Even among the salvage operators—who collectively used *none of my business* as a mantra, for fuksake—someone had tried to pick a fight and, as far as he was concerned, Torin had already done more fighting than any two people should have to.

By morning, the whole station would be talking about her, but by morning they'd be gone.

"Are we playing or talking?" he asked the table at large as Nat dug bloody fingernails into her scalp.

Sleep when you can was not one of the Corps' official mottos, but Torin had always figured it should have been. Head pillowed on her jacket, she woke when Craig approached their air lock. Ankles crossed, she rolled up onto her feet.

"They charge us every time we use the lock," she reminded him as his brows rose.

He grinned and spread his hands. "I wasn't going to ask."

"How'd you do?"

"I won big." He moved closer when she turned to code in.

Torin leaned back against his heat. The floor had been a bit cold. "And then?"

"How do you know there's an *and then*?"

Torin said nothing as the telltales turned green.

"Okay, there's an *and then*." He shifted, trying to get a look at her face. "Are you smiling?"

She was. "So you blew your winnings on racing stripes for the *Promise*?"

"Not quite." Torin felt his chest rise and fall against her back as he took a deep breath. "I used my winnings to buy the coordinates for a tech field from a cargo jockey."

"Magic beans were going to be my next guess."

FOUR

Craig blinked up at the top of the bunk, wondering what had woken him. He shifted, realized he was alone, and from the lack of residual heat, probably had been for some time. Rolling up onto his side, he could see the back of the pilot's chair silhouetted against light rising from the control panel and assumed Torin was in the chair.

"Sorry, I didn't mean to wake you," she said before he could speak.

It would never not be fukking creepy when she did that.

"Your breathing changed," she added, spinning the chair around far enough so he could see her against the lit screen.

Craig thought about pointing out that most people wouldn't have noticed, but Torin wasn't most people, never would be. The hour seemed to call for the direct approach. "What're you doing?"

"Threat assessing. Go back to sleep."

Yeah, like that was going to happen now. "Are we in danger?"

Torin huffed a laugh. "Most of the time." One hand rose up through the light to wave at the fuzz of Susumi through the front port. "Screw up a basic trigonometric function, and that shit eats you for breakfast."

Old news. "Specific danger?" he prodded, covering a yawn with his fist.

He couldn't quite see her shrug, but her tone told him she had. "The data stores have nothing on the *Heart of Stone*."

"No reason they should. It's a cargo ship I've never run into before."

"I don't trust this… *Nat*. I don't trust that she sold you the coordinates for so much less than they could be worth."

"*Could* be worth," Craig repeated, adding emphasis. "And she sold them for as much as she could get. Nat did okay, more than, given that she can't bring in military salvage without tags. She got a sure thing. We're taking the chance. And I checked the math before I paid her— the odds of it being a debris drift from the destruction of the *Norrington*, the *M'rcgunn*, and the *Salvanos* are high. Very high, even. But you know that because I showed you the numbers." Eyes narrowed, he strained unsuccessfully to see her expression. "What's really wrong?"

For a moment, he thought she wasn't going to answer. Finally, she sighed.

"I knew Marines on the *M'rcgunn*. Most of them are still MIA."

"*…three hundred and seventy-one thousand, two hundred and twenty brought home. And counting.*"

"You're wondering if we'll find them."

"It had crossed my mind."

Craig knew that one of Torin's hands rested on the place the tiny cylinders holding the ashes of the dead would fit into a combat vest. He suspected she still carried every Marine she hadn't been able to bring home alive. He wanted to tell her she could put them down. Knew it wasn't his place. But he'd do what he could. "Come back to bed. Celebrate life."

He could feel her stare. Heard her snort. "That may be the corniest pickup line anyone has ever used on me."

"What can I say?" He grinned. "You're a sure thing; I've stopped trying."

Torin had always thought that, given the chance, she'd prefer to be at the controls during a Susumi fold rather than have her survival depend on another's ability to get the equation right. Far as the Navy's Susumi engineers were concerned, Marines were meat in a can. Not that Torin had ever actively worried about them getting it wrong. No point. Nothing she could do, strapped down in one of the Marine packets, would affect the outcome. She preferred to save her concern for things she *could* affect.

Turned out, being at the controls gave her exactly as much satisfaction as she'd thought it would. It felt good to have external responsibilities again.

The last time, she'd merely been at the controls when they emerged. This time, it was her fold, start to finish.

As the Susumi wave faded, she brought the front thrusters on to slow their emergent speed, and then checked her boards. "We've arrived at the coordinates we were aiming... Shit!"

"What?"

A piece of duct tape tore as Craig's grip on the top of the chair actually tightened. Given the white-knuckled grip he'd been using as they came back into normal space, Torin hadn't thought tighter was possible. "Scanners are reading dispersed Susumi radiation."

"Our wave..." he began, but she cut him off.

"No." Enlarging the display, she frowned at the scrolling numbers. "That's the edge of our wave there. See the overlap?"

He was close enough that his sigh of relief moved her hair, breath lapping warm against her scalp. "Oh, thank fuk. Levels that low, we ignore."

"Ignore?" With the *Promise* now essentially motionless, she twisted around to face him, putting them nose-to-nose. "Are you serious?" Susumi radiation wasn't just nasty, it was variable at the molecular level, and results were never the same twice. The scientific community had agreed that only *run away, run away* was the wisest response.

Shifting to the right, Craig reached past her and enlarged a different display. "During the battle, three Confederation ships blew within five thousand kilometers of these coordinates—this is just residue. And, Nat, the cargo jockey who pointed us this way told me they'd had a hinky fold. Might be nothing more than that. We can pull salvage at twice this level."

"And you have?"

He snorted. "Sure."

Torin took another look and still didn't like the numbers.

"Tell me you've banked sperm."

"I've banked sperm."

"Good." Both branches of the military required the banking of reproductive material upon enlisting, given the hundred percent probability of being exposed to hard radiation while serving. Torin had an ovary in storage back on Paradise. Civilians who went into space made their own choices. Most of the mutations weren't viable.

An incoming communication pinged the board.

"Fukking figures." Craig scaled the radiation readings down so he could bring up the code. "Looks like there's already a tag registered."

Torin surrendered the pilot's chair. "If this is a one-on-one with another CSO, you'd better take it."

He grinned and sat. "You have to learn to talk to them sometime."

"The moment they learn communication protocols."

"You know some people would consider the term *hot mama* a compliment."

"Some people think the H'san are cuddly, I'm not responsible for their delusions either." She took the position he'd been holding behind the chair, just as glad she had no farther to walk as her first Susumi fold had left her legs feeling embarrassingly wobbly. Ex-gunnery sergeants did not wobble.

"It's just the code for the tag coming through—no one I know. Seems they don't want to talk."

"Is that standard operating procedure?"

"We're a little skint with those." Craig pulled up a keyboard. "If they're working alone, maybe suited up outside—they won't want the distraction of talk. I'm registering second tag," he added, before she could ask. "Whoever they are, their registration says they're on the other side of that lopsided planetoid with the ring, so I'll do a long-range scan and see if there's anything worth investigating about 500 kliks from their…"

The scanner pinged.

"We found debris?" Torin frowned. "That was fast." It was a hell of a lot faster than their first trip out. Vacuum being short of friction, objects in motion, like pieces blown from battle cruisers, tended to keep moving. Made them harder to find.

Usually.

"Damn!" Craig reached back, yanked her head down by his, and kissed her enthusiastically.

Torin grinned as she pulled away. "While I enjoyed the sitrep, I'm going to need more details."

"There's tech potential in this clump. Nat was right."

"I'm sorry I distrusted her."

"No, you're not."

Her grin broadened. "No, I'm not." Maintaining a little healthy distrust would go a long way to keeping them alive. "So, do we head to the clump?"

Craig shook his head. "Not yet. We give first tag a chance to object to us working those coordinates."

The CSO with the first tag could reject second tag's first three choices. Should a third CSO arrive, the approval of both previous tags had to be acquired. Torin couldn't decide if she appreciated the fact they had a system in place—given their whole *my business is none of your business* attitude—or if she was appalled by the inefficiency.

She made coffee while they waited. As she filled the first mug, Craig brought *Promise's* engines back on-line. She hadn't thought they'd been pinged. "No news is good news?"

His teeth flashed white as he smiled broadly. "Every damned time."

First tag's registered coordinates were behind the lopsided planetoid. Out of sight. Scanners blocked. Torin stood by the control panel, stared down at the scrolling numbers still registering the Susumi radiation, and tapped a fingernail lightly against her mug until Craig reached up, wrapped a hand around her wrist, and stopped her.

"What?" he demanded.

"They might not be answering because they're in trouble."

"Then we'd be picking up a distress call from the ship or the suit." He sat back and swept his free hand over the board. "No distress call."

True as far as it went, but she'd learned to trust her instincts. "Would pirates give them time to send a distress call?"

"A distress call'd have bugger all to do with the pirates; the ship'd send it automatically. Once he got close enough, Brian was up and aces finding the *Firebreather*," Craig added. "What took the time was Jan and Sirin. Here…" Still holding her wrist, he used his free hand to tap the edge of the small screen showing the steady blip of the other CSO's tag. "A registered tag but no distress call means the alleged pirates destroyed the ship completely but left behind some of the tagged cargo. Not likely, love."

"I know." They'd discuss the endearment another time. "But it wouldn't hurt to go check on them."

"It'd use resources…"

"Then take it out of my share," she snapped.

"Torin…" He sighed, tightened his grip slightly, and shook her arm—not quite hard enough to spill her coffee. Smart man. "…I know this is hard for you to get your head around, but you're not responsible for every fukking thing that happens in known space. Most people, they don't need you to ride to the rescue. They can live their lives all sunshine and puppies without you giving them…"

The corners of his mouth twitched up, and Torin almost heard him say, *Why not…* in the pause.

"…context."

The little plastic aliens, the polynumerous polyhydroxide alcoholyde shape-shifting molecular hive mind, had deep scanned both their brains—hers and Craig's—during the Recon investigation of the unidentified alien ship known as Big Yellow. The organic plastic bastards had then hitched a ride inside their skulls in order to give *context* to observations about the centuries-long war between the Confederation and the Primacy. A war the little plastic aliens had admitted to both starting and maintaining. A lot of Marines had died while they'd been along for the ride, and sometimes Torin would sit in the control chair, listen to Craig sleeping in the bunk behind her, watch the stars, and find herself second-guessing every choice she'd made since that day on Big Yellow. Wondering if it had actually been her making them.

CSOs were able to doubt the lives they'd lived, but gunnery

sergeants accepted responsibility for their decisions and moved on. They didn't dwell. And, yeah, she'd left the Corps, but the Corps would never really leave her.

Twisting her hand above Craig's grip, Torin poured the coffee into his lap. They'd gotten dressed before emerging from Susumi space, so it didn't make as much of an impression as it could have.

"Fukking hell, Torin!"

Still, it was a fresh pot. Hadn't cooled much.

Torin knew a lot of different ways to kill people. She could come up with three ways, off the top of her head, using the mug as a weapon. All things considered, a crotch of coffee rated minus five on a scale of one to ten.

When she stepped back, Craig hung on. She could have broken his hold. She didn't. Minus five or not, she figured she owed him that much.

He met her gaze, ignoring the liquid pooling in his lap. "Okay, it's too soon to joke about context. I'm sorry. If it means that much to you, we'll go check on the other ship."

My business is none of your business.

HE suits screamed for help if their wearers got into trouble they couldn't get out of. Beacons in the suits were slaved to the ships and when they went off, the ship would go off as well, extending the suit's range. If the ship was damaged, its own distress call would sound.

The *Promise* wasn't picking up a distress call.

But she was picking up registered CSO tags.

Pirates would take the tagged debris, or what the hell was the point of being a pirate.

"No, you're right…"

"If I'm right," he interrupted, "why am I absorbing caffeine through my ass?"

Four ways with the coffee mug. "You're right," she repeated, "that I need to start thinking more like a salvage operator."

Craig nodded, relaxing slightly. "Without a distress call, they wouldn't thank us for dropping by."

That surprised a laugh out of her. "I was a Marine. I didn't expect to get thanked."

* * *

The battle debris had drifted into an interlinked mass, the smaller, more salvageable pieces fused to huge sheets of twisted metal and slabs of ceramic. Given the parts she could see, given the protection offered by the large, outer pieces of hull, Torin was willing to bet her pension that the odds of finding DNA remnants would be high. Maybe not the specific Marines she counted as her friends, but Marines.

"This first trip out, we eyeball the puzzle pieces," Craig reminded her, waiting by the air lock as Torin checked his helmet seals. "We tag what'll give us the best resale price, maybe set a few small charges to break things up so that we can get a better look inside. DNA scans come later." He checked her seals in turn, then moved his hands to her shoulders and left them there. "We're not wearing propulsion, so we stay tethered to the ship or the end of the grapple at all times. Eyeballs on where I'm attached before you unhook. It's safer if we're not both off the ship at the same time."

The urge to respond to this latest repetition of common sense masquerading as instruction with a noncommittal *"Yes, sir"* was intense, but that wasn't a dynamic she wanted to set up with Craig—he'd earned her respect a long time ago. And, in all fairness, in spite of her previous performance out by the pens, she understood why he erred on the side of caution. She'd been equally unwilling to trust his skills, all evidence to the contrary, when he'd been on her turf. Since the CSOs didn't have any kind of basic training to meld individuals into a unit, and would likely be appalled by the thought, all she could do toward being thought one of them was give it time.

So she said, "You think eight charges will be enough?" They were each carrying four.

"We're not out here to fight a war."

"Please," she snorted. "I could win a war with seven." They were close to the edge, as likely to run into a Primacy ship making a foray into Confederation space as a Confederation ship on patrol.

"Eight should be aces, but there's only one way to find out

for sure." He opened the air lock's inner door. *Promise*'s interior lights shifted red—they were now a lot closer to vacuum than the ship's sensors were happy about. "After you."

They used the heavier grapple to first tether the ship to the largest piece of wreckage and then to winch it closer, the wreckage winning the mass sweepstakes.

Standing beside Craig on the edge of the deployed pen, Torin couldn't see his expression through the helmet's polarization, only her own blank silver reflection, but she could hear the smile in his voice when he gestured at the massive triangular piece of metal above them and said, *"Race you,"* as he released his magnetic soles and pushed off.

She considered jerking back on his safety line. Didn't. But it was close.

In the end, she won only because her suit was newer and, when she flipped, she remagged her boots at full charge, allowing them to drag her down past him. She was moving fast enough at impact that she was glad she had her tongue tucked safely away from her teeth.

Landing beside her two seconds later, Craig grunted, *"Cheater."*

"Don't start with me, Ryder. Usually, there's a three count before a race."

"Just assumed, you being an ex-gunnery sergeant and all, you should be handicapped to make it fair."

She grinned and flipped him off. "Handicap this."

They were standing on a piece blown out of the outer hull, roughly eight meters by four meters at the longest points, and half a meter thick—the two visible Susumi contact points on the metal no longer radiating.

"You don't find that odd?"Torin leaned over to check that the information on Craig's sleeve matched hers. She didn't completely trust his aging tech. "Given the initial radiation readings?"

"Dispersal," he said absently, his attention having been pulled deeper into the tangle. *"Damn! Take a look there."*

"You want to be a little more specific?" *There* covered a lot of ground.

"That piece, the blue-green one just past the cable end." His voice was as animated as Torin had ever heard it. *"That's Other... Fuk it, Primacy tech. Premium scoop, babe! We get that out and we're building a deck."*

"Babe?" *Love* she could cope with. Lines had to be drawn.

"Heat of the moment." She heard the grin in his voice.

One hand gripping the edge of the hull, Torin turned until she could pull herself headfirst a short distance into the debris. "Piece we want looks fused to that link section, but I can't get a good enough angle on it to see for certain." With the magnification on her faceplate at maximum, she could see pitting caused by tiny pieces of debris but still couldn't see the point where the Primacy tech butted up against the link.

They were going to have to blast it clear.

"Do we tag it for later?" she asked reaching for the tagging gun strapped to her thigh.

"We tag it for now." Craig pulled one of his charges from the pouch. *"This, we don't wait for."*

Maybe she was a little more excited about that than she needed to be, but so far, the crazy, dangerous life of the civilian salvage operator had been a bit dull.

"They're both suited up and climbing around the debris, Captain. We can go on your order."

"We need Ryder." Cho gripped the edge of his board. "He's the registered CSO. Doc says the woman was Corps long enough for it to mark her, so cut her free when we take him." Only a fool brought that kind of trouble on board and Mackenzie Cho's mama had raised no fool.

"You got it. Or him." Dysun made a small adjustment to her scanners and sat back, looking pleased with herself. "One of them is enough larger to account for Human gender differences and is in a significantly older suit. The smaller one, she's wearing a Marine design, no more than a year old. Sending specifics to cargo."

"Almon?"

"It's enough data to aim the net around him if you can get him out in the open, Captain."

Dysun answered before Cho could. "I take out their tethers, and send the next shot into the debris. That'll shake them loose. That is if Huirre can keep us pointed the right way."

"I could fly this ship right up your ass," Huirre growled.

"Promises, promises."

"Move in fast," Cho snapped. "Dysun, you take out the ship as soon as their proximity alarms go off. We don't want them getting back to it and fukking dying on us. Then take out the tethers, then hit the debris. If you've got a clear shot at the woman, take it. Get her out of Almon's way."

"Aye, Captain." The ends of her hair flipped back and forth.

This was going to work, he could feel it. This time, Craig Ryder would give them the information they needed. Cho could see the armory opening. He could almost feel one of the Corps' ubiquitous KC-7s in his hands, bucking back as he switched it to full auto and squeezed the trigger. Ships in orbit could EMP more complex weapons but no one on either side had been able to dream up a way to stop a basic chemical reaction from happening. Armed with KC-7s, they could take over any station they docked at.

This time, nothing would go wrong. "Dysun, whatever happens to their drive, happens to you."

Her hair stilled. "Aye, Captain."

"The fuk!" As *Promise*'s proximity siren screamed through his suit's comm link, Craig, slapped his last charge down, and worked his way backward along the path of his tether as fast as possible. Unfortunately, as fast as possible was too fukking slow, but a hole ripped into his suit by a jagged edge would slow him more. "Torin! Have you got a visual?" He didn't have to shout to be heard over the siren, the comm would take care of volume levels, but it felt good. Like he was doing something.

"Negative. Still obscured by wreckage."

"It's probably the wreckage that set it off." He jerked his line off a twisted cable end. "If we got it moving…"

"Not unless you've been putting on weight," Torin snorted. *"Four meters and I'm out."*

He could see the patch of stars that marked his entry to the clump's inner labyrinth. "I'm out in three."

They emerged at roughly the same time. Torin popped out and kept rising at about 120 degrees to his zero, clearing the slab of metal cutting up like a fin out of the tangle and then remagging her boots to snap down onto the upper edge. *"I've pinged the Promise. The debris hasn't moved."*

"Then what the fuk…" His boots demagged, he pushed off, grabbed a loop of piping, swung around it until he pointed the right way, then bent his arms and shoved off. As he landed three meters from Torin's position, the top of the *Promise*'s cabin blew off, debris spraying out as she decompressed into vacuum.

He didn't remember moving, but Torin's grip on his ankle said they both had.

"Let me go, damn it!" He had to get to his lady. She wasn't answering, but he knew she wasn't dead. Holed, yes, open to vacuum, but nothing crucial had been hit.

"Craig! Listen to me! There's a ship…"

The next shot took out the line holding *Promise* to the wreckage.

In order to set the charges around the piece of tech, they'd both tethered to the grapple head. With that gone, the only thing holding him in place was Torin's grip.

He could see the incoming ship. Ex-Navy with a cargo hold attached like half the small freighters in known space. But the guns said…

"Pirates!"

"No shit!" The next shot slapped into the slab of metal just under Torin's boots. Craig whipped backward as her knees buckled, but she hung on. "They want the salvage! We need to get clear!"

"No! It's not the salvage they're after!"

"Damn it, Torin, you don't know…"

The next shot slid behind the slab and into the wreckage.

The clump shuddered.

He felt Torin's grip shift as her body adjusted to the movement under her feet.

Then the charges blew. Shards of debris flew past. Hit his shoulder. His suit absorbed most of the impact, but it fukking hurt.

He heard Torin grunt, more an exhalation than an actual sound as though, just for that moment, she were breathing inside his helmet with him.

Then he felt her grip fall away.

She'd never have let him go were she still able to hold on.

"Torin!"

He saw stars, the attacking ship, his poor wounded lady, debris flying off in every possible direction, Torin caught up in it—the bright orange of her HE suit, visible then obscured by wreckage as he pinwheeled. He reached out. Stupidly. She'd absorbed more of the blast. Was moving away faster than he was spinning. Red lights flashed around the edge of her helmet.

Red lights...

Air leak!

Craig tasted blood as he slammed against the mesh of a cable net, jaw impacting with the hard edge of his suit's collar. His faceplate, crossed by four cables, creaked but held. He couldn't turn his head, but if they'd netted him, they planned to haul him in. The ship he'd seen while spinning had to have been two kilometers away, minimum. Two kilometers of cable gave him time...

His charges were gone, but he had a cutting tool on his belt. Much smaller but the same basic principle as the Marine's bennies.

Don't think about Marines now.

Right arm trapped between two loops, he shoved his left between his body and the net.

Torin's trained for this, he reminded himself. *Situations like this.*

Fumbling the magnetic clasp out, he managed to shove his first two fingers into the tool pouch.

If Torin were conscious, she'd have her suit patched before she lost enough air for it to matter.

With the charges gone, it wasn't that hard to hook out the cutter.

If Torin were conscious, she'd be talking, implant to implant, to keep the pirates from overhearing. If she'd been hit hard enough to damage her implant…

The cutter was harder to use with his left hand, and working so close to his body, there was always the chance he'd hole his own suit.

Didn't stop him from aiming it at the net and turning it up to full burn.

All he could hear was his own breath. In. Out. A little too fast. A little too hard.

Three strands through.

Four.

One more…

A sudden shadow caught his attention. Craig turned his head to see the edge of a cargo door go by on his right. He'd barely been pulled over the threshold when the gravity generators kicked in and slammed him down hard onto the deck, the edge of his tank driving into his kidneys with enough force to ensure he'd be pissing blood. Teeth clenched, he flopped over onto his side.

And saw…

He wasn't sure what it was, but it was fukking huge and explained why they'd dropped him so close to the door. There wasn't room to drop him any farther in.

A siren wailed as the doors started to close, and he fought the weight of the net to raise himself up onto his hands and knees. *Promise* still had power. Craig could see her lights flashing in the distance. If he could get to her, he could get to Torin.

Then the door closed, the halves coming together hard enough he felt the vibrations through his gloves. Through his knees. As he watched, still crawling forward, the telltales turned green.

He kept crawling. Inching forward. Muscles screaming.

That was the way out, and he was Goddamned well going out it.

Suddenly, the floor receded as the net lifted about half a meter into the air. He grunted as his weight drove the cables into his chest, making it hard to breathe. His right leg slipped through the gap he'd cut, but his left remained hung up.

When they came to get him out, he'd get one chance.

He went limp, cutting tool hopefully hidden behind the curve of his gloved fingers. With luck, they'd think he'd taken damage and was a little out of it.

With luck, they'd be quick about it because he didn't know how long he could overcome his need to move, to get free, to get to his ship, to get to Torin.

The net started to swing almost immediately. Maybe his luck was changing.

He turned his head inside the helmet, the polarization making the movement invisible from the outside, and saw boots approaching. HE boots. They hadn't pressurized the cargo bay, then.

As the wearer of the boots peeled the net away, and he could feel himself begin to fall, Craig flicked his cutter on. Letting gravity win, he dropped free of the net, landing back on his hands and knees.

He made contact, that much he knew, but he had no idea how much damage he'd done. No idea if he'd bought himself enough time to get to the door.

Surging up onto his feet, he'd taken only two steps forward when something jabbed his thigh, and the jolt snapped his head back, driving the edge of the suit's collar into the back of his neck.

Torin would've made sure the bastard stayed down, he thought as he pitched forward, slamming face first into the deck, mouth filled with blood from where he'd driven his teeth through his tongue. Next time…

"You had to fukking knock him out?" Cho glared up at Almon, who glared back, the ends of his hair carving short choppy arcs over the collar of his suit.

"The *ablin gon savit* tried to take Nadayki's leg off." Almon jerked his head toward the deck where Doc had the gash sealed and was working on getting the younger di'Taykan out of his suit. "I didn't have time to fukking mess around being pleasant."

The problem was that not everyone reacted well to the *tasik*—where *not well* could be defined as *turned into drooling, brain-dead meat*. Originally developed to control the large, flightless birds that were the main source of animal protein on the Taykan home world, they were a cheaper "personal weapon" to acquire than black market military guns, and Cho had two on board. "If you've broken him…"

"Then he's broken," Almon interrupted flatly, most of his light receptors closed, his eyes pale yellow, lid to lid. "And we'll get another one. And if that one tries to kill my *thytrin*, I'll break them, too."

He wasn't going to back down, Cho realized. Not when it came to protecting his *thytrin*. If Almon hadn't been already suited up and on his way into the cargo bay, Nadayki would have bled out and Almon would likely have ripped the helmet off their captured CSO and spaced him. Pushed now, he'd push back and he was still wearing the *tasik* clipped to his suit. Lucky for him, Cho knew that the trick to turning the kind of people who were willing to do the things the job required into a functioning crew, was knowing when not to push. And when to shove the offender out the air lock.

Stretching out a foot, Cho poked the body slumped against the bulkhead. Everyone looked bigger suited up, but Craig Ryder was clearly not small. "Get your suit off," he snapped at Almon. "Then get his suit off and get him secured to the chair before he comes to. Doc, how will we know if Ryder's still functional?"

"Functional is usually pretty fukking obvious," Doc grunted without looking up, his hands leaving bloody prints all over the ruin of Nadayki's suit.

Head lolling forward, too heavy for his neck to hold, Craig felt like he had the worst hangover in the history of hangovers. Worse than that time back when him and Kurt and Nicole had grabbed the first bottle they could get their hands on out of Nic's dad's liquor cabinet and gotten stupidly drunk on crème de menthe. Only a drongo could have decided that that particular green poison, of all the many ways the Human species had created to get shitfaced, needed to go with them into space. Took months before Nic had stopped puking at the smell of mint.

He remembered a card game. Except he never drank to excess when he was playing.

After?

He tried to move his arms and legs. Couldn't. How fukking drunk had he gotten that he couldn't...

Couldn't because there were bands around his arms. He could feel the pressure against his skin. Bands around his ankles, too. Warm liquid pooled on his right thigh, but it was his left thigh that hurt. Blood?

Hospital?

No. He was sitting up.

Station lockup?

No. Torin wouldn't...

Torin!

He saw stars, the attacking ship, his poor wounded lady, debris flying off in every possible direction, Torin caught up in it—the bright orange of her HE suit, visible then obscured by wreckage as he pinwheeled.

Memory surged back hard enough it slapped against the inside of his skull, causing starbursts of brilliant white against the inside of his lids. The attack. The explosion. The net. Pain...

They'd hit him with some kind of current.

Pain radiated out from the burning circle in his left thigh where they'd jabbed the contact point into flesh. The dull pain across his lower back matched up to where his tanks impacted. The ache in his mouth—Craig remembered spasming, teeth closing on his own flesh. Last but not least, a red-hot iron spike had been jabbed into each temple.

Only not actual spikes since he was apparently still alive.

He was pretty sure he was breathing.

He was naked. No surprise, if they'd just peeled him out of his suit.

Tied to a chair. He couldn't lift his head or open his eyes.

Torin's suit had been leaking air.

No way she'd survived a war and been taken out by pirate scum.

No fukking way.

But she hadn't been conscious.

And her suit had been leaking air.

He recognized the vibrations he could feel through the soles of his feet. The Susumi engines were on-line. The pirates had folded away from the debris field.

Away from Torin.

This wasn't the first time he'd been expected to believe Torin had carked it. Last time, the Primacy had taken out most of a battalion, melted Marines and equipment and the ground they were standing on into a sheet of gray-green glass. He hadn't mourned Torin then. He wouldn't now.

Muscles knotting across his shoulders and upper back, he forced his head up and his eyes open.

"Finally."

Craig blinked, closed his mouth around a line of pink drool— the warm liquid on his thigh explained—and looked for the source of the voice. The young male di'Taykan standing by the hatch had pale yellow hair and a nasty expression. As Craig watched, he raised one long-fingered hand to his throat, and turned his masker off.

"Fuk you." Even to his own ears, it sounded garbled, but Craig figured he got his message across.

The di'Taykan sneered. "I'll remind you of that in a few minutes when you're begging me for release."

Dragging his tongue across dry lips, Craig managed a snort. "Are di'Taykan even able to withhold sex?" The plastic cable ties that held his forearms and his lower legs tight to the chair had no give in them. Fukking sentient alien plastic, never around when needed. The chair had been secured to the deck. No matter how he threw his weight—forward, back, side to side—he couldn't budge it.

When he rocked his hips forward, his ass came off the seat, skin ripping up off the plastic with a disgusting sucking sound. If these were the same pirates who'd tortured Rogelio Page— and he almost wanted them to be if only to keep down the numbers of bugfuk crazy sons of bitches cruising around known space—he had a good idea of what made the seat sticky. Maybe not a *good* idea…

The di'Taykan watched him, eyes dark, so he rocked his hips forward again, trying to bring the bastard close enough that he could rip his throat out with his teeth. He'd never considered himself a violent man, but for this lot, he'd make an exception.

He felt himself beginning to respond to the pheromones. They'd crank him up until he was so sexually frustrated he couldn't think straight and then go after whatever the fuk it was they wanted to know. Had they started that way with Page?

Tough old bastard had held out, though, forced them to bring out the knives and live wires.

Had died in this chair.

This chair.

This inert plastic chair. Fukking figured. Insult added to injury.

Craig began to fight the bindings. Held nothing back.

Felt his knee pop. Kept fighting. Had no idea when the struggle turned to rut. His skin felt on fire, and if he didn't get some release, soon, he was going to…

The fist that smashed into his face snapped him back to himself. He'd never had any interest in tying sex to pain. Although, by the third blow, he couldn't remember why.

Out in the corridor, Cho frowned down at the monitor and the image of Almon beating their prisoner. "This can't go the way the last one did."

Beside him, Doc shrugged. "Then make him an offer."

"An offer?"

"Traditionally, in this way of life, if the captured seaman had needed skills, it was join the crew or die."

"Join the crew?"

"Or die."

"What if he decides to die?"

Doc sighed. "No one decides to die. Page was a crazy old loner who stood on principle, but his actual death was an accident."

"You accidentally *questioned* him to death?" Cho asked dryly.

"It happens. The point is, it won't happen to this guy if I don't have to *question* him." Doc repeated the emphasis exactly. "Ryder's ship has been destroyed, his woman is dead, what does he have to return to? Nothing. Offer him life."

"As a part of the crew? We won't be able to trust him."

"So? When push comes to shove, we don't trust anyone."

It was, Cho acknowledged silently, opening the hatch, a valid point.

* * *

"Almon! Back off!"

The di'Taykan drove his fist into Craig's stomach one last time, then backed away breathing heavily, his arousal evident. Craig's own arousal had been dealt with twice. Vomit descending from half a meter up provided sufficient friction. Who knew? The relief had been temporary; he could still pound nails with his donger.

"Hose him down, he stinks."

He turned his face into the splash of water to get the blood out of his eyes and managed to focus on the Human male by the door. Shorter than the di'Taykan by about half a meter, he had a cap of glossy black hair, dark eyes, a rivet through his right earlobe, and, behind the glimmer of a filter over his mouth and nose, an expression that suggested Almon's fists had been merely the prologue. Given the condition they'd found Page in, Craig had already figured that out for himself.

"Now get out."

Almon bent closer to the other man and said something too quietly for Craig to catch.

"Do I look like your *sheshan*? Go to the infirmary and check."

The di'Taykan shot Craig a look of such loathing on the way out the hatch, Craig wondered how much damage he'd managed to do with his cutter. Damage to someone Almon cared about. That would explain the personal touch.

He wasted the time while the new guy crossed toward him wondering if this was what a crazy person looked like. Almon sure as shit hadn't been the guy who'd done Page.

"Craig Ryder. Yes, I know who you are," the new guy said, stopping at the edge of the mess on the deck. "You're probably wondering why you're here. I need your codes."

Craig spat out a mouthful of blood. "Could've just asked for them, mate."

"Would you have given them up?"

"No, but you still could've asked." More than the beating, the red-hot spikes through his temples, left over from whatever the fuk they'd taken him out with, were making it hard to think. What the hell had Sirin and Jan locked down? What was big enough for three people to die to protect?

"I don't like to waste time, Ryder. Which is why I've come to make you an offer." He had to be the captain, Craig realized, no one else would have had the authority to make an offer. "Join my crew."

"What?"

"Join my crew, and your codes become part of our..." He looked slightly pained. "...booty. Refuse and you die. There's a lot more salvage operators out there and, while I'd rather not have to put more time into this, frankly, you're not that hard to grab."

All things considered, Craig had to agree with that. "What do you want my codes for?"

"That's none of your business."

"Hey, my codes, my business." The blow took him by surprise. He hadn't thought the captain would be willing to get his hands dirty.

When Craig managed to focus on the captain's face, he smiled. "You decide to join us and you'll find out what I need the codes for."

"You couldn't possibly trust me if I joined you."

The captain's smile twisted. "I have it on good authority that when push comes to shove, we don't trust anyone. You'll be outnumbered, and even if you could get away from the rest of the crew, where are you going to go? We're in deep space. You could make a run for it when we reach a station, I suppose, but should we dock at a station that might offer sanctuary, I suspect I'm smart enough to lock you down for the duration."

"Being a member of your crew sounds a fuk of a lot like being your prisoner."

"Beats the alternative. And you have nothing to go back to, remember? Your ship was destroyed, your woman left for dead."

"Left for dead?" Torin wasn't dead.

The Captain shrugged. "She was alive when we folded, but her suit had been breached, and vacuum has a way of taking care of these things. Think the offer over," he added, turning toward the hatch. "It's open for a limited time."

Torin wasn't dead!

Craig heard the hatch slam and looked up to find himself

alone in the small room, bruised, bleeding, still hard enough to pound nails, and tied to a chair.

Torin wasn't dead. She'd been left for dead, but when talking about ex-Gunnery Sergeant Torin Kerr, that was a long way from *being* dead. All he had to do was stay alive until she found him.

Damn, but she was going to be pissed.

"That went well," Doc said thoughtfully, looking up from the monitor as Cho joined him.

Cho glanced down at the screen and frowned. "Why is he laughing?"

"...unless one of you lot has learned how to breathe vacuum. Private Kerr!"

Torin jerked awake and onto her feet. Since she'd arrived at Ventris Station, her days had been filled with intense physical and mental training and her nights had held no more than four to five hours of sleep. She wasn't the only one dozing off in quiet moments—or even not so quiet moments. Tom Wiegand had fallen asleep during drill. His body had managed to keep marching in a straight line, but an order to *about face* had caused a pileup and resulted in an extra 5K run for the entire platoon.

But Wiegand wasn't the one on the hot seat now.

She blinked and managed to bring Staff Sergeant Beyhn into focus. His eyes were dark—most of the light receptors open— and his hair—which was honest-to-gods scarlet and not auburn or strawberry blond— jerked back and forth. She'd never met a di'Taykan until she got to the Marine Corps recruiting center on Paradise and was amazed to discover that the stories about them were mostly true. She'd never met a staff sergeant either, and the stories about them were *definitely* true.

When he saw he had her attention, Staff Sergeant Beyhn smiled and said, with exaggerated patience, "Perhaps Private Kerr would like to tell the platoon what she would do should she find herself in vacuum in a leaking HE suit."

Oh, thank gods, this was something she knew. "I'd patch the leak, Staff Sergeant."

"You'd patch the leak, Private Kerr? That's it?"

Torin had no idea what he was getting at. "Yes, Staff Sergeant. I'd patch the leak in the suit." Since he seemed to be waiting for more, she added, "Or I'd die."

"And you don't intend to die, is that it?"

She squared her shoulders and lifted her chin. "No, Staff Sergeant, I do not."

His eyes darkened further and she wondered how much more there was for him to see. After a long moment he nodded, and said, "Good."

Wait...

She frowned. She had a leak in her HE suit? Not good.

Leak in suit...

As soon as the pressure dropped, the internal patching material would have been released. If the leak was large enough, a further drop in pressure would release the secondary IPM.

Conscious personnel were instructed not to wait for the release. Conscious personnel needed to preserve more air. Torin's first attempt resulted in an inarticulate croak. No good enough. She wet her lips, swallowed, and tried again.

"Command! Patch release!"

Better.

It was cold. She remembered that from training. Cold and a little slimy.

"And then what, Private Kerr?"

Staff Sergeant Beyhn's red eyes were blinking. Off.

On. Off. On. Off.

Torin blinked when the lights stopped and the surrounding stars came slowly into focus. The surrounding stars and quite a bit of moving debris. Calming her breathing, she worked back from what she knew.

She was in an HE suit. In space. Surrounded by moving debris. There'd been an explosion. Frowning, she opened and closed her right hand. She'd been holding something.

Craig. She'd been holding Craig. The tethers had been cut.

She couldn't see him. Not even with the helmet magnification on full.

"Craig! This is Torin, do you copy?"

A ship had come out of nowhere, shot out *Promise*'s cabin, cut the tethers, and blown up the clump of wreckage she and Craig had been tagging.

"Craig! Damn it, answer me!"

The wreckage had blown as spectacularly as it had because the shot had set off the eight small charges they'd set to free up that piece of Primacy tech.

"Command! Run diagnostics on communication unit."

By tucking her head down, she could see *Promise*'s lights flashing in the distance and her own cut tether pointing back the way she'd come. She was moving away from the ship. Diagnostics told her there was nothing wrong with the comm.

"Craig!"

No answer.

No sound at all but her own breathing. Usually, Torin found that comforting.

She'd been carrying twelve hours of air when they left the ship. They'd been out for ninety minutes when the shooting had started. Her suit said she had four hours and twenty-three minutes left. The leak had not been a hallucination. Or not only a hallucination.

Four hours and twenty-one minutes before the scrubbers were no longer effective and the oxygen levels dropped below what the suit considered air. She could manage for another ten to fifteen minutes after that as long she didn't need to do anything too complex.

Even more fun, two layers of internal patching hadn't quite stopped the leak.

"Shit."

Had she been wearing jets, it wouldn't have mattered; she'd be back to the *Promise* before she ran out. But she'd been wearing a safety line. Jets and a safety line were redundant.

Apparently not.

Had she been in Craig's suit instead of one of the new military-tested designs, she'd have been screwed. And this was not the time to think about Craig in Craig's ten-year-old suit, unconscious, unable to make repairs. "Command! Foam release."

The foam—more or less the same material that protected Navy fliers in disabled pods—filled in all the space between Torin and her suit, started warm, got very hot for seven seconds, then semi-solidified, becoming, in essence, a second suit. She could still bend her arms and legs but not without effort. Design flaw—fix a leak, but then make her work harder, breathe harder. To add insult to injury, the foam itself was a brilliant pink. So was the skin under the foam. On the other hand, insulted beat dead. The collar seals bulged up against the bottom of her chin but held.

Giving thanks that she'd bothered to hook up the plumbing this trip, Torin considered her next option.

She wasn't moving particularly fast, but she was moving away from the ship. Fortunately, the tagging gun was still strapped to her leg and...

Her tanks hit first.

Given the amount of debris around her, moving at differing angles and speeds, it was inevitable she'd make contact with a piece of it. This felt like a big piece. And, in this instance, *make contact* was clearly a euphemism for *full body impact*.

Her tanks, or tanks like them, had been dropped out of a low orbit and continued to work when the defense contractors dug them out of six meters of dirt. Torin had seen the vid; she wasn't worried about her tanks.

Instinct said, brace for impact.

Training said, relax.

Torin had seen Marines thrown about like rag dolls by unexpected explosions, ending up bruised and battered but without major injuries. Rag dolls didn't break. The foam pressing against the collar seal held her head in place.

Her brain, unfortunately, continued moving until it was stopped by the inside of her skull.

"If the collision is relatively elastic, then object A is going to rebound much like a rubber ball, traveling now back along its original course." Sergeant Roper paused, turned away from the formulas on the screen, swept a weary gaze over the training platoon and said, "Here in the

Corps, we call inelastic *collisions crashes. Try to avoid them."*

"Yes, Sergeant!"

Torin really wished people would stop shouting. She had one fuk of a headache.

Opening her eyes, she squinted her surroundings into focus and slowly realized something was wrong.

No, right.

Most of the wreckage continued to follow the blast radius, moving out and away.

She was on her way back.

That was good.

Four hours and six minutes of air.

Okay, the concussion she seemed to have wasn't optimum, but as long as she could avoid slamming into anything else that massed out significantly higher than she did, she could work around it.

Evidence seemed to suggest an HE suit full of semi-solidified foam made collisions remarkably elastic.

Unfortunately, because her tanks had hit first, she'd lost enough energy during the crash that she'd slowed considerably. She pinged the *Promise*—114 kilometers— then waited five minutes and pinged again—113.27 kilometers. She'd traveled .73 of a kilometer in five minutes, .146 in one minute, so in sixty minutes she'd travel 8.76 kilometers.

"These things need a fukking speedometer," she muttered, redoing the math.

Math never lied.

When she ran out of air, she'd be a little under 80K short of the ship.

She needed to be moving three times faster. Roughly three point three times faster, but who was counting.

Not entirely convinced she could keep it down, Torin took a sip of tepid water and swallowed carefully. Ignoring the unpleasant reality of—she glanced down—three hours and forty-one minutes of air—the two liters of water would recycle for days until the laws of diminishing returns caught up to her. The concentrated sludge in the emergency food pouch would keep her from starving. Craig had mocked her when she filled it. His was empty.

Mouth moistened, she tongued his codes into her implant. Her comm was working, but his might have been damaged in the explosion. "Craig! Answer me!"

Still nothing.

Torin ran her magnification back to full, trying to see between the pieces in the thicker parts of the debris field, but she had a bad feeling she wouldn't find him without the ship's scanners.

She froze. Barely breathing.

One of the charges hadn't blown. A ping read it at 2.6 kilometers away at 320 degrees to her zero. Without maneuvering thrusters, it might as well be in the next system.

Three hours and thirty-seven minutes of air.

If she could get to the charge, she could use it to shoot herself at the ship.

Shoot...

Her brain must've taken more damage than she'd thought.

Forcing her arm down to her side, she slid the first finger of her right hand through the trigger guard and pulled the tagging gun free of the holster. Still ninety-seven tags in the magazine. She drew a mental line along the path the piece of debris carrying the charge would take. Another along the line she'd have to take to meet up with it.

Aimed the barrel back along that line.

Adjusted to account for the debris' speed.

Adjusted to account for her speed.

Adjusted to account for any additional speed that might be added by the tagging gun during the course correction.

Realized there was no way in hell she could do that kind of math in her head.

And pulled the trigger.

Better to die attempting the impossible.

A full magazine held a hundred tags. She'd used three while they set the charges. She used another twenty-two before her path looked like it would cross the debris' path. Maybe. Probably.

"Fuk it."

Three hours and four minutes of air.

Two hours and fifty one minutes.

It was going to be close.

Another six tags made it closer.

Moving slowly and carefully, Torin stretched out her left arm…

Two hours and forty-seven minutes.

…and closed her thumb and forefinger on the edge of the debris.

At this point, spin didn't matter—she'd have to aim herself at the ship regardless, so she moved as quickly as she could, arming the charge and then using the remains of her tether to strap the piece of debris across her back. By the time she managed it, she'd used up another forty-nine minutes of air.

Fourteen tags lined her up facing the *Promise*'s lights.

Fifty-one tags left to adjust her course—she was aiming a projectile at a target almost a hundred kilometers away by eye— and to keep her from slamming into the ship at a speed that would do neither her nor the ship any good.

It all came down to whether or not the blast would supply enough push to get her to the *Promise*'s tanks before her air ran out.

"Fire in the hole!"

Teeth together, tongue safely out of danger, she detonated the charge.

"Escape pods…" *Captain Farmer slapped the curved metal of the pod beside her. "…are not designed for comfort. They are designed to get you away from your transportation and the battle that's destroyed it as quickly as possible. You will be pulling close to 4 gs during the initial thrust, so if you've taken any injuries during the time the Navy has been getting the shit shot out of it, it's going to hurt." She smiled out at the training platoon. "Here in the Corps, we feel a little pain is preferable to going down with the ship."*

When Torin came to, a nosebleed had gummed her lips together. She checked the time—she'd been out for twelve minutes—worked her lips apart, and licked them mostly clean. Good thing she'd never minded the taste of blood.

Most of the debris field had moved past her at this point. This was a good thing because slamming into random pieces of wreckage currently filled the top spot on her list of things she'd rather not do.

A ping put her at 84.6 kilometers from the ship. She'd traveled 14.4 kilometers in the twelve minutes she'd been out. That was

1.2 kilometers a minute and 67 kilometers an hour.

She'd reach the *Promise* in an hour and thirty-six minutes.

This left her a little better than thirteen minutes to get inside and hook up to the ship's tanks. At full magnification, it appeared that only the cabin had been holed, but she couldn't be a hundred percent positive the tanks were intact until she actually got there.

Decelerating would also eat up some time, but she had a plan.

If not for the concussion, she'd catch a quick nap—setting her comm to wake her in an hour. As that wasn't an option...

The Susumi radiation they'd read on arrival had undoubtedly come from the other CSO's ship, destroyed more thoroughly than the *Promise*. That explained why there'd been no answer. Nat, the cargo jockey who'd pointed them at this field, had been on station because her ship had taken a bad fold. Not a huge jump to suspect it hadn't been a bad fold at all but that they'd been caught in the blast radius. No one deliberately put themselves in the radius of a Susumi blast. The destruction had been an accident.

Rogelio Page's injuries told her they wanted information from a CSO.

The blast had destroyed any chance of them picking up a new operator.

So they'd had to look elsewhere.

Craig wasn't answering his comm or his implant. There was always the chance he'd died when the charges blew.

Torin didn't think so.

Didn't want to think so.

Nor did she think she'd find him when she finally got to the ship's scanners.

The pirates needed him. They—Nat and her crew—had scooped him up and left her for dead.

She was more than a little pissed about that.

Turned out, an hour and a half later, her course didn't need much correction.

"Let's hear it for paying attention on the heavy ordnance range."

Torin took three shots to slightly change her angle of approach and spent the rest of the tags to slow herself as much as possible.

She hadn't aimed herself right at the ship but just over it, her boots barely clearing the metal. As it passed under her, she took a quick look at the hole in the cabin. The control panel looked intact and the odds were very good the main cabin had been sealed off immediately from the rest of the ship. There'd be air. If she could get to it.

The moment her body cleared the ship on the far side, she remagged her boots. Full power. They slammed her down onto the ship working against her forward momentum.

To a certain extent, the foam continued to protect her.

Swearing seemed like a good idea except she had to concentrate on basic functionality. Given that she was in the cabin, she assumed she'd managed to stay conscious through docking maneuvers, but she wouldn't have bet her pension on it. And the tank hookup seemed stupidly complicated until she realized she still had the piece of wreckage tied to her back.

Things started to spin while she worked it loose and she only just got her mouth over the puke tube in time.

"You haven't had fun until you've had a helmet full of puke." Staff Sergeant Beyhn frowned down at her. *"You're sucking carbon dioxide, Kerr. Get your godsdamned tanks in the fill position."*

"Work... ing on... it, Staff."

"Work faster."

"Yes, Staff Sergeant."

She didn't so much push her tanks into the fill niche as collapse back into it.

"Lucky these things are idiot proof," the staff sergeant muttered.

Torin turned off the scanners, started to sit, and remembered her suit didn't exactly bend anymore. She'd been right. The scanners had picked up no sign of Craig. If he'd been blown to pieces, they'd have picked up the DNA signature. The pirates had him.

The way they'd had Rogelio Page.

But Craig had something Page hadn't.

He had her.

All he had to do was stay alive until she came for him.

FIVE

"**I** are not hanging around here indefinitely. I are having more important things to be doing than to be watching her breathe, so for the last time before you are suddenly being part of your own not very complimentary vid about medical personnel who are being deliberately obstructive to the media, you are needing to be telling me when she are waking up." Imperious, demanding, and self-righteous with an order of scrambled syntax on the side; Torin knew that voice. Couldn't figure out how Presit a Tur durValintrisy, ace reporter for Sector Central News, had managed to push her way into Med-op but figured the duty noncom would have her furry little ass out of there so fast it wasn't worth worrying about.

Torin couldn't hear the response to Presit's demands, but she did hear the reporter's reply.

"Fine. But I are not going anywhere until you are telling me where Civilian Salvage Operator Craig Ryder are being. His ship are here, and his ship are being damaged, and he are not with his ship. Or with her."

And it all came back to Torin in a rush of sound and light and pain.

She'd punched up the Susumi engines, hoping that the panel she'd spot welded to the hole in the control room wouldn't throw off the equation too badly. As the patch's sole purpose was to bring *Promise*'s external variables back to the dimensions in the default equations, it was a long way from airtight. Torin would have to remain suited up during the short fold back to the station and help. She had water and could easily go a day and a half on her emergency rations.

Not pleasantly, but easily.

The military had done tests on the protection an HE suit offered against Susumi radiation by strapping a suit filled with sensors to the outside of a ship during a fold. After twenty-seven hours, the suit had begun to fail. After thirty hours, levels were fatal for di'Taykan. After thirty-two hours, for Humans. After thirty-seven hours, for Krai. Torin's fold would take thirty-four hours, but she figured she had two things going for her. First, the military had never performed testing on live subjects and while thirty-two hours might be fatal for a Human, that didn't necessarily mean it was fatal for this Human. Second, the patch would block a portion of the radiation, buying her time.

That was the last thought she could remember. The silent hope that the patch would buy her enough time had segued right into Presit's less than dulcet tones.

Torin had messaged the reporter back on Salvage Station 24. If Presit had time to both find her and get to her out on the edge, then how long had she been out?

Fuk!

Craig had been taken by the pirates. She had no time to lie around.

Her eyelids felt like they weighed a hundred kilos each. Forcing them open, she dragged her tongue over dry lips, and asked, "How long?"

A startled med tech spun around toward her, feathers ruffled, pale-green crest rising. "You're awake!"

"She are obviously awake!" Presit snapped, moving closer to the bed and gripping the railing with a small hand that looked like a black latex glove emerging from the cuff of a thick fur coat. "You are being unconscious in this medical facility for seven hours. I are being here for three of them."

"The pirates have Craig." Teeth clenched, Torin sat up.

"You are having proof of that?" Presit demanded. Behind her, the tech spoke into her slate.

Torin stared at her reflection in the reporter's mirrored glasses. Even taking the curve of the lens into account, she looked like hell. Fuk it; she'd given sitreps in worse condition. Her brain was still too scrambled to separate out time spent sideways of reality in Susumi space and apply it to time passed, so she settled on listing the events that had brought her here in order of occurrence. "Recently, two Civilian Salvage Operators were killed attempting to keep their salvage from pirates." Her voice sounded like she'd been swallowing glass. Her throat agreed that was a valid observation. "This is not standard operating procedure; salvage operators drop and run, but these two found something worth dying to protect. A short time later, another CSO was tortured to death. The only thing a living CSO would have that a pirate might want is information. His death suggests they didn't get it."

"And you are knowing these two things are connected because... ?"

"I don't believe in coincidence."

"Oh, well, that are all I need to be knowing."

Torin ignored the sarcasm and continued. "Approximately thirteen hours ago, pirates captured another CSO—Craig—in what is most likely a second attempt to get the information they did not get from Rogelio Page. I was left for dead."

"They are leaving you for dead? They are being fools for not being sure. And all that," Presit added, tapping one metallic-blue claw against the railing for emphasis, "are being a theory, not proof. Word around this station are being that you were attacked by the Primacy. You were being in a debris field very close to the edge, were you not?"

"I saw the ship," Torin said tersely, forcing the railing down and Presit back. The bright-pink skin on her hand startled her and startled her again when she swung her bare legs out of bed. Right. The foam. The color would fade in time, but time was what she didn't have. "It wasn't a Primacy ship."

"And your word are being good enough because you are being Gunnery Sergeant Torin Kerr."

The floor beside the bed was freezing. "The *Promise*'s computer wasn't damaged. There may be a record of the attacking ship in her data stores, but it doesn't matter if there isn't. I know the ship. It was docked here, at the station, repairing damage from Susumi radiation at the same time we were here selling salvage. Our sensors picked up residual Susumi radiation when we first arrived at the debris field. The debris field one of the crew of the attacking ship suggested we check out."

"That are perhaps being a few too many coincidences."

Torin grinned; she knew that tone. Presit sensed a story. "No shit."

The room spun when she stood and she sat back down considerably faster than she'd risen.

"Speaking of damage from Susumi radiation," Presit added, "they are telling me you are having been damaged yourself when you are arriving. If you are having to be in Susumi space much longer, they are not being able to fix things. As it is, you are being mostly fine. Oh, and they say you are smelling terrible when they are peeling you out of the suit," she added with a toothy grin as the doctor fluttered into the room and came to a sudden stop.

Katrien were omnivores, but Presit had an impressive mouthful of sharp, white teeth, and Torin didn't blame the doctor for not moving any closer.

"You…" A slender finger pointed at Torin. "… shouldn't be out of bed." He snapped the halves of his residual beak together in irritation.

"Will it kill me?" Torin asked.

"Being out of bed? No, but…"

"Presit, that pile on the chair looks like my clothing. Pass it over."

"What are your last slave dying of?" She trilled something to a slightly larger Katrien, bringing him out of the far corner of the room and into Torin's field of vision. "I are lending you Ceelin a Tar guPolinstarta…

Confirmation of gender; a Tar was the male designation. Secondary sexual characteristics were hard to read on a species with fur a minimum of ten centimeters deep.

"…but you are understanding he are being my assistant, not yours."

"I just want my clothes," Torin pointed out, taking them from Ceelin with a nod of thanks. "I don't need…" The pile slid out of her hands as her thumbs refused to work properly.

Ceelin caught the clothes before they hit the floor and set them beside her on the bed. "I are not minding helping you," he said quietly, muzzle crinkling in a tentative smile. "If I are handing you one thing at a time, it are maybe being easier." The darker fur on his brow folded into a deeper vee, dipping down behind the top edge of his dark glasses, as he frowned at her bra. "But I are not knowing what this is."

"It's a place to start," Torin told him, peeling off the medical shift.

"Excuse me!" The doctor snapped his beak again, the dark-green feathers of his crest now at full extension. "This one just said you shouldn't be out of bed! If you'd been in Susumi space for any longer, you would have taken irreparable damage."

"I are having told her that already," Presit murmured.

The doctor ignored her, continuing to glare at Torin. "This one has only just been able to clear the radiation from your system and repair the effects."

Torin nodded once in his general direction. "Thank you."

He blinked, translucent inner eyelid sliding across, then back. "There may still be small amounts of damage at the cellular level."

"Small enough amounts for me to survive them?"

"Yes, but…"

"See any sign of molecular gray plastic aliens while you were in there?"

"No, but…"

"Then again, thank you." Pushing head and arms through the correct holes of her sweater took longer than it should have, but eventually Torin managed it.

"You seem to be deliberately misunderstanding me. You're not completely recovered. You need rest."

"Or else?" she asked as Ceelin guided her feet into the leg holes in her underwear. Time spent in the close quarters of the Corps conquered nudity taboos; not that either Katrien or Rakva, with fur and feathers, would have cared had any lingered.

"Or else you will recover more slowly."

"I can live with that." One hand on Ceelin's shoulder, she stood and used the other to drag her trousers up over her hips.

"This one cannot allow you to leave until the Wardens arrive." He turned to the med tech, who checked her slate and shrugged.

"This one has no ETA."

"I don't have time to wait." Slate on her belt, boots fastened, Torin took a careful step, didn't fall flat on her face, and counted it a win.

"The Wardens will want to take your statement."

"Presit can record it and send it back to the station." One bright-pink hand on the bulkhead and one on Ceelin's shoulder, she could walk at almost a normal speed.

"Where are you going?" Presit demanded, scrambling to catch up.

"Do you have a ship?" She touched the top curve of the plastic chair as she passed by.

"Yes, I are having a ship, but…"

"Then that's where we're going."

Crest still up, the doctor stepped between her and the hatch. "This one objects," he began, but stopped at the expression on Torin's face.

"Did the Wardens tell you to detain me?"

"No, but…"

"Do I owe you for my treatment?"

If he'd had a lip, he'd have curled it. "Health care is a basic right for citizens of the Confederacy."

"That's what I thought. Move."

He'd never been in the Corps, or he'd have moved a lot faster, but he still moved.

"This one needs your statement that you are released from this facility without this one's approval," he grumbled, slate held out.

"I understand that I am released from this facility without my attending physician's approval," Torin said as clearly as possible as she passed him.

"You are best letting her go," she heard Presit say behind her. "She are not being a very nice person even on her good days. Ceelin!"

His shoulder tensed under Torin's hand.

"I are hoping you are planning to come back for the camera?"

"Go on, kid." Torin nudged him back toward the room, wondering just how much of her regaining consciousness he'd recorded. "I can manage."

The long hall leading toward an open hatch with a red exit light above it seemed to be tilted forty-five degrees. Torin took a deep breath, got the hall straightened out about twenty degrees and figured *Fuk it, close enough*. The series of open hatches along both sides of the bulkhead nearly defeated her, but her arms were just long enough to bridge the gaps.

Most of the facility's other patients watched with interest as she lurched past their rooms. One shrieked. Torin ignored them all.

"The only reason the Wardens are not asking the medical facility to be detaining you," Presit told her matter-of-factly, "are because they are assuming any reasonable being are planning on staying right where they are until the Wardens arrive."

"Waste of time," Torin grunted, swayed slightly, and found Presit's shoulder suddenly under her flailing hand. She looked down to find the reporter looking up at her, teeth showing.

"You are assuming, in turn, that I are allowing you to use my ship."

"I'm giving you one hell of a story."

"Your opinion…" Her muzzle wrinkled. "It are not buying me *hurinca*."

Torin neither knew nor cared what *hurinca* was. "Your biggest stories have all involved me in some way." And the polynumerous polyhydroxide alcoholyde shape-shifting molecular hive mind. There was a chance that the pirates were another one of their social experiments but, bottom line, who the fuk cared. The pirates had Craig. "This story is about the pirates, and it'll be huge."

"I are not seeing how."

Torin pulled her lips back off her teeth in an expression that in no way resembled a smile. "I'm going to destroy them."

Presit reached up to pat the hand on her shoulder. "Of course you are."

She didn't sound condescending—or no more condescending than usual. She sounded pleased.

Stumbling toward the docking ring, Torin learned that her patch *had* affected the equations and *Promise* had emerged from Susumi space close enough to the station to set off the proximity alarms.

"It are being a good thing, too," Presit said, steering them around a corner and along the outside curve of the central hub. "They are finding you fast, before you are being dead. Ex-Gunnery Sergeant Torin Kerr are dead are being a story, sure, but not enough of a story for me to have been dragging my ass out to the edge. Ex-Gunnery Sergeant Torin Kerr are removing the pirate scourge from known space, now that are being a story. A better story than merely an observational piece about pirates are being bad," she added, turned, and waved off two people hurrying across the concourse toward them. "Yes, this are ex-Gunnery Sergeant Torin Kerr who are helping to discover the little gray aliens and are helping to be ending the war. Yes, she are smaller in real life. No, her hands are not usually being pink. Yes, she are being in a hurry right now, but my assistant are giving you my burst and you are watching Sector Central News for what she are up to next. Presit a Tur durValintrisy are having the whole story. Ceelin!"

Torin concentrated on walking and taking the slate off her belt at the same time. After three tries to input the codes, she finally managed to access the *Promise*'s data storage. Requested as evidence by the Wardens, the ship had been tethered to a buoy just off station.

"What are you doing?"

Actual Federate syntax out of Presit's mouth sounded wrong. "I'm copying everything from the last three tendays to my slate."

"What are you going to be doing with Craig Ryder's ship?"

"Nothing. It'll be here, waiting, when I get him back."

"You are being sure about that?"

"Given the speed the Wardens work at? Yes." If she couldn't free Craig any faster, if wouldn't matter what she did with the ship; he'd never be returning to it.

"He are not going to be happy about the hole," Presit said thoughtfully.

Torin would kill to hear Craig be unhappy about the hole. Literally.

Presit's pilot was also Katrien, his fur paler than both Presit and Ceelin, the markings around his eyes extending down into his ruff. He was sitting outside the air lock chewing a stim stick when they arrived.

"Merik a Tar konDelasinskin are being at your service." He tapped his index fingers together, a gesture Torin had never seen before. "I are being a big fan. I are watching your vids a hundred, no, two hundred times."

"It are being my vids," Presit snarled, pushing past him and into the air lock. "She are just being on them!"

The ship had been configured for Katrien. Torin couldn't stand erect in any of the three compartments.

Fine with her. Sitting was also good. Torin had nothing against floors.

"Hey!" Presit's eyes were level with hers, the light levels low enough she'd removed her glasses. Had they not been narrowed so dramatically, Torin could have still seen her reflection in the gleaming black. "Where to now? The pirates who are having Craig Ryder could be being anywhere. Space are big."

"No." She decided against shaking her head when she felt her brain wobble. "They have treasure. They've gone to ground."

"Again, could be being anywhere."

"True. So we do this one step at a time. The salvage operators are taking the damage. They'll have the most information. We need to go to Salvage Station 24; the coordinates are on my slate." She couldn't get her slate off her belt. "Fuk."

"Ceelin!"

Small fingers snapped it free and pushed it into her hands. Torin frowned at the screen.

"If you are not able to find the equation, I are taking you back to the doctor who are no doubt going to be unbearably smug."

Torin refused to rise to the challenge in Presit's voice. "I don't need to find it." Activating the DNA reader by pressing her thumb twice in the lower right corner, she unlocked the memory. When she held the slate toward Presit, the reporter actually took a step back.

"You are being sure? This are giving me access to... everything."

"I don't have time to be unsure. Get us to the station. They'll give us the pirates. I'm..." Katrien feet—the same matte black as their hands—had long, prehensile toes. They didn't look as dexterous as Krai feet, but they were close. Presit's toenails were also metallic blue.

"Hey!" A small finger poked her shoulder. Hard. "Torin?"

She couldn't remember her eyelids ever being so heavy. The doctor had been right about her needing to rest. "Just get us there," she murmured, watching the light show on the inside of her lids. "I'm sleeping now."

Twelve hours and thirty-seven minutes later, Torin woke up enough to crawl to the head—easier than standing given the ceiling height. Easy was good given the complex maneuvers needed to urinate in a Katrien toilet. After crawling back to the control room, she sat cross-legged, braced against the wall, and worked both thumbs over the screen of her slate.

"You are listing what you are doing to the pirates when you are catching them?"

"Fuk, Merik!" The pilot was nearly the same shade as the pilot's chair. The low lighting made him remarkably hard to see. Torin had thought she was alone and that thought was a good indication of just how fried she still was. In the Corps, that kind of oversight could be fatal. "No, I'm not listing what I'm going to do to the pirates because that would be a very short list."

Find them.

Destroy them.

"I'm calling in reinforcements," she continued, saved the file, and crawled over to the board. "I need to hook in so the packets go as soon as we emerge."

"Presit are going to want approval," Merik pointed out as the comm screens lit up. "But Presit aren't being here. Be laying your slate down there and I are hooking you in."

"Because Presit shouldn't always get what she wants?"

He smiled, pointed white teeth gleaming. "That is what I are thinking, yes. Are there being anything else I can do for you?"

Torin's stomach growled as she placed her slate on the control panel. "I could eat."

* * *

"I thought the point of the exercise was to get Ryder to join us," Cho pointed out. "Why the fuk would the crew take a vote about him joining if he's already agreed?"

Doc shrugged, eyes locked on the monitor. "If he thinks we don't want him, he'll want us more."

"But we do want him!" Cho snapped. He glanced down at the screen. Beyond the labored rise and fall of his chest, their captive hadn't moved in the last ten minutes.

"No, we don't. We want his codes and, like you said, we can get those from anyone."

"But we have *him*. And we have an armory we can't get into. And I've waited long enough." He'd waited long enough eight years ago when those fukking Marines had taken their own sweet time hooking their packets up to the ship. He'd been the one taking the crap when they weren't ready on the captain's schedule, so he'd had every right to hit the all clear. It hadn't been his Goddamned fault their seals weren't locked.

"Don't think of it as waiting, think of it as amusing yourself by fukking with his head. Ryder can't start on the armory until we're back to Vrijheid," Doc pointed out calmly. "Not unless you want to give him a chance to kill us all."

"You said no one chooses to die."

"He'd be choosing to kill. There's a difference."

"Between dying and killing? No shit." Still, Cho had to admit getting the armory the hell off his ship before Nadayki began his hack had a certain appeal. Except... "If that thing blows, we'd need to be in the next system."

Doc shrugged again. "Big Bill said he had an explosives locker. That should contain most of the blast."

When he said nothing else, Cho shook his head, muttered, "Should. Most. That's very reassuring."

Craig had no idea how long they'd left him alone, but his erection had gone down and the ache to get off had eased by the time the hatch opened again, so they must've been waiting for the air scrubbers to clear out the Taykan pheromones. Made sense. He'd never met anyone who'd actually enjoyed wearing a filter. Then again, he'd never met anyone who tortured people to death before, so what did he know.

Same guy who'd made him the offer came back in and stood by the hatch. Craig tested his restraints. Still no give and the bruising under and around the straps hurt like hell. Seemed like the guy was just being careful.

"Have you thought about my proposal?"

This was a way to stay alive until Torin came for him, but Craig knew he couldn't seem too eager. He swallowed, trying to get a little moisture down to the abraded tissue of his throat. The screaming had done some damage. "Your proposal to join up and become a murdering, thieving pimple on the ass of known space? So fukking tempting, how could I think of anything else?"

Dark brows drew down. "I don't remember phrasing it exactly that way, but yes, that proposal. Join." He held out his left hand, palm up, and then his right. "Or die."

"Great choice there, mate."

"It's *a* choice. And as I said, the offer is on the table for a limited time."

Craig let his head slump forward, then raised it again, figuring the damage from the Taykan's fists as well as the sudden spike of pain the motion had caused would add a certain realism to his despairing expression. "It's not like you've left me anything to go back to. Fine. I'm in."

"Not quite. Now, we take a vote to see if the crew wants you."

"The fuk? I thought you wanted my codes!"

"I want codes." The dark-haired man twitched a nonexistent crease out of his tunic. "Not necessarily yours. You've made your choice. Now it's the crew's turn. It should be an interesting vote. I suspect Almon will be all for stuffing your ass out an air lock. You nearly took his *thytrin's* leg off."

"I nearly…" Craig couldn't believe this was happening. "You blew up my ship! You killed my partner! You fukking kidnapped me!"

"And you might be more trouble than you're worth." Smiling slightly, he turned his head to the side and yelled, "Doc! Come and help our potential crewmate out of this chair."

When the hatch opened again, Craig recognized the man who

came into the room. Hair tied back, muscles straining against the fabric of his gray sweater, fukking freaky thousand-meter stare— he'd been with Nat at the poker game. He hadn't played; he'd just leaned up against the bar and watched. "You set me up!"

"You were convenient, and Nat showed some initiative. It was nothing personal."

"It is from where I'm sitting."

"Yes, and speaking of where you're sitting..." Standing directly in front of the chair, Doc pulled out his slate. "...how much damage did Almon do?"

He sounded like he actually cared. A little confused, Craig took stock. "Nothing's broken."

"Are you sure? Your nose is distinctly crooked."

"Did that six years ago."

"Well, all right, then." Doc tapped the screen, and the straps holding Craig to the chair fell away.

There were only two of them, and neither of them was armed. Torin wouldn't thank him for sitting around on his ass, waiting for her to arrive.

Craig surged up onto his feet and would have fallen flat on his face had Doc not caught him as his right knee gave out. The pain in his leg caused the pain in his head to spike, and if he'd had anything left in his stomach, he would have spewed all over the other man.

His grip surprisingly gentle, Doc lowered him back into the chair. "I can't help if you don't tell me where it hurts." He sounded annoyed.

"Forgot I did... that." It hurt to breathe. First time Craig ever knew his knees were connected to his lungs.

"*You* did that? Ah!" Doc nodded before Craig had a chance to answer. "Fighting to get free. You can't get free. No one can."

Just for an instant there was enough crazy under the concern that Craig, in spite of being a good six to eight centimeters taller and just as heavily built, flinched away from his touch.

The cabin they locked him in had a bunk, facilities that folded up into the wall, a blank vid screen, and a good-sized locker.

It smelled like disinfectant, but that might have just been the lingering fragrance of what they'd sloshed him off with. Ship this size would have been designed to give everyone a bit of privacy, so Craig had no way of telling if the cabin had belonged to officer or enlisted.

Half the secondhand ships in known space were decommissioned Navy ships; weapons removed.

Of course where weapons had been, weapons could be again. *Promise* hadn't been... wasn't armed—*wasn't* because he would get back to her and his injured lady would fly again. Not that a salvaged weapon had done Jan and Sirin any good. Probably got them killed. If they hadn't had the weapon, they'd have cut and run.

Survived.

Let the Navy and the Corps play silly bugger with their lives. Civilians were supposed to be smarter than that.

Stretched out on the bunk, Craig shifted his bad leg and noted with fuzzy appreciation that nothing hurt.

"I'm not going to bother with a healing sleeve until we know we're keeping you, but there's no reason you have to be in pain."

Something in Doc's voice gave Craig the impression that, *should* there be a reason, Doc had no problem at all with pain.

The bunk was surprisingly comfortable. Or he was remarkably stoned.

Either/or. Both.

He woke when the hatch slammed open. The thrum of the engines hadn't changed; they were still traveling through Susumi space.

"Thought you'd like to know..." Nat grinned at him from the open hatch; her expression lecherous enough that he realized he was still naked, "...we've decided to keep you. Welcome aboard, gorgeous."

But she relocked the hatch when she closed it.

It hadn't occurred to Torin that the salvage station might not give a ship from Sector Central News permission to dock.

"Oh, for fuksake!" Her head still throbbed, but sleeping

through most of the fold had done her good. "Are we within a hundred kilometers?"

"Yes." Merik glanced down at his board. "But we are being…"

Torin cut the pilot off. "Keep heading in. I've got this. My codes are on file." She tongued her implant. This was the station's business whether they wanted it to be or not.

Pedro met her at the air lock, arms open, cheeks wet. As soon as the docking beacon had locked, she'd contacted him directly and told him the story. No point in wasting travel time. "*Chica*, I'm so sorry!"

Because Torin had been afraid, in the pause before he'd answered her, that it had been his ship the pirates had destroyed at the debris field, she went into his arms and hugged him hard enough to feel his heart beating. Hard enough to feel he was alive. Then she pulled away and said, "I need everything you know about the pirates."

"*Madre Deos*, why are you pink?" He lifted her hand to eye level.

"Suit sealant." She twisted free. "Focus. I need a list of every pirate attack; I need sightings, rumors, hearsay. I need it all."

"Torin…"

"And we need to get everyone on this station together in the market. I'll need access to the internal comm. No…" She shook her head, editing as she headed for the center of the station, "…better you do it. They know you."

Pedro fell into step beside her. "Torin, what…"

"We're going after Craig."

"What?"

Before Torin could expand on her plan, a small hand grabbed the back of her tunic and yanked her to a stop. She turned far enough to see Presit glaring up at her.

When she saw she had Torin's attention, Presit shifted her gaze to Pedro. "You are probably knowing me, Presit a Tur durValintrisy of Sector Central News. Torin are not exactly having manners. Mind you, I are not exactly happy about leaving my assistant behind, so things are balancing out."

The salvage operators had agreed to Presit's presence but had refused to allow her to record within the station. As the law stated recording devices had to be visible to most species at ten meters, regardless of the actual size of the device, Ceelin's absence was considered a gesture of good faith.

Pedro frowned, scrubbing a hand over damp cheeks. "Torin, why is she here?"

Torin opened her mouth to say something about the story but realized that wasn't actually the reason. Wouldn't have been the reason even had Ceelin and the equipment been with them. "Craig was her friend."

Presit snorted. "For all he are having a patchy pelt and a dubious love life."

"Dubious?"

"...and we know he's on the *Heart of Stone*. The image *Promise* recorded matched on all points the ship docked at the station at the same time we were. The pirates have what they need now, so they'll have gone to ground somewhere they feel safe. We find the *Heart of Stone*, we find Craig."

"They're fukking pirates!" someone yelled from the concourse. "They feel safe with other pirates."

"That's my point," Torin told him. "You need to band together and create an opposing fleet. We not only rescue Craig but eliminate a good portion of the pirate threat."

One of the overhead fans had a loose bearing and made a metal on metal *burr* with every rotation. The *people* on the concourse were silent. Faces that had been turned toward her turned toward the deck.

"Torin. Craig's dead." Over against the bulkhead, Alia waved her hands as though she thought she needed movement to attract Torin's attention. As if her name and the declaration weren't enough.

"We can't know that."

"They've had him..." Her voice broke. "They've had him for hours."

It had taken roughly four and a half hours for Torin to get back to the *Promise*. Seven hours spent unconscious. Forty minutes to walk from the medical facilities to Presit's ship. Ninety minutes to get far enough away from the station to fold.

Ninety minutes to get from the point where they'd emerged to the salvage station. Thirty-three minutes to gather the salvage operators and their families in the concourse. Torin had been up on the stage in the corner, talking for half an hour. Craig had been with the pirates for sixteen hours. Roughly.

Except...

She'd been used to living her life like time spent in Susumi didn't count—ships emerged seconds after they folded regardless of how long they spent inside. Time in the Corps, time spent being ferried from battle to battle and home again, had probably aged her another five to seven years. Med-op kept records. She'd never checked.

But time in Susumi counted when time in Susumi was spent at the mercy of people who'd already killed three innocents. Torin hung onto the certain knowledge that they'd killed Rogelio Page very slowly. Craig was younger. Stronger.

"He's not dead."

"Torin..."

She wasn't sure who'd said her name, but she thought it was Jenn. Craig had been the next thing to a part of their family and they wanted to mourn. Torin wasn't going to let them.

"Two reasons he's not dead. One..." She resisted the urge to raise a specific finger. They were wasting her time. Craig's time. "The pirates need him alive, and they'll have learned from their handling of Page." Handling. A neutral way of saying torturing to death. Torin squared her shoulders and swept her gaze over the crowd. Craig had been well liked—they were listening, but she needed them to do more than that. "Taking salvage is one thing, but taking the salvage operators is something else entirely. Too much of that *will* get the Wardens moving and they won't risk it."

"You don't even know it's the same pirates!" shouted a di'Taykan, dark orange hair in constant movement.

"In the Corps, we called those kind of coincidences a reason for artillery."

A woman in the front row shook her head. "You aren't in the Corps now."

"And we don't have artillery," added the man beside her.

Torin stared at him, brow up.

"Much artillery," he amended, rubbing the back of his neck.

"You said there were two reasons." One arm around Kevin's waist, the other across Jenn's shoulders, Pedro stared at her over Alia's head. "What's the second reason?"

Torin met his gaze. "He'll do everything he can to stay alive because he knows I'm coming for him."

"You also said there was an explosion. He probably thinks you're dead."

"He are not being so stupid," Presit snorted, moving forward and answering before Torin could. "I was being with Craig Ryder the last time Torin was being thought dead and even when he are being told she are dead by the Commandant of the Corps, he are not believing it. When he are standing on the glass that are having been a battalion of Confederation Marines, he are still not believing it." She stroked her claws through the silver fringe of her ruff and glanced up at Torin. "As it are happening, he are right."

"And what are being your part in this?" a Katrien perched up on one of the kiosks called out, sounding suspicious. The reporter was a stranger. Even more than Torin.

Presit's ears flicked, the Katrien equivalent of a shrug. "I are being brought in to expose the pirates so the Wardens will be getting the Navy involved. It are being for your benefit."

"Oh, yeah, like you are doing us a favor!"

"I are benefiting you," Presit responded dryly. "It are not the same thing. I are also planning to be benefiting from the story."

"There is no story." Pedro's voice cracked. He swallowed and continued. "Craig is dead—just like Jan and Sirin. Just like Page. If we band together and go after him, if we go after the pirates, more of us will die."

"Let the Navy do their job!" spat a dark-haired woman.

"The Navy has to be called in by the Wardens," Torin snapped.

"So let it!" someone yelled from the back.

"Some of you have military experience…"

"And we got the fuk out, didn't we?" snarled a di'Taykan. Torin had met her at Sirin and Jan's funeral. Kiku; served one contract in the Corps as a comm tech. She'd told a few "war" stories then. When it became obvious Torin wasn't interested, they'd talked together about one of the guys in the band. "You think you can just waltz in here," Kiku continued, "all 'I'm Gunnery Sergeant Torin Kerr and I survived a prison planet and I found the little gray aliens,' and now we have to march in straight lines and do what you say? Fuk that. We don't fight. We prefer to survive."

"We have families," Pedro added before Torin could respond.

They weren't going to help, she realized. Her business was none of their business.

"You are losing them," Presit murmured as people began to shuffle from the shuttle bay.

"I never had them," Torin admitted, cutting her losses. She didn't have time to convince them of the obvious. She raised her voice until it filled all the empty spaces. "I need to buy a ship. And I need it now."

That got their attention. Every face turned back toward her. To her surprise, the first question was, "Why?"

"The *Promise* is damaged, and pirates aren't likely to welcome reporters."

"Everyone are playing to a camera," Presit snorted quietly.

"You're going after Craig alone?" Kiku again. When no one laughed with her, she flushed, her hair flattening, but she didn't look away. "You don't even know where the *Heart of Stone* is, do you?"

"I'll find it."

"Because you're Gunnery Sergeant Torin Kerr?"

"Because they have Craig." At least some of those in the room who were ex-military had served with combat troops in a time of war. Pulled a trigger and seen a distant body fall. Torin had killed up close and personal. People near the stage backed up as they heard that in her voice.

"How," asked a narrow-eyed woman with three black lines tattooed down the center of her forehead, "are you planning on paying for this ship?"

Given the audience, that was the question Torin had expected to hear first. "I'll cede my military pension."

"How much of it?"

"All of it."

"Oh, yeah. That's just great." A mocking voice rose above the murmur as the man with the ginger mustache who'd confronted her at the funeral moved to the front of the crowd. "You take that ship off to play hero against the pirates, and we'll get sweet fuk all because you'll be dead, and they don't pay pensions to the dead."

"I don't plan on dying."

"No one plans on dying."

"You'd be surprised."

He had his mouth open again, and Torin was seconds from putting her fist in it when Pedro called out. "You can have our small ship."

He didn't mean have as *have it to save Craig*, he meant have as in he'd take the pension. She could hear it in his voice. "I need a ship with a weapon mounted."

"The *Second Star* has a recessed BN-344. We use it to cut debris apart."

The BN-344 was the big half sister of the BN-4, the cellular disrupter/tight band laser the Corps carried in those places a projectile weapon would be unwise. Without the cellular disrupter attached, the big laser could *also* be used as a cutting tool. Her lip curled, but she nodded. His small ship was almost the same base model as the *Promise*. She could get it from point A to point B. "Deal."

The crowd parted as she jumped off the stage. For a moment she wished they hadn't—laying hands on even one of them would have helped her mood—then she ignored them. Their business wasn't her business. The crowd stayed parted behind her, and she could hear Presit following. The reporter had sharp claws and no compunction about using them.

"If you come back, *chica*..." Pedro closed a hand on Torin's shoulder. "We'll do another deal."

Words that would wound rose to her tongue. She could see the damage stitching across his chest, spraying blood. Teeth clenched, she settled for shrugging out from under his touch and saying, "I'll arrange for the transfer on the way to the ship." She pulled out her slate. "Let's go."

"I are still coming with you," Presit announced before Torin could move. "As much as I are hating to admit it, you are being right. This are going to be an amazing story." She closed her hand on Torin's wrist—claws dimpling the skin, fingers barely making it halfway around—and held her in place as she turned a sneer on the listening crowd. "And besides, as are having been mentioned before, Craig Ryder are being my friend."

"There's information on the pirates coming in from all over the station—I've directed it straight to the ship." Pedro stood by the air lock, arms folded. "People want to help."

Torin ignored him. She knew defensive when she heard it.

Merik, what the hell is taking Presit and Ceelin so long?

They are being on their way. Presit are making sure she are having full remote access to Sector Central.

Of course she was.

"You've got supplies on board for a tenday—there's ice in the converter, you shouldn't have to capture more. Torin…"

Torin was fully capable of looking out over a platoon of Marines and keeping her opinion of the situation—of any situation, good or bad—from showing. Here and now, she didn't bother.

Pedro winced. "It's your life to throw away, but you're delusional if you think he's alive. Craig's dead."

"No, he isn't!" Helena pushed past her parents—the other three had gathered at the far edge of the cargo bay, unwilling to be contaminated by hope. She ran across to the air lock as they shouted her name and followed. Instead of her usual station overalls and soft shoes, she wore scuffed boots and a jacket that was just a little too big for her. A small green duffel bag hung over one shoulder. "I'm going with you. I'm probably a better pilot than you are," she added quickly, "and I know what to do if the *Star* gets weird."

"I'm sorry, Helena," Torin stepped forward, physically cutting off whatever Pedro had been about to say. "But you're too young."

"I'm not!"

She closed her hands on the girl's shoulders, met her gaze, and held it. "Thank you for offering. I don't doubt your courage or your commitment, but I can tell you right now that in order to get Craig back, I'm going to do things no fourteen-year-old should have to deal with. Even if you survived the experience, parts of you would die. I won't be responsible for that, and you're three years away from taking responsibility for yourself."

"But I want…"

"I know." And she did. She'd seen it a hundred times. Kids who'd lost friends or family in the war—a station destroyed, a colony attacked, a ship lost—and had joined up because hitting back was the only way they could make sense of what had happened. It wasn't as simple as just taking revenge—although she'd seen plenty of those kids, too—they didn't join because they hated the enemy, they joined because they'd loved something and lost it.

Helena searched her face for mockery and finally nodded, eyes glistening. "You'll bring him back?"

"I'll bring him back."

Leaning in a little closer, she peered into Torin's eyes. Torin knew what the girl was searching for and she let her look. Finally Helena nodded, one corner of her mouth twisting up, and she said, "They don't know what they're in for, do they?"

Torin gave her back the smile she'd been attempting. "No, they don't."

"The child are not going with us, right?" Presit's voice carried.

"No, she isn't." Torin gave Helena's shoulders a final squeeze and released her, the space where her hands had been almost immediately taken by Alia, who clutched her daughter to her protectively. Helena shook her mother off, eyes rolling.

"Good. It are an old vid adage never to be appearing with the young of any species. One way or another, they are always going to be making you look bad." Presit patted Helena's arm approvingly as she passed. The girl looked startled but pleased. "Ceelin, you are being careful with the camera. It are being the conscience of the cowardly."

The Elder Races may have brought Human, diTaykan, and Krai into the Confederation to fight their war, too pacifist to take up weapons and keep themselves from slaughter, but some of the Mid Races were clearly willing to draw blood.

"He agreed to come?" Torin asked quietly as Ceelin crossed the cargo bay all but buried under an impossible amount of gear.

Presit snorted. "Please, I are practically having to lock Merik in the ship to keep *him* from coming."

"Merik has his..." She closed her teeth on *orders*. "...part to play before he meets us at Val Doron Station. But Ceelin..."

"Ceelin are knowing the odds. He are also knowing you and I are where the career-building stories are being. He are ambitious. Also..." She fluffed her ruff. "...I think he are having *jurnifa* for me."

"You honestly don't think they'll be any help," Pedro muttered as Presit disappeared into the ship. "And don't give me that bullshit about her being Craig's friend."

Torin thought about flattening him. Didn't. But it was close. "You'd be amazed at how few people shoot at the media, all things considered." She nodded again at Helena—*Good-bye* and *Thank you* and *Don't worry, we'll bring him back* all layered onto the movement—then paused, just inside the *Second Star*'s air lock. "You went out after Jan and Sirin."

Alia had the grace to look embarrassed. "To find out what happened. We know what happened to Craig."

Torin laid her palm against the control pad, one finger bent to touch the plastic trim. "No," she said quietly, "you don't. Craig told me once that you took care of your own. He was wrong. All you're willing to do is throw parties for the dead."

Pedro's small ship was the same basic model as the *Promise*—rectangular cabin with the control panel and two chairs across one narrow end, bunk and the hatch into the head across the other. The air lock and suit storage took up the majority of one long wall while across from it were general storage, cooking facilities, and a half-oval table with two chairs that snapped out from recesses in the wall. Because the *Second Star* had an additional three-by-three module, some of the storage space had been replaced by another hatch across from the air lock.

Presit claimed this space as hers and graciously permitted Ceelin and their equipment to share it.

"I are willing to support you in front of fools and cowards," Presit announced, climbing up into the second control chair and tucking her feet under the thick fringe of her fur, "but now it are just you and me, I are wanting to be assured you are knowing what you are doing."

"The station's docking computer is in control until we clear the panel array," Torin told her without looking up from the board. She'd been surprised to learn the station *had* a docking computer and wondered if they hadn't trusted her to leave on her own without causing deliberate damage. Fair enough. She didn't trust herself.

"Not what I are asking. You are having a plan?"

A call from the station pinged the ship before Torin could answer. Unlike the steady stream of data still being downloaded through Pedro's personal comm to the *Second Star*, this message was addressed specifically to her.

"Kerr, go."

The Krai on the screen looked nervous, his nose ridges opening and closing so quickly they seemed to be fluttering. "Gunnery Sergeant Kerr, this is Kenersk. We uh, spoke, back at the funeral."

"I remember you." An ex-Marine who'd done two contracts, Kenersk had fought with the Four Three, holding the line during the evacuation of the Denar Colony, so she let the form of address stand. Turned out, he'd also been the Krai who'd allowed Winkler to get his hands on the cup of *sah*—which was why she remembered him.

"I don't know if it'll help, but I can tell you where you can find a pirate ship."

Torin waited.

After a moment, Kenersk rubbed a hand over the bristles on his head and continued. "It's a Krai ship, the *Dargonar*. All Krai. Captain Firrg hates Humans, I mean, really, really hates them. Don't know what she thinks about di'Taykan, but Humans, Humans she obsessively hates."

"I got that, Kenersk." The information might have been a

warning. Or possibly merely Kenersk trying to talk himself into the betrayal.

"Yeah, well, they say she likes to pick off the occasional ore carrier—just the drones, though, and never often enough to set off alarms—and they say she sells the ore at the Prospect Processing Station. They say, she'll be at Prospect in two days."

"Who are saying…"

Kenersk broke the link.

Presit snorted. "If he are not supplying his sources, I are not trusting his information."

Torin drummed her fingers against the control panel's inert trim. "Good thing it's my call, then."

"Why are you trusting him? Because he are stroking your ego and calling you Gunnery Sergeant."

"No. Because he feels guilty about Winkler getting the *sah*, and he owes me for not calling in the Wardens. Salvage operators don't like to be beholden. It makes them feel dependent."

"They are not liking to be dependent on the kindness of others. It are a quote from Human literature," she added, sounding annoyed that Torin hadn't recognized it. "I are having read it at university in Xeno History. You are being familiar with it?"

"No." She slid her hand between Presit's fingers and the board. Presit's claws caught against her knuckles but didn't break the skin. "Don't touch that."

"I are turning light levels down! Humans are always keeping the lights too bright."

"I'll turn them down after we fold. Until then, I need to see the board."

"I are thinking that the station's docking computer are doing the hard part," Presit sniffed.

A ship the size of the *Second Star* was no harder to fly than an APC was to drive. Easier, since dirtside driving provided a lot more solid objects to hit. Also, APCs were seldom empty, the driver responsible for every Marine on board. APCs, however, didn't have Susumi engines. Torin had read somewhere that eighty percent of all accidents in space were a direct result of a Susumi error. "Firrg's taking the unmanned drones because they're the most likely to go missing in a fold." No computer could compensate one hundred percent for the unexpected.

Presit made a noise that sounded remarkably like the Katrien version of, *Well, duh.* and then said, "Who are being his source, I are wondering."

"He said it's an all-Krai ship," Torin muttered, studying the charts to place Prospect in known space. "Fourday fold from here…"

"Four days are not so long, but even you, *ex*-Gunnery Sergeant Kerr, even you are not being able to go up against a ship full of Krai pirates on your own. Not even if they are out of their ship and under the influence. You are being weighed down by numbers alone. Although," she added thoughtfully, head cocked to one side, "that would be having amazing visuals."

"I don't have to go up against a ship full of Krai pirates. I only need to get one of them alone."

"You are probably needing to be getting the captain alone," Presit scoffed. "You are not able to guarantee anyone else are having the information you need."

"Then I'll get the captain."

"And it are being just that easy for you?"

Torin pulled up the charts with the Susumi equations. Remembered Craig bitching about her basic-level math. "I'm motivated."

SIX

"So, I are thinking that while we are being trapped together in Susumi space and are having time, you should be filling me in on the Silsviss."

Stretched out on the bunk, replaying her last moments with Craig over and over, Torin had been paying next to no attention to Presit's background babble, but that got her attention. "I should fill you in on the Silsviss? Where the hell did *that* come from?"

"If a large, aggressive, reptilian species are joining the Confederation..." One foot pressed against the edge of the control panel, Presit rocked the pilot's chair back and forth. Unlike the chair in the *Promise*, the pivot point was mercifully silent. "...I are thinking smaller mammalian species are wanting to know about it."

She had a point, Torin acknowledged. On Silsviss, small mammalian species were considered snacks. "Well, you're out of luck because I can't talk about them."

"Can't or won't."

"Both." Sitting up, Torin scraped a clump of silver-tipped fur off the blanket and wondered just why she'd agreed to have Presit come along. They'd established beyond a doubt that the reporter was Craig's friend, but she wasn't Torin's. No more than Torin was hers.

The enemy of my enemy is my friend. Faulty logic from a military point of view, where nothing prevented the enemy of an enemy from also being an enemy, but Torin supposed it worked in this instance. Craig had given them common ground; perhaps it was time to move beyond that and establish a connection of their own.

One of the basic tenets of the Corps was that no Marine got left behind, that in the midst of violence and death, in spite of rank or lack of rank or species or gender, they were all in it together. For whatever reason, Presit had stepped up when no one else had.

"There are being stories about Staff Sergeant Torin Kerr and the Silsviss. I are thinking you are wanting to set the record straight. Ceelin are just sleeping. He could be setting up..."

"No. I was senior NCO of the platoon accompanying the first lot of diplomats," Torin told her, rolling the fur into a tight silver cylinder. "That's all."

Presit snorted. "That are not what the rumors are saying. I are knowing what you are doing on Big Yellow, and I are knowing what you are doing on Crucible, and I are knowing what you are doing on the aliens' prison planet, so, given what I are knowing, I are wondering if there are being any truth to those rumors."

"Exaggerations..."

"I are not doubting that," Presit snorted. "But I are also not doubting there are being truths at their core and a story people are wanting to hear."

"It's not a story I can tell." It had been a military exercise, and for all the law said full disclosure to the press, the brass had kept the final facts need to know only. As Presit opened her mouth, Torin held up a hand. "But when I can tell it, I'll tell it to you. Okay?"

The lights were low enough that Presit hadn't put on her glasses, but her eyes were as unreadable as the mirrored lenses would have been. After a long moment she nodded, fluffed her ruff with her claws, and said, "Okay."

Progress. As her head began to tip forward of its own volition, Torin stretched back out on the bunk. The random moments of weakness came less frequently but were still a disturbing reminder that she wasn't yet at a hundred percent. The one good thing about time wasted in Susumi was that it gave her time to finish healing.

"I are hating this."

Pedro, or a member of his family, had scratched *Sonrisa de señora Luck sobre nosotros* in the painted metal above the bunk. "You hate what?"

"Waiting. We are having gone through the information the CSOs are sending us. We are having researched the Prospect Processing Station, not that there are being much available information to research. We are having decided I are being distraction while you are being muscle."

It hadn't so much been a decision, Torin amended slightly, as it had been the only possible division of labor.

"Now we are having nothing to do. Unless you are telling…"

"No." The plastic trim around the small light over the bunk still had no reaction to her touch. She closed her eyes. "Sleeping now."

"I are knowing why you are sleeping!"

"Still healing. Go talk to Ceelin."

"Oh, no. I are knowing that you are trying to be ignoring me…"

Torin had spent a high percentage of her adult life sleeping in war zones and not even Presit could match an artillery barrage for either volume or duration. Although she tried.

The computer countdown ended and Craig felt the ship's vibration change as they came out of Susumi space. With his last meal sitting like salvage in his stomach, he prayed to the gods of his childhood that with him and his codes on board, the ship had gone to ground rather than gone hunting for new prey. If he were captain and he had a crewmember he didn't trust and had just picked up a new captive he needed to brutalize, he'd put that crewmember back in the room with the chair. Only, this time, the new crewmember would be the one standing. And that new crewmember would cross a line they couldn't cross back or they'd take a short walk out the air lock. Craig liked to think he knew what his choice would be, but he was honest enough with himself to realize it wasn't something he could know until he actually had to make the decision.

Kill or die.

Sounded like the same choice Torin had made for years.

Close, but not quite.

The locked door said Cho didn't trust him. That maybe Cho figured injuries be damned, if let loose, Craig would overpower the entire crew and fly the ship to the nearest Warden's office. Torin might—fuk it, Torin would—but he wasn't Torin.

But if Cho thought three days of minimal contact would soften him up, the captain knew sweet fuk all about how salvage operators worked. Before Torin, Craig's default had been two or three tendays with no one to talk to but *Promise* and the space between the stars.

Doc had brought him a pair of overalls on his last visit to check his knee. They stank of di'Taykan and Craig reacted to them just being in the room.

"You wouldn't fit into mine or Nat's or the captain's," Doc had growled, his hands gentler on the bruised flesh than his voice. "You're too damned tall. Rest of the crew's Krai or di'Taykan. You do the math."

Sure, might have been as simple as that.

Might have been Almon continuing to fuk with him.

Either way, he hadn't put them on. Not like he was packing anything the crew hadn't seen. Nat's casual lechery as she delivered his food—blatant enough to distract him as he ran his fingers over the gray plastic tray—made him reconsider; even the dubious shield of pheromone-drenched cloth became better than no shield at all.

He rubbed his palms against the navy blue fabric stretched over his thighs.

No point in counting his heartbeat to keep track of the time between emerging from Susumi and arriving at their final destination—distance between emergence and final destination depended on the equation used and the standard emergent point was ninety minutes out. Even if pirates refused to conform to standards, counting wouldn't change a damned thing.

Torin would probably count.

Craig stretched out on the bunk, hands behind his head.

Torin was a tad anal at times.

He'd just close his eyes for a quick kip.

He had no idea how much later the familiar soft bump of a

ship making contact with a docking nipple woke him.

Weird how the internal dampeners never seemed to compensate for that.

They'd be coming for him soon.

Prospect was a Krai colony planet, settled for barely two hundred years. The city clustered around the spaceport was a splash of light, but the rest of the land mass under the station's geosynchronous orbit was dark, even though it was just past sunset in that hemisphere. Low population density explained part of it, the Krai's preference for living in actual high forest canopy rather than high-tech imitations explained the rest.

The planet's Krai name was in a dialect Torin had never mastered although she was fluent enough in most to ensure the Krai who'd been under her command had assumed the worst. Her vocabulary in any dialect skewed toward profanity and comfort.

"It are making a better impression if you are able to be throwing the species' name in," Presit admitted, fluffing out her ruff as Ceelin packed the brushes away. "But only if it are pronounced correctly, otherwise, stick to Federate. Prospect are being a perfectly fine name."

Prospect Station was not only the link between the planet and the rest of the Confederation but the ore processing center for the planet below.

"Apparently, planets that are being capable of growing such enormous trees are being short of certain minerals. Who knew?" Presit's tone suggested someone was an idiot.

The ore processing made it a lot rougher place than most planets' primary stations, which probably explained why Firrg and her crew thought it safe to hang around after unloading their stolen ore.

As the station's sysop brought them in, Torin examined the three other ships on the docking arm. The *Dargonar* was registered as a C-class cargo vessel the same as the *Heart of Stone* had been.

"It are not looking like a dangerous pirate ship," Ceelin noted, standing up on his toes to see out the port. "It are having no weapons. Not even as much as this ship."

"The weapons are preConfederation Krai," Torin told him. "There…" She used a light pen to circle the forward guns. "There. There. And there for sure. People forget the Krai, like the Taykan, like Humans, were in space before the Confederation emissaries arrived, and they took all their really dangerous toys with them."

"PreConfederation weapons are being antiques," Presit scoffed.

"Fine. Copies of preConfederation weapons."

"And you are just *happening* to be able to identify them?"

"Me and a couple million other Marines. We don't spend all our time dirtside shooting at things," she added off Presit's look.

But all Presit said was, "Didn't spend all your time."

Hard to remember given the assault she was planning.

To Torin's surprise, one of the other ships was Silsviss.

Presit combed gleaming copper claws through her ruff. "I are maybe knowing they going to be here," she admitted. "There are being small integration attempts before they are being given full citizenship where studies are being done on how they are dealing with other species off their planet as well as on. They are wanting to look into orbital smelting, and Prospect are small enough and isolated enough if it are all going wrong, damage should be at a minimum. I are hoping you are giving me enough background to be picking up the story."

"You have a story."

"Good thing," the reporter snorted. "Because you are being no help at all."

Moments after the *Second Star* had attached to the docking nipple, Torin had the board shut down and the air lock sequence initiated.

"I are needing to go out first," Presit reminded her, digging a sharp elbow into Torin's thigh. "I are the reason we are being here, remember?" She nodded toward Ceelin and the camera.

Torin drew in a deep breath. "Almost an hour to get onto the *Star*. Ninety minutes to get far enough away from the salvage station to fold. Two hours from emergence to docking. Not counting time in Susumi, Craig's been gone twenty hours."

"I know. But you are not helping him if station sysop are not agreeing you have a reason to be breathing their air. This are not a place anyone are going without a reason…" Her muzzle wrinkled. "…or at all if possible, and your reason are likely to have someone calling the Wardens or have whoever are working here with Captain Firrg giving her warnings, so it are better if you are being invisible behind me." The air-lock telltales went green, and Presit settled her mirrored glasses on her muzzle. "Show time."

"You have got to be fukking kidding me." One hand braced against the bulkhead to counteract the dizzy spells he was still having, Craig stared at the screen outside the cargo bay as the eye moved around the gray-green metal rectangle taking up most of the room. "That's a weapons locker. A Marine Corps weapons locker."

A sealed Marine Corps weapons locker—double sealed, in fact with both the Corps' seal and the CSO seal intact. That meant there were weapons inside. KC7s at the very least, the chemical-powered, practically indestructible primary weapon of the Corps. Primitive enough they couldn't be neutralized at a distance the way more high-tech weapons could be and dangerous enough that even in spite of an interfering plastic molecular hive mind, the Corps had nearly fought the Primacy to a stalemate with them.

Torin wasn't big on war stories, but sometimes, lying with her head on his shoulder as the sweat dried and stuck them together, she'd sketch out what he knew were the bare bones of her life before he became a part of it. He'd seen her in action on Big Yellow. He'd seen what she survived on Crucible and the prison planet. He didn't really want to know any more than what she was comfortable telling him. In fact, given how she'd looked the first time he'd seen her in the tank after Crucible, there were things about her previous life he wished he could forget.

At least now he knew why Jan and Sirin had died trying to keep their salvage from the pirates. This could shift power in the whole sector, maybe far enough that other sectors could fall. Craig didn't have Torin's eye for ex-military, but of the members of the crew he'd met—where met included having the shit beat out of him by—he'd bet both Captain Cho and Doc had served. From a violent life to a violent life; no great stretch to assume more pirates would be ex-military than not.

There went any hope that a high proportion of the people who'd end up with these weapons wouldn't know how to use them.

Torin had to find him fast; it was no longer just his life on the line.

And fuk but the universe had a sick sense of humor. What kind of sick joke was it that pirates would happen on this particular cargo in the minimal amount of time between the sealing of it and sending the packet to register salvaged weapons with the military. It hadn't been registered, that was for damned sure, or he wouldn't be here because the Navy would. Torin'd call that kind of a fukked-up coincidence a reason to call in air support...

Torin wouldn't believe that kind of a fukked-up coincidence.

"You intercepted the registration packet."

Almon glanced up from the controls of the eye and smiled unpleasantly. "We did."

"That's not possible."

"Surprise." The di'Taykan moved closer. Craig gritted his teeth and ignored his body's reaction. Even with Almon's masker up to full, he'd taken such a hit of pheromone he'd be feeling the effects for days. Hopefully only days. "My *thytrin*," Almon continued, voice dropping into a near growl, pale-yellow eyes darkening as more light receptors opened, "the one you nearly killed, he can make a comm unit beg."

"Kinky. That why you're here? Because your *thytrin* is more into machines than meat?" Craig blocked Almon's blow. "I'm crew now. You don't get to touch me."

"You don't get it, do you, Ryder?" He was standing close enough now that the ends of his hair stroked Craig's cheek. "*You* don't get to touch *me*."

"Enough." Cho's voiced backed Almon all the way to the screen. "I need him able to think with something other than his dick." The captain stopped just behind Craig's left shoulder. "Can you crack it?"

Craig had little doubt that if he said no he'd be out the air lock—probably in the kind of condition that would make a fast death in vacuum a gift. He rubbed at the small patch of stubble on the edge of his jaw. "My codes will get me into the guts of the seal. After that, it's grunt work." Sentient species were incapable of being completely random, a pattern always emerged. Find the pattern, work the code. Open the lock.

"Once you're in, we can hook up a slate and…"

"No." Craig wanted to smile but doubted smug satisfaction would go over well. "Hook in anything the seal reads as a random-number generator, and you'll fuse it. Usually, that'd mean hacking the seal off the salvage physically and ringing every bell in the yard when you tried to sell it. You… we," he amended, "don't have to worry about sales. We have another problem." He tapped the screen. "Fusing the CSO seal will melt it into the Corps' seal. The Corps' seal will read that as an attempted forced entry and self-destruct."

"So when you say grunt work?" the captain growled.

"We can use a slate to input, but what we input will have to be worked out the old-fashioned way."

"So why do we need him again?" Almon sneered.

The captain raised an eyebrow that asked the same thing.

"Without my codes, you'll fuse the seal trying to get in." Craig spread his hands. "Boom. And I have a better chance of recognizing the locking pattern than someone with no background in the way salvage operators do things. It'll save some time."

"How much time?"

"No idea. Faster with me than without me, that's all I know."

Cho stared at him for a long moment. Craig tried to look like a man who didn't want to be thrown out an air lock. Finally, the captain nodded. "Your slate stays with me. I'll supply a scrubbed slate and you'll be working with Nadayki…"

"Captain!"

"And you can shut the fuk up about it." Cho moved up into Almon's space. "Ryder didn't lure the kid into a dark alley and stick him for his beer money. Ryder fought back. Nadayki didn't haul ass out of the way fast enough. End of discussion."

Almon looked like he wanted to argue, but to Craig's surprise, he kept his mouth shut.

Maybe by the time a person decided to be a pirate, there was nowhere else to go. Get thrown out of the crew, and survival became unlikely. Life at rock bottom explained how a shitkicker like Cho could maintain command. And who'd be stupid enough to challenge him with Doc at his side?

"You…" Pivoting on a heel, Cho turned his attention back to Craig. "Once we've got the locker secured on the station, you'll provide the raw data and Nadayki'll make it dance. Nat."

"Right here, Cap."

It was more than a little creepy how Nat *was* right there whenever the captain called her.

"Take Ryder back to his quarters and secure him." The smile he shot at Craig was nearly as unpleasant as Almon's had been. "I don't want our new crewmember running around loose while we're moving the locker. He could get hurt."

"I'll stay out of the way."

"I'll make sure of it," Nat muttered, taking Craig's arm. "Come on, gorgeous. If you're lucky, I'll tuck you in."

Still aching from the effect of Almon's pheromones, Craig gave it half a thought. If he wore her out, he could make a run for it. Except that any station welcoming this particular ship onto its docking arm and offering a secure location for the illegal entry into a Marine weapons locker made the oldEarth observation about frying pans and fires depressingly relevant.

"…but by far the greatest benefit to processing the ore here in orbit is that we have greatly reduced airborne pollutants in our planetary atmosphere."

"I are seeing how that are being a benefit, but you are having to admit that an orbital facility are adding distinct dangers to the job and that…" Presit reached out, and Ceelin, who continued walking backward without breaking stride, slid a slate into her hand. "…station logs are reporting you are having eight injuries in the last ten tendays and one of them are being fatal."

Although Torin could only see the top of his head, she knew Rergis, the facility's manager, had slammed his nose ridges shut. His whole posture screamed overdone, righteous indignation.

"There were extenuating circumstances…"

"And here are being one of them," Presit said brightly as they drew even with what was clearly the station's roughest drinking establishment. Halfway between the docking arm and the processing plant, against the outer skin of the station, it was perfectly situated for easy access. Easy to get to, after work. Easy to get away from, should the need arise.

Rergis pulled himself up to his full height, barely reaching the middle of Torin's chest and towering over Presit by a full six centimeters. "Are you insinuating that these accidents might have been the result of stimulant abuse?"

"I are not suggesting anything of the sort. I are merely observing that stimulants are often considered extenuating circumstances and…" She glanced down at the slate and back up again while Rergis stared at his reflection in her glasses "…are being cited in two of these reports. So let's be taking a look." Her gesture sent Ceelin in through the hatch, leaving Rergis no choice but to follow the camera or allow Presit to wander unsupervised. He'd been with her for less than ten minutes, and Torin could see he'd already discovered that was a bad idea.

The ore processors ran 28/10 and few, if any, incoming ships would have matched their clocks to the station's, so it was no surprise the bar was fairly crowded although station time was officially midafternoon. Most of the clientele were Krai though there were a few Niln. The bartender was Human. So were two of the people sitting at the bar. Nearly everyone had at least part of their attention on the three Silsviss sitting at a table in the corner.

They were young males and, from the slight distension of their throat pouches, they were here to prove a point—which, given how incredibly hierarchical their society was, was pretty much the point of being a young male Silsviss.

"This are not seeming like a problem," Presit announced, her voice cutting through the ambient noise with an ease Torin had to admit she admired. Although no one became less aware of the Silsviss, they all became entirely aware of Presit. And the camera.

Odds were good pirates would prefer to remain off the evening news; Torin noted which Krai were keeping their faces hidden as Ceelin panned the camera around the room. Then she noticed that all three Silsviss were looking at her. When one started to rise, Torin glared his ass back onto his stool.

"I don't know what you were expecting," Rergis began, but Presit cut him off, the points of her teeth barely showing.

"Pretty much what I are finding, actually." Turning to look up at Torin, she added, "You are being too big to be following normal-sized people around. You might as well be staying here while Rergis are showing me the facility and explaining what actual extenuating circumstances he are referring to. Ceelin!" She chivied the camera back out the hatch, giving Rergis no choice but to follow her, trying to explain.

As everyone but the Silsviss returned their attention to their drinks, Torin walked over to the bar, silently acknowledging that Presit had effortlessly put Torin right where she needed to be. Odds were good Firrg was in this bar. No one continued to pay docking fees for the privilege of staying on board their own ship and since the captain's contact for unloading stolen ore had to be someone fairly high up in the power structure of the processing plant, she wouldn't drink anywhere they might run into each other. Or, for that matter, anywhere where she might have trouble getting back to her ship.

Finding her in a dim room full of Krai when most non-Krai couldn't even tell the genders apart— di'Taykan excepted— would be no problem. Torin had planned to find her by doing some eavesdropping among the Krai who'd hidden from the camera but, fortunately, there was a faster way. Firrg hated Humans. The bartender was Human. The fact that the Corps spent a long time teaching recruits to look beyond nearly universal default species parameters meant said parameters were alive and well in the general population.

Torin sat down, pointed at the beer spout, and said as the bartender put a glass of pale draft in front of her, "Which one is Captain Firrg?"

Dark brows rose toward the polished, mahogany dome of the bartender's head—he was old enough he might have been caught up in the permanent depilatory phase that had been popular with male Humans two decades ago or he might have just felt that in an establishment that catered mostly to a species with minimal bristling across their scalps, hair was a bad customer-service idea. Didn't matter. He leaned toward her and growled, "Who wants to know?"

Torin took a long swallow of beer, then met his eyes as she put the glass back down on the bar. "I do."

After staring at her for a long moment, he snorted and shook his head. If he recognized her, that was the only indication he gave. "You planning on starting something?"

"Not in here."

His grunt was noncommittal. He might have approved, or he might have wanted to see Firrg get hers. Again, didn't matter. Torin had no intention of taking the captain down in a place where a fight would be so distinctly to the Krai's advantage.

"Table just inside the door," he said after Torin took another swallow and set the glass down again. "Firrg's in the red, got the jagged scar across her head. But those five she's with? They're her crew and they're male and they'd die for her."

Torin nodded her thanks.

"I don't care how good you think you are," he added when she stood. "You can't take them all."

"I won't have to," Torin told him, sliding her slate across the credit reader and turning to go. "The thing between us is personal."

Torin knew how to walk across a room and draw every eye toward her. She also knew how to blend, look like she belonged. No one noticed her by Firrg's table until she pulled another chair up, sat down, and said quietly, "I hear you hate Humans. The *Heart of Stone*, which has, at the very least, a Human captain and two Humans in the crew, has taken a friend of mine captive. I plan on killing whoever gets in my way when I go in to get him back. I figure Humans killing Humans should make you happy, so you'll be willing to tell me where I can..." She twisted out from under the hand of Firrg's crewman reaching for her arm, grabbed it, drove her thumbnail into the nerve cluster on the inside of the wrist as hard as she could, slammed the spasming hand down onto the table, and said to the groaning crewmember still attached to it, "Piss off. The grown-ups are talking."

On anyone but a Krai, Firrg's expression would have been a smile. When a Krai showed that many teeth, something or someone was likely to end up eaten. "Why should I tell you anything when you're damaging my crew?"

Torin shrugged. "I could have driven my elbow into his nose ridges and assumed someone would keep him from drowning in his own blood."

"You could have," Firrg agreed, her nod throwing the jagged scar zigzagging across her forehead into relief. The edges looked too even to be accidental and Torin had a suspicion she knew the source of at least some of the pirate captain's hatred. Scars being easy enough to remove, that was a statement. It said, *Hi, I'm completely bugfuk!* among other things. "And you're right," Firrg continued, her expression holding the rest of her companions in place. "Humans killing Humans makes me very happy. But you're Human, and I don't do favors for Humans." She spread her hands. "So I can't help you."

"Last word on the matter?"

"Yes." Firrg looked happy to be turning her down. Her crew laughed.

Torin had really hoped they could do this the quick way. She didn't have time to fuk around and no choice but to take the time. Leaning forward, she said in thickly accented Krai, "I've heard that the reason you hate Humans is because it was a Human who laughed as you ran like a coward from a fair fight." Then she stood and walked out of the bar, trailing her fingers over the gray plastic frame around the big menu screen on her way by. Behind her, chairs scraped against the floor as they were shoved back, and there was a lot of loud swearing that Torin would bet serious money came from everyone but Firrg.

Hating Humans—or any other species as a whole— wasn't that unusual, no matter how often the H'san sent out slightly sad messages insisting that the member species of the Confederation were one big happy family. Everyone knew someone who hated their family, but no one seemed willing to clue in the H'san. Had Firrg just hated Humans, the odds were good, given that it had been established Firrg was a pirate and pirates were violent and unscrupulous thieves, she'd give the order to have Torin killed before Torin made it back to the *Second Star*.

"Captain Firrg hates Humans, I mean, really, really hates them. Don't know what she thinks about di'Taykan, but Humans, Humans she obsessively hates."

Obsession meant she'd do Torin herself. Obsessive hate meant she'd get up close and personal to do it. Rational people were a lot harder to manipulate.

Just past the *Dargonar*, about twenty meters from the *Second Star*, Torin stepped into a large storage alcove, half filled with replacement parts for ore processors unloaded from the fourth ship on the docking arm—the ship that didn't belong to the Silsviss, pirates, or an ex-Marine hunting pirates. When it came down to it, it was a wonder the station got any work done. The alcove wasn't entirely private, but the angles would interfere with the security cameras. The two Krai already using it took one look at her face, grabbed their clothes, and ran.

Then she waited.

But not for long.

Firrg hadn't come alone. The five males from the bar moved into a semicircle behind her, eyes locked on Torin, lips drawn back off their teeth, their presence clearly saying that if a random hell should happen to freeze over and Torin should just happen to win, she'd still lose. Had Firrg stopped to pick up reinforcements, that might have been a problem, but five was doable.

Firrg's scar drew an angry red line against the mottled green of her scalp. Her nose ridges flared once, twice, then clamped shut. "I am going to kill you," she snarled and charged forward.

Torin took half a step out to meet her, then slammed her as hard as she could in the side of the head with the iron pipe she'd been hiding behind her leg. Craig didn't have time for her to fight fair.

Krai teeth were among the hardest substances in known space, and Krai bone came a very close second. Firrg was unconscious and bleeding when she hit the floor but probably not badly hurt. By the time Torin had her boot on the captain's throat, the three Silsviss males—who'd arrived about the time the pipe made contact—had taken care of the crew.

"I need one conscious," she snapped, and the claws stopped just on the surface of the Krai's eyeballs.

It took the pirate's brain a few seconds to catch up to his

155

situation, then he pissed himself and sagged in the Silsviss' grip.

"We were there," one of the others said, using the metal ring on his tail to smack down a bleeding pirate trying to rise, "when you accepted the pack's defeat."

Given the way they'd been looking at her, Torin had figured as much. If they'd learned Federate before their trip, they weren't bothering with it. The cylindrical comm units on their harness translated simultaneously with her implant. And thank tech support that her new translation program had lost the extra sibilants.

"These little ones were not very good fighters," another said. Like the two reptilian species already part of the Confederation, they flicked their tongues around an impressive array of pointed teeth when they spoke. "The little ones you had with you in the preserve were better."

"They're called Krai, not little ones, and these Krai aren't used to fighting for their lives," Torin told him. When male Silsviss reached the age that their body chemistry required them to challenge for position, they were sent to wilderness preserves where they formed packs and fought it out—pack to pack as well as within the pack for position. It was as much population control as training. If these three had been there on the hill when Torin accepted the pack surrender and had become, for all intents and purposes, their pack leader, then they were only just off the preserve. Fighting for survival was still very close to being their default setting.

She figured they'd been brought on this trip, not only because of the flexibility of youth, but because they'd had at least some contact with other species even if that contact had consisted primarily of trying to kill them.

Switching her attention to the only conscious pirate—although she suspected one of the others of faking—Torin leaned in until the watering eyes behind the points of the four-centimeter-long claws focused on her face. "Tell me where I can find the *Heart of Stone*, or I'll kill your captain."

"You are inedible!"

"It's ruder in Krai," Torin explained as the Silsviss looked confused by the translation. "Tell me where I can find the *Heart of Stone,* or I'll kill your captain and have your eyes gouged out slowly."

At Torin's nod, the Silsviss tightened his grip slightly.

Nose ridges flapping so quickly they sounded like crumpling paper, he gasped. "Vrijheid!"

"Coordinates?"

"I don't know where it is exactly! I'm not helm! The government thinks it was destroyed during the war, but it wasn't!"

"Was the name changed?"

"Why the fuk would they change the name? I told you, the government thinks it did a crash and burn!"

That was enough information to find it.

"Big Bill Ponner runs it now! He'll fukking kill you!"

"You can drop him."

As he hit the floor, Torin took her foot from Firrg's throat and pulled her slate off her belt. "Presit, I've got it. Head back."

"There are still being more to the story here. Those accidents…"

"Can wait. Craig can't."

"On our way."

"What do you want *us* to do?" Given positioning, this was the dominant male of the three. They were all a little twitchy. The instinct to fight her for control had only barely been overlaid with more adult socialization.

"Wait with this lot until security arrives." Firrg groaned as Torin rolled her out into the camera's line of sight. "Tell them to check the load of ore that just came in with the *Dargonar*. The numbers on the sled will match the numbers on a drone that recently went missing during a fold. Someone in the station is accepting stolen goods."

"When they ask how we know this?"

"Tell them you heard it from Presit a Tur durValintrisy's pilot. If you convince them, you'll all gain status for bringing it to their attention."

"Then why do you leave this opportunity with us?" the dominant male hissed.

Torin smiled as she passed them. "I have a bigger enemy to take down."

Three tails tapped against the floor in unison. To the Silsviss mind-set, that made perfect sense. And they were another species who recognized the baring of teeth for what it was.

The exposure of someone on the station dealing in stolen goods, not to mention the capture of the thief, her crew, and her ship, would bring in the Wardens, and when Torin's involvement came to light—if not through the Silsviss then through the payment she'd made in the bar—it might actually light a fire under the ass of the law, given the finding of Page's body and the attack on the *Promise* that the Wardens already had on record. The problem was Torin no longer wanted the Wardens suddenly going all gung ho—enthusiasm from that quarter could easily provoke the pirates into killing Craig. Involving the Silsviss— who were not yet members of the Confederation—would slow things back down to diplomatic speeds.

"Strategy and tactics," she muttered, stepping into the *Star*'s air lock. "Your tax dollars at work."

"There are being a lot of shouting happening down the docking arm," Presit said, leading Ceelin back into the ship. "I are being hustled past it at full speed. Apparently this station are not wanting what could be a diplomatic incident on the news. You are being responsible?"

"I am." Torin sealed the air-lock doors behind the Katrien.

"I are suspecting as much. The Silsviss are seeming to be very involved, and I are seeing how they are watching you in the bar. Rumors are saying that with your platoon being pinned down and outnumbered, you are challenging the lizard leader to mortal combat and are having been ripped off his head."

"Not quite what happened," Torin told her, sending a request to disengage from the docking arm. But, given that she had a Silsviss skull in her quarters, she could at least see how that rumor had gotten started.

"I are really wanting to hear that story someday." Presit pulled herself up onto the other chair and added her codes to the request. "They are not locking down the press, no matter how many unconscious pirates they are having at the feet of large lizards. Not if they are not wanting a world of trouble."

Torin had hoped they'd get clear before any lockdown happened. Maybe they had, she acknowledged as the clamps released, but it was equally possible Presit had just kept them moving. "Thank you."

Feet tucked up under her, Presit lowered the light levels in the cabin and took off her glasses. "Thank me by telling me what the story of the Torin Kerr and the Silsviss are being. But later," she added, raising a hand to wave off Torin's protest. "Right now, you are first telling me that we are having a location?"

"We are. Do. Have. Vrijheid. The government thinks it was destroyed by the Primacy during the war. Crash and burn, my informant said, so it's a station."

"The government thinks?" Presit snorted. "That are being unlikely. Still, that are being enough information even for you to be finding it. Fortunately, you are not having to. Ceelin! Run a search."

Because Confederation law stipulated that all recording equipment must be large enough to be seen by the general public and carry obvious network identification, Ceelin's camera also included as much or more data storage than the *Second Star*, an ability to hook into any nearby network, as well as, he'd confided to Torin on the trip out, every game made by Kwin Industries. That was one hell of a lot of games.

"So when we are finding Vrijheid Station," Presit continued, "you are having a plan? Or are you just docking and telling murdering pirates they are giving you back Craig Ryder now."

"Yes," Torin told her, frowning down at the Susumi charts.

"Well, which is it being?"

"Both."

The crew of the *Heart of Stone* had moved the armory to a heavily reinforced storage pod near the station's old shuttle bays. If Craig had to bet, he'd say the pod had been designed to hold explosives of one kind or another. Stations usually stored explosives in support of mining facilities on the planet they orbited and that told him absolutely sweet fuk all about where he was. There were enough uninhabitable planets being mined that most of them didn't even have names and, even if this one did, he sure as shit wouldn't find it written on the wall in a storage pod.

As large as the armory was, the pod was just enough larger that Craig could walk all the way around it.

"The seal is on the front," Cho snapped.

"On the front of a locker potentially containing enough explosives to fracture this pod, hole the station, and kill us all," Craig reminded him, reaching out to brace himself against the metal as his vertigo returned. "I've lived most of my life in vacuum and I have no intention of dying in it because I didn't take a couple of minutes to make sure I knew what was I doing."

"Why would salvage operators even need a seal this complicated?" Nadayki sniffed. He hadn't been happy hearing about the possibility of fusing the lock and exploding the armory. Although Craig suspected he was less happy about not being able to hook in his slate than he was about blowing up. The youngest of the ship's di'Taykan had lime-green hair and eyes, and an attitude Craig wanted to smack off his pale face. Where the di'Taykan default leaned toward elegantly slender, Nadayki bordered on skinny and that, combined with the not entirely healed leg, made him appear as close to awkward as one of his species ever got. "It's like you're expecting to be robbed," he added sulkily.

"Yeah, well, we don't play well with others, and eyeballing this thing..." Craig patted the metal. "...isn't about the seal. What we have here is an armory that hasn't been treated with the respect it deserves." He eyeballed the dent beside his hand. "If something inside is damaged and leaking, it could blow before we get a chance to fuk it up."

"That's...possible," Nadayki reluctantly acknowledged after a long moment.

"I've already examined it," Cho growled.

"And I've got more experience with debris blown off a battle cruiser." Craig tapped a fingertip against the metal and almost laughed as Nadayki's eyes lightened. "I know exactly what kind of stress fractures that causes, and I know when it's safe to hang around and when the only thing to do is haul ass and pray."

Cho folded his arms and glared first at Nadayki and then

at Craig. Craig waited patiently for the captain to deal. Every second he took coming to a decision brought Torin one second closer. "Fine," he said at last. "Inspect it."

"Thank you."

Ignoring the sarcasm, Cho only growled, "But make it fast."

Unfortunately, the locker was in amazing shape considering what it had been through. In spite of his best attempt, Craig could spend only so long checking out a line of slag that ran diagonally across the bottom third of the locker's back to tail out along the lower edge of one side. It looked like part of whatever had secured the locker to the Marine packet had melted.

"Well?" Cho had moved back beside the pod's closed door.

There was barely enough damage for Craig to lie about.

"Looks like the slag's attached to the locker's surface. With luck, it hasn't melted in." Down on one knee, he reached back to where Nadayki hovered, making less than helpful comments under his breath. "Give me a screwdriver, kid."

"Why would I have a screwdriver? That's hardware. And don't call me kid!"

"Fine, a stylus then. Just something solid and pointed so I can get a bit of this slag off and make sure there's no structural damage."

"Use your *kayti*," Nadayki snorted dismissively. "And it's obviously not melted in. Even pathetic Human eyes should be able to see that."

Craig grabbed for the approaching foot but missed as his depth perception twisted. Naydaki's kick wasn't hard, not given that the kid was supporting weight and movement on his bad leg, but he hit the armory with enough force to break off a six-centimeter length of melted metal. It took a bit of enamel with it as it fell to the deck.

"See? No structural damage. Can we get on with it?"

"An excellent suggestion. Move, Ryder; on your feet."

"Forgive me for wanting to start with *not* blowing up," Craig muttered as he stood. Halfway up, the pod tipped sideways, and he slammed back against the locker.

"What is the matter with you?" Nadayki snarled, yanking him forward.

Okay, maybe not the pod that tipped, he thought as those metaphorical red-hot spikes got shoved back through his temples. Jackknifing forward, he spewed the contents of his stomach over the young di'Taykan's uninjured leg. Shoved hard, he bounced off the locker, vomited again, then headed for the floor, impact jarring both knees. At least he avoided putting his hands down in his own puke.

I've got to learn some more di'Taykan profanity, he thought as the pod tipped again and he fought to keep from toppling over. It sounded like the kid had hidden depths and an impressive vocabulary.

"Well, are you surprised?" Doc asked, as he half carried a semiconscious Ryder past the captain and out of the pod. "Given the amount of juice Almon hit him with, I'm amazed he has brain function. Intermittent dizziness and vomiting is no big deal."

"It's keeping him from what I need him to do," Cho growled.

"Doesn't the boy wonder have Ryder's codes? Tell him to get started. Tell him to change first," Doc amended, nose wrinkling.

"Ryder's codes are only the first step," Cho began, but Doc cut him off.

"Yeah, well, that's where most people start. Now, I'm going to take my patient to sick bay and make sure there's no brain damage I missed."

"If he's brain damaged…"

"Station medic is looking for organs. I'll take care of it."

"Good."

Cho stared into the storage pod, stepped aside as Naydaki shuffled out, and tried not to show how much he'd been startled when Big Bill said conversationally behind him, "Smells like puke down here."

"Ryder had an accident."

"Ryder? Your salvage operator?"

"Lingering effects from when we took him."

"You need to learn to play more nicely with your toys." Thumbs in his belt loops, Big Bill nodded toward the pod. "So that's what's going to change the world as we know it?"

"You can take a closer look," Cho allowed reluctantly, even as he moved to put himself between Big Bill and the pod.

Big Bill's expression suggested he could do whatever he damn well pleased. "No, I don't think so. I'm not a part of this. Remember?"

Because Big Bill only allied himself with schemes that had a hundred percent chance of working, Schemes where a mistake wouldn't blow a hole into the station that, one way or another, Cho definitely wouldn't survive.

"I wasn't even here," Big Bill added before Cho could reply.

Nose ridges closed, the Grr brothers followed their boss toward the nearest hatch.

Cho amused himself by thinking of feeding them a missile, launching it, and watching their guts spraypaint the outside of the station.

"So if Merik are not having what you sent him for, what then?" Presit demanded, as Ceelin ran the brush down the center of her back with long, firm strokes.

"He'll have it," Torin told her, scowling down at the tufts of undercoat on the floor as she did her second set of push-ups.

"Wishing are not making it so."

"If I were wishing for something, I'd wish I was going in as part of a full Marine boarding party with cruiser backup."

"If you are wishing," Presit snorted, "why not be wishing Craig Ryder safe and being here? Never mind," she added, as the five-minute emergent warning sounded and Torin got to her feet. "You are Gunnery Sergeant Torin Kerr, and you are not taking the easy way. Fine. If Merik *are* having what you sent him for, what then? You are not having the fleet you were thinking you would."

Torin appreciated the sneer Presit used when referring to the absent salvage operators. "I know."

"So you are planning to be doing what?"

"I'm going after Craig."

"Oh, that are being a brilliantly developed plan," she muttered.

Torin ignored her, wiping at her face and arms with a towel as she threw herself down into the chair. "Have you got that packet ready to go to the Wardens?"

"It are going automatically the moment we are being back in real space. You are thinking it'll help?"

"It can't hurt."

"Even given that I are having pulled the information on the pirates into some kind of coherency, they are not likely to be suddenly thinking you are right and they are not actually needing to conduct an investigation before they act. They are not going to be sending the Navy in at the last minute to be saving the day."

"They can't if they don't have the information."

"They won't even if they are having it."

Torin sighed and turned to look at the reporter. "Black."

Muzzle wrinkled, Presit climbed into the other chair. "I are having no idea of what you are talking about."

"Just wanted to see if you'd say white."

Ceelin snickered, tried to turn it into a cough, and all but ran into the other cabin prodded by Presit's glare. "Oh, yes, you are being very funny."

They were forty minutes out from Val Doron Station when they got the message from Merik. All three answers to the packet she'd had him send out on the way to the salvage station were positive.

"You are never doubting?" Presit asked, studying her face.

"Not this," Torin told her. "This, I believed in."

She didn't have much beyond belief to keep her going. Belief in her own ability. Belief that Craig would know she was coming and do what he had to in order to stay alive until she got there. Belief that after everything they'd been through, after everything the polynumerous polyhydroxide sons of bitches had put them through, they were not going to have their lives ruined by a group of pissant pirates.

Val Doron Station was one of the larger OutSector stations. Torin had originally chosen it as a meeting place both because it was busy enough that only the station sysop took note of every coming and going and because it was a very short fold from the salvage station.

Merik was waiting on the other side of the air lock when they docked.

"They are not being happy," he said, grinning broadly. "My ship are having too low ceilings apparently. But they are being here."

As Presit pulled him aside to fill him in on their new information—or possibly to complain about how the dry air in the ship had made her fur brittle, it was impossible to tell with Presit—Torin looked past them at Ressk, Werst, and Binti Mashona, all three of them smiling and obviously glad to see her. Her chest hurt. In the months since she'd seen them, in the months since she'd left the Corps, Ressk had slimmed down, Werst had bulked up, and Mashona had added half a dozen small gold rings to the upper curve of her right ear where the light spilling off them painted gleaming highlights against the dark skin. Before she could move, Mashona dragged her into a hug while both Krai charged forward and slapped at her arms. It seemed strange not to be keeping the distance rank and the Corps demanded. Strange, but not unpleasant. "Thank you for coming."

Ressk spread his hands as they separated. It was strange to see him—to see all of them—in civvies. "All you had to do was ask, Gunny."

"Whatever you need us for," Mashona added. "Merik told us the CSOs won't help. Do we convince them, or…"

Torin opened her mouth, but Werst, eyes locked on her face, spoke before she could. "We're going after Ryder."

The other two looked from him to Torin, who finally nodded. Years of training couldn't keep the anger from leaching into her voice. "Werst's right. We don't have time to convince the salvage operators Craig isn't dead. And they won't put themselves and their families in danger for a dead man."

Metal clanged farther down the docking arm. Someone shouted. Someone else laughed.

Mashona snorted. "You believe he's alive, Gunny, that's good enough for me."

"Us," Werst growled, nose ridges flared. "Good enough for us."

"We're it," Torin reminded them. "It's one thing to ask you to help train a sizable fleet, it's another thing entirely to ask you to get involved in a retrieval of personnel from behind enemy lines."

"Yes, it is," Ressk allowed. "But Merik told us up front, and we're still here." He grinned. "It's not like we have anything better to do."

Mashona matched the grin. "Who knew I'd miss nearly dying on a regular basis?"

"I," Werst snarled, "am looking forward to kicking the ass of someone who undeniably needs their ass kicked. Since you haven't found those gray plastic fukkers yet, pirates will do."

"They'll do in a pinch," Mashona agreed. "How are we going in?"

They didn't have time—Craig didn't have time—for Torin to tell them what this meant. She suspected they already knew or they wouldn't be standing there.

"We'll go in as pirates. Given what they saw on the vids," Torin expanded, lifting the first case of supplies Merik had also delivered, "no one's going to be at all surprised if the four of us are bitter, twisted, and seriously pissed off."

"Ryder was on those vids, too," Ressk pointed out, heaving a case up onto his shoulder.

"Not too much, he are mostly being behind the camera, and he are hiding most of his face behind a patchy pelt. Besides, he are not being a big hero like you three are being. Hello." Presit smiled up at the ex-Marines. "I'm sure you are remembering me."

"Hard to forget," Werst muttered, a case under each arm. "Is she coming, too?"

"No." Torin nudged Presit away from the *Star's* air lock.

"Yes," Presit corrected, shoving back.

"Okay, then." Mashona picked up the last case and followed Torin, the two Krai, and all three Katrien onto the ship. "So we're pirates."

"In this?" Werst snorted, setting the case on the floor and tossing his duffel onto the bunk.

Torin turned and looked around the cabin, which seemed significantly smaller now it held seven warm bodies, three new duffel bags, and a stack of supplies. "All right, so we're not very successful pirates."

SEVEN

"**I**f we were going in, guns blazing…"

"We have guns?" Ressk asked Mashona quietly. She slid the case of food into storage and smacked the top of his head.

"…that would be different, you'd be as welcome to join us as you would be in a war zone."

Werst snickered.

"If we could insert the team undetected," Torin continued, ignoring him, all her attention focused on convincing Presit she wasn't going in with them, "again, no problem. But the only plan we have to get Craig out alive is to pretend we're something we're not and you're too well known."

"I are not pretending to be something I are not!" Presit declared, drawing herself up to her full height.

"I wouldn't ask you to." Years of similar conversations with officers kept Torin's voice level. "You're our backup. Once we're in, if we run into trouble, we'll need a distraction. Something to keep them off-balance. *That's* when you signal the station, say you tracked my ship and…"

"And you are not telling me how to do my job," Presit snapped. "Why are we not being a ship you are having captured? We are tracking you and you are capturing us; *that* are proving you are being pirates."

"They could demand we kill you to prove we've crossed the line."

"As I are understanding it—as you are having been telling me," she added before Torin could interrupt, "the pirates are being more thieves than murderers."

"Other salvage stations may have lost personnel. These pirates may have been killing for some time."

"Then wouldn't the surviving salvage operators have been reporting them to the Wardens?"

"Maybe. But the odds are as good they didn't; Station 24 didn't report Jan and Sirin's deaths. You were there when…" Her nails were too short to cut into her palms, but Torin could feel them pressing against the skin. "You know the salvage operators are independent to the point of isolationist. We know one set of pirates kills without hesitation. We can't know how many more do."

"Fine." Presit combed her ruff with one hand. "I are holding back until you are needing a distraction. But you are carrying a camera." She thrust an imperious hand at Ceelin.

He shot an apologetic glance at Torin as he laid a disk about the size of Torin's smallest fingernail on Presit's palm. Matte black, if not for the gold edging, it would have been almost invisible against Presit's skin.

"It are having been designed to look like fasteners what are having been fashionable last season. In fact, it are looking like the fasteners on both tunics and the sweater I are having had Merik pick up for you."

"You didn't need—" Torin began.

Presit cut her off. "You are having only the clothing you are standing up in. Everything else are still being on the *Promise*. Also, I are knowing you. That are making me certain from the beginning that you are not allowing what you are seeing as a civilian to be going into danger. But you are also promising me a story, so I are being prepared. I are willing to have my ship be waiting at the edge of its range," she declared, holding the camera up to Torin. "But that are as far as I are willing to be from the action."

"A camera that size is against the law, and—"

Presit cut her off again. "Pirates are being very much against the law. Theft are being against the law. Murder are being against the law. I are willing to be your backup, but I are not taking a chance that you are being unable to be calling when you are needing me."

Torin heard one of the Krai move, heard Mashona murmur something, and tried to unsuccessfully look past her reflection in Presit's glasses. She looked like shit. After a long moment, she nodded, held out her hand for the disk, and flipped it over to Ressk.

"They'll monitor signals in and out of the station," he said, pressing the disk into his slate. "You don't successfully hijack a government station without being paranoid as all fuk. Question is, do they monitor all frequencies and, more importantly, are they monitoring this frequency? This thing has its own DSP with one fuk of a high compression rate and then it embeds the transmission steganographically in what looks like static, sending stored information out at random intervals."

"But…"

"Random is better," he interrupted, apparently getting the gist of Werst's protest from the single word. "A constant signal is more than likely to be artificially generated and therefore worth monitoring; it *will* attract attention. The question is…" He looked up at the reporter, nose ridges flared. "…why would you even have this technology?"

Presit flicked her ears. "If it are in a large enough case that are marked with a network signal, it are fully legal."

"So you pulled this out of his case?" Ressk demanded, glancing over at Ceelin, who was doing a good job of hiding his opinion behind his dark glasses and under the thick mask of his fur.

"Don't be being ridiculous."

"You happened to have it handy?"

"I are being in a very competitive business," Presit told him dryly.

"But—"

She cut him off. "Are I asking you to be telling me all *your* secrets?"

"If we carry this, you're going to know them," Ressk pointed out.

"No, I are going to know hers." She nodded toward Torin.

"And if they are monitoring signals, then how are you thinking you are going to signal me without they are knowing? This way, I are knowing, they are not."

"Well?" Torin held out her hand, and Ressk tossed the camera back.

"She has a point." He frowned, hung up in the syntax. "I think."

"All right." Torin looked past Presit to Merik. "Err on the side of caution when adjusting your equations…"

"Wait!" Presit grabbed the front of her sweater. "Adjusting what equations?"

"There's a good chance the station will monitor Susumi portals. Even if Merik thinks he can tag in through the same portal…"

Merik waved a *Maybe, maybe not*.

"…they'll pick up the second ship. You need to emerge outside their sensor range. If Merik believes he can bring you closer without discovery, that's up to him."

Presit adjusted her glasses. "In the interests I are having of not being killed, I are willing to be sneaking up on the station until we are blazing in to be saving your collective asses."

"Good." Torin moved her toward the air lock. "Werst, inform the station sysop we're ready to release. Merik, you have the final word on how close you can safely move in. Don't let Presit pressure you."

"I are also interested in not being killed," the pilot told her as he followed Presit into the air lock. "Don't worry, I are more interested in surviving than I are in having a story."

"You are remembering you are working for me," Presit snapped.

He flicked his ears. "Not if you are being dead."

Torin hit the controls and realized she was going to miss, not Presit exactly but, at the very least, the reporter's annoying ability to drag her out of her own head. "You're part of this story, Presit. That changes things. Don't forget that."

"I are having downloaded some games for you!" Ceelin called out as Presit waved off Torin's comment and the air lock's inner door shut.

"Station says we have a green on go." His foot against the control panel because he couldn't reach the deck, Werst pivoted the second chair around to face the cabin. "When the air lock reseals, the docking computer will take control."

"You have a plan, Gunny?" Mashona asked from the bunk. "Something with a little more detail than the lot of us pretending to be pirates?"

Torin dropped into the pilot's chair, back straight, refusing to relax. She had no one to relinquish control of the situation to. "Not really."

"Well," Ressk said slowly after a long moment where the only sound was the muffled thud of the clamps releasing, "it has the benefit of simplicity."

"We've got a four-day fold to Vrijheid," Torin reminded them. The ship seemed significantly larger without Presit on board. Without Presit, she'd lost another connection to Craig. "We have time to refine it."

"And time for you to tell us why you're pink. Pinker," Werst amended.

"But he was fine!"

"No, he was functioning. Not the same thing." Doc turned from the screen, folded his arms, and stared up at Nadayki. Who took a step back, his hair flattening against his head.

From where Craig lay on the examination table, it looked like the kid was actually scared—in spite of having an extra twenty centimeters in height and the di'Taykan pheromone advantage—rather than merely giving way to a stronger personality. He adjusted his opinion of Doc a little further toward the unstable end of the scary, bugfuk crazy spectrum.

"Well, if he was functioning before," the young di'Taykan all but whined, "can't he function again?"

"Depends. How fond are you of being puked on?"

Nadayki took another step back. "Not much."

"Then learn to get the hell out of the way," Doc told him, "because it's going to continue to happen at random intervals." He half turned toward Craig and indicated he could get up. "Short circuit, puke, collapse in pain. Rinse, repeat."

"Rinse?"

"Never mind. He'll also be unable to see yellow."

"Really?" Nadayki's eyes darkened as Craig searched the room for yellow and realized he could see it fine.

"No, I'm just fukking with you. You, Ryder..." Doc frowned as Craig moved carefully around the end of the table toward the door. "If your brain doesn't slag itself, you're likely to dehydrate so keep your fluids up."

"And how do I keep my brain from slagging itself?"

"Build a time machine, go back, and stay the fuk away from that poker game."

Considering how things had turned out, it wasn't bad advice. On the upside, random brain spasms were definitely going to slow things down. And how much shit was he in, that random brain spasms had an upside?

Nadayki wasn't happy about the pace Craig set leaving medical, but when Craig pointed out that a faster pace raised the odds of immediate puking, he decided to cope. He tapped a syncopated beat against the bulkhead as they moved and just as they approached the *Heart's* air lock, said, "There's a theory among the really out there experimental astrophysicists that, if the math is right, Susumi space can be used for time travel."

"Well, that's the trick, isn't it, kid; getting the math right."

"Stop calling me kid."

The air lock's inner lip seemed one hell of a lot higher than usual. Craig didn't so much step over it as lift one leg and then the other, maintaining a white-knuckled grip on the edge of the lock. He'd planned on exaggerating his condition as much as possible, but it looked like he might not have to.

"That's pathetic."

"Yeah, well, bitch to your *thytrin*. I didn't ask to have my brain scrambled."

"You tried to cut my leg off!"

"Don't rubbish me, mate, I'd just been shot and netted." Craig repeated the one leg at a time maneuver over the outer lip. "I'd have preferred to have cut your throat."

The expression on the kid's face suggested he'd never considered he might end up on the receiving end of the violence he helped dish out. "You fukking deserved to be zapped!"

"So live with the result."

They walked in silence for a few moments, about as long as Craig figured the di'Taykan *could* be silent. "I've applied your codes to the CSO's seal, but they only opened the upper levels. There's no pattern in the lower levels."

"No, you can't find a pattern in the lower levels."

"There is no logical pattern."

"You might be right. A CSO's seal is more art than science," Craig continued before Nadayki could protest the qualifier.

"That makes no sense."

"They tell me you're good with code."

"I hacked a defense satellite and had it burn Nadayki di'Berinango…"

Nine letters in his family name. Given that the Taykan social system favored those with the shortest names, it was no wonder the kid had turned to crime.

"…half a meter deep into the Prime Progenitor's lawn with a laser," he bragged.

Craig frowned. Didn't sound like much to be all big note about. "You signed your name?"

"I was making a point. They said it couldn't be done, and I wanted them to know who'd done it."

"And how'd that work out for you?"

"We got away," Nadayki pointed out smugly as they reached the storage pod and Nat stepped out of the shadows.

"About fukking time you got here," she muttered. "Cap says before you get started again, Ryder, you get to clean up the puke." She nodded toward the shovel leaning against the bulkhead next to a mop and bucket.

"It's got kind of rubbery, so if you want my advice, start by scraping."

"I have to clean up my own chunder?"

Her brows rose, but she picked up the slang from context. "It's your puke, gorgeous. Who the hell else is going to clean it up? At least I opened up the maintenance station and got things ready for you. Deodorizer's already in the water."

Since his original plan of staying alive until Torin got him out had turned into the slightly more specific *delay opening of the weapons locker until Torin arrived to neutralize the threat*, Craig supposed that, on some level, he appreciated the delay involved in scrubbing dried vomit off the deck. But only someone stalling for time would accept the job without whinging. "Have Almon clean it up. His pathetic need to use the *tasik* as an auxiliary donger is the reason I chucked."

"Cap says you do it." Nat squeezed his shoulder, and he hoped it wasn't with the hand she usually used to scratch. "When you're done, get moving on those seals before he decides to encourage you by letting Doc take a pair of bolt cutters to your toes."

His toes curled under in his borrowed boots. She didn't sound like she was kidding. "In what universe is that encouraging?"

"The one where you don't want it to happen. So don't dawdle. Keep him up to speed, kid."

"Don't call me kid," Nadayki muttered.

"Oh, yeah. Put the larrkin in charge." Craig rolled his eyes as he picked up the plastic shovel and headed for the hatch leading into the pod. The shovel remained inert. If the fukking plastic aliens were still around, they had no sense of timing. "Kid's on the run for high-tech graffiti."

"He told you that, eh?" Nat sounded amused. "He tell you those lasers sliced and diced three people who just happened to be on the Prime Progenitor's lawn at the time?"

"No..." Craig glanced over at Nadayki who shrugged. "...he didn't skite about that."

Taykan noses were much more sensitive than Human noses.

Nadayki's reaction to the half-dried vomit nearly made the job worthwhile. The time he spent cleaning the chunky puddle off the deck was the longest Craig had ever spent with a di'Taykan without being propositioned.

"That wasn't exactly fast," he whined as Craig dumped the soiled water down the reclamation chute.

"Oh, yeah, because I like to take my time cleaning up puke."

Hand over his mouth and nose, Nadayki muttered, "Whatever. Can we get the fukking seal open now?"

"Don't get your panties in a knot, kid, I still have to wash the gear."

"Wash the... What the fuk for?"

"You want the smell to linger?" Ignoring the muttered response, he did a thorough job. Unfortunately, there was a finite time he could spend cleaning a shovel, a mop, and a bucket, slotting them back into their places, and closing the maintenance area down. Because the ore docks would be open to vacuum every time a carrier came up from the planet and loose items were dangerous, the lockers were built to withstand accidental decompression. Beside the maintenance area was a tool locker holding only a broken pipe wrench and seven identical screwdrivers. Beside that, an empty suit locker with space for six although only three hookups were live. Tucked into the far corner by the rear bulkhead was a hatch that led to an actual head.

If maintenance reclamation worked, then the toilet should, so Craig used it. And took his time.

Finally, after increasingly sullen reminders that toes weren't necessary to break code, Craig skirted the wet area of the deck and returned to the storage pod. Holding his borrowed slate up to the seal, he linked in. He gave half a thought to cutting the safeties in and blowing the armory, but he knew Torin was on her way and she'd be pissed if he died. His code opened the first level and slid them through the second. Then he watched the lines of new code scroll by and frowned.

"See!" Nadayki waved his own slate in front of Craig's face. "It makes no sense!"

"Sure it does. You can hack a defense satellite and slaughter three people, but you can't hack this seal."

Nadayki's eyes darkened as his lip curled. "What's your point?"

"Given that the point of a seal is to keep people out, an unhackable seal makes perfect sense."

After a long moment, the di'Taykan nodded. "Yeah, okay."

"Yeah, okay?"

"Yeah, okay, you're right," he expanded reluctantly. "It does make perfect sense." His eyes had lightened but he still sounded sulky when he asked, "*Can* you get in?"

It came down to pulling out recognizable bits and building on them. Craig shrugged. "Won't be easy, but I know how CSOs think."

"They think? Really? I can get through the Marine seal, no problem," he muttered.

"Yeah, well…" Craig patted the dent in the armory. "…not to knock your code fu, kid, but in my experience, Marines are a lot less complex."

"So we're disillusioned and pretending to be pirates." Werst took a long swallow of beer and shrugged. "Should work."

Stretched out on the bunk in the cabin, one arm tucked up under her head, the other holding a beer of her own, Mashona asked, "How many of these pirates are you planning to kill, Gunny?"

Torin thought about the way Page had died. "As many as I have to."

"I'm not sure I can kill other people. Not anymore," Mashona added as Ressk glanced up from his slate and shot her a look. "War is different."

"What if those people are trying to kill you?" Werst wondered, picking the label off the beer pouch.

"That's different, too," Mashona acknowledged.

Ressk nodded. "They try to kill me, all bets are off."

"You three shouldn't have to kill anyone," Torin told them flatly. Ceelin had found her the original schematics of Vrijheid Station. They'd use Susumi time to commit as much of them to memory as possible. "If there's any killing to be done, I'll be doing it."

The other three exchanged a glance that held a whole conversation.

Werst gave it a voice. "We've got your six, Gunny."

"Why?" She hadn't planned on asking, but now it was out there. "You had lives and now…"

"I wouldn't say we had lives." Mashona swung her legs off the bunk and sat up. "We were all kind of drifting. We're used to being a part of something bigger, you know, and not having that anymore was… Well, it wasn't. I guess what I'm trying to say is you give us…" Mashona looked at Ressk. Ressk looked at Werst. Werst half shrugged, making the usual Krai cock-up of the movement. "…grounding. Direction."

But Torin had heard, *Something to believe in…* in the pause.

* * *

"It's difficult to make plans until we know what's actually in the locker," Big Bill said thoughtfully, indicating that Cho should sit. "But in order to expedite the eventual arming of the free merchants, I've made a list." He slid a piece of paper across the desk.

"A list?" Visitors to Big Bill's office deep in the center sphere of the station sat in chairs that were both closer to the ground than Big Bill's own and deliberately uncomfortable. Already fuming at being summoned like an erring ensign called before the officer of the watch, this lack of subtlety pushed Cho's mood further into the black, and he fought to keep his expression neutral.

"A list of who'll be willing to pay top dollar and potentially for what; where *what* is based on the content of the armories my boys remember from while they were in."

The Grr brothers had been in the Corps. Cho couldn't say he was surprised. *"I've seen your type before, boy. You wanted Recon or Ranger, but you were too crazy even for those crazy fukkers."* Page's voice in memory. *"No one tried to convince you too hard to stay, after your first contract ran out, did they, boy? No, it was: 'So long, Private, have a nice life. Hell, have a shitty life, just have it away from us'."*

He wondered if that was where they'd met, brought together by sanctioned violence. Their own brutal tendencies honed and refined.

Well, as refined as a fondness for eating people alive got.

Rather than think about the screaming, Cho picked up the list. Big Bill was a manipulative son of a bitch but vested self-interest would see to it that Cho got the best price for his weapons. He attempted to think of the list as helpful instead of as an attempt to wrest away control. A really fukking annoying attempt. He frowned down at it.

"You can't hack paper," Big Bill told him, misinterpreting the frown. "Some smartass will find a way into the tightest system but that right there, you need eyeballs for that and eyeballs can be controlled. You remember not to leave it lying around where any idiot can read it, and it's about as secure as it gets. Helps, of course, that no one expects anything of import to be on paper these days. How much longer to get through the seals?"

Cho recognized the sudden change of subject as an attempt to throw him off his game. Yeah, like he'd let his guard down that much around a power-crazy fuk like Big Bill. "Ryder, the salvage op, is back at work."

"Good."

"Doc says his brain got a bit fried by the *tasik* when we brought him in."

"Doc would know." Even Big Bill was... maybe not cautious but definitely *aware* around Doc.

"It's slowed him down some," Cho continued, "but he's functional, and Nadayki reports they're making progress." Nadayki had reported nothing of the sort, but Cho had no intention of showing weakness of any kind. Even secondhand.

"Again, good." Big Bill's smile didn't reach his eyes. Didn't even reach his cheeks. Or any other body part. "But I asked you, *how long*?"

"No way of knowing."

"I see. As we have no idea what's in the armory, we have no idea how much you'll be paying me for the use of that storage pod. We don't know the specifics of my fifteen percent," he expanded when Cho frowned. "Given that, I'd like to know how long you plan on taking advantage of my generosity."

Slouching back in the chair, Cho hoped he looked like he didn't give a H'san's ass about eye lines or the unfortunate fact that his own ass was going numb. "Allowing me to use that pod is you minimizing the risk of blowing a hole in your station while still maintaining a certain amount of control over the contents of an armory you have no responsibility for. Length of time spent is irrelevant."

Big Bill stared across the deck at him, like he was actually seeing him for the first time in this conversation. "That's a valid point."

He made it sound like it was first valid point Cho had ever made in his hearing.

"Keep me informed." Eyes narrowed, Big Bill nodded toward the piece of paper. "Take the list with you."

Only a suicidal idiot would mistake that for anything but a dismissal.

By the time Cho had heaved himself up onto his feet, Big Bill had a channel open to what sounded like one of the shops in the Hub, enquiring about last quarter's drop in profits, and therefore a drop in his fifteen percent. As far as he was concerned, Cho had already left the room.

In the outer office the Grr brothers lay tangled together on a leather sofa, drinking *sah* and watching news vids, the big screen split into the top four networks. They'd been watching news vids when Cho went in to talk to Big Bill. And sure, he hadn't been in there long, but they'd been watching news vids every time he'd been called to the inner sanctum.

Could've been worse. Could've been a cooking show.

No surprise the little freaks didn't watch porn like normal people.

Craig could see that as far as di'Taykan went, Nadayki was a lime-green geek-and-a-half, but he was still a di'Taykan and di'Taykan were hardwired to default to sex. Sex seemed to be an obvious tactic to delay the opening of the seal, with the potential to be a repeat performer. As his stomach had steadied and the red-hot spikes were not currently being driven into his temples, Craig figured it made sense to get the initial encounter out of the way.

"The thing with CSO codes," he said, looking up from his slate, "is that they're hard to put in and even harder to take out."

"Unless you know the sequence," Nadayki snorted, eyes locked on his screen, ignoring the potential for innuendo.

Craig fired off a second attempt. "Give us time and we'll get it off."

"Fukking right. There's no way some stupid scavenger is going to create a seal I can't break."

Any other di'Taykan would have made a proposition and started the foreplay by now. Raising his assessment of the kid to a geek-and-three-quarters, Craig upped his game.

The seal had been positioned in vacuum, which put it at an idiotically awkward angle with gravity applied. Upper body bent at about forty-five degrees, with the kid standing so close the movement of his hair kept Craig thinking of spiders and slapping at the back of his neck, it was easy enough to brush his ass to Nadayki's groin with every position shift.

And yeah, they still hadn't talked about where they stood with di'Taykan before the *Heart of Stone* had blown their lives apart, but Craig knew where Torin stood as far as staying alive went. She'd expect him to do what he had to. So, when Nadayki finally got with the program—and seriously, he had never expected to use the word *finally* when it came to a di'Taykan and sex— Craig responded with, if not enthusiasm, at least interest. First chance he got, he dialed the kid's masker back a couple of levels and enthusiasm became moot.

Then the kid decided to prove he could evoke the same response without the pheromone boost and Craig took back every disparaging thing he'd ever thought about geeks.

"What the hell do you think you're doing?"

Nadayki muttered in Taykan against wet skin—maybe a description of the specific act or maybe bitching about the interruption, Craig had no idea and really, really didn't care— but kept going until Cho grabbed a handful of hair and yanked him back.

"No gods damned fukking on my time! I catch you again, and I'll have Doc cut your damned *kayti* off. And then I'll have Doc cut his off…" Half a dozen lime-green hairs floated to the floor as Cho released his hold and jabbed a finger toward Craig. "…and fukking feed it to you. Put your damned clothes on and get back to work!"

Craig had hoped Nadayki would argue, but the mention of Doc acted like a cold shower, and the kid complied without protest, his eyes pale, one hand rubbing at the side of his head. Di'Taykan hair wasn't actually hair. It was part of their sensory system, and losing some of it must've hurt like hell. Given three dead on the Prime Progenitor's lawn, Craig couldn't bring himself to care. Still… "You couldn't have taken another fifteen minutes to show up?" he grumbled, shooting the captain a disgruntled glare as he shrugged back into his overalls.

"You can fuk on your own time, Ryder," Cho snarled. "And your time is mine until that armory is open." He jerked his slate off his belt. "Huirre, get down to the locker."

"Now, Captain?"

"Yes, now!" Cho smiled unpleasantly. He jabbed a finger into Craig's chest. "I am warning you, do *not* fuk around on me. You forget why you're here while Huirre's watching and I'll let him pick a part to snack on." The jab became a shove.

Fingers curling into fists, Craig wondered how long it would delay things if he took a swing at the captain. Given the way he felt, he'd get the shit kicked out of him in any fight, but, hell, as long as he was alive when Torin found him, that only mattered in the short term.

Something in Cho's eyes stopped him. Something that said *Go too far and you'll be out the air lock wearing bruises and fuk all else.*

Because the trick was to stay *alive* until Torin found him.

A second shove, to prove Craig wouldn't respond, then Cho backed up snarling, "Now, get back to work before I start carving bits off myself!"

"This is all your fault," Nadayki muttered sullenly as they bent over the seal again.

True enough. "Takes two to tango, kid."

"What the fuk is a tango? And stop calling me kid!"

"What if Presit's little protégé found the wrong Vrijheid Station?" Mashona asked, saving one of Ceelin's games as the *Second Star* began her ten count before emerging into normal space.

"How many Vrijheid Stations that supposedly took a dirt dive during the war could there be?" Werst demanded from the second chair.

Mashona shrugged. "Space is big."

The stars reappeared.

"Ceelin found only one Vrijheid Station, and full disclosure laws give Presit access to government databases." Torin lifted her hands up off the control panel and started working the stiffness out of the fingers.

"She could be sending us on a fool's errand while she heads in to get the story," Ressk said thoughtfully, rubbing a thumb along the edge of his slate. "I mean, she said she knew you weren't going to let her join us. She could've set up equations to a different station and then faked her protests."

Werst shook his head. "You always this paranoid?"

He glanced over at Torin. "Just trying to cover all bases."

In the old days, being paranoid was a part of Torin's job. Now… "I trust her. I'm not one hundred percent positive she wouldn't screw me over, but she'd never risk Craig."

Mashona's brows rose and fell in exaggerated lechery. "You need to worry about her making moves on your man, Gunny?"

"Not everything crosses species lines, Mashona, di'Taykan excepted." Her response to Mashona's joking almost sounded normal. Under the circumstances, it was the best she could do.

"Gunny…"

Grateful for something to focus on, she gave Werst her full attention.

"At least some of the *cark* in this station will know you from Presit's vids."

"I'm counting on it. Me, and the three of you."

"Yeah." His nose ridges flared. "And they'll know Craig from that last vid."

"No, probably not. Like Presit said, he was behind the camera about ninety-five percent of the time, and when he wasn't, Presit was all but shooting up his nose. He had the beard then, and the edits…" Under the old adage of know thy enemy, she'd seen all the vids once. "…focus exclusively on the gray running out of his eyes." Sometimes she dreamed about the way the polynumerous polyhydroxide alcoholyde shape-shifting molecular fukwads had felt, slightly cooler than body temperature as they oozed out of her tear ducts. She'd wake up furious and have to leave the bunk before she took it out on Craig. Sometimes she wondered if it had felt the same to him, if he'd felt the same about it. After she got him back, she'd ask. Add it to the list of all the things they'd intended to talk about *later*. No more waiting for later. "Odds are good no one looked away from the emerging aliens long enough to identify him and, under personal privacy laws…" Which did not extend to members of the military under the full disclosure act. "…he was never identified by name."

"And Nat, the woman who…"

"The woman off the *Heart* who set us up for the ambush that took Craig," Torin growled. "I remember her."

"She saw you."

"Only for a minute, and she was paying no attention to me. Had her eyes on the game. The man who came into the bar with her, he might be a problem."

"The guy with the crazy eyes," Mashona put in.

"Yeah, him. But I'm not sure he saw me as an actual person— he threat assessed, he moved on. Who'd expect to see Gunnery Sergeant Torin Kerr on a half-finished OutSector station? I suspect that, as much as economic factors, was why Craig chose it. Here, at Vrijheid, who we are becomes the larger part of our reason for being here and being that obvious will act like camouflage; all they'll see is the *obvious*—not the people behind it and certainly not a specific person glimpsed for a few seconds in another part of space."

The three members of her assault team stared at her for a long moment. Finally, Ressk said, "Maybe you could change your hair?"

Torin closed her fingers around the plastic vertical that held the padded arm to the pilot's chair. "The only reason I'd go anywhere near that man is if he ends up between me and Craig. Otherwise, I'll avoid him. It's a good-sized station, I'm willing to play the odds."

"Make your bet, then, Gunny. Long-range sensors just picked up a station." Werst swept his palm across the board. "No details, though."

"Distance?" Mashona asked.

"If we can ping them, distance doesn't matter. Not everyone sends out a tourist brochure, but, if nothing else, we should be receiving information about docking and fees. And what's more, I'm reading ships, but their registries aren't coming up. There's no way to tell if the *Heart of Stone* is there."

"It's there." The *Heart* was there, and Craig was there. Because they had to be.

"If we can ping them…" Mashona began.

"They can ping us." Werst agreed.

"And they'll get what I want them to," Ressk said, smiling

broadly. "Which is the same as what they're giving out."

"I wonder how close they'll let us get?"

They were still moving fast, riding the exit surge, maintaining their emergent speed until they knew where they were going.

"No point in talking to us until they can stop us," Werst pointed out, "and unless they've got some big fukking guns, we need to be a little closer for…"

"Hi there." The young di'Taykan male on the screen had hair so light a blue it was nearly white and his pale eyes looked paler still given the amount of black they were lined with. Makeup had turned his skin the same shade as his hair—Torin assumed it was makeup—and he had two black rings piercing the center of his lower lip. "I'm pulling sweet fuk all off your signal, so you've got three minutes to make your case before I blow you to kingdom come. Which, by the way, is not an actual place but an oldEarth term meaning *up*. So, three minutes before I blow you up."

Torin centered herself on the screen. "I heard Vrijheid Station was a refuge from government bullshit."

"Really." He leaned a little closer to the pickup and grinned. Torin had never see a di'Taykan with dimples. "Who'd you hear that from?"

"Krai named Firrg."

"I don't think so."

"I had my foot on her throat at the time."

"Well, that endears you to me, trin, but there's…" His hair stilled and he frowned. "Wait, do I know you?"

Torin smiled.

"Fuk me. I do know you. You're that gunnery sergeant who had the little gray aliens in your brain and then got captured and found out the little gray aliens were in the plastic and actually making us all run around like we were neivins or something. I saw the vids. You were like crazy kick ass. Seriously, fuk me."

"Little hard from way out here."

"Right." His hair flipped forward over his face, then back— like his whole expression had blinked. "Okay, there's a lock free on the delta arm. You're going to have to give control over to the docking computer if you want to come any closer. We can't risk you ramming the station."

"That happens a lot?"

"Hasn't yet. But if it did, Big Bill would fukking space me."

"How do I know I'll get control back?"

"We start randomly taking ships over and it's bad for business, isn't it? Big Bill doesn't like things being bad for business. You leave here in good standing, and you get control back about when you would be leaving any station. Your standing ends up being not so good, well, you don't leave and you don't actually care about who's flying your ship." He glanced down at his screens. "Okay, really, you have to give control over now or you're fukked. And not in a fun 'I think you're fukking amazing because you did that whole plastic alien thing in your underwear' kind of way."

Teeth gritted, Torin sighed and surrendered control.

The *Second Star* shuddered as her forward jets fired to slow her approach.

"Wow, nice firewalls. I can't get squat off you." He sounded honestly impressed. "Look, when you get in, I'm pretty much guaranteeing Big Bill's going to want to talk to you, being who you are and all, so if it takes a while to get the lock open, that's why. Oh and don't forget..." He leaned closer to the screen, one hand dropping down off camera into his lap. "...seriously, *trin*, fuk me."

And the screen went black.

"They listening in?"

Ressk snorted. "They're trying to."

"Sounds like you've got a fan, Gunny." Mashona stretched out her legs, crossed her booted feet at the ankles, and grinned. "He's kind of cute in a slightly crazy way. What's *trin* mean?"

"Beats me. Must be new slang."

"Context makes it sounds like sweetheart, or babe."

"Yeah, well, he's all yours," Torin told her, keeping most of her attention on the boards. "My focus remains on Craig."

"But di'Taykan don't count. They're like drinking that watery Niln beer—you get to have the experience with none of the effects."

"And if I have to fuk my way past him to get to Craig, I'll consider it for as long as it takes me to snap his neck."

It took her a moment to realize it had gotten so quiet she

could hear one of the Krai scratching through the bristles on the back of his head. She could feel their eyes on her as she turned the chair.

"We'll get him out, Gunny." Werst had his lips pulled back off his teeth. So did Ressk. Mashona nodded.

"I know." Because to think in terms of anything less than one hundred percent would send them in handicapped.

On his hands and knees, expecting to see chunks of his stomach lining hit the deck at any moment, Craig was vaguely aware of Huirre telling Cho he'd lost it again. Huirre was wrong. He hadn't so much lost it, as deliberately thrown it away. The work they'd done on the seal over the last few hours had proved Nadayki was almost as good as he believed he was. Although Craig had been as obstructive as he thought he could get away with, the kid had connected a few too many dots.

With sex off the distraction menu—Huirre was a verbal cold shower at the slightest innuendo—Craig had used hard and fast contractions of his stomach muscles plus the sense memory of cleaning the vomit to force his already unhappy system to rebel. It was a trick he used to use to get out of mandatory early morning classes when hung over.

Let's hear it for... Holy fukking crap! The vomiting had driven the red-hot spikes back through his temples... *higher education.*

"What I wouldn't do for even a KC-7 with a scope," Mashona muttered, tucking a third sheathed knife up against the small of her back. "I mean, I'm a sniper, right? You'd think they'd let you take something useful with you when you leave."

"Guess they figured there's not much use for a sniper in civilian life," Ressk said thoughtfully.

"And apparently, they'd be wrong."

Torin noted that Mashona still considered herself to be a sniper in spite of months out. Given that all three of them were still calling her Gunny that was hardly surprising. She needed them to think of her as their gunnery sergeant if this was going to work, so she let it stand.

"Not much use for a sniper inside a station," Werst pointed out. "Nothing like a hole shot through the bulkhead at high velocity to remind you that pressurized atmosphere is a good idea. Station work is up close and personal."

"All right," Mashona allowed, "I'll give you that one. Gunny, what about demolition charges?"

Werst snorted. "They aren't exactly up close and personal."

"They are if you drop them down someone's pants."

"All right," he grinned, "I'll give you that one."

"We're not taking charges in because we'll lose them," Torin pointed out. "If I were running a refuge for people who live off violent crime, I'd make damned sure to control the amount of damage they could do. I'd be fine with them beating the shit out of each other, blades even, but no one wanders around with the ability to damage the station."

Ressk tapped his head. "Got my ability right here."

"I'm betting he's got his system protected against every attack he can think of. Of course," she added before Ressk could respond, "I'm also betting you can think circles around him."

"He's got brains," Ressk allowed. "Government records say this station doesn't exist. But living on a station that doesn't exist means he's been out of the data stream for a while." He patted his slate. "I can guarantee I have a few tricks he's never seen."

Ressk was a combination of tech support and a stealth weapon. She trusted Mashona and Werst to have her back.

Werst was right, and up close and personal meant hands and feet and head. Torin was bringing in a knife in her boot sheath, fourteen years in the Corps trained to fight a war that had turned out to be a lie, and the certain knowledge she wasn't leaving this station without Craig Ryder.

"Two things," she said as the docking clamps clanged against the ship. "One, expect some of the people we'll meet to have spent time either in the Navy or the Corps. They'll be the ones who joined for the sanctioned violence and won't have lasted more than one contract, if that, but they'll have had some training. Take that into account when you engage." Not if; when. "Second, sometimes the salvage operators find weapons."

"You mean small arms? You think they ever keep them?" Mashona wondered, left elbow hooked over her right arm as she stretched out her shoulders.

"Doesn't matter what they do." Torin's snort dismissed every salvage operator in known space but one.

"So you're saying there may be weapons on this station," Werst translated. "In the hands of people who think they know how to use them."

"Probably in the hands of the so-called authorities." If there was no honor among thieves, then force or the threat of force would be needed to ensure compliance with even the minimal rules thieves and murderers were willing to live by.

"So if we need to arm up, we know where to go."

Torin glanced over at Mashona, who shrugged.

Werst snickered. "Okay, not where you were going with that, Gunny, but still a valid observation."

The telltales showed that the ship had been secured to the docking arm, but the station hadn't released control of the air lock. "Now," she said, hands locked behind her back to keep from slapping down the override, "we wait for Big Bill."

"Gunny, if the man in charge is coming out to greet us, we could take him. Exchange him for Craig."

"You think he's going to be that easy to take?"

"I think we shouldn't dismiss the possibility out of hand."

She had a point.

"What *again*?"

"Just started, Cap." It sounded as though Huirre had moved as far away from the watery, pale-yellow puddle as possible. "One minute he was fine, the next puke city."

"How much of the seal have you got left to go through?"

"One level, Captain." Nadayki sounded smug. "But I don't need him anymore. It'll take longer without him, but with the base he's laid, I can work out the remaining pattern on my own."

"You're sure?"

"Aye, Captain."

"Because if you're not, you'll…"

Craig missed the rest of Cho's warning as he coughed out a mouthful of bile, his skull attempting to collapse in on itself. When the ringing in his ears cleared enough for him to hear, Nadayki was saying, "Plus he was breathing hard."

"Hyperventilating?"

"I guess."

Plus? Had Nadayki spotted the stomach clenching and realized he'd made himself sick? Was the little shit dobbing him out?

He could hear Cho breathing heavily through his nose, hear the scrape of his thumb through the stubble on the edge of his jaw. Hell, he could practically hear that stubble growing. Every little sound set off another spike of pain. This was a ripping new side effect he sure as shit hoped didn't last long.

"Take him to Doc," the captain growled at last. Craig gave thanks he wasn't a screamer.

"Thought there was nothing Doc could do about this, Captain?"

"About this, no."

In Craig's experience, enigmatic was never good. He fell away from the puddle when Huirre kicked at his legs, taking the impact on his shoulder to keep his weight off the borrowed slate he'd instinctively snapped onto his belt as he dropped to his knees.

A smart man would have puked on the seal; *that* would have gained Torin some time.

"Welcome to Vrijheid Station, Gunnery Sergeant Kerr. Please remove all weapons before entering your air lock. In the interest of not fatally disrupting business, we prefer our violence to remain at the hand-to-hand-to-foot-to-teeth level."

Torin bent and pulled the knife from her boot sheath. "You heard the man."

"But, Gunny…"

"He's clearly got more control over this place than I thought, but everything I said about weapons relates to hand-to-hand. Some of them will be trained, but you're better."

"*I'm* better," Werst muttered. Ressk elbowed him. Hard.

"Just stay away from anyone who works directly for Big Bill," she reminded them, checking that Presit's camera was in place as the telltales went green.

Big Bill was actually big. About a meter nine, Craig's height, and heavier. Fat over muscle, considering the way he carried his bulk. In spite of the name, that hadn't been a given; Torin had served with a man universally known as One Ball for no physical reason. Big Bill had thick brown hair combed back off a high forehead, gold-flecked brown eyes, and he smiled like a Krai.

The two Krai flanking him—also smiling—came as bit of a surprise. Not many people used the Krai as muscle—and Torin had no doubt that's what these two were. It explained the hand-to-hand-to-foot-to-teeth comment. Odds were the rules that governed Krai eating habits in most of known space weren't in effect here, and it was hard to win a fight with a Krai when they literally took bites out of their opponents.

Hard. But not impossible.

Given their size and the mottling on their scalps, she'd bet they were both male.

"Well, it really is Gunnery Sergeant Torin Kerr. I hate to call any of my people liars, but…"

Torin knew he'd examined the recording of the conversation. Knew that there'd *been* a recording of the conversation. Big Bill didn't seem like the type who'd appreciate secondhand news.

"…but Alamber, the little shit, is a chronic liar so you'll forgive me for doubting him." Big Bill beamed a smile just past Torin's shoulders. "And Corporals Mashona, Ressk, and Werst. I'm pleased to see you've recovered from your stay on the prison planet."

Confirmation that he'd seen the vids.

"And here you are. Running away from your old lives." He spread his arms. "Disillusioned by discovering that rather than fighting an honorable war against an implacable foe, you were being screwed over by a collective of plastic aliens. Is that what I'm supposed to believe?"

He reminded Torin of Harnett, the staff sergeant who'd called himself colonel and taken over one of the pods in the prison, building his power base with the lives of other Marines. Torin had no doubt that Big Bill's power base had also been built with death. With many more than the three deaths she personally knew of. She'd killed eight of Harnett's thugs and finished the day by snapping his neck and, now, with this man implicit in Craig's abduction, she fought to keep that memory from showing on her face. No problem if Big Bill thought her threatening, but for this to work, he couldn't consider her a personal threat.

As the pause lengthened, Big Bill's brows rose, barely breaching the breadth of forehead. "That wasn't a rhetorical question. Is that what I'm supposed to believe?"

Torin shrugged, and locked her gaze with his. "That's up to you. Me, I discovered everything I believed was a lie. That my whole fukking life was a lie. That almost everyone I knew died for that lie." Colonel Mariner. Major Ohi. Captain Rose. Lieutenant Jarret. First Sergeant Tutone. Sergeant Hollice. Private Gradon. The list went on. And on. This anger, it was safe to show. "You can believe it or not."

He stared at her, head cocked. The two Krai behind him shifted in place.

"I believe it," he said after a long moment. They continued to stare at each other for a moment longer, then by a silent and mutual decision, looked away. Big Bill looked over Torin's shoulder again. "And you three?"

"We're with her," Werst answered.

"Obviously." He brushed his palms together. "So this is a salvage operator's ship. I can see where the pens attach. How did you come by it?"

"So this is a mining station," Torin replied flatly. "How did you come by it?"

He stared at her again, then he laughed. "I like you, Gunnery Sergeant Torin Kerr. That may change, but right now, I like you. So if you're going pirating…"

"I'm considering the best use of our talents."

"Which are?"

"We're trained killers." It was the tone Marines learned not to argue with.

Big Bill made a noncommittal noise and dropped his hands to the shoulders of his Krai companions, moving them closer together. "The people who use this station call these guys the Grr brothers."

Behind her, Werst snorted.

Torin ignored him when Big Bill did. "Think you can take them?" he asked.

"Yes."

Both brows rose. "You're that sure."

Torin looked at them. They looked amused. They won as much on reputation as skill, then. She didn't give a flying fuk about their reputation. "One at a time or both together?"

"Always together." When she returned her gaze to Big Bill, he looked amused as well. "And you alone."

Of course. "I'm that sure."

"They've never lost a fight, and they prefer to eat my enemies alive. Around here, people believe they devour souls with the flesh."

Torin heard both Werst and Ressk shift in place, but they held their position. Before receiving her third chevron, Torin'd had to learn a number of obscure details about the three species who made up the Confederation Marine Corps. Belief systems, philosophies, religions—if people believed the Grr brothers were eating souls with the flesh, then it was because the Grr brothers had told them they were.

"Still think you can take them?"

Crackpot religious beliefs further warped by a pair of amoral believers didn't frighten her. "Are you asking me to prove it?"

"You have no gun. No blade. None of the means to kill that Marines are so fond of." Under Big Bill's hands, the Krai shifted, ready to prove a point. "I think you overestimate your..."

Eyes still locked on Big Bill's, Torin put a hand behind each of the Grr brothers' heads, twisted, and slammed their faces together as hard as she could, glad of the chance to spend some of the anger she'd carried since Craig had been taken. Krai bone was one of the hardest materials in known space. Krai faces, without warning enough to get their nose ridges closed, were a weak point.

Taking them on one at a time, she might have had a problem. She didn't—Craig didn't—have time for extended posturing.

As expected, they pushed away from the source of the pain first.

By the time they turned to her, gasping for breath through the blood, blinking it out of their eyes—and, noted for later encounters, it was a short time—Torin grabbed the brother reaching for her and dug into the bundle of nerves at the base of his thumb. As he hit the deck, arm stretched up over his head, his brother wrapped a foot around her ankle and a hand around her arm just as she drove her fingertips in under the edges of the nose ridges he couldn't close.

He froze.

"Your choice how this finishes," Torin said quietly. The Krai could do Big Bill's dirty work with half his nose ridges destroyed, the scarring would add visual intimidation, but he couldn't win this fight.

Big Bill considered it long enough, she felt the grip on her arm tighten just a little. Finally, he sighed. "Stand down."

When the standing Grr released her, she pulled her hand away, stepping back as he did, freeing his brother. Stepping back until she felt a warm, solid body against her left side. Werst; the other unarmed combat specialist in the group, had moved to a support position.

Both Krai flashed bloody teeth as they moved to flank Big Bill.

Torin bit through the back of her left index finger, showed them the drop of blood, and rubbed it against her own teeth, saying in Federate because she didn't know the Krai, "Your defeat feeds me."

Part of the catechism.

When their eyes widened, she knew she'd gotten lucky. They were true believers, not crazy fuks using an unpopular religion to spread terror. Or, at least, not *only* crazy fuks using an unpopular religion to spread terror.

They clearly didn't like it, but they nodded and said in unison, "*Zer ginyk satalmerik.*"

Based on the article Torin had studied, "We are tree-down" was the correct reply to her statement. For an arboreal species, it meant, "We are finished." If the cultural xenologist had it right, she'd symbolically just eaten their souls, and they wouldn't move on her or hers—an insurance policy against a random attack.

Unless Big Bill gave a direct order, in which case all bets were off. Commerce trumped religion nine times out of ten.

"So are we welcome here or not?"

Big Bill glanced down at the Krai and back up again, this smile purely Human. "If you can afford to breathe." The rates were murderous, but they wouldn't be there long enough for anyone to discover the account Ressk had set up was imaginary.

"We can afford it."

"Good." He should have been furious that his bully boys had been defeated, but, if anything, he looked speculative. Behind the smile, he was clearly making plans. "All right. What are your immediate needs?"

I need to know if the Heart of Stone *is docked here. If it is, I need you to stay out of my way while I take back what's mine.*

Torin bit back the words, kept them from showing on her face. The price for Big Bill's cooperation would be far too high. She'd pay it if she had to, sell herself to save Craig, buy him and her people passage away from Vrijheid, but not until she'd spent everything else.

"Ship could use restocking," she said.

"Then let me escort you to the Hub. I'm going that way."

No one spoke during the sixty-meter walk down the arm to the Hub. Torin walked at Big Bill's right, the two Krai, still bleeding from their nose ridges, followed on their heels, Werst, Ressk, and Mashona behind them.

The arm was narrow, clearly a later addition to the station, and although there were other ships docked between the *Second Star* and the Hub, none of their crews were out and about. Either Big Bill preferred not to be approached in a confined space, or people preferred not to approach him—Torin didn't plan on being around long enough for the difference to matter.

A wave of sound hit as they stepped out through the decompression doors into the central cylinder on the lowest level. Torin could see four bars and half a dozen small businesses around the outer curve. Two large screens on either end showed sports and what looked like music vids—play-by-play and instruments competing for ears. There were people in the concourse—Human, di'Taykan, and Krai—talking, conducting business at small kiosks, moving from one place in the station to another. Torin thought she saw the bottom segment of a Ciptran disappearing into a vertical. A few people were drunk, and a couple of voices were raised in an argument heading for a fight, but they could have been in any one of a thousand stations.

Heads turned as they emerged, and although no one seemed to be overtly watching them, suddenly everyone was. Even the drunks.

No, not watching them. Watching Big Bill.

The ambient noise level dropped further when the Grr brothers emerged, still spattered with blood. Even the volume of the big screens seemed lower.

For a moment, Torin thought Big Bill was going to clap her on the shoulder. When she turned to face him, he thought better of it and let his hand fall back to his side. He made it look like it had been his decision. "If you need anything, Gunnery Sergeant, Mashona, Werst, Ressk," he said jovially, his voice carrying, "let me know. Good luck finding work."

"Good luck finding work?" Mashona repeated, coming in closer as Big Bill and his companions moved out of eavesdropping range. "What the hell does that mean?"

Torin watched people watching Big Bill and the injured Krai as they passed. "It means he's identified us, all of us, as his. No one will hire us, the cost of being here will put us dangerously into debt, and we'll have no recourse but to go to work for him."

"He wants us for something specific. You, anyway, Gunny," Werst amended.

"And that means no one will question us being here, so it works in our favor." As Big Bill moved off the concourse, all eyes turned on them. Lip curled, Torin swept her gaze around the space and noted reactions. Not as many ex-Corps as she'd feared.

"Gunny, about the… them." Ressk sounded worried, so she turned. "You ate their souls?"

"They believe, Ressk, I don't." Glancing between the two Krai, she exchanged raised eyebrows with Mashona and said, "And?"

"And they're lovers," Werst snorted. "Not brothers."

"Actually…" Ressk's nose ridges opened and closed. "They

might also be brothers. Their scents are so tangled."

"Yeah, well…" Werst waved that off. "…consenting adults. Who the fuk cares. More to the point, no one smells like that living on protein patties and vat steak. Big Bill, he wasn't kidding about them eating his enemies."

"I doubt Big Bill kids about much," Torin pointed out. "Now, let's find the *Heart of Stone*, find Craig, and haul ass out of here before it matters."

EIGHT

"**S**o where do we start, Gunny?"

"With the bars. Drunks aren't known for their discretion. The *Heart of Stone* scored big with Jan and Sirin's salvage. People brag. They got hit with a Susumi wave. People talk. And I'm betting…" Torin remembered the look on the gray-haired woman's face as she pushed past her toward the game. "…that *Nat* owes money to more than one person on this station."

Mashona snickered. "Interesting emphasis, Gunny. I like how you make her name sound like a target."

The four of them had taken half a dozen steps away from the docking-arm hatch when the hatch of the bar directly opposite them opened and a roar of laughter spilled out onto the concourse, closely followed by a flailing Human—traveling about a meter and a half off the deck and covering an impressive distance before landing.

"Gravity always wins," Ressk observed as the middle-aged man hit the deck, rolled twice, and finished flat on his back.

Arms and legs splayed out, breathing heavily, the man waved a stained finger in the general direction of the bar while a turquoise-haired di'Taykan yelled, "And don't come back!" out the open hatch. He jerked as the hatch slammed shut, announced with the overly precise diction of the very drunk that it had totally been worth it, flopped over onto his left side, and went to sleep.

"We'll start there," Torin said.

The Vritan Kayti was a di'Taykan bar, and the trick with di'Taykan bars was to take a good long look into the corners, realize that sex was not a spectator sport, and get on with things.

Not a spectator sport for *most* people, Torin amended, dropping into a chair at an empty table and ordering a beer from the center screen. Took all kinds. Werst was at the bar, Mashona had disappeared behind a drape of multicolored gauze, and Ressk had joined a game of darts. Torin doubted she had any subtle left, and since the last thing they wanted to do was give the game away and spook the bastards into killing Craig, it seemed like a better idea to let people come to her.

She ran her thumb around the inert plastic edge of the screen.

As more of them recognized her, someone would.

It was merely a matter of time.

Or would have been if she'd had any time to spare. Not counting time spent in Susumi space, Craig had been with the pirates for approximately twenty-eight hours. If they'd folded directly here after scooping him out of the debris field, he'd spent anywhere from three and a half to five days in Susumi—couldn't be more precise without the exact equations but three and a half days minimum.

The militaries of oldEarth had a saying: *Everyone breaks on the third day.*

But Craig had information they needed. Page's death had been an accident, an accident that said they'd wanted him alive more than they'd wanted him dead. They'd take their time with Craig.

Three and a half days minimum in Susumi. Another day in real space.

Four days.

If it was true that everyone broke on the third day—and Torin had no way of judging because the Primacy hadn't taken prisoners—what happened on day four? Did they keep him around, keep him alive, in case they had other questions?

What if she was wrong?

What if he was dead?

What did she do then?

Destroy the people who killed him. Easy answer. But what happened after?

"...think you're too fukking good to pay attention?"

The voice had been a constant background drone for a few minutes, but that last bit had volume enough to break through her thoughts. The grip on her shoulder snapped her the rest of the way back to the here and now.

The slam of bone against the table brought a moment's silence, a roar of laughter, then the business of the bar carried on.

He was Human, Torin's height, and his bare arms were heavily muscled. He might have been attractive, but the blood running down his face from above one eyebrow made it hard to tell.

Torin grabbed a fistful of vest and hauled him up onto his feet. Looking past him, she spotted three di'Taykan and a Human who were still finding the situation funny. "He with you?" she asked, raising her voice slightly. When one of the di'Taykan indicated he was, she shoved him in their general direction, sat down, and accepted a fresh beer from Werst.

"Price of these things is fukking proof piracy isn't confined to space," he said as she took a drink. They sat silently, watching an orange-haired server clean up the blood with practiced efficiency. "Seems like you've solidified your more badass than thou reputation, though," he continued once they were essentially alone again. "Nicely done, Gunny. I know how you did it and barely saw you move. You okay?"

"Thought you said you were watching?"

"Not what I meant."

"I'm fine."

"Really? Because I'd be willing to bet you haven't bothered doing anything since Ryder was taken but try to get him back."

"Your point?"

"I'd be willing to bet," he repeated, "you haven't ranted or raged or used any of the time you spent in Susumi to fall apart for a few minutes."

"Who would that help?"

"You."

Torin thought about sticking with the party line, gunnery sergeants didn't fall apart—not for a few minutes, not at all—but gunnery sergeants had the entire Corps helping to hold them together, and she'd given that up.

"All that pressure you're under..." Werst tapped a fingernail against his glass. "Cracks are starting to show, Gunny."

A missed drop of blood gleamed a translucent crimson in the light from the menu.

"I'm not under..."

What if Craig was dead? What if they were too late? Fuk it. Torin took another swallow of the overpriced, watered beer. "Trust me, I'll use that pressure, let it blow when we find the *Heart*."

Werst shrugged. "As long as it doesn't use you. The *Heart's* here. It was here with a cargo. It went away. It came back sometime yesterday."

"But while they were here the first time," Ressk added, sitting down, "word is, they were acting strange. Rumor has it they'd scored big but weren't sharing. Were selling only a small fraction of what they had, and weren't talking about the rest. And then Big Bill got involved. That Krai ship, the *Dargonar*— you questioned the crew..."

"I know what I did, Ressk."

"Right, well, it left the same time as the *Heart*. Sent out with the *Heart* by Big Bill. They aren't back yet."

"Given their last meeting with the gunny, that's a good thing," Werst muttered. "And now the *Heart's* docked down where the processed ore used to get loaded onto the drones. It's not on an arm, it's sucking on the actual station. And no one docks way the fuk down there without Big Bill's approval."

"No one docks at this station without Big Bill's approval," Torin reminded them.

"Yeah, but where the *Heart* is now, that's off the beaten path."

"Considerably off," Ressk agreed. "Question still outstanding is why?"

"You could always ask Mackenzie Cho, ex Naval officer, current captain of the *Heart of Stone*." Mashona grabbed an empty chair from the next table and sat carefully. "Seems he finds di'Taykan service *distracting*." Her teeth flashed white in the dim light of the bar. "He drinks down the concourse at the Sleepless Goat."

* * *

Mashona watched Werst go into the Goat through narrowed eyes. "You sure this is going to work?"

"You've known me almost ten years," Ressk snorted. "If we switched clothes, could you tell the two of us apart?"

"Are you likely to switch clothes?" Mashona's brows went up. "Is there something you want to tell me?"

"Fuk off. Point is, it's a Human bar. Werst asks the bartender if he's seen Cho because the *serley chrika* stiffed a friend of his, bartender's not going to suddenly ID Werst from the furball's vids."

"You know she can hear you, right?"

"Doesn't scare me."

"And you're supposed to be the smart one."

"Smart enough not to sit on that bench. Your nose is just decorative, right?"

Leaning back against the recycling chute, eating a steamed momo she'd bought from a food cart, Torin kept the camera attached to her tunic pointed toward the door of the Goat and listened to Mashona and Ressk fill time with meaningless chatter. She chewed a little more vigorously than the minced filling required, the burn of the chutney almost covering the familiar taste of the vat. Years in the Marines had taught her how to wait but didn't change the fact that waiting sucked.

Craig was on the station. Or on a ship attached to the station. So close.

When Werst finally emerged, although objectively he hadn't been more than ten minutes, he stopped by the same food cart for a kabob before joining them. Torin had known he was going to do it, throw off any attention he might have gained, but she still had to bite back an order that he get his ass in gear and deliver the damned sitrep.

"Cho hasn't been in since the *Heart* got back to the station." Werst took a look at the bench and stayed standing. "None of his crew have. Whatever they needed your boy for, it's keeping them at the ship."

Ressk held out a hand and Werst dropped the last bite of kabob into it.

"Seriously, guys..." Mashona's brows were back up. "...is there something you want to tell me?"

"You're sitting in…"

"Not about that."

Torin crumpled the momo's wrapper and tossed it down the chute as she straightened. "They're all in one place. Let's go."

"I warned him about fukking around." Cho's voice was an ice pick that slammed into Craig's head beside the hot pokers.

Hot and cold shifted when Huirre let go, and Craig's knees hit the deck. Feeling like his head was about to explode, he curled forward, hands digging into his hair trying to relieve some of the pressure. Somehow, he managed to get an eye open as footsteps approached and stopped, and he found himself staring down at the toe of Doc's stained boots.

"He was alone with a di'Taykan, Captain." Doc sounded amused. "I'm not surprised."

"Not actual fukking!" Cho snarled. "Not this time. Nadayki says Ryder forced himself to vomit."

"And Nadayki's an expert on Human physiognomy now? Beyond the obvious? Isn't it more likely," Doc continued, before the captain could answer, "that as he defines himself by his skills, he hates needing Ryder's help to get into the armory. Odds are high he's lying."

"Doesn't matter if he is. He says he can get through the last layer on his own. You said the station medic needs organs…"

Cho's foot connected with his ribs. Craig slammed down on his side, gasping for breath. The way he felt right now, they could take his brain. He wouldn't miss it.

"While breaking him down for parts…"

Oh, fukking hell. Craig tensed, sending muscles into painful spasms. They weren't kidding about the organs.

"…would bring us a tidy profit," Doc agreed, "consider two things." Even through the pain, Doc sounded terrifyingly reasonable. Craig tried to crawl away, but another kick from Cho dropped him flat on the deck. "All right, three points. One, stop bruising the merchandise. And two, at this point in the proceedings, I have to reiterate that Nadayki could be talking out of his ass. He says he can get through the last layer on his own, but you have no reason to trust that and every reason to believe it's what he wants you to believe to maintain his place in the crew. It might be wise to keep Mr. Ryder around until the job is done."

Cho snorted. "In case Nadayki is, as you say, talking out of his ass."

"As far as his organs are concerned, a few more hours will make no difference."

"And your third point?"

"Ryder's crew. No one gives a shit if you kill a prisoner, but you can't kill a member of the crew for puking."

"Doc's right, Captain." Huirre sounded pretty much exactly the way Craig imagined a man caught between a rock and a hard place would sound. "I mean, you've got to keep discipline, sure, but if puking's a killing offense, whole crew'd be dead a couple of times by now."

"I can kill anyone I want to!"

"Yeah, but…"

Craig cracked the eye again. Huirre was looking to Doc for support. Surprisingly, he got it.

"You can kill anyone you want to," Doc agreed. "But that's not a philosophy people will follow, and you need a minimum of four crew to keep the *Heart of Stone* profitable."

Huirre shifted nervously back and forth, toes flexing against the deck, but it seemed that Cho was actually thinking about what Doc had said. From anyone else, the observation would have sounded like a threat, but it hadn't taken Craig long to learn that Doc didn't make threats.

Breathing shallowly, one arm wrapped around the newly rebruised ribs, Craig began to relax. He didn't want to die and now it seemed as if he might get through this little adventure in one piece. Not counting the pieces of his gut he'd already hurled to the deck down in the pod.

"You're right," Cho said at last. "If Ryder's crew, he gets treated like crew. Nadayki could be full of shit about his chances of getting through that last bit of code, and he could be bullshitting about Ryder doing this…"

The toe of his boot jabbed the bruise rising from the earlier kicks. Pain surged out from the contact like waves of flame. In its wake, his body felt burned.

"…to himself, but maybe he isn't. Maybe Ryder's worried that once he gets me into that armory we won't need him anymore, so he's fukking around. Fukking around delays the payout to the crew. We can't have that." Cho sounded pleased with himself.

"No, we can't." Doc still sounded reasonable.

"He needs to be taught that the crew comes first. That we don't fuk around and delay payouts. Take a toe."

Huirre had him held down before Craig realized what *take a toe* meant. He got an elbow up, Huirre grunted, then Huirre's foot closed around his forehead and slammed the back of his head into the deck. Struggling to escape became weak flopping between the four points Huirre had locked down.

Doc got his boot off with terrifying efficiency.

He felt cold air against his sole.

A strong hand closed around his ankle, grinding the small bones together.

Metal pried the smallest toe on his left foot out from the one next to it.

Given the spikes of pain in his head, it wasn't the new pain that dragged the cry out of him. It was the crunch of the blades going through the bone.

The salt-copper smell of blood.

Closely followed by the crunch of Huirre's jaws.

Then the new pain hit.

Over the years, the squatters had made very few changes to the layout of the station. Outside of the additional docking arms, most changes seemed to be a case of areas being used in ways the planners hadn't intended.

"Not much they can do to the internal structure," Ressk noted as he climbed out the lip of yet another double decompression hatch. "This thing's been designed to break apart into independent segments rather than hole and blow in case of an explosion. Limits the damage. It used to be the default for stations supporting mining operations, but these days, not so much."

Mashona shook her head as she stood just the other side of the opening, watching back along their six. "You're just a font of knowledge, aren't you?"

"Knowledge is power."

"I think you're overcompensating for something."

"You *think*?"

"Less chatter, people." They weren't saying anything Torin gave a H'san's ass if Big Bill heard, nothing about Craig or the *Heart* or why they were actually here since they'd left the masking noise of the Hub, but she saw no point in sending up flares, giving him sound on top of everything else.

"Big Bill's got this whole place under surveillance, Gunny." Ressk brushed a hand over his slate. The gesture would have meant nothing to anyone watching, but it told Torin he was mapping that surveillance out.

"Eyes and ears in the whole place limits him," Werst grunted, dropping down into the new section. The double decompression hatches were wide enough the Krai found it easier to climb over than step over. "He can't watch the whole *serley* place at once."

"We get into an area that's off limits, we'll trip a sensor. Talk, don't talk; doesn't matter. He'll know we're here."

Werst waved it off. "He didn't say this area was off limits. He didn't say any area was off limits."

"He's too smart to lay down those kind of rules for these kind of people," Mashona said, falling back into position behind the two Krai.

"You head out here when you're tired of rules," Torin reminded them. That was why they'd told Big Bill they were on Vrijheid. Better to leave it at bad things happen to people who go where Big Bill doesn't want them to; that implied choice.

Each new section as they moved away from the Hub had been less used than the one before. The pale-gray bulkheads of this section had been scored and dented by old machinery—Torin neither knew nor cared how they got machinery over the hatch lips—but it felt as though it had hardly been used since. Every other light was out in the band along the ceiling, and the black rubber treads running down the center of the deck were barely worn. It felt abandoned.

This was the most direct route to the ore docks. Once the ore carriers stopped, there'd been no reason to use it.

"They're still using the smelter," Mashona said suddenly, as though she'd been following Torin's thoughts. "Not the actual smelters but the area they were in. Machinery's gone, and it's a big open space like… a parade square. They use it for things that affect the whole community. Trials and shit. Oh, and fights every now and then."

"Fights that affect the whole community?" Ressk asked.

"Fights the whole community makes book on, you ass."

Torin picked up the pace. According to the original schematics, this was the last section before the storage pods. This was the last hatch, last pair of hatches, between her and Craig.

The first hatch was closed.

And locked.

The lock had been added recently.

"Ressk…?"

His nose ridges flared as he exhaled long and loud, fingers stroking the screen of his slate. "That's a good question, Gunny. Under normal circumstances, no problem, but this isn't going to take a simple digital jimmy. I need a way into the system, and this place is locked down tight. So far, no cracks."

"Not surprising," Mashona acknowledged, "given the rumors about how Big Bill scored this place."

"Yeah, exactly. I can break it. I can break anything eventually, but it'll take time."

How much time did Craig have left?

"How much time?" Torin asked, voice hard.

Given Ressk's expression, he'd heard the first question, too. "From outside the system? I couldn't tell you."

The gray plastic housing around the lock remained a gray plastic housing under her touch.

"Let's go." She pressed her palm against the hatch—Craig was on the other side—then turned and headed back the way they'd come.

"Where to now, Gunny?"

"We're going to see Big Bill."

"Okay." Mashona fell into step beside her. "Why?"

"We're going to take him up on that job offer."

"You're probably wondering why I didn't just have Huirre bite the toe off." Doc removed a wad of blood-soaked bandaging, sprayed sealant on the stub, and began to apply an old-fashioned dressing. "Thing is, I can't trust him to stop and the loss of an entire leg becomes a bit more than an inconvenience."

Breathing heavily through his nose, Craig stared at the other man in disbelief. "Inconvenience?"

"Comparatively."

"It fukking hurts!"

"It's fukking supposed to. If I gave you something for the pain, there'd be no point in taking off the toe." He stroked down the last bit of gauze, the heat in his thumb causing it to adhere to the layer below, then straightened, leaving a thin smear of blood across his cheek as he pushed his hair back off his face. "This way you'll remember that no one likes a delayed payout and you'll stop fukking around."

Doc had tended to the amputation like he hadn't been the crazy-assed psycho wielding the tin snips. Watching him switch back and forth made Craig feel like he should add whiplash to his list of injuries.

"Now things are tidied up, I'd hustle your ass back to that storage pod before the captain thinks you're less than committed to the job and that it's not fair Krisk didn't get a bite. When you get to the pod, try and keep the foot elevated."

"Sure. Elevated." Balanced on the edge of the table, Craig took a moment to try and get enough air into his lungs, trying not to remember the sound of Huirre chewing on his toe. "How do I *get* back to the pod?"

Doc smiled, cracking the dried blood on his cheek. "Walk carefully. Keep your weight on your heel."

Big Bill had claimed the station's central old admin area as his own and disabled all but one access.

He wasn't stupid, Torin reminded herself as they crossed the Hub to the one vertical that would take them up to his level. She needed to remember that.

"Hey, you!" The woman staggering toward her was very drunk. "You're the bitch who found the plastic aliens."

Torin kept walking.

The drunk managed to keep up. "Whole thing was a fukking fake. I seen vid shows before, you know. I know when shit is fake."

Torin ignored her.

"Hey! I'm talk—" The rest of the sentence dissolved into a pained shriek that lingered for a moment, then disappeared into the ambient noise behind them.

"She made a grab for you, Gunny," Werst explained.

"I didn't ask."

They had the vertical to themselves between the Hub and the admin level although they could hear whooping and laughter drifting up from below.

"Didn't pull out of the dive in time," Mashona guessed when the whooping ended in a thud and a scream and the laughter grew louder.

"Kids," Ressk snorted.

"Drunks," Werst amended.

The section leading into admin had been recently painted a pale blue, the deck treads a darker blue, and the area between the treads and the bulkheads patterned with polished steel. The hatch at the end of the section was closed, and Torin would bet big it was locked. To the left of the hatch was a sensor pad that clearly hadn't been part of the station's original equipment.

Alamber waited on the right.

"That's weird," Werst muttered.

"Which?" Mashona asked, moving up behind Torin's left shoulder. "His hair blending with the bulkheads or the way the black makeup makes his eyes look white?"

"Either. Both."

The di'Taykan smiled as they approached, gaze locked on Torin's face. "Saw you get into the vertical. Not all I saw either; saw you down by the ore docks."

"And?" He wore black, like a Marine, but the similarity ended with the color. His legs were covered in fabric so tight it looked more like paint. He wore at least half a dozen layers of different styles and lengths over his torso, sleeves ending in either fingerless gloves or excessively frayed cuffs. On his feet... Torin had no idea why a di'Taykan, a species that topped two meters by default, would wear boots with thick soles and heels that high.

The rings in his lip glinted when he smiled. "Big Bill's going to want to know what I saw. I won't tell if you *ser vernin ta lambelont*."

Werst snorted. "You double-jointed, Gunny?"

"You could always tell him you're old enough to be his progenitor," Mashona snickered.

"When have you ever known a di'Taykan to give a crap about age?" Ressk asked.

Alamber ignored them, shoved his hands in his pockets, and leaned back against the bulkhead. "So, what's it to be, *trin*? You and me, or me and Big Bill?"

Torin laid her palm against the sensor pad. "You and me and Big Bill."

His eyes darkened and his hair stilled. "That's not..."

"We were heading in anyway, might as well make it a party."

"Heading in? No one goes in to see Big Bill without an invitation."

"Got one."

He shook his head and laughed. "Oh, *trin*, you forget I'd know if you..."

The lock disengaged with an audible clang, probably for effect. The hatch swung open.

"Let's go." Torin stepped past him, over the lip. When only Alamber remained in the first section, she paused, and turned toward him. "Well?"

"Strange, but it seems I just don't want to share you. So..." He spread both hands. "...I'll pass."

Torin had spent enough time with new second lieutenants to know when a confident smile was a fake. To recognize when bravado twisted the curve and softened the edges. And fuk, the kid was young. What the hell was he doing here? "I won't mention this to Big Bill."

"You don't share either. All right." This smile was the real thing. The fingernails on the hand he waved had been painted black. "When you realize I'm the best thing that could happen to you, you can find me in Communications. No surveillance on the surveillance; sets up a feedback loop. You can do what you want with me, *trin*. Go crazy wild."

As the hatches slammed shut, Torin sighed and said, "Don't push it, kid."

"At least he only wants to get into your pants," Mashona pointed out as they moved toward the only open hatch in the corridor. "Whole lot simpler than Darlys wanting to deify you."

Torin snorted. It *was* a nice change.

The open hatch led into a large outer room dominated by a wall of vid screens all playing a news feed, and the Grr brothers sitting together on a heavy, black leather sofa.

As she stepped over the threshold, one of them looked up, eyes swollen nearly shut over visibly bruised nose ridges. His lip curled as Werst, Ressk, and Mashona followed her into the room. "Boss wants your people to wait here." He nodded toward an inner door. "You go on in."

"They're watching you, Gunny," Ressk said quietly.

"Yeah. I noticed." All of the screens were playing one of Presit's reports. Torin shifted so the camera she wore could catch it. It never hurt to stroke Presit's ego. "Don't let them provoke you into a fight." This mostly to Werst. "You take the first swing, and it doesn't matter if I ate their souls on toast. It's on."

"How do you know so much about a freak cult most Krai have never heard of?" Werst demanded, curling his toes under and cracking the joints.

"I used to be a gunnery sergeant." Torin squared her shoulders and headed toward the inner door. "And I still know everything."

The walk back to the storage pod became extended torture. Every time the heel of his left foot hit the deck, the impact sent a jolt of pain up his leg. By the time Craig got to the air lock, the muscles of his back had knotted. By the time he got to the pod, every other muscle on his body had knotted; his back had moved on to spasms.

Nadayki had gone to his knees in front of the seal, his eyes now at the same level as the tiny screen. He shuffled around when Craig lifted his injured foot over the hatch lip, the muscles of his other leg trembling with the effort.

The slow sweep of Nadayki's hair stopped. When it started moving again, it flipped around his ears in short choppy arcs. "I'm not sorry. It was your own fault. You shouldn't have been fukking around."

Somehow Craig managed to get enough air into his lungs to snort. "Yeah. So I've heard." Sweat dribbled down his sides. His skin was cold and clammy under the overalls. "And I heard you say... you don't need my help... anymore. So I'm just going to park my ass over here... and put my foot up like the doctor ordered." Everything from his left hip down throbbed and burned. He didn't so much sit as collapse to the deck. It still stank a bit of chunder, but that was a minor inconvenience compared to being horizontal.

When he finally turned his head toward the armory, Nadayki was staring at him, eyes dark.

"What?"

Nadayki's eyes lightened. "Nothing. This coding is complete crap. Don't get comfortable because I'll be through any minute now."

"Great."

"Asshole!"

"You had your chance, kid."

"That's not what I... Fine. Whatever." Eyes narrowed to lime-green slits, he jerked back around to face the lock.

Craig made himself as comfortable as he could and, if he hadn't thought it would hurt like fuk, he'd have smiled. Were he a betting man, and he was, he'd bet the kid wasn't getting through that last layer any time soon.

Having refused the chair, Torin stared across the desk at Big Bill—directly at him, not at a point just over his shoulder, he was no officer of hers—and wondered if she'd heard him correctly. "You want me, us, to train... pirates?"

He raised a hand. His palm was pink and, as far as Torin could see, completely free of calluses. "I prefer the term free merchants."

"Fine. You want us to train free merchants to fight? As a unit?"

"Yes. We'll start by training the crews who frequent this station, but once word gets out, I expect our numbers will grow." Head cocked, he studied her face. Fortunately, Torin had long since learned to keep her opinions of even more asinine plans to herself. After a moment, he sighed, and shuffled a pile of paper around without actually moving it anywhere. Torin had never seen paper piled on a desk before. How did he access his screens? "Things are going to hell in a handcart, Gunnery Sergeant Kerr," he said at last. "You should know, you pushed the cart off the cliff. You and your discovery of the gray plastic aliens. I've been watching you, you know, and during the short time you've been in this room, you've managed to touch most of the visible plastic."

Torin curled her fingers in toward her palms.

"You're looking for them." Big Bill picked up a plastic stylus, spun it at eye level, then put it back down. "You know they're still around. You know they're still fukking with us. And you ask why I want you to train these people? I should think it would be obvious. We're going to take what's rightfully ours. What the gray plastic aliens have taken from us when they involved us in this war."

Had she been here for any reason other than to get to Craig, she'd have asked him what the hell he thought had been taken from him. She could almost hear Presit demanding an answer from Big Bill's image on the monitor. As it was, she didn't give a flying fuk. All she wanted to do was move this conversation as quickly as possible toward Big Bill giving her an all-points-access pass. "Why me? You have muscle."

"Muscle. Exactly. Ignoring for the moment that their present job keeps them surprisingly busy, the Grr brothers have a reputation with the people who use this station that would ensure compliance but little actual learning. Your reputation, on the other hand..." He leaned toward her. "You brought the Silsviss into the Confederation. You fought the enemy to a standstill in the depths of the Big Yellow ship. You escaped from an inescapable prison. You're someone people listen to, aren't you? You can turn the free merchants into a force that a government who lies to us over and over and over will have to take notice of."

It was almost funny—in a bitterly painful way—that the salvage operators and the free merchants wanted the same thing. To have the free merchants noticed by the government. Sure, the salvage operators wanted them noticed by a battle cruiser, and who the fuk knew what kind of notice Big Bill had in mind, but still the similarities were hysterical. Interestingly, Torin could feel hysteria beckoning. "What will this force be armed with?" she asked, her reaction safely locked behind the gunnery sergeant. "Harsh language?"

Big Bill's chair creaked a protest as he leaned back and steepled his fingers. "I just happen to know where I can gain access to a Marine Corps armory. Still sealed. Contents intact."

Torin heard a nearly audible click as the last piece fell into place. Jan and Sirin had scooped an armory up out of their debris field, and everything else made perfect sense.

Still sealed.

"You haven't opened it?" Even to her own ear, she sounded like she couldn't quite catch her breath but figured there were valid reasons enough, given a sealed armory. Big Bill wouldn't question it.

He didn't. Asked only, "What difference does that make?"

They hadn't opened it. But it was on the station and the *Heart* was docked, so that could only mean they were working on getting it open. Working on getting past the seal the original CSOs had used to lock it down. Using the CSO they'd grabbed to break the code when Page had died before giving them what they needed. Using Craig. Who was alive. After a moment, Torin realized Big Bill was waiting for her to answer his question. Back in the day, it had been part of her job to remain calm regardless of the situation. Surrounded by a couple hundred juvenile sentient lizards. Trapped in the belly of an unidentified ship. Under fire by their own training equipment. In a prison that shouldn't exist. She could do this. She could sound like she didn't want to dive across the desk and grab Big Bill's ears and slam his head into the wall over and over and over until he agreed to take her to Craig.

Torin regained enough motor control to shrug. "It makes a difference because you don't know what's in the armory."

"We don't know exactly what the contents are…" Glancing down, he shuffled a few papers on his desk and looked up again. "…but I'm sure you could draw up a reasonably accurate inventory."

"I'd have to see it. There's more than one type of armory. Platoon support, armored support, hell, even air support."

Craig was at the armory.

"So you'll take the job?"

If she agreed too quickly, he'd get suspicious. If she agreed too slowly, there'd be yet another delay in getting to Craig.

"Depends. On what kind of an armory you've found," she expanded when his brows rose. "No point if it's carrying the wrong gear. And," she added before he could speak, "it depends on what's in it for me."

"You'd be at the forefront of the revolution."

"And?"

"And?" He laughed. "And do you have any idea how much fifteen percent of everything amounts to, Gunnery Sergeant? You'll be very, very well compensated."

"*After* the revolution. I'm not taking a job that offers nothing more than the possibility of being well paid."

"You do your job right, and that possibility is a certainty."

"Chance is always a factor."

He stared at her for a long moment. Torin kept her expression absolutely neutral. And here she thought she'd never have anything to thank General Morris for.

"You and yours stay here free," Big Bill said at last. "Air, food, water—you work for me, I pick up the tab. Plus extra credit you can spend on the station."

Thus tying them to the station.

"No deal until I see the armory."

Big Bill smiled that smile he'd learned from the Krai. "Seems like you've already attempted to take a look at it. My station, Gunnery Sergeant," he added, more teeth coming into view as his smile broadened. "I know everything that happens on it. I assume you had a good reason to be down by the old ore docks?"

"We did."

He waited and, when Torin didn't expand on her answer, finally snarled, "Let's hear it, then, and I'll decide how good it is."

"We heard rumors that the *Heart of Stone* had come in with a big haul and wasn't sharing. No one mentioned the word armory, but we thought we might convince the captain to share. For a small finder's fee."

"Running percentages." He nodded. "I do like you, Gunnery Sergeant Kerr, but only I run percentages on this station. Understand?"

Torin had seen warmer expressions on corpses. "Perfectly, sir."

The "sir" pulled out a real smile. Torin had known it would; it was the most manipulative word in a NCO's arsenal. "Right, then. Let's go take a look at the armory, and you can tell me what we have." Pulling a pile of paper toward him, Big Bill added, "Wait for me in the outer office." An order given to establish the chain of command. "There's no need for your people to hang about; send them back to the ship. Do not mention the armory. You can fill them in when we have all the details worked out."

The vid Presit had shot on the prison planet filled all screens when Torin went back into the outer office. Each screen showed a different feed, a different point in the recording. She could see herself, Mashona, Presit, the plastic alien, and, given the HE suit, Craig's knees. Two screens had subtitles in languages Torin didn't recognize.

The Grr brothers sat staring at the screens, ignoring the other people in the room.

Appearing to ignore the other people in the room.

Keeping the two Krai in her peripheral vision, Torin beckoned Werst, Ressk, and Mashona in close, a hand signal moving Mashona far enough to the left to block the pertinent details of their interaction from Big Bill's muscle. "We've been offered a job. Training the *free merchants* to fight."

Werst recovered first. "With what?" he snorted.

"I'm about to find out." Hands on her hips, Torin stretched out her index finger and wrote *armory* on the screen of her slate. Ressk's eyes widened slightly and she stroked the word away. "Go back to the ship, I'll fill you in when I know what's going on." Wrote *locked*. "If you stop in the Hub for a drink, don't mention the job offer where you could be overheard. There's no guarantee we're taking it." Stroked the word away.

"Haven't had any better offers," Mashona muttered.

"Granted, but we're not going in blind."

Werst's nose ridges were nearly shut. "What's the payment?"

"For now? We get to breathe and eat."

"Activities I'm fond of," he admitted. "However..."

"Still here?" Big Bill asked, stepping out of his office.

Torin shifted slightly, just enough to put herself directly in Big Bill's line of sight. "They were just leaving."

"Gunny?" Werst didn't quite growl the word.

"Don't worry. Standing next to Big Bill is the safest place on the station."

"It's true." He brushed a bit of nonexistent dust off his shoulder. "Everyone loves me."

Ressk gave him a look that suggested he was wondering how the large man would taste with a nice red sauce. Given Big Bill's amused expression, Torin suspected he'd been looked at that way before.

"You're wasting... Big Bill's time," Torin pointed out. The pause had been small enough it could be explained by any number of reasons. If Big Bill asked, she'd think of one. He didn't ask. They were wasting her time. Craig's time. Big Bill could shove his time up his ass for all she cared. "Go."

They still recognized an order when they heard one.

When they heard the hatch close at the end of the corridor, the Grr brothers snapped off the screens and stood.

Big Bill shook his head. "If anything comes up, the gunny'll take care of it. Right?"

Torin shrugged. "Your first one's free."

"I *do* like you."

The Grr on the left made a noise Torin nearly echoed.

The Grr on the right rolled his eyes and dropped back onto the sofa, grabbing for the remote.

As she stepped out into the corridor, Torin heard the sound come up on one of the screens and Presit say, "You are having aliens and he are having aliens in your heads—being lovers who are being reunited and who are discovering way to be saving the day. Very romantic."

And Big Bill said, "Whatever happened to that lover you were reunited with?"

"We had aliens in our heads," Torin growled, stepping through the hatch.

When he laughed, Torin resisted the urge to turn and slam him in the throat, crushing his windpipe. But only just.

No one approached them when they crossed the Hub although everyone tracked their progress, voices rising and falling as they passed in a wave of sound that had become familiar to Torin over the last few years.

"Feel free to use your implant," Big Bill told her as they started toward the ore docks, his voice pitched intimately even though there was no one around to overhear. "Many of the free merchants do, although, given that free merchants are strongly individualistic, very few of them have tied into the station. In the interest of security, I've had to have the station's sysop capture and record all signals, even those using ship's computers as SPs."

Torin moved her tongue away from the contact points. None of her crew had implants—the Corps installed them in sergeants and above—but Craig did and Craig was alive on the station. Walking half a stride ahead of Big Bill in an empty corridor, it had seemed like a good time to let Craig know she was there. Just a ping. A moment's contact. And now her codes and Craig's had been captured by the station. They wouldn't know who he was, not yet, but the moment they did, they could connect him to her, and that could be fatal.

"Over the years I've noticed a specific muscle twitch, just here..." Big Bill touched his own face, not hers. Good thing. She didn't have a Krai's jaw strength, but she'd have made a damned good attempt to bite his finger off. "…when an implant is in use."

The bastard didn't miss much.

"Of course, when you agree to work for me, I'll need your codes."

Nadayki slapped his palm against the locker, his hair standing out around his head in a lime-green aurora. "The last eight digits are a fukking date!"

It hurt to laugh; the vibrations felt like glass ground into the stump of his toe. Craig didn't let that stop him. All his delaying had been completely fukking pointless.

Patterns could be sussed out and, once found, broken, but finding a random date without hooking up a slate, with no way to tell if the first seven numbers were correct until the last number was in—time to pack a lunch. Not all CSOs added that extra layer of protection, but it wasn't uncommon. Birthdays. Anniversaries. He'd changed his to the day he'd walked late into the briefing room on the *Berganitan* and first saw Torin staring down at him like he'd just crawled out of a H'san's ass. Those who knew him had a chance of figuring it out. A stranger? No fukking way.

It was the digital version of a steel bar across the door.

"You're a salvage operator, this is a salvage operator's seal. Did you know them?"

Craig actually had his mouth open to answer when he realized Nadayki didn't know that Jan and Sirin had been friends. No one knew. Up until now the crew of the *Heart* had gone by the old truism that space was big and hadn't asked. "Sure I did, kid. You know di'Akusi Sirin? You're di'Taykan, they're di'…"

"Fuk you. And if you think the captain'll stop at a toe, you're wrong. If he thinks you're screwing him over, he'll have Doc take out organs. And sell them."

Lovely. Craig shifted, trying to ease the burn in his left leg. "Why would you crew under someone who'd allow that?"

"Are you kidding?" Fingers paused on his slate, Nadayki grinned down at him. "That's hardcore. No one fuks with the captain."

What kind of upbringing did the kid have, Craig wondered, that he was impressed by casual cruelty? Looked like the Taykan were just as capable of fukking up their kids as every other species in known space. "Seems to me," he said, grabbing his thigh and shifting his leg, "that it's more like no one fuks with Doc."

Nadayki shook his head, hair flipping in counterpoint. "Yeah, but Doc signed on with Captain Cho, so…"

Craig missed the rest. He could see Nadayki's mouth moving, so the kid was still talking, but all he could hear was the *ping* of his implant coming on-line.

Torin.

Had to be Torin.

She was close. She'd found him.

He couldn't answer, not with Nadayki staring right at him, eyes dark, as he laid out all the reasons he admired a thief and murderer. His hands were shaking, so he dug his fingers into the leg of his overalls and hung on. Hung on so tightly to the bunched fabric that his knuckles were white.

He couldn't answer, but he could listen.

His throat was dry. He swallowed. Waited.

Except Torin never spoke.

Just the ping.

One small noise.

One small noise that could have been caused by the damage the *tasik* had done. A random firing of neurons that just happened to sound like an implant coming on-line. A familiar noise created by hope and applied current.

"…and when I get this thing open—because I fukking will…" Nadayki half turned and slapped the side of the weapons locker. "…the captain will lead us as we take back what's rightfully ours!"

"What's rightfully yours?" Craig repeated when the pause seemed to indicate he was expected to respond. "What's been taken from you?"

"The universe! I am meant for more than this crap," Nadayki continued, arms and hair spread. "I'm smarter than all of those *tregradiates* who said my attitude wasn't right for their academy, and the captain'll help me prove it. They're going to pay!"

"Yeah, okay." Craig smoothed down the two handfuls of crumpled overall. "How old are you, kid?"

"Stop calling me kid! And I'm old enough to know who has the power and that's more than you can say."

"You have a…"

A hatch clanged in the distance. Too far away to be at the ship, so it had to be the point where the ore docks joined the station.

Nadayki's ear points swiveled toward the sound, his hair following the movement. "Sounds like two pairs of boots."

"Probably people in them, too," Craig grunted, shifting around so his back was against the wall and a corner of the armory stood as bulwark between him and the storage pod's open hatch.

"Captain's on board, so it's got to be Big Bill. He's the only one allowed down here."

"Big Bill? You're bullshitting me, right?"

"What? No. It's what they call him." He fumbled with his slate. "I need to tell the cap… *Ablin gon savit!* Lost the last fukking screen. Good thing I can… Captain? Big Bill's on the dock. "

Craig couldn't quite catch the captain's answer. It was just another layer of sound.

"Yeah, but… I know, but… Yes. Okay, I will." Forefingers and thumbs tapping on the screen, Nadayki kept his eyes locked on his slate as he said, "Captain's on his way."

"Joy." Craig let his head fall back against the bulkhead. He could hear a man's voice, a deep burr of monologue growing louder and ending in a question eliciting a monosyllabic answer from his companion.

He knew that grunt.

He knew the tone and the timbre.

He knew the feel of the lips and the taste of the mouth.

Torin.

Torin.

Torin.

It hurt to breathe.

* * *

Torin had never seen the docking bay of an ore processing facility, but she assumed they were all much the same. Large enough for loading and unloading ore carriers and probably a lot more interesting when they hadn't been left unused for years. These ore docks weren't that large, the ore wasn't stored but passed through to the smelters while supplies went the other way onto the ships, but it was empty enough that their footsteps all but echoed.

She'd just spotted the air lock where the *Heart* was docked—visible lights were green—when Big Bill pointed toward an open hatch.

"I've had the armory moved into that pod. Originally designed for storing explosives until they were needed dirtside, it's the best place to both control access and minimize damage to the station. If it blows, any force the pod can't contain will be blown out along fault lines here and here." His gesture followed shadows that moved out to the outer hull. "Depressurizing this part of the station and possibly damaging any ship at the lock, but it's an allowable risk given the payoff, don't you agree?"

Torin made a noncommittal noise. The hatch on the pod needed to be closed in order for it to contain anything, but since she'd be perfectly happy watching this station broken up into its component parts and everyone on it sucking vacuum, it seemed hypocritical to point out the problem.

When she picked up the pace, he said, "Must be strange going unarmed after all that time in the Corps. Bet you can't wait to get your hands on a weapon."

He thought he knew her, and she could use that. Was using that to hide the truth. *If I didn't need you to get to Craig, I'd kill you with my bare hands* wouldn't get her far. When they reached the open hatch, Big Bill waved her on ahead.

Torin stepped over the lip into the pod and froze.

It was one thing to be told that Cho, and by extension Big Bill, had a sealed armory. It was another thing entirely to stand in front of it. A sealed armory meant people she wouldn't trust as far as she could spit a H'san were in possession of enough firepower to do significant damage. The kind of death and destruction she'd spent her adult life trying to prevent, the only difference being the Primacy's forces had been made up of soldiers just like her, not amoral assholes.

Torin ignored the green-haired di'Taykan and stepped closer. She couldn't walk away from this. She had to...

Craig.

He was sitting on the floor, wearing a pair of ugly navy-blue overalls, his eyes bloodshot and darkly shadowed, his lips chapped, his face bruised, his hair looking like it hadn't been brushed in days.

Alive.

His lips were pressed together, and he was breathing fast and shallow.

Torin had seen enough pain over the years to recognize it now.

He was in pain.

But alive.

He didn't seem surprised to see her.

There wasn't enough air in the pod.

Torin locked her leg muscles and braced one hand against the armory to keep from throwing herself into Craig's arms. Both Big Bill and the di'Taykan were behind her by the hatch. There were footsteps approaching.

There were a thousand things she wanted to say in the seconds she had. Craig would know that whatever it looked like, she was there to get him out. He'd know she couldn't just leave the armory. He had to be told the implants were tapped before he tried to contact her. He'd know they were live, he must've heard the ping.

So out of all the thousand things she wanted to say, she mouthed, *Implant tapped.*

He swallowed, she watched his Adam's apple rise and fall. He nodded; a small, careful movement.

And that was all the time they had.

"Captain Cho, excellent timing." Big Bill was smiling his Krai smile, Torin could hear it in his voice. "I hope there's been some progress made."

Captain Cho.

Captain of the *Heart of Stone*.

The captain who'd given the order to take Craig. Torin began to turn. Paused. Craig wore a standard soft-soled boot on his right foot, but his left was bare of everything but a bandage folded over…

…the empty place where the smallest toe should be.

Craig felt as though his heart had stopped when Torin came into the pod. It stopped again as she looked up from the bandage and turned toward the hatch.

He knew that expression.

Last time he'd seen it, Doc had been wearing it.

NINE

"**W**ho's she?" Captain Cho frowned up at Torin, obviously trying to remember where he recognized her from.

Hands locked together behind her back, her body between Craig and the pirate captain, Torin tried to work out what would happen if she locked them around Cho's throat instead. Craig was in pain. The injury could have been accidental, but allowing the pain, that was something else entirely. That was purposeful. That was torture. That was the reason she should kill the son of a bitch right now.

Except...

If she killed him...

"*She* is the H'san's mother," Big Bill said. "This is Gunnery Sergeant Torin Kerr."

The roaring in her ears made it sound as though Big Bill had answered the captain from the bottom of a vertical.

"The one who discovered the gray plastic aliens?" Cho's eyes narrowed. "I thought she left the Corps."

"She did."

"Doesn't that make her an *ex*-gunnery sergeant?"

"Not possible."

"What's she doing here?"

Torin could snap Cho's neck before Big Bill realized she'd moved.

Then…

She tried to shift the flood of pros and cons into some kind of order, into some kind of strategy, but the anger kept getting in the way. She couldn't kill Cho, no matter how much she wanted to, until she knew she could get Craig off the station. And she couldn't plan a way to get Craig off the station when the need to make Cho pay pushed everything else aside. It was almost funny how, temporarily, the anger was the only thing keeping Cho alive.

"*She* is going to teach the free merchants how to use the weapons in the locker as *I* have no intention of allowing untrained persons to carry weapons inside my station. Projectile weapons," Big Bill added, "in case you've forgotten what the Corps carries."

Even while speaking to Big Bill, Torin noted Cho kept part of his attention on her; although he very deliberately didn't look her in the eye. "She works for you?"

"She will. When your people finally get this thing open." Arms folded, Big Bill half turned toward the locker. "About that, Captain; do we have a time frame or am I giving you access to my station indefinitely for no apparent reason?"

"Nadayki!"

The young di'Taykan was unarmed, Torin noted as he stepped forward, adding a fourth point, shifting their triangle. He favored his left leg and moved as though he were uncomfortable in his body—unusually graceless for a di'Taykan. If it came to a fight, he couldn't protect his captain.

Depending on how he got the wound, he might not *want* to protect his captain. Nothing said Craig had been the only one taken and tortured.

"We're down to the last section, Captain, but…" Nadayki's hair lay flat against his head. "…it's a date."

Cho blinked. His attention split three ways between Torin, Big Bill, and Nadayki and unable to watch all three of them at once, he couldn't seem to get a handle on the information he'd just been given. "A date?"

"Yeah, a date. Eight numbers, two sets of two and a set of four. And I can't run a number from a slate without slagging the seal, and slagging the seal will set off the Marine seal and that'll blow the armory."

"We know all that." Cho made the statement a threat. Torin barely stopped herself from a fatal reaction. She shifted her weight forward, back muscles knotting when she didn't throw the blow. Craig moved behind her, she could hear him breathing heavily through his nose, but she didn't dare turn. It helped that the movement sounded deliberate not involuntary. Not controlled by the pain. Hopefully, he'd remained sitting on the deck to conserve his strength because if it turned out he was unable to stand, she'd have to...

Have to...

She bit through the inside of her lip. Focused on the taste of iron and Nadayki's voice as he said, "Without the slate hooked in, coming up with a specific combination of eight numbers, that's impossible. Well, technically, not *impossible*, but the time I'll need to..."

Big Bill cut him off with a raised hand. "Dates are relevant to the people who set them, are they not?"

Nadayki glanced over at Cho and when the captain didn't respond said, "Yeah, almost always, but we know shit about the people who set this."

"You know the name of their ship," Big Bill sighed. "A little research into public databases and you'd learn several possible dates I'm sure. However, in the interest of saving some time, which you seem to believe I have an indefinite amount of..." He nodded past Nadayki at Craig. Torin turned to follow the gesture. Enough to see Craig's face but not enough to remove her primary focus from Cho. "He's a salvage operator. Perhaps he knows them?"

Craig rolled his eyes; all familiar attitude, like he hadn't just been tortured. Torin began silently listing the parts of a KC-7 to keep herself from doing something stupid. "Oh, sure, all salvage operators know each other," he muttered. "It's not like space is big or anything."

He was right, Torin realized. The sons of bitches who took him had no reason to believe he knew the CSOs who'd lost the original cargo. Space *was* big. Trite but true. And Craig could bluff a table off a substantial pot while holding nothing more than trip eights.

Cho muttered something in a Human dialect Torin didn't

know, then took a short, jerky step toward Craig and snarled, "I should have left your toe where it was and cut off your useless fukking nuts."

Craig saw a muscle jump in Torin's jaw and decided to save Cho's life.

More importantly, he was saving Torin's.

"It's a long shot, kid, but try 23, 14, 1552. Date of the first big civilian salvage find," he explained as they all turned to stare at him. Where *all* did not include Torin; she continued to stare at Cho like she was deciding how to cark him. Odds were high she was doing exactly that. "The first find that wasn't just scrap. We…" He snorted, remembering what side he was supposed to be on. "*They* use it for luck."

In point of fact, he had no clue when the first salvage find had happened. The date he'd given Nadayki was the day Jan and Sirin had finally saved enough dolly to buy their license. He'd just happened to have been on station for the party and knew the date only because it had also been the day Jeremy'd been born. If that wasn't the code, well, he knew a couple of other dates it might be and, more importantly, he'd distracted Torin long enough for her to get a grip.

"Aren't you helpful," Big Bill said.

"Aren't I?" he muttered, watching Torin's fingers flex. He knew her rep. He knew her life before joining him had been spent dealing with the kind of shit that would have most people bringing engines on-line to get away. Hell, he'd seen her get her people off a sentient spaceship and then attempt to save her surviving enemies as well. He'd seen her angry, but he'd never seen her so close to losing control.

He supposed he should be flattered that she'd gone this close to the line for him. All things being equal, not so much.

"What if he's decided to blow us up?" Nadayki asked, taking a step toward the armory then a step back toward the group at the hatch.

"He'll be blowing himself up as well," Big Bill pointed out. He stared at Craig for a long moment while Craig attempted to look like his foot hurt so fukking much he didn't give a H'san's ass about what Big Bill thought.

Not exactly acting.

Big Bill didn't look convinced.

"He doesn't want to blow himself up." Torin made it a definitive statement. No others need apply. If Craig hadn't known he didn't want to blow himself up, she'd have convinced him.

When Big Bill turned to look at her, so did Craig. The station manager... head pirate... everyone's chum... whatever the fuk his actual title was, *Big Bill* stared at her for a long moment and she looked away from Cho long enough to meet his gaze. Craig had no idea what game Torin had to play to get onto the station, but in spite of maintaining a mere fingertip hold on her temper, she seemed to be playing it well.

Of course she was playing it well. *Ex*-Gunnery Sergeant Torin Kerr was still the walking definition of overachiever.

And as possessive as all hell.

He wanted to tell her he was good, now she was here. That he'd known she'd come for him. He hoped she already knew all that.

Big Bill finally nodded and spread his hands. "There you go, then," he told Cho genially as Torin locked her narrow-eyed gaze back on the captain.

Cho looked like he smelled something foul. "She can't know..."

"I say she can."

"But..."

"I can't provide free air to this part of the station indefinitely," Big Bill sighed.

"Nadayki!"

"Captain?"

"Do it!" Cho snapped, unable to stop his eyes from flicking toward Torin.

Yeah, Craig acknowledged, the captain had pressing personal problems that put being merely blown up into perspective. Under the circumstances—and he could only see part of Torin's expression—Craig gave him credit for not pissing himself.

Nadayki entered the eight numbers—he didn't need to have them repeated and Craig made a mental note about the kid's memory to go with previous notes about his unfortunate powers of observation—then jerked back, propelled by an ominously final-sounding click.

The CSO seal split and dropped to the deck.

The Marine seal, still securing the armory, beeped once.

After a long moment that did not end in being blown to his component atoms, Craig started breathing again.

Big Bill cocked his head. "Can you get into it, Gunnery Sergeant?"

"No." Not a refusal. "My codes have been retired."

Craig wondered if he was the only one who heard, *You're a dead man* when Torin opened her mouth, regardless of what she actually said. Cho twitched randomly, so probably not.

"Retired codes," Torin continued, "will initiate the armory's self-destruct."

"The government doesn't trust anyone," Big Bill said with exaggerated distress. "And that's just part of the problem. How long to get in?" Playacting done, he whipped the question at Nadayki.

Nadayki flinched, his eyes lightening. "Twenty-eight hours."

Big Bill glanced at his slate. "It's 0230 now. You have until 1630."

"Station time?"

"Unless you were planning to leave." When Nadayki made no response, Big Bill turned to Cho. "Of course, as you owe me fifteen percent of what's in that armory, I wouldn't advise it. You have fourteen hours. Gunnery Sergeant…"

Torin didn't want to walk away and leave Craig in enemy hands, but she couldn't just grab him and go. With no exit strategy, even if they got off the ore docks, they'd be dead before they got back to the ship. She could tell Big Bill that she wanted Craig as part of her payment for the job she wasn't going to do, but that would give Big Bill a weapon he could use against her.

Putting Craig in an entirely different kind of danger.

She paused at the pod's hatch and, before he could look away, locked her gaze with Cho's. Jerking her head toward Craig, still sitting on the deck by the armory, she snarled, "What happened to his foot?"

"It was an accident," Craig said before Cho could answer.

Why was he defending the son of a bitch? Torin actually felt her lips pull back off her teeth as though she had no control over her expression.

Cho's pupils dilated. "An accident," he agreed. "Couldn't happen again."

Big Bill's footsteps placed him almost halfway to the exit. Torin ignored him and listened to Craig breathe. She wanted to say that she'd get him out just to hear him say he knew it. She wanted to hear him say a lot of other things. She needed to touch him.

Wouldn't be able to let go if she did.

"It couldn't happen again?" She watched beads of sweat form along Cho's hairline. "Good."

Cho waited just inside the storage pod until they heard the hatch leading into the station close, then he took a deep breath. Craig half suspected it was the first breath he'd taken since Torin's final comment.

"He's going to try for more than his fukking fifteen percent."

Not what Craig had expected the captain would say. While he hadn't thought Cho would suddenly spill his last will and testament, some acknowledgment of the danger Torin posed to him might've been a more *aware* response.

"He's up to something," Cho continued, fingers tapping against his thigh. "Big Bill thinks we're all going to end up working for him."

From Craig's understanding of how the station worked, Cho seemed to have come to that realization a little late. Big Bill might be blatant about taking his fifteen percent off the top, but the station master grabbed fifteen percent off the back and sides as well. The pirates paid fifteen percent to Big Bill, but so did every service on the station, and they got their money from the pirates with prices adjusted up to cover Big Bill's share.

Nice gig.

"You." Cho's attention jerked suddenly back to the here and now. He pointed at Nadayki. "What the fuk are you looking at? Get to work. Big Bill thinks he's getting into this armory in fourteen hours. I want it open in twelve."

"But…"

"I thought you were good at this?" Cho sneered. "The best, they told me. That's why I agreed to take you and your *thytrins* on. Fukking di'Taykan, lie soon as fuk you."

Nadayki's hair flipped out. "I am the best!"

"Prove it!"

The young di'Taykan glanced down at his slate and then up again, squaring his shoulders. "You'll have it in eleven," he said, turned, and bent over the seal.

Funny how *young* and *stupid* were so much alike.

"And you…"

Craig could tell Cho wasn't really seeing him. Suspected he hadn't seen Nadayki either in spite of the crude manipulation. That he was still worrying at what Big Bill might be up to. Or Torin had rattled him, and the Big Bill reaction was a cover. Wouldn't do to look rattled in front of the two junior members of his crew, would it? Might give them ideas.

"You get over here." Cho pointed to the deck at his feet. "Anyone comes through that hatch…" He pointed down the docks. "…*you* let me know immediately. No matter what happens, the kid keeps working." Pivoting on one heel, he stepped out of the pod without waiting for a response.

Interesting, Craig thought, listening to the captain walking quickly back toward the *Heart.* He'd seen Torin make that exact same move and that made him think Cho was military. Navy, though, not Corps. Craig had been up close and personal with ex-Corps long enough to be able to eyeball their ticks. Navy might explain Cho's reaction to Torin. Junior officers defaulted to terrified by senior NCOs and, unless the Navy was a lot more fukked than was safe, Cho had never held anything close to command rank. Maybe he found the kind of terror Torin evoked familiar. And so ignorable.

Holding his left leg up, sucking air through his nose, teeth clenched on the whimpers that threatened to escape, Craig scooted across the deck on his ass—dignity be damned—until he could see out the hatch. It just happened that Cho's orders dovetailed with what he'd planned to do anyway. Watch the hatch Torin had left through. And would return through.

For him.

And for the armory.

She'd no more leave weapons with these people than she'd leave him.

When he finally stopped feeling like he wanted to cut his whole fukking leg off—it was just a toe for fuksake, moving two meters shouldn't make him feel like shooting himself—he glanced at the stripped slate he'd been given. Twenty-six fifteen ship time. No wonder he felt stuffed. It had been one fuk of a day.

He looked up to see Nadayki watching him, eyes so dark barely any green remained. With the light receptors that open, he wondered what details the di'Taykan could see.

"Twelve hours," Craig reminded him.

Nadayki blinked, and his eyes lightened enough they looked green again. "She's fukking scary, isn't she? I mean…" His hands sketched impossible meanings in the air. "She doesn't look that scary in the vids."

"Yeah, well…" Craig stretched out his legs, sucked some air in through his teeth, and set his left heel gently down on his right ankle. "The vids add almost five kilos and a veneer of civilization."

"What can Big Bill do with fifteen percent if we control the other eighty-five? I mean, basically it's fifteen guns to eighty-five guns, isn't it?" Nat lifted her hand to scratch, glanced across medical at Doc and lowered it again.

"Look what he's already done with fifteen percent?" Cho snarled. "Made himself his own little kingdom. Having any gunnery sergeant train his people would give him an advantage, but that gunnery sergeant? She's got a rep outside the Corps. This lot'll actually listen to her."

"This lot," Doc sighed, "will challenge her repeatedly to see if she's all the vids say she is."

"Not repeatedly," Cho corrected grimly. "*Once*."

Nat opened her mouth, frowned; her gaze flicked across sick bay to Doc—who continued to tidy away medical instruments—and closed her mouth again. The quartermaster wasn't the brightest star in the cluster, Cho knew, not by a fukking long shot, but she had excellent instincts for self-preservation. "Like that, then," she murmured. "Good to know."

Doc had been challenged *once* by someone too stupid to recognize the difference between threat and certainty. The fight had lasted seconds. Doc had dropped the fool's eyeball on the body when he walked away.

Kerr's eyes held the same certainty Doc's did.

"But *ex*..." Cho came down hard on the ex. "...Gunnery Sergeant Torin Kerr isn't our problem. Her kind's shit without an officer..." According to the vid, she'd even followed an enemy officer out of the prison, more than proving his point. "...and Big Bill's holding her leash. Big Bill is our problem. He threatened me with her. Reminded me that he's in control."

"His station," Doc pointed out mildly.

"This goes beyond the station. He says he knows where I can sell the weapons to my best advantage, that my best advantage is his because it increases his fifteen percent. I say, any sale Big Bill sets up is to *his* best advantage, period." When neither Nat nor Doc disagreed, Cho continued. "He thinks he can sit here in his web and send us out to do his bidding. I walked away from that kind of shit once." They hadn't *needed* to court-martial him; he'd been all but gone when the MPs had shown up.

"We sail under no colors but our own. A phrase the ancient sea pirates used to use," Doc added when Cho turned toward him.

"Exactly." Cho might be seeing other ships move out through known space under his colors, under his command, but command wasn't like control. "You two need a drink."

Nat grinned. "Well, aye, Cap, but didn't you say we were to stay with the *Heart*? Loose lips and all that. Don't want folk to find out what we have until we're actually holding it and can return fire, you said. Don't want them ganging up on us."

"I know what I said!" He wiped the grin off her face with his tone. "Now I'm saying get out there and find out what the fuk Big Bill is up to. Something this big, there has to be someone who can't keep their mouth shut."

"Someone who knows what's going on." Nat nodded. "Loose lips in our favor. So, we won't be actually drinking then?"

"You'll keep your fukking mouths shut." Huirre had hit his bunk and couldn't keep his mouth shut besides, Krisk was a brilliant engineer and a useless shit if dragged from the engine room, but the di'Taykan... "Find Dysun and Almon, make sure they know they're to be listening during sex, not talking. I'm sending the code to get back in the docks to your slates, don't fukking lose it. And you all stay away from ex-Gunnery Sergeant Kerr."

"Once," Doc murmured, closing the equipment drawer and activating the lock. "That's a fight I'd like to see.

"You're very quiet," Big Bill said as they crossed the Hub.

Mapping alternative routes from the docking arm to the *Second Star*, Torin unclenched her teeth. He'd said nothing after she'd caught up to him at the hatch; it wasn't like she'd been ignoring his conversation.

They skirted a mixed group yelling profanities at a large vid screen showing the *Dar peed* finals on the Taykan home world. Torin had watched the finals on Paradise. With her family. And Craig.

"You must have questions, Gunnery Sergeant."

The distinctive sound of half a dozen or so di'Taykan working out logistics drifted down from an upper level. Torin pitched her voice under the argument. "Neither the time nor the place."

"You think this lot..." Big Bill's gesture included both the seen and the unseen. Those behind bulkheads in the pubs and the shops and the pleasure palaces as well as those actually out in the Hub, drinking, dealing, and fighting. "...hangs on our every word?"

It took every moment of every year of experience to plant a gunnery sergeant face firmly in place over her rage before Torin turned toward Big Bill and raised a brow.

Big Bill laughed as he stepped over a Krai lying in a puddle of mixed blood and vomit. The sound sent a ripple of imitation laughter through the Hub. "All right, then. We've covered that we're both smarter than we look." He paused and raised his voice only little. "Can we get this mess cleaned up before the stink adds to the load on the ventilators? Remember you pay extra for repairs."

The vertical smelled of unwashed bodies. Torin hung onto a rising strap and listened to Big Bill greet everyone who passed. No one seemed too thrilled by the attention although everyone did a reasonable job of faking it. About half of them recognized her, which made a station full of thieves and murderers more observant than the general public.

When they got back to the outer office, the Grr brothers were still watching news vids. This time, only one screen had anything to do with her. Both Krai looked up as she entered, stood as Big Bill came in, and headed out into the station as soon as the hatch was clear.

Torin saw no hand signals. Big Bill and the Grr brothers had implants, then. But Big Bill wouldn't want his conversations recorded by the station—too much risk—so there had to be a way of opting out. A way for her to be in contact with Craig. Ressk would know.

"So." Big Bill settled in behind his desk and smiled up at her. He didn't look like a man heading into his second 28-hour day. Maybe he didn't sleep on the station's day / night schedule. "Your best guess as to the armory's contents."

No reason not to tell him, Torin acknowledged silently. He'd never get a chance to use the weapons.

The way Craig saw it, he now had a few options.

He had somewhere to go if he made a run for it. He'd made it from medical out of the ship to the storage pod; he could make it to Torin. Now he knew she was on the station, now they weren't watching him so closely—or at all—he could get to her.

Except there was a chance that Nadayki could crack the seal in the eleven hours he'd claimed—the kid was almost as good as he thought he was. Once the armory was open,

Craig didn't trust Cho not to siphon off guns immediately regardless of what Big Bill's plans were.

If that happened, Torin had to know.

The farther the guns got from the armory, the harder they'd be to destroy or remove or whatever Torin planned on doing with them.

As much as he wanted to be anywhere else, anywhere Torin was, he had to stay here with the *Heart* to keep an eye on things.

Torin's eyes inside. Undercover work.

"What are you smiling about?" Nadayki demanded petulantly.

"Grown-up stuff." He hadn't realized he'd been smiling.

"Fuk you."

"Missed our chance, kid."

Problem: if Cho started moving the weapons, how did he let Torin know?

The only thing Torin had been able to tell him in that first instant of contact was that the implants were tapped. He didn't know how the fuk that was even possible, although Nadayki might, but he had to respect the importance of information given top billing over everything else she'd wanted to say. Over everything he'd seen on her face.

No matter how frustrating it might be.

Torin attracted more overt attention crossing the Hub back to the *Star* than she had crossing the other way with Big Bill. No surprise. He was a known factor. She had yet to define her place. If she were staying, if she were planning to do the job, she'd have to prove to the locals it was in their best interests to listen to her.

The pair of di'Taykan watching her from over by the verticals, the Krai and Human on the bench by the kiosk selling *cumot'd*-on-a-bun, and the Human crossing diagonally from her, laden down with boxes—even a cursory sweep identified them as having spent at least one contract in the Corps. The ex-Navy were a little harder to spot, but the three Krai who'd paused to stare before going through the hatch into one of the bars, definitely.

Ex-military had specific responses to senior NCOs conditioned in, but the ex-military on this station had *you're not the boss of me* shoved so far up their collective asses it had impacted on their thinking. Yet another parallel between the pirates and the CSOs.

Because the ex-military thought they knew what she was, they'd see to it that the first challenger wouldn't be a loser with more balls than brains but would be hand-picked to beat her.

Wouldn't happen.

The first fight would also be the last fight. Fear would give her the control she needed; respect could come later.

If she were staying. If she were she planning to do the job.

If Big Bill hadn't decided to wait until the armory was open to announce her position, she'd be fighting right now. Beating her frustrations out on a thieving murderer no better than the bastards who took Craig. Tortured Craig. Bastards she couldn't yet touch.

In a just universe, she'd be accosted by another drunk declaring she didn't look like such hot shit, but although they were staring, the scum in the Hub were giving her a wide berth.

Recent events, she decided, reaching the decompression door unaccosted and digging her thumbnail into the gray plastic trim, had proved that the universe was anything but just.

"An armory? Intact?" Mashona swung her legs out over the edge of the bunk and sat up, her gaze never leaving Torin. "Fuk."

Werst's nose ridges flared. "Good thing we dropped by."

"An intact armory in the hands of pirates would light a fuse under the Wardens," Ressk pointed out from the second chair. "They'd send in the Navy for that."

"And what would the Navy do?" Torin asked, stopping in front of him. Unable to remain still, she'd paced the cabin while she filled them in. "Send a warhead into the station to blow the armory? Kill citizens of the Confederation no matter how *misguided*? No. Confederation law states explicitly that the military will not be used against citizens of the Confederation."

"But the Wardens can send the Navy against pirates," Ressk protested.

"Specifically pirates," Torin reminded him. The damned cabin was too small. "Not everyone on this station is a pirate." She started pacing again. "Some live off theft and murder second- or thirdhand. The Wardens can't legally send the Navy after them, and the Wardens are all about the bureaucracy. What's more, even if the Wardens get their slates out of their asses and send out the Navy, the Navy will argue for landing Marines to take the armory back."

"The Corps' armory, the Corps' problem," Mashona muttered.

"Exactly. Even if Presit allowed Merik to fold the moment they got the first image..." Presit's camera now rested on the edge of the control panel with no way for them to tell what Presit's reaction had been to the new information. "...what are the odds of the Corps getting out here in under fourteen hours when they're not going to be able to cut the orders without a Parliamentary decree?"

"Slim," Mashona offered.

"Slim," Torin agreed.

"So it's up to us." Ressk nodded at whatever plan he had unfolding inside his head. "We rescue Ryder. We get the armory far enough from the station to blow it without the explosion sending pieces back through the station."

Torin stared at Ressk for a long moment. "We figure out a way to blow the armory," she said at last. "We're not military, and I don't give a H'san's ass if the station goes with it."

The silence thickened until it dragged at her legs. Six paces across the cabin. Six back. That was weird. Seven paces across *Promise's* cabin and the *Star* was larger. One. Two. Three...

"Gunny." Werst stepped out in front of her. No room to go around him, so she stopped. "Bartenders. Waiters. Whores. Shopkeepers. Maintenance personnel. Techies. Hell, even that weird black-and-white di'Taykan with the hots for you. Okay, sure, they live off theft and murder second- and thirdhand like you said, but they don't deserve to die. And you don't get to make that decision." His nose ridges opened and closed, slowly. "You don't *have* to make that decision. Not this time."

Werst didn't look bad, all things considered, but his natural mottling couldn't hide the bruises, one eye was swollen almost closed, and Kyster had definitely been supporting him as they moved toward her. Torin could see abrasions on one wrist and knew there'd be a matching set on the other wrist and both ankles. He hadn't just laid there after he'd been staked out, he'd fought the bindings. A bloody scab weighed down one corner of his mouth, but his lips still rose off his teeth. "Harnett?"

"Dead."

"Edwards?"

"Also dead."

His grunt suggested he found the news of Edwards' death disappointing. Torin assumed that was only because he'd had plans to take care of it himself. "How many total?"

"Seven. Eight, including Harnett."

A sudden impact jerked Torin out of the memory. She blinked and stared at the blood smear marking the place where she'd slammed her right fist into the bulkhead.

The pain hit right after the visuals.

"Gunny?"

Raising her left hand, palm out, she drew in two deep breaths and let them out slowly. Clear and bright, the pain sliced through all the shit in her head and left only three things behind. Craig. The armory. The certain knowledge that *this* couldn't happen right now. The shit couldn't win. She had to hold things together for just a little while longer. One more deep breath, then she let her left arm fall back by her side and nodded.

She'd barely finished the motion before Ressk, holding her right wrist in a gentle grip, pushed her back into the pilot's chair. Mashona knelt beside her and opened the first-aid kit.

"That was stupid."

"Werst!"

Looking over their heads, she locked eyes with Werst.

"No, he's right. Seeing Craig threw me, but I'm thinking clearly now."

"So you punched the wall to clear your head? Bullshit."

"And yet, my head is clear." Her tone told him to drop it. Trouble was, Werst hadn't listened back when she had actual rank to enforce the order. And now...

He folded his arms, his tone matter-of-fact. "If you're losing it, Gunny, we need to know."

"Fuk you."

"He's right, Gunny." Mashona's hand rested warm on her thigh. "You don't have to prove anything to us. We're here."

Yes, they were.

Ressk flashed Werst a look that made Torin suspect Mashona might be right about something going on between them then, nose ridges flaring, asked, "What would you say, Gunny, if one of us pulled a dumbass move like punching a bulkhead?"

Good question. The pain blocker he'd shot into her hand dulled the edges of the clear and bright but not so much the shit could creep back in. It was all still there—Cho, Big Bill, Craig's injury, a station not entirely full of thieves and murderers—but she owned it now, not the other way around.

"I'd tell you to not let it get so bad again."

"Yeah," Mashona snorted. "But you'd be more emphatic."

She'd have been as emphatic as required for them to hear her. "True."

"So, consider yourself told." Werst's teeth flashed white. "What's the plan?"

"First…" This was the easy part. "…we need to be able to communicate with Craig. Not only to get him out, but because he's with the armory." She sucked air in through her teeth as Ressk's thumb pushed at cracked bone.

Ressk's grip tightened. "No point in bonding the knuckle when it's halfway down your fukking hand," he reminded her. "Stop twitching. If Big Bill's blocked his codes, then I can block yours and Ryder's. I just need to get into the sysop. Once in… Gunny!"

"I'm not twitching."

He snorted noncommittally and maneuvered the bone into place. The pain flared bright and clear for an instant, then settled back to a constant reminder of why punching bulkheads was definitely dumbass.

"Once in," he began again, "I can lock our slates out, too."

Mashona handed him a tube of sealant and sat back on her heels. "Wouldn't it be easier to just lock out the *Star*? Since we use her as our SP?"

"If I lock out the *Star*, the docking clamps release because the station thinks we no longer exist."

"So you'll be locking out the codes." With the split skin over Torin's knuckle sealed shut, Mashona dropped the empty tube back into the kit. "Good thing you're an evil genius."

"Doesn't take a genius to lock out codes," Ressk snorted, frowned down at the repair, then set the hand gently on Torin's knee with a look that said it was the best he could do. "But it'll take time to get into the system unnoticed."

"We now have less than thirteen hours for the entire mission." Torin reminded him.

"Then I need to get to one of the station's boards. Easy in from there."

"I have an all-access pass to the station—apparently the *free merchants* need to see I have Big Bill's trust," she explained as she handed Ressk her slate. "But whatever I do, wherever I go, Big Bill will be watching. That's a given."

"Then we need him to look away." Ressk dropped back into the second chair and worked both thumbs across the screen. "Or we need him to believe he's seeing something he isn't. This…" He tapped the lines of code. "…is almost too simple. Your slate will identify you to any locked hatch. The lock, in turn will record your presence."

"Tracking me."

"Yeah. But it's not hard to see Big Bill's point. He's just given the most dangerous person he's ever likely to meet the run of the station. He's going to want to know where you are."

"*Serley* suck-up," Werst snorted.

"Best part of it is," Ressk continued, ignoring him, "I can separate out the ID code that makes this work. These things aren't random, they're sequential. I copy the whole thing into my slate and give myself the next lower number, and I now also have an all-access pass."

Mashona held out her slate. "Do one for me."

"The next lower number that Ressk is using already belongs to someone." Torin took her slate back as Ressk began messing about on his own. "Let's send up as few flares as possible."

"So how does *chrick* and geeky here get to a board?" Werst asked.

"Alamber."

Torin stopped checking the movement in her hand— eighty percent, she could work with that—and stared at Ressk. "No."

Ressk shrugged. "At worst, Big Bill will think you're heading to Communications to build and consolidate a power base."

"Fukking a di'Taykan is like breathing air," Werst pointed out. "Evidence suggests Big Bill's too smart to see anything else in it."

"Then he'll just think Gunny's getting some." Mashona raised her hand. "I volunteer to get some."

"Weirdly, Alamber wants Gunny."

Werst unsuccessfully hid a snicker. "You'll have to use your wiles, Gunny."

"I don't have wiles," Torin snapped. Unfortunately, she couldn't think of a better idea. "What if Alamber was lying and Communications *is* under surveillance? You think Alamber and I getting it on will make Big Bill look away?"

Ressk looked up at that. "Who notices a di'Taykan having sex? If Big Bill happens to stumble over the recording, he'll think nothing of it. And, if it turns out he's still up and watching live, you'll be distracting him while I slip in and crack his system. More to the point, you'll distract Alamber."

Unfortunately, Ressk was making sense. "If I'm there to see Alamber, why would I bring you with me?"

"You wouldn't. Aren't. I'm bringing myself." Ressk patted himself on the chest. "Most of the station maintenance is done by Krai wearing blue overalls much like these. Unless they're into seams and pockets, anyone watching will just see another maintenance worker. Humans usually can't tell us apart."

"True." Mashona rolled back up onto her feet and moved to stow the first aid kit.

Gross physical features like height and weight aside, Humans—with their substandard sense of smell—could only identify individual Krai by the pattern of mottling on their scalps. Put them in uniforms, remove the individuality of clothing choice, and the Humans working with them when they were integrated into the Corps had to learn new recognition skills. Fast. Outside the military, most Humans never bothered.

"If the Grr brothers are watching?" Torin asked.

"Acceptable risk."

Werst suddenly grinned. "So he slips in while Alamber's slipping in?"

"Oh, fuk you," Torin sighed.

"That would make a stronger man than Big Bill look away," Mashona pointed out, rolling back up onto her feet and moving to stow the first-aid kit.

Werst raised both arms and flexed. "Not the first my *cernit*'s scared off."

"Deformed?"

"Enormous."

"Enormous would *be* deformed on a little guy like you."

It sounded like business as usual, but Torin could hear the concern under the banter. She was the one thing they shouldn't have to worry about. Be a whole lot easier if people started shooting at them. That, she could deal with in her sleep.

Speaking of… It was 2426 ship time, and there'd be no chance of rest until this was done.

She stood, flexing her hand. "I hope you caught some sleep while I was gone. Werst, Mashona, go back out into the Hub and find out everything you can about the *Heart of Stone*. How many in her crew, who they are, what kind of training. How many weapons they have. Their captain, Cho…" The bonded knuckle pulled painfully but held as her fingers curled into a fist. "…he's ex-Navy. And there's a young di'Taykan named Nadayki working the seal, doing the same sort of shit Ressk can. If necessary, use that information to get people talking. Take into account that anyone off a ship is an amoral s.o.b., and the support staff isn't a lot better. If you're done before Ressk and I are back, the armory is in an old explosives storage pod off the ore docks, up against the back bulkhead, maybe ten degrees off from the lock.

"The *Heart*'s at the lock. Go into the schematics of this place and find the fastest way to get the armory off the station. Quick and dirty, we've got no time for finesse. And speaking of no time for finesse…" She sighed and headed for the air lock. "Come on, Ressk. Let's see if Alamber really does spend all his time in Communications."

"What are you going to…?"

Torin cut him off. "I'll decide when I get there." She glanced down at the camera on the edge of the control panel, thought briefly about pretending to forget it, and changed her mind. Ultimately, rescuing Craig trumped her ego. "Whatever happens," she muttered, reaffixing the camera to her tunic, "you're editing this bit out."

Torin would have preferred to have avoided the Hub entirely, but it was the only way to get from the docking arms into the station. "Remember," she said quietly, pitching her voice under the noise of the games on the big screens and a fight between two di'Taykan under the nearer one, "play nice. Recon only. Do not engage."

"If they swing first?" Mashona asked, arms folded.

"Win." Torin swept a disdainful gaze around the Hub. At first glance, she couldn't tell the pirates from the station crew. The thieves and murderers from the support staff. Fukking Werst. "Might makes right with this lot." The two di'Taykan were rolling around on the deck. Given they were di'Taykan, it wouldn't be a fight much longer. "If it comes to it, I want this lot to think twice about pissing us off."

Wrest flexed his toes against the deck, cracking the knuckles. "Just twice?"

"Twice is fine. It's 0341 now; if we're not back at the ship by 0830 station time…" Five hours was more than twice the time Ressk said he'd need. "…assume we've been caught. Abandon subtlety. Blow the docking clamps, haul ass, and call in the Marines to deal with the armory."

"This is subtle?"

"Werst."

His nose ridges flared. "These are bad guys, Gunny. You get caught doing bad things, they'll assume it's because you're a bad guy, too. Not because you're a good guy trying to screw them."

"Figuratively speaking," Mashona muttered under her breath.

"You get grabbed," Werst continued ignoring her, "precedent suggests you'll haul your ass and Ressk's out of the fire. We'll wait."

Torin opened her mouth to tell him she'd just given him an order and, from his expression, he knew exactly what she was about to say. Easy enough to figure out his response. With less than fourteen hours, they didn't have time to argue. "Fine. Presit can call in the Marines. She'll know before you do." Nodding toward the nearest bar, she added, "Put your drinks on my tab."

Mashona grinned. "So we can skip out without paying it."

"Cherish the small things," Torin agreed. "Now go before I get any older and this plan gets any more ludicrous."

There were three ways to get to System Administration from the Hub. With no reason to be anywhere near the staff quarters or the maintenance tubes, Torin took the obvious and most public route. *What was your business in Admin?* would be a lot easier to answer than, *Why were you skulking about?* should her journey come to Big Bill's attention in the next…

Torin glanced at her slate.

…twelve hours and forty-one minutes.

The section of corridor directly off the vertical was utilitarian. Gray. Cleaner than the public areas, granted, but also less streamlined. Not all the mechanicals were hidden and it reminded her of the engineering sections of a battle cruiser. It was stupid o'clock in the morning station time, between shifts, so she expected to be alone, but four meters away at the access to a second vertical, a Krai in maintenance overalls stood swearing at an open panel. Glanced up as Torin's boots hit the deck, dismissed her as unimportant, and returned to profanity. Big Bill could almost definitely pick the Grr brothers out of a crowd, but his maintenance workers? Not likely. Not unless they were behind on their fifteen percent. Ressk would get to Communications right after she did, and no one would see him coming.

System Admin had its own set of decompression doors.

According to the schematics, Communications was at the end of the next corridor, the last in a line of closed, unlabeled hatches leading to Records, Finance, and Weapons Control.

Torin couldn't see the surveillance cameras, but she didn't

doubt they were there. To be on the safe side, she stayed as far from the locks as the corridor allowed. Her new code opening them in sequence would sure as shit attract the wrong kind of attention. Enough attention to justify waking Big Bill should he have gone to sleep.

The hatch to Communications was already open.

Unable to see how it could possibly be a trap, Torin stepped in over the lip. A glance at her slate showed Ressk's sweeper program had picked up no surveillance in the room. So far, so good.

Communications was long and narrow. Two extended boards ran along both side bulkheads with a double row of monitors over each. The monitors offered a tour of the station's surveillance cameras, three seconds on each view. Torin noted four different angles on the Hub, the interior of half a dozen bars or half a dozen interiors of the same bar, interiors of the shops—Vrijheid had a masseuse? Pirates got stressed?—and one fuk of a lot of empty corridors. Looked like a dedicated monitor on the last hatch before the ore docks. Each monitor had its own station. The room also held two wheeled chairs; minimum staff to cover maximum distance. An ocher-haired di'Taykan sprawled in one chair. The other chair was empty.

The di'Taykan looked up and frowned. Although the Taykan showed few visible signs of aging to non-Taykan, Torin's experience with Staff Sergeant Beyhn on Crucible made her think this was a di close to turning qui. That meant she wasn't here because she was young and stupid. She was here because she chose to be here.

"Who the fuk are you?" she demanded.

New plan.

"New hire," Torin said, moving closer, careful to make it look like she was watching the monitors.

"And I'm supposed to train you? At this hour? Fuk that. Wait..." Her eyes darkened, most of the ocher disappearing as the light receptors opened. "...I saw you with the boss. Couple of times."

"That's what I said. New hire."

"What, and you're here to keep an eye on me? I don't fukking think that..."

As a species, the Taykan had long slender necks. Easy to get an arm around. Lots of room to cover the mouth and nose. Easier for Torin to kill her than disable her, but Werst had made that impossible. Ignoring the fingers clawing at her sleeve, Torin wondered if she should thank him.

As the ends of agitated ocher hair stung her face, Torin moved her mouth in close and murmured, "Big Bill sent me."

The di'Taykan stiffened momentarily before finally going limp. Message received.

The thin plastic panels fronting the vertical bottoms of the control boards—solid and unchanging under her touch—were easy enough to slide off although Torin had to open up four sections before she had room for the unconscious di'Taykan. Stretching her out on her side, Torin turned her masker up full, slid the panels back on, and stood. No way the di'Taykan would be out for the full twelve hours and thirteen minutes, but she'd be out of the way for a couple of hours at least. And when she came to, she'd remember Big Bill had been responsible and she wouldn't raise the alarm.

For a while.

With any luck.

If the vids were right about bad people being willing to suspect other bad people without question.

With luck, with her masker turned up, Alamber would consider any whiff of the other di'Taykan just a part of the ambience of the small room.

"I knew you couldn't resist me, *trin*."

Speak of the devil. Torin turned to face the young di'Taykan as he closed the hatch behind him and leered at her, pale hair fluffed out in anticipation.

And, back to the old plan.

Before Torin could speak, he frowned, his hair flattening. "Where's Nia?"

"I told her to leave."

He smiled and his hair lifted again. "That's right. You don't like to share. Doesn't mean you can order people around, *trin*. Naughty, naughty."

"Big Bill's hired me on."

"A man with taste, our employer." If anything, Alamber's mannerisms broadened at the mention of Big Bill, a shield he could hide behind. "He's hired you on to do what?"

"Can't say. Not yet." She could deal with him the way she'd dealt with Nia. Faster, definitely, but she suspected that rather than slink off to safety, Alamber would raise high holy hell when he came to.

In order to save Craig and destroy the armory in less than twelve hours, *high holy hell* topped her list of things to avoid.

Not to mention that taking out both people in Communications would leave no one watching the store and definitely attract unwelcome attention.

"You can't say, but Big Bill's hired you to a position that not only lets you tell Nia to leave but has Nia actually listen? Interesting." Alamber dropped into the chair, sprawled out with effortless grace, and looked up at her from under half lidded eyes, more blatantly seductive than di'Taykan usually wasted time bothering with. "Well, if you're here to see me, *trin*, I'm all yours."

Torin sat on the edge of a board, rested one boot in the space between his spread knees, and held him in place. "How old are you?"

His smile picked up edges. "None of your damned business."

It was hard to tell under the black-and-white makeup—Torin had never seen a di'Taykan use makeup, so she had no basis of comparison—but up close he didn't look old enough to join the Corps, and that was far, far too young to be here on this station although Torin knew better than to assume lack of years meant lack of life experience. Humans had a tendency to be delusional about the Taykan because of the way they looked. Torin didn't. There were bastards in any species. She shrugged. "You know about me. You want me. I want to know about you."

He spread his hands, the fingers nearly bone white against the dark, fingerless gloves. "I'm awesome."

"Details?"

"Recordings, if you like." A nod toward the monitors, hair moving fluidly out over his face and back again. "I like to leave my quarters active."

"I'll bet." That might mean he could turn the surveillance

cameras off. It also might mean SFA. "How did you get the hell and gone out here? Tagged along with *thytrins*?"

"Tagged along?" He sighed, the sound suggesting he'd expected better from her. Long fingers stroked her ankle above the boot. "I came with my *vantru*, okay?"

Torin hid her reaction. A *vantru*? The rough translation may have been primary sexual partner but the way Alamber said it layered on shades of meaning that took it a Susumi fold from the relationship Jan and Sirin had. And for a di'Taykan to choose to have a *vantru* with or without shading at Alamber's age? Not impossible, but...

"She died in a bar fight almost a year ago." His eyes darkened so they nearly blended with the thick band of black makeup around them. His lips were pale enough his tongue looked shockingly pink as he swept it along the lower curve, rising and falling over the piercings. "You could make me feel better about it."

"Why me?" Torin wanted to hear his answer, but she didn't need to. Not all relationships were between equals. His *vantru* had definitely been older. Female. Stronger personality. In charge. Almost a year ago, Torin's presence on Presit's vids about Big Yellow and Crucible had been inescapable. Alamber didn't want sex—actually, he was di'Taykan, so of course he wanted sex—but he was also looking to her for familiarity. Comfort.

"What happened to that salvage operator you hooked up with?" he asked, running two fingers up the back of her calf.

"We're spending time apart." The pull on the broken knuckle reminded her to relax her hands.

"You don't sound happy about it." His voice dropped to a purr. "I can make you happy."

Considering the way he was working this, working her, Torin had started to be happy his *vantru* was dead. Particularly, given the suspected age difference. Particularly, because Vrijheid was a place where bad people ended up. "You can make me happy by teaching me how the communications system for the station works."

"Not what I meant."

The panel by the door flashed green and in her peripheral

vision, Torin caught sight of a Krai outside a closed hatch on one of the monitors.

Ressk.

She stood and went around behind Alamber's chair, one hand on his shoulder, keeping her body between him and the door. "But it's why I'm here. We'll start at the far end." No surprise the chair ran smoothly along the deck.

"What exactly did Big Bill hire you to do?"

As she swung him up to the section of control board farthest from the door, still blocking his view with her body, she leaned forward until she could have touched the curve of his ear with her tongue and whispered, "Not you."

"Too bad." His gaze dropped to his hands on the board. "You could do me during your free time."

This close she could see the fine tremble underlying his cocky delivery and she felt a little dirty watching him react as she growled, "You can do as you're told." But not as dirty as she would have had she let him talk her into applying the power he granted her to sex.

Sitting on the deck, propped against the edge of the hatch, fighting endorphins and the hour to stay awake, Craig straightened as the exit to the station opened. He sagged in place again as Almon came through carrying a shallow box. As Almon crossed the docks toward the pod, Craig wondered if he should be worried. If the big di'Taykan decided to bail him up, he was in no condition to fight back.

On the ups, he had one less body part to have beaten than the last time.

The box turned out to be the bottom cut from a supply container. Inside, smaller containers.

Hair flicking back and forth, Almon stopped just before he'd have had to step over Craig's legs and peered into the pod. His hair sped up as he looked down and snarled, "Where's Nadayki?"

"Went to take a piss."

"I don't like you being alone with him."

"Yeah, well, I don't like being alone with you, so it seems neither of us can have what we want." He was still reacting to Almon's pheromones, but the effect had gone from painful to endurable.

"Smart mouth on you, Ryder." Almon set the container bottom down on the deck. "Maybe I should smack you in it a couple more times. Teach you to keep it closed."

Maybe I should have my girlfriend kick the crap out of you. Craig snickered. *And now he's going to ask...*

"What's so fukking funny?"

"You're just very predictable, mate."

"And you think you're..."

"Leave him alone." They turned together as Nadayki closed the hatch behind him and hurried across the dock. "I'm serious, Almon. Back off."

"He tried to kill you."

"Yeah, but he didn't."

"You're still limping." Almon sounded confused.

"Doc cut his toe off and fed it to Huirre. I win. Now move." He shoved the larger di'Taykan out of the way, and stepped into the pod. "I don't have time for anything if that's what you're here for. This fukking seal has fail-safes on the fail-safes."

Almon's hair flattened slightly. "I got you some takeaway from that kiosk you like."

"Give it to Ryder. He can divide it up." Hands in the small of his back, Nadayki stretched, moving his hips in a sinuous curve that—if he was translating the noise Almon just made correctly—put Craig on the same page as Almon for the first time ever.

"I didn't fukking bring it for him."

"Whatever."

"Nadi, dir sal veranin ka bor savitor."

"No." Dropping to his knees, Nadayki pulled out his slate.

"Nadi..."

Eyes locked on the Marine seal, Nadayki ignored him.

Almon growled something Craig didn't catch.

"He told the captain he'd have the seal open in eleven hours," Craig said quietly. Not because he gave a shit about Almon feeling rejected, but defusing the big guy's temper seemed like the smart thing to do. "He's good, but..."

"You saying he can't do it?"

"I'm saying you're a distraction he doesn't need."

"And you?"

"I don't smell like 'Baby, baby, fuk me,' do I? Besides," he added, as Almon's hand rose to his masker. "Captain's orders. I stay until he tells me to go." He leaned around the di'Taykan's legs as the air-lock door opened. "And speaking of the captain…"

"What the fuk are you doing back?" Cho yelled, his voice echoing in the empty docks.

Craig thought about tripping Almon as he turned and headed for the air lock, but his sense of self-preservation kicked in at the last minute.

"No one's saying anything specific about Big Bill, but I heard that little freak Alamber is chasing after the gunnery sergeant with his *kayt* in his hand."

"Ex-gunnery sergeant," Cho snarled.

You keep telling yourself that like it matters. Craig kept his eyes on the drama across the docks while his hands worked over the nonreactive plastic containers. The captain all but dragged Almon into the air lock and although Craig could hear his voice, he couldn't make out the words. He sounded pissed, though. Good. Craig had a long list of body parts he'd like to see Almon lose.

"So he responds to slutty authority?" Ressk asked, falling into step beside her as Torin crossed the Hub on her way back to the *Heart*. "I'm not judging," he added when she growled wordlessly. "It certainly seemed to work."

When Alamber had finally scented a Krai in the room, a growled command and Torin's grip on his chin had been sufficient to turn his attention back to teaching her the boards.

"Did you clear the codes?"

"I did. According to the station sysop, all our slates and yours and Ryder's implants don't exist."

Torin seemed to be having a little trouble breathing. She could talk to Craig. Now if she wanted to.

"Gunny?"

"I'm okay." When he glanced at her injured hand, she used it to smack him lightly on the back of the head. "Good job."

Given the placement of the surveillance cameras, she waited until they were through the decompression doors and into the docking arm before she tongued her implant. If Big Bill was watching, the angle in the arm wouldn't allow him to see her fukking jaw muscles move.

"Our codes are blocked. If you can talk, it's safe."

She'd been trained to use her implant and not be overheard while surrounded by the enemy. Most civilians weren't able to subvocalize to that extent, but translating the mumble was part of the training. If Craig couldn't talk out loud…

Who the fuk is Alamber? He sounded amused. He sounded alive.

Ressk grunted, and Torin realized she had a death grip on his shoulder.

TEN

*A*lamber?*

"Hear he's following you with his *kayt* in his hand."

He's di'Taykan. And young. Are you jealous?

"No."

Then why the hell…

"Torin." With all the other things fighting to be said, asking her about Alamber had seemed the least weighted. In retrospect, Craig realized that might not have been the best idea he'd ever had. He'd never heard Torin sound so thrown. "I just… there's just…" Fuk it, start over. He glanced over his shoulder into the pod, but Nadayki was still bent over the seal, muttering Taykan profanities, hair in constant movement, concentrating so hard on cracking the code he'd be unlikely to notice H'san opera let alone a little mumbling. "I knew you'd come."

Craig actually heard her draw in a breath through the open link. Could see her straightening her shoulders and pulling her shit together because Gunnery Sergeant Torin Kerr didn't do mushy.

Are you okay?

Loaded question. "Am now."

*What… * Another breath and a clear decision to move away from the personal in the pause. *Do you think Nadayki will make the deadline?*

No surprise she remembered the kid's name. "Yeah."

*Damn. Okay, it's 0653 station time. That gives us nine hours and *forty-three minutes to get you to safety and blow the armory.*

"Six hours and forty-three minutes."

What?

"Cho wants it open earlier." Not the time to go into the kid's ego, cutting yet another hour off their time. When he heard Torin repeating the new information, he realized she hadn't come alone. If she'd brought Pedro into this mess... the man had kids for fuksake. "Torin, who's with you?"

Ressk, Werst, and Binti Mashona.

She'd called in the Marines. Big surprise. All three of them had climbed out of that hellhole of a prison with her, and all three of them would follow her right back in if she asked them to. If he had reason to be jealous of anything... of anyone...

"You have a plan?"

We have a goal. Get you to safety and blow the armory with as little loss of life as possible.

That was a little less detail than he'd hoped for.

*Maybe... * Something had clearly just occurred to her. *Vrijheid was built to survive explosions—I've never seen so many decompression doors on a station. Plus there's emergency fracture lines built into the docking bay. If we blow the armory in the storage pod, between the pod and the design, the station might just blow into its component parts. I'm sure that's the only reason Big Bill allowed it on board. Wait... *

Where was he going to go? Nadayki had stopped swearing and started whining. Even without knowing the language, Craig would bet that every other sentence started with: *It's not my fault.* A better man might have felt sorry for the kid; as good as he was, it was obvious Nadayki was in over his head and afraid he wasn't going to finish in the eleven hours his ego had locked him into.

Ressk ran the numbers. And Torin didn't sound too happy about them. *Even at minimum potential, if we blow inside, the odds are uncomfortably high that we lose the station. We have to get the armory outside and... what?* The question had clearly not been to him. *And far enough away that the debris will disperse beyond the point where multiple impacts will chop the station into pieces. Do you know how they moved it from the Heart into the pod?*

"No."

All right. If you find out, get back to me. We'll try and work it from this end.

He thought for a moment, that was it.

Craig...

She said his name like it held a hundred questions but finished up an answer short. "I know. You know... ?"

Yes. Even through the implant, he could hear how close that tiny bit of personal connection came to cracking her composure. Knew she'd let him hear it. It wasn't necessary; he'd seen how much she wanted him safe, but under the circumstances he'd take the little extra to hold on to. *We can't stay connected. When Ressk pulled our codes out, he noticed the log shows random signal sweeps. Big Bill doesn't seem to like the idea of anyone trying to beat the system. Long odds there'll be one in the next six hours, but let's not make it easy for him.*

"Deal." Connection wasn't necessary. It was enough to know she was there, on the station. That she'd come for him.

Ping me when you've got something. I'll do the same.

"Yeah, okay."

He smiled as the extended pause reminded him of sitting at the table in Pedro's kitchen, hearing Helena and her current crush muttering, You pop off. No, you pop off first. And wouldn't Torin appreciate being compared to a fourteen-year-old.

The smile faded when the implant pinged the connection closed.

"All right." Torin took a deep breath and turned to face her team. Ressk and Mashona had their eyes locked on their slates. Werst had stretched out on the bunk, eyes closed. All three of them pretending they hadn't been trying to hear as much of her side of the conversation with Craig as possible. Torin appreciated the effort, but she'd needed Ressk *during* the conversation and could have gone into the *Star's* additional threeby or into the head if she'd required privacy. "Listen up, people; we figure out how to get the armory off the station. We work everything else from that."

Ressk waved his slate, although in the close confines of the *Star's* cabin the extra effort to get her attention wasn't necessary. "We can pull up the schematics and work them from here, Gunny, if you want to head down to the docks and check things out."

"Why would I do that? Where *I* refers to the person Big Bill just hired to teach his free merchants how not to blow holes in the bulkheads."

"This job you're not doing," Mashona began. Frowned. Began again. "This job *we're* not doing, right? He's hired all of us?"

"Technically," Torin told them, "he's hired me. I've hired you lot."

"How much are you not paying us?" Werst wondered, sitting up.

"Exactly what you're worth."

"I need next week off."

Torin sighed, sagging back until her shoulder blades hit the bulkhead. "Mashona, you were explaining why the person who's paying Werst more than he's worth would head down to the docks."

"You can't start doing the job you're not doing until the armory's open. Therefore, you'd like it to be open." Mashona shrugged. "Hatches are locked, you can't send one of us down, so it makes sense that you'd personally check on their progress. While *that* you is being impatient about the wait, the you that's here to take care of business can spend some time with Ryder."

"I don't..." Except she did. They were on the same damned station and that wasn't enough. She'd just spoken to him and that wasn't enough. If she'd been able to touch him, that would've helped convince her that he was... not *all right*, it was obvious he wasn't all right, but that he didn't blame her for what happened to him.

Most of her adult life had been spent at war, and now she was out, it seemed like that violence had followed her. Rationally, she knew what had happened to Craig had nothing to do with her, and guilt over it was self-indulgent bullshit she had no time for, particularly not given their new shortened schedule. Rationally, she knew that if Craig hadn't been with her when he was taken, there'd be no one coming to pull his ass out of the fire now.

Rational had nothing to do with the way she'd felt when she saw him.

Or heard his voice.

But *rational* was what would destroy the armory and get them all off of Vrijheid in one piece.

"While Ressk pulls the schematics up, tell me about Cho and his crew."

Werst and Mashona shared a look Torin didn't care to examine too closely, then Mashona said, "Captain because it's his ship. Mackenzie Cho is ex-Navy. Made lieutenant before they court-martialed him for abuse of power."

"There's about fifteen different versions of what he actually did," Werst put in. "Doubt that any of them are accurate, but they all agree that Marines died. He's got two Krai on crew. Most of the Krai here—on station and on the ships—are here for the same thing, eating sentient species, but that said, Huirre's apparently just a guy with no military training, used to fly cargo ships smuggling body parts, and Krisk never willingly leaves the engine room."

"Three di'Taykan." Mashona flipped fingers up. "Dysun, Almon, and Nadayki di'Berinango."

"Nine letters in their family name?" Torin frowned. Taykan society was hierarchical. The more letters in the family name, the lower the class. Alamber was a di'Cikeys; six letters, solidly working class, and making up a high percentage of the di'Taykan in the Corps. Prodded by Parliament, the Taykan were working toward equalizing their society based on merit and more or less succeeding on the colony planets.

"Unfortunately, the poor bastards come from home world," Mashona continued as though she'd been following Torin's line of thought. "With nine letters stacked against them, I'm amazed they even got off the ground. By all accounts, Nadayki, the youngest, is some smart. Ressk-level smart. And, like you said, Gunny, he does what Ressk does."

Ressk snorted.

"Cho has Nadayki breaking the seal on the armory, so he *could* be Ressk-level smart," Torin pointed out. "But he'd have had to fight for any opportunity to prove that at home."

"Could've joined up," Ressk muttered, pulling the big screen up from the *Star*'s board.

"Crime's easier. Are they siblings?"

Mashona shook her head. "No. *Thytrins*. Almon, the oldest, he's a big guy and apparently pretty damned protective of the kid. Competent street fighter; no training but if he fights, he doesn't tend to lose. Only thing I heard about Dysun was that she took to pirating like the H'san took to cheese. She's on the bridge of the *Heart* doing pretty much everything Huirre doesn't."

"I got told she's likely to have her own ship someday." Arms folded, Werst met Torin's gaze. "If she survives. They're none of them too *serley* old, Gunny."

Torin thought of Alamber and ran both hands back through her hair. "And Nat?"

"Okay, she's old. Well, not young anyway, not by Human standards," Mashona amended. "When Cho showed up looking for a crew, she was the first to sign with him. There's a lot of rumors about what she used to do but I'm guessing ninety-nine percent of them are bullshit. Me and Werst compared stories and think she was probably quartermaster corps back in the day and cashiered out for black marketeering."

"And the other one?" Torin asked. "The Human male I saw with her?"

With the schematics hanging in the air over the board, Ressk spun the chair and joined the conversation. "That's Doc."

"Definitely ex something," Mashona continued, "but no one agrees on ex what. Everyone figures the military broke him, but no one's willing to risk getting caught talking about him because he's completely bugfuk. Disturb his calm, and he'll hurt you. Someone with more balls than brains challenged him to a fight once. At the end, Doc gouged his eyes out and dropped them on the body."

"Showy," Werst snorted. "But effective."

"Good thing I'm not actually taking Big Bill's job," Torin muttered.

The three ex-Marines murmured varying agreements.

* * *

He'd watched Dysun stagger back to the *Heart* just after Torin had pinged off, and now, watching Huirre cross from the air lock to the storage pod, Craig wondered if the two things were connected. Had Dysun brought news in from the station? News about Torin? Had someone finally realized he was the bearded man in the vids from the prison planet?

Then he wondered how true all those stories were. *Once a Krai tastes your flesh, they'll do anything to get more of it.* He straightened, rolled his shoulders to loosen stiff muscles. If Huirre wanted more, Craig would start him off with a mouthful of fist.

"Captain says you're to pull some rack time."

Braced for a fight, that wasn't the opening line Craig had expected.

"Oh, fukking great," Huirre sighed. "I eat your toe, you get all weird around me. Well, pull your shit together, and go grab a few hours' sleep."

Pulling his shit together sounded like a good idea. So did sleep. Craig dug the heel of his hands into his eyes. "The captain told me to watch that exit to the station, let him know immediately if Big Bill returned."

"And he sent me here to replace you, you *serley chrika*." Holding the edge of the hatch, Huirre leaned into the pod. "Not done yet?"

"Asshole," Craig heard Nadayki mutter. "Ryder was talking to himself."

When Huirre leaned back out to snort a wordless request for an explanation, Craig shrugged. "Trying not to fall asleep." He rolled his shoulders again, cracking his upper back. "He's lucky I didn't sing."

"Yeah, well he's lucky about a lot of things."

Craig heard boots ring against the deck then Nadayki stood in the open hatch, scowling down at the Krai, the ends of his hair flicking back and forth in short, jerky arcs. "What's that supposed to mean?"

Huirre ignored the question. "You going to get that thing open in time?" His nose ridges flared and closed, slowly, deliberately, and—although Craig realized his perceptions might be colored by lack of sleep—he suddenly sounded dangerous. "Cap'll pitch a fit if you promise and don't deliver. You don't want to piss him off, do you?"

Nadayki's eyes darkened. "If the captain does anything to keep me from working, he'll never get through this seal. Not when I'm the only one who understands the groundwork I've laid."

"Was that a threat, kid?"

"No." Nadayki's chin rose, but his hair flattened. Mixed messages. "It's a simple if/then statement. If he hurts me because I haven't finished, then I can't finish. Cause and effect."

"Yeah?" Huirre flexed his toes against the deck. "Does it effect you if he hurts one of your *thytrin* to motivate you?"

"Affect," Nadayki snapped. Craig had to suppress a completely inappropriate desire to laugh. "And no. If he hurts one of my *thytrin*, I won't finish." This, he was sure of. His hair started moving again.

"If you're not going to finish," Huirre pointed out thoughtfully, "he might as well hurt you."

"What?" Nadayki's hair stopped moving again.

Craig sighed. "Huirre's fukking with you, kid. Getting you to waste time. Then he tells the captain, and he's golden while you catch shit."

Huirre snickered. "You're no fun at all. Tasty, but no fun."

Eyes darkening, Nadayki frowned, then smirked in triumph. "You hate that I'm more important right now than you!"

"Moment of glory. Enjoy it." The Krai dipped a hand into his pocket and held it out, a stim on the tip of one finger. "Captain wants you to take this."

"I don't need a…"

"Yeah, you do, kid." Back against the bulkhead, Craig worked himself up onto his right foot, keeping his weight off the left until absolutely necessary. "You get tired, you'll make mistakes. You make a big enough mistake, we all die. Bottom line, that's what the armory blowing up means. We all die. I don't want to die. You don't want to die. Take the stim."

"Stop calling me kid!" But he took the stim.

Huirre picked up one of the takeout boxes with his left foot and tossed it up into his hand. He sniffed the stained interior and took a bite. "*Chrick*. Just like my *jernil* used to make. Now get lost, Ryder. And you might want to fukking shower. You stink."

Considering he was still breaking out in a sweat every time he moved his foot, Craig wasn't surprised. He hadn't thought of showering until Huirre mentioned it, but right now, there was only one thing he wanted to do more than stand under hot water. Torin's implant could reach dirtside to a ship in orbit. It could reach him in the *Heart*.

He took a careful step away, weight on his left heel, and remembered Torin had wanted him to check on how they'd moved the armory into the pod. The deck was smooth. They had to have shifted the armory from the ship's cargo bay doors in through the big decompression doors—it was too gods damned big to get it to the storage pod any other way—but they hadn't moved it on rails.

"Hey, Huirre." He nodded back toward the pod. "You know how they got that thing in here?"

"The armory? Yeah."

Craig waited.

Huirre snickered. "I'm not going to tell you. Ask the captain. Or Almon. He could beat you up again before he fuks you." He took another bite of the box. "I don't give a shit about Doc's pirate guidelines. Far as I'm concerned, you're not crew until you're in deep enough you can't screw us over with the Wardens. Until then, you're walking snack food."

After showering, Torin felt a lot more Human. They still had ice in the hopper, and the *Star* had a top-of-the-line recycling system; they'd have plenty of water to get them through the next…

She glanced at her slate.

…five hours and seventeen minutes. Given what Big Bill charged for water—up front—that was no small thing.

The station schematics had proved without a doubt the armory had come through the ore dock's decompression doors— the armory was just too big to have gotten onto the station any other way. But how had they maneuvered it from the doors to the storage pod? That was the question. The schematics showed nothing capable of maneuvering that kind of...

Her implant didn't so much ping as ring loudly enough she felt her jaw vibrate.

Good morning, Gunnery Sergeant. I hope I'm not waking you.

Torin had survived under fire more times than Big Bill had charged his fifteen percent. No way was she going to show that the son of a bitch had startled her. "I'm up."

Good. Meet me at the old smelter in thirty. I'll send a route to your slate. The ping when he broke the connection was at a volume significantly closer to the default.

Torin fought the urge to beat her head against the bulkhead, reached for clean clothes instead, and began dragging them on. She couldn't believe she'd forgotten that Big Bill had her codes. Technically, he *was* her employer, so she'd had no good reason to refuse when he'd asked. Actually, she'd had any number of good reasons, but none she could give him.

She paused, one arm through her shirt. Big Bill's implant codes didn't go into the system. As far as the station sysop was concerned, that call hadn't happened. Therefore, her codes hadn't been put into the system and she could still contact Craig without putting him in danger.

"Probably," Ressk agreed as she put her boots on. "I'll go in and check. Easy enough to take them out now anyway."

"Easy enough?"

"I set it up as a link to the communications boards." He waved his slate. "Full access from here."

"Can you eavesdrop on Big Bill's implant?"

"Not yet. But I'm working on it."

"Good." Second boot on, she took a moment to lay her head on her knees and get her shit together. "I'm a soldier," she muttered. "I fukking suck at this undercover shit."

"You're doing okay so far, Gunny."

She straightened then and glared across the cabin at Ressk. "Just okay?" That pretty much proved her point.

He grinned. "I'm sure you'd be happier if someone was shooting at us." He held out his hand, a familiar white dot on his palm. "Mashona found stims in the first-aid kit. Look like ours—the Corps'—don't they?"

They did. She crossed the cabin and lifted the tiny white pill on her fingertip. "How many?"

"Two. I took the other one. Mashona and Werst'll have to do it the old-fashioned way. They've fought a war on less sleep."

"War." Torin swallowed a mouthful of saliva caused by the familiar, bitter taste of the stim. She shrugged into her tunic, checked that Presit's camera was secured, and headed for the air lock. "War has rules. Whatever this is, it could use some rules."

"Harder to break an arbitrary decision," Ressk agreed as the lock cycled closed.

Five hours and six minutes. They needed a plan.

The route Big Bill had sent to her slate would have taken her more than thirty minutes even if she'd left the ship immediately after receiving it. With only nineteen minutes remaining, she took a short cut. First up to the Hub's mezzanine level, moving quickly through the public areas—senior NCOs did not run in order to reach their destination on time. At least not where they could be seen. Once through a locked hatch, Torin picked up the pace, racing down the pale-gray corridor that led to the staff quarters, left at the T-junction, then past twenty identical darker gray hatches...

"Hey! What the fuk are you doing up here?"

Torin ignored him, opened the maintenance access she'd been aiming for, and stepped into the darkness, closing the access behind her. Using her slate as a light, she hooked two fingers under a bit of gray plastic conduit, and, having given it as much time as she could spare to respond, pushed herself down toward the smelter level—for representational rather than gravitational values of the word *down*. Like the verticals, the maintenance shafts were kept at zero g—one of the reasons so many maintenance workers were Krai. The Krai, as a species, suffered no nausea, no disorientation; without gravity, they were able to use both hands and feet to double their efficiency.

She skimmed her free hand along the plastic cables. One deck. Two. Three.

Snapping her slate back on her belt, Torin snagged another conduit to stop her descent and flipped the access panel open with her free hand. She swung her feet out onto the deck, twisting sideways to clear her shoulders as gravity took over and her weight pulled her clear.

Six seconds to twitch everything into place, and she walked around the corner to the smelter with a minute and a half to spare.

The Grr brothers noticed her first, turning slowly, nose ridges flared, hands out from their sides. The position was half reassurance that they weren't reaching for weapons, half loosening up for a fight. The swelling had mostly gone down, and although the mottling made it difficult to tell for certain, it looked as though the bruises had begun to darken.

Bruises made her think of Craig and the evidence of violence still marking his face.

Both sets of nose ridges slammed shut. Torin fought to get her expression under control before she faced Big Bill.

He started to turn as she passed his bodyguards, frowned when he saw her, then glanced back in the direction he'd expected her to arrive from.

Torin fell into parade rest and waited, counting the seconds they were wasting. She'd counted to six when Big Bill said, "I see you found your own way."

It wasn't a question, so she didn't answer it.

His slate chirped.

One of the Grr brothers snorted.

Big Bill had intended her to arrive late, putting her on the defensive, allowing him to give her shit or grant clemency depending on his mood. Torin kept her expression neutral. Compared to General Morris, he was a complete amateur.

"Why didn't you use the route I sent you?"

When she looked directly at him, his gaze slid off hers—not so obviously it seemed deliberate but consistently enough Torin knew it had to be. "You expected me in thirty."

"And you always do what's expected of you?" His tone sounded more speculative than curious, no doubt wondering how he could use that information.

"It's part of the job."

And the camouflage.

"Well, as you're here so promptly, let's use the time you

saved and have a look at the smelter. Boys, open the hatch. It's a community arena now," he added as the Grr brothers hurried to obey. "Used for courts and fights and the like, but I thought you might use it as a training facility."

The small decompression hatch led into a large rectangular area, with high ceilings and nearly as much floor space as the central part of the Hub but empty except for black metal bleachers around the bulkheads. At first, Torin thought the walls had been allowed to rust. A moment later, she realized they'd been painted a dark red-brown—the shade somewhere between rust and dried blood. A double set of glossy black decompression doors broke up the seating at ninety degrees from her zero. Patches rough welded into the floor showed where large machinery had been removed.

She doubted there was much difference between the *courts* and the *fights*.

There was no visible plastic. That was less comforting than she'd expected it would be.

"The seats can come out if you don't need them, or they can be rearranged into more useful configurations." Big Bill slapped a meaty palm against the bulkhead. "Industrial reinforcing— it's the best place on Vrijheid to put a range even with targets designed to absorb the impact."

Not everyone would hit the target. On military stations, they built a barrier designed to neutralize the rounds from a KC-7 and set the targets in that. As Torin enjoyed the thought of pirates shooting holes in their own station, she didn't bother correcting the flaw in Big Bill's design.

"For the larger weapons, we may need to set up something on the planet. Although it's not like the big stuff needs precision shooting, right?"

He was waiting for a response. "Just needs to be pointed in the right direction," she agreed. Pirates blowing themselves to hell with heavy ordnance would also be celebrated. She scuffed her sole against one of the welds, frowned at the big double hatch, and laid out the station schematics in her head. "The smelter machinery; how did you get it out?"

"Why?"

Torin gave him her best *That question is too stupid to require a facial expression.* "We'll need to move some large equipment back in."

"Of course." Big Bill moved out into the center space. "The double hatch leads to the ore dock. We cut the gravity in both sections, opened the hatches, ran leads in from the runners in the ore dock and floated them out. Then we cleared the ore dock by putting a couple of crews in HE suits and shoving the machinery—stripped of anything useful, of course—out the big exterior hatch the ore carriers used. The crews that did the work got to grapple the scrap in and sell the metal to my recycling contacts. You'll merely need to reverse the process."

Or repeat the process to get the armory off the station.

Torin nodded. "It's a plan." She needed to get the hell back to the *Star*, but Big Bill wasn't finished.

"It's more than a plan, Gunnery Sergeant, it's a beginning." He faced her, arms spread. "The Navy can shoot at individual ships the Wardens designate pirate—bureaucracy runs slower than a H'san in the sun, so no ships have yet been designated, but it's only a matter of time before the Wardens get their opposable digits out of their anal passages and convince Parliament to declare the free merchants enemies of the Confederation. Ships will therefore only take us so far. But, if we take over stations, who's to say who's a free merchant and who's part of the station crew? If we control stations, the government will have to talk to us. We can form a Free Merchant Alliance." His voice bounced back off the metal surfaces, layering on a patina of aural crazy. "When we control enough stations, we'll sue for representation in Parliament."

Torin stared at him. There were holes in his plan a battle cruiser could slide through, but the son of a bitch thought big, she'd give him that. "And all you get from this…"

"Is fifteen percent."

When Torin raised a brow, he smiled. She glanced over at the Grr brothers who looked more bored than impressed by the rhetoric. If she had to guess, she'd say they'd heard it before.

"Problem." She made it sound like a single problem, not a problem with the crazy-ass concept in general. "Even with the armory on the station, doesn't Cho control most of the weapons?"

"Captain Cho will, of course, be one of the leaders of the Alliance, and he'll sell the weapons he and his crew don't personally need."

"To people you've chosen."

"To the people who will give him the best price." Smiling, Big Bill beckoned her closer. When she was an arm's length away, he said, "I'd like you to have the training facility ready to use the moment the free merchants have weapons in their hands, but the ore dock is off-limits until the armory is open, so that'll limit any large-scale changes." With his volume dialed back to conversational levels, he might have been discussing sweeping out the Hub instead of the first steps toward violently commandeering stations and holding their inhabitants hostage. "It's eight fifty-three now…"

Four hours and thirty-three minutes until Craig said Nadayki would have the armory open.

"…I'd like to see a design by 1130," Big Bill continued, unaware of the change Cho had made in his schedule. "Include a list of everything you'll need to make it happen—material, tools, workers—and once I've approved it, you can begin."

"Then I'd better get started." She pivoted on one heel and headed for the hatch, roughing out a plan that would not end with the Free Merchant Alliance gaining representation in Parliament or Big Bill using the weapons in the armory to gain fifteen percent of anything.

As Torin stepped onto the *Star*, Werst handed her a mug of coffee. "We cut the gravity, open the exterior decompression doors, use the overhead runners to get the armory out of the storage pod and out the doors, grapple it, use the *Star* to tow it away from the station, blow it up, and fold before any of the pirates come after us, illegal weapons blazing?"

Torin nodded. "Bare bones."

"What about Ryder?" Mashona asked, breaking the seal on a packet of eggs.

Torin gripped the mug tighter, pulling at the bonded knuckle.

"I said, bare bones." With no time to waste, she'd filled them in while returning to the ship. Assuming Big Bill was watching, or would be watching at least fifteen percent of the time, she'd tried to look like she'd already begun to design a training facility for thieves and murderers. Ressk's tracking program kept her face turned away from surveillance cameras.

"Okay, one and zeros." Ressk cracked his toes and took a long swallow of *sah*. "Moving training equipment would be a great cover. Any chance of Big Bill changing his mind about waiting until the armory's open?"

"No." When it looked like he was going to pursue it further, Torin raised a hand and cut him off. "You've cracked the station sysop, can't you shut down the gravity and open the exterior hatch from your slate?"

"I'm in Communications, Gunny."

"Not what I asked you."

He straightened, responding to her tone. "Yes, I can shut down the gravity and open the big hatch from the slate. But it'll take time to find the right subroutines and more time to subvert them."

"How much time?"

His nose ridges opened and closed. "Probably more than we have."

Torin narrowed her eyes. "You hacked through ship security every time Sh'quo Company was deployed."

"Yeah. But, Gunny…"

"Are you telling me Big Bill Ponner is more paranoid than the Navy with Marines on board?"

"Gunny, he created a digital history that convinced everyone who mattered that Vrijheid was destroyed in the war. He's either written or adapted every program running on this station. I'm telling you he's *better* than the Navy."

"Better than the Navy doesn't make him better than you."

"Well, no, but…"

"No buts. Get to work; we need the gravity off and the hatch open." Torin dropped into the pilot's chair and set her mug on the edge of the board. "All right, before we can open the ore docks to vacuum, we have to get Nadayki and Craig away from the pod. I'll talk to Craig." She frowned. "There's no blast wave in vacuum. Does that change the result if we blow the armory in the pod?"

"Not enough. Atmosphere or no atmosphere, the pod's not designed to contain large chunks of shrapnel. Pieces of the armory will go through the pod and then the station like cheese through a H'san. We have to get it, on an absolute minimum, thirty kilometers away and even then the station will take damage."

Every mission came with collateral damage. The brass tried to pretend it didn't, but the people on the front lines knew better.

"Let's hope the interior decompression hatches work as planned, then. You two..." Torin spun the chair to face Werst and Mashona at the table. "Get down to the Hub and watch for Big Bill. We can't risk him going to the ore docks and finding out he's got three hours' less time."

"Why would they tell him?" Mashona asked, shoving the last spoonful of scrambled egg into her mouth and shoving the tray in the recycler.

"From what I saw of Nadayki, if asked, he's likely to brag about it."

Werst emptied his mug. "Would it matter?"

"Big Bill believes nothing will happen until 1630. If he learns the armory's due to open at 1330, our cover story tightens up. Without those three extra hours, we blow our cover with Big Bill or we lose the armory. Either way, we're screwed."

"Or Cho is. Cho's betraying him," Werst expanded off Torin's look. "Pulling weapons out early."

"If Big Bill finds out before the armory's open, Cho'll argue he was just being gung ho. Wanted to surprise Big Bill with how efficient he is." Pain from her injured knuckle reminded her to loosen her fist. "If we control the information, we can aim and fire it when it'll do us the most good, so we have to keep Big Bill..."

"From the docking bay." Werst laid his palm against the air lock's inner panel. "Check."

"And if we see him?" Mashona asked, falling in beside Werst.

"Ping me." So far, the plan had more variables than actual points of reference. A few more variables couldn't hurt. "Let's mix things up a bit. Drop a few subtle rumors about Cho while you're out there."

"About how this big mystery haul of his is big enough to finally piss off the Wardens and have them kick the Navy into action, putting the station and everyone on it in danger?"

"That's good."

Mashona smirked. "More than just a pretty face, Gunny."

Huirre and Nadayki were at the storage pod; Krisk apparently never left the ship. Cho wasn't going any farther from the armory than the *Heart*. Craig suspected he wasn't standing at Nadayki's shoulder only because he didn't want his crew to think he had nothing better to do—even though until the armory was open, he *had* nothing better to do. Dysun had returned not long after Almon, but Nat and Doc were still out.

With half the crew gone, the ship felt empty.

Craig didn't much like the ship having a *feel*. It smacked of familiarity. Of becoming a part of something he wanted no part of.

Sitting on a bench outside the showers, he nearly fell on his face while carefully easing the overalls past his injured foot. Fuk, he was tired. As he bent to pull the dressing off—Marines used sealant alone in the field—small spikes tapped into his temples and, although Doc had bonded the ribs Almon had cracked, breathing became less an automatic function and more a painful chore.

But Torin was here. On the station.

It was almost over.

Craig. We know how they got the armory in—they cut the gravity, floated it out of the Heart *and in through the exterior hatch. We'll take it out the same way.*

"Great." He stepped over the lip into the shower and pressed *hot/strong*. "You can take me out with it."

He thought for a moment the hot water pounding down on his head and shoulders had drowned out her reply. Impossible given that the implant was jacked directly into his ear.

Are you up to it?

He didn't know where his suit was, and he very much doubted Cho would just hand it over. Or allow him to unhook a suit from the *Heart*. "Are you serious?"

Easier to get you out the exterior hatch than through the station. Craig, are you up to it?

She didn't think he was, or she wouldn't have asked again. But she'd take his word for it, or she wouldn't have asked the first time. One of the first things he'd learned about Torin was that when she asked a question, she wanted an actual answer to it.

Stepping out from the wall, changing the angle so the water could pound at the base of his spine, he took inventory. Everything hurt. But if he could walk out to the fukking storage pod right after Huirre ate his toe, he could do what he had to in order to get the hell away from the *Heart*.

"Yeah, I'm up to it."

Do you have access to a suit?

"Not right now, I'm in the shower. Naked. Soapy." Actually, he hadn't even started soaping. So as not to be telling a lie, he pushed a little into his palm and began to carefully rub it around the bruising.

Ressk says the schematics show a suit locker on the ore dock, by the head. It sounded as though she was smiling and trying not to. He really hoped it was because she was thinking of him naked and not because of Ressk. That would just be... wrong.

"Yeah, I saw the hookups. No suits, though."

Shit.

"At least some of the stations are live. Maybe I can get a couple suits out there."

How?

"Captain Cho already thinks Big Bill is up to something. I'll use that."

Don't take any unnecessary risks. I need to know you're...

"Safe?" He regretted the word the moment it left his mouth. Okay, maybe not the word itself but the tone, the sarcasm, that he regretted. "Sorry, I'm tired. It's been a long day."

Pain is tiring. Regrowing a toe requires only a small sleeve.

Worst of it was, she probably thought she was being comforting. Loss of body parts was no big deal in the Corps. *Bam! Lose your head? Just regrow it.* Pain? Pain was an inconvenience. *Suck it up, Marine. You've got a job to do.* Craig knew he was being unfair; he'd seen Torin's reaction, but he was just too tired to care. Losing a body part, even a small insignificant one, might not be a big deal to Gunnery Sergeant Torin Kerr, but it was to him.

"Trust me, I won't provoke the captain."

Good. Her intent to make Cho bleed seeped out around the edges of the word. Craig wasn't one hundred percent positive that if it came to it, he'd be able to stop her. He wasn't one hundred percent positive he wanted to. *Ping me when you've got at least one HE suit moved out into the ore dock. Make it sooner rather than later.*

She took it for granted he'd succeed. He liked that. Braced against the tiles, he bent to wash his legs. "You have a time frame?"

Depends on Ressk.

"He's got to take control of the program."

Programs. Gravity, hatches, and the runners—the cables that'll help control the armory.

"Zero g; it won't weigh anything."

It'll still mass one fuk of a lot.

"Right." They were talking just to hear each other now. Since he knew it, Craig assumed Torin knew it, too. "Well, give me a heads-up and I'll go out with the armory. While you're getting the grapples on it, I'll hit *Promise*'s air lock and be inside before they even notice I'm gone."

This new silence felt different.

"Torin?"

I'm not on Promise. *I'm on Pedro's* Second Star.*

"God fukking damn it, Torin!" So much for her just calling in the Marines. And how nice she didn't mention it until now. "Pedro has kids!"

Pedro's not with us. Her voice gave nothing away. Absolutely nothing. She never pulled that shit on him, never, so if the situation was so bad she couldn't not... Craig shifted into a more stable position as she continued. *I bought the* Star *from him, from the family, because the* Promise *was too badly damaged to use.*

"What? Damaged?"

Cho shot the shit out of it when he took you.

His skin pebbled as a chill slid down his spine. Torin wasn't hiding how she felt about the *Promise*—or Cho's part in it at least. And she'd clearly gone back to the station if she had Pedro's

Star. What would Torin have done when...

"You tried to turn the salvage operators into a ragtag battle fleet, didn't you? I could have told you that wouldn't work."

You weren't there.

"They're not Marines, Torin," he said gently, turning the water off and reaching for a towel. "You can't feel betrayed because they didn't act like Marines."

Not the time to talk about it.

"Granted." He added it to his mental list of things they needed to talk about after the rescue. The list, not exactly short before he'd needed rescuing, had grown to the point where whatever this was between them needed to last for a good long time or they'd never get to everything. He crumbled the towel between his hands and sagged back against the bulkhead. "Torin, where the fuk is my ship?"

*The Wardens have her. Evidence. The damage is external. Structural—not functional. I patched what I could in order to fold her back to the station... *

"You what? Never mind." Not a story he needed to hear now. Even thinking of the possibilities had begun to knock sharp edges onto the throbbing in his skull. "We're going to have to break her out, aren't we?" At the speed the Wardens worked, both he and Torin would be dead of old age before they were ready to release the *Promise* back into his hands.

I'll add it to the list.

Not a big surprise to discover that Torin also had a list. Hers probably involved a lot more hitting and a lot less talking.

We need to break this off. Chance of random scans...

"Right."

Three hours, forty-six minutes and it'll all be over. One way or another.

Craig stared down at the place his toe had been and wished she hadn't added the qualifier.

"Fukking hell, Cap, I have no idea where Doc is." Nat dropped into one of the eight chairs surrounding the big galley table and stared into a mug of coffee like she wasn't entirely certain what it was. "I'm not his fukking mother, am I?"

Cho folded his arms and leaned back against the counter. "How drunk are you?" he growled.

"Not very. I took a party-pooper pill on the way back to the ship. Be sober as a C'tron any minute now."

"And while you were out there drinking, did you remember what I sent you out to do?"

"Sure." The fingertips on the hand she waved were stained with fresh blood. "Find out what Big Bill's up to without giving anything away. Shit, I couldn't do that without drinking because me being in a bar without drinking would raise suspicions you don't want raised. That last one, that was not the first party-pooper pill I took and my stomach would like... oh, fuk." Nat set the mug carefully on the table, stood, walked to the sink, and puked up a thin stream of colorless bile.

Barely maintaining a fingernail grip on his temper, Cho sidestepped farther from the sink as she splashed water into her mouth. "And?"

"And there's a lot more talk of that free merchant crap going on." Nat spat and straightened. "How we're going to change known space and won't they be sorry they were mean to us and boo fukking hoo." She downed a glass of water and belched. "High percentage of them talking that way. Too high to be random."

Now that was information he could extrapolate from. "The people Big Bill has lined up to buy our weapons are gathering."

"If I had to guess, I'd say, yeah."

Cho paced the length of the galley and back, trying to work out Big Bill's plans. He needed to compare the ships in dock to the ships on the list Big Bill had given him. "He's putting together a fleet..."

"Nope. From the sound of it, and given that gunnery sergeant is definitely on the payroll, I'd say he's putting together assault teams." Hissing through her teeth, Nat pulled her fingers out of her hair and wiped them on her hip. "What do you figure he's going to assault, Cap?"

Frowning, Cho juggled the pieces. Smiled as they finally snapped into place. "Stations. Like this one was. Stations with no planetary government, so they're under the Wardens' jurisdiction. The Navy can't attack a station…"

"No way of separating the good guys from the bad guys." Nat nodded, returning to her chair and picking up her mug.

"So they have to negotiate." Cho leaned back against the counter, clutching the edge so tightly the plastic creaked. "It's exactly what I was going to do. But if Big Bill takes enough stations, he'll be negotiating from a position of power. And once he's established, he'll get rid of those ships who didn't sign with him."

"And we're not signing with him, right? But he said you'd have a place in the forefront of the revolution," Nat added before Cho could answer.

"*His* revolution." Cho curled his lip at the thought of being under Big Bill's command. "I don't like being told what to do."

"Okay, so we don't sign with him, but why would he turn us in?"

"Turn us in? To the law? No, he won't do that. Won't risk pissing off his captains. But if we continue to use this station—and he knows there's fuk all other stations we can use—he'll put a surcharge on ships that didn't play his game. We sign to serve under him, or we pay until he owns us anyway."

"That's…" Cho could all but see her ticking the list off in her head. "That sounds possible," she admitted at last. "But, Cap, odds are the armory's not holding the kind of weapons we can arm the ship with. In order to be of any use at all, they've got to be in someone's hands. Someone who gives us money for them. Big Bill's people'll give us the most money because that means he gets the most money. You're willing to make the hard choices, Cap, that's why we ride with you. And because of those choices the paydays have been good so far, but none of us are going to give up this kind of a payday now on the chance, however possible, that Big Bill might screw us down the line."

He should have known it would come down to the payout. He not only made the hard choices, but he was the only one who had any foresight. "If Big Bill controls the market, Big Bill controls the price."

Nat opened her mouth in the pause, then closed it again without speaking, indicating that he should go on. "The whole concept of the *free merchants…*" Cho sketched quotes around the words. "…means more to Big Bill than money, so he has to get the weapons into the right hands. The weapons change everything. This is the one time Big Bill is not going for the immediate payoff." He cut Nat off with a raised hand. "Yes, he'll get his fifteen percent, the fukking universe would be imploding before he gave that up, but he'll get fifteen percent of one fuk of a lot more if his plan works. So Big Bill is screwing you out of part of your payoff because Big Bill is setting the prices."

"Okay, so…" She stared into her mug as if it might have the answers, then up at him as if it actually had. "In order to get the payoff we're entitled to, we need to set the prices."

"Yes." And because Nat had come to it herself, she'd sell it to the rest of the crew. As often as possible, Cho believed in giving orders he knew would be obeyed. Greased the way for those times the orders were less palatable.

"How?"

It all came back to the weapons. "We get the weapons off the station, out of the territory Big Bill controls—it's hard to take a stand when the person you're standing against can turn off the air—and we renegotiate based on how important we know the weapons are to Big Bill's long-term plans."

"Yeah, but if we set the prices, Big Bill can just suggest no one buys."

"He won't. The weapons change everything."

"Okay." She nodded slowly, forehead folding into well-defined lines. "I can see that. But we can't get the armory off the station with the gravity on. Big Bill controls the gravity."

"The armory doesn't matter."

Nat rolled her eyes and slapped both palms down on the table. "Damn it, Cap, I thought the armory was the whole fukking point!"

"The contents of the armory are the whole fukking point. When Nadayki gets the seal open and we have three hours Big Bill doesn't own to unload everything onto the *Heart*."

"So Big Bill's station, not the *Heart*, took the risk of Nadayki blowing the armory," Nat said slowly, "and we end up free and clear with a load of weapons."

It sounded good. Simple. Foolproof. Profitable. "And we

renegotiate a better price. Our price, not Big Bill's."

"Why, Captain Cho," Nat grinned, bloodshot eyes gleaming, "that's practically piracy."

Nat made him feel good about command. Always had. She was never obsequious the way Huirre could be and she always, eventually, understood what he was doing and why. For the first time since that gunnery sergeant had clued him in to Big Bill's betrayal, Cho felt back in control.

The weapons were his, not Big Bill's.

He might sell them to Big Bill's people, he might not. His final decision would be based entirely on whether or not they could pay the price. That was what kept the system they had out here working.

Cho didn't begrudge Big Bill his fifteen percent—not of the weapons, not of the price he got for them—the canny bastard kept the station running, a safe haven in a universe that tried to choke a man with rules, but Big Bill had to learn he didn't control the other eighty-five per...

"Ryder." He managed to stop before slamming the salvage operator to the deck. His eyes were red, face was still bruised, his hair was wet... the man looked like shit. "What the hell are you doing?"

"Looking for you." He swayed in place and laid a palm against the bulkhead. "You think Big Bill's trying to screw you, right?"

"Go on." No point in denying it, Cho realized, Ryder had been right there in the pod when Big Bill had tipped his hand.

"Okay, suppose Big Bill thinks that the hard part's done. The CSO seal is the hinky one; the Marine seal is straightforward in comparison. He convinced a government that this station didn't exist; surely he can get through a Marine seal. Why should he settle for fifteen percent when he can have the whole enchilada?"

"What the hell is an enchilada?"

"When he can have the whole thing," Ryder amended.

"Why do you think...?"

"Weapons change everything," Ryder interrupted flatly.

Cho's eyes widened. His own words, thrown back at him.

"All he has to do is open the exterior hatch," Ryder continued. "Any crew by the pod has sweet fuk all in the way of time to get to the air lock and into the ship. They're sucked into vacuum. Nadayki's brain is explosively decompressed pudding. Result—Big Bill's the only one with the mad skills to get the seal open. And you know what they say: possession is nine tenths, not fifteen percent."

"Fuk him!" Cho snarled. He could see Big Bill spreading his hands and smiling and saying exactly that.

"You can't stop him," Ryder pointed out, and kept going before Cho took off his whole fukking foot for being obvious. "But you can screw him in return. There's a suit hookup right by the storage pod. You put suits in it and they're just hanging there, charging behind closed doors, not giving anything away if Big Bill comes down. But, if the exterior hatch opens…"

"There's no time to get into a suit."

"Those are big heavy doors with a big heavy seal. There's not much time, but there's time."

"Could you do it?" Cho looked him up and down. Right at the moment, Ryder didn't look like he could get into a bunk without falling on his face, but before Almon had started in with his fists, Ryder's body had worn the marks of long hours suited up. "Could you get into a suit in time?"

"Hell, yeah! Why do you think I'm telling you? It's as likely to be my ass on the line as anyone's."

Cho thought for a moment while Ryder sagged against the wall. "Take two suits out and hook them up," he snapped at last, using his voice to jerk Ryder vertical. "One for you, one for Nadayki."

"Oh, no." He actually had the balls to wave a dismissive hand. Cho glared it back down to his side. "Huirre said he was relieving me, that I could get some sleep…"

"That was before you got useful. Nat's in the galley. Have her pull you a stim and, Ryder, if it comes to it, make sure Nadayki gets into a suit or, as you float by, I'll let Almon use you for target practice."

* * *

"No, Gunny," Ressk scrubbed a hand back over his scalp. "Big Bill's got code set up like he expects people to try and crack it. It'll throw alarms. Bastard doesn't trust anyone."

Torin sagged against the bulkhead. "So what you're saying is…"

"I need more time."

"Gunny." Werst's voice out of the comm panel. *"Big Bill's heading across the Hub."*

"Toward the docking bay?"

"There's really no way of telling where the hell he's going until he's gone too far for us to stop him."

"Right." She pushed herself up straight. "Delay him."

"Tell him you want to talk to him?"

"No. He won't wait. He'll expect me to find him." Given it was Werst and Mashona, Torin could think of only one solution. "Start a fight. Make it inclusive."

ELEVEN

The wave of sound hit the moment Torin cracked the hatch from the docking arm. Yelling. Screaming. The soft slam of flesh on flesh and the slightly louder, moister noise of flesh making contact with a harder surface. Given the numbers, a couple of the bars had to have emptied and it looked as though every warm body in the Hub had gotten involved. Those not actually fighting screamed encouragement and made bets. As Torin stepped out of the docking arm and the door closed behind her, a di'Taykan with scarlet hair came flying out of the melee horizontally and took out three of the watchers. All four of them threw themselves back into the fight.

Big Bill stood untouched, chaos bending around him like he was a rock in a stream. He didn't look pleased. Torin caught a glimpse of Mashona over by the falafel cart but couldn't see Werst. Given his size, that wasn't surprising. She couldn't see the Grr brothers either but didn't doubt there'd be a few people using the mayhem to try and get their own back.

"About to charge in and rescue the boss, *trin*?"

"Doesn't look like he needs rescuing." She took another step into the Hub, making more room between her and the bulkhead.

"I need to talk to you," Alamber murmured, sliding into it, his hands on her hips.

"Turn up your masker."

"What?"

Torin would've sighed, but taking a deep breath with the young di'Taykan all but plastered against her back and attempting to influence the situation with unmasked pheromones would have been the definition of a bad idea. "If you want to *talk*, turn up your masker. And make it fast," she added. "I have things to…"

Twisting out of his grip, she grabbed the front of his tunic and yanked him down to the deck as a stool moved through the space they'd just been filling and slammed into the bulkhead.

"…do."

Getting a di'Taykan horizontal was never a problem. Torin took the opportunity to turn up Alamber's masker while they were lying face-to-face. Getting back up again required a jab in a sensitive place.

"Ow!" His hair flattened. "What's your hurry?"

"I told you. I have things to do." She held out a hand and, when he took it, heaved him up onto his feet. The di'Taykan were tall but not usually very heavy, and she still had the benefit of the station's lower gravity. "So talk."

He twitched his tunic back into place, adjusting the layers until it looked exactly like it had when he started as far as Torin was concerned. "It's about your implant," he said, leaning in— although, given the noise level, he could have been shouting and not significantly raised the odds of eavesdroppers.

The Corps installed implants in sergeants and above. As everyone knew who Torin was, the electronics built into her jaw were no secret. She raised a brow.

Alamber's gaze flicked out over the Hub, settled on Big Bill for a moment, then returned to Torin's face, his smile as self-satisfied as a cat's. "I found Nia after you left." He touched the side of his nose.

It seemed Nia's scent, even with her masker turned all the way up, had been stronger than her ambient scent in the room. "And?" Torin prodded, keeping most of her attention on the fight.

"What went on between you and Nia—if I'm not invited to join, well, that's none of my business. But it did make me wonder what you were up to, *trin*, so I checked things out. I could smell Krai by the boards. Not on the boards." Alamber wiggled his fingers triumphantly at her. "He wore gloves but not boots so I know where he stood, I know how he got in. He's good, but he doesn't know the system like I do. I haven't cracked the wave yet, but you're using your ship as an SP, blocking the station's rider. If you've got someone on the side who can crack Big Bill's code—and, hello, you do—I want in on whatever shit you're doing." He pursed his lips in a mockery of a kiss. "Or I tell Big Bill what's up."

"And you haven't already told him because... ?"

His shoulders rose and fell, the movement all grace and faked nonchalance. "Big Bill's got this nasty habit of taking bad news out on the messenger. Just figured I might get a better deal from you."

She didn't have time for this.

"All right, fine. I have to..." Torin yanked him sideways as an unlaced boot slammed into the bulkhead. "...prove I'm invaluable right now, so go to the *Star* and wait for me there."

"Nice try, but I'm going to need the entry codes, *trin*."

"Nice try, but if you don't already have the entry codes, you're of no use to me." As his eyes darkened and he grinned, telling her everything she needed to know, Torin grabbed his shoulder and spun him around to face the hatch. "Go. Ressk's still at the ship. Tell him I sent you."

The moment the door closed behind him, she tongued her implant, direct to the *Star*. "Ressk, Alamber's incoming. Take him out, stuff him in the head. I'll deal with him later."

Take him out? How?

"You're an ex-Marine, his balls have barely dropped. Try not to hurt him." Breaking the connection, she moved into the fight.

Torin could have taken the path of least resistance to Big Bill's side, read the movement of the brawl and put herself where it wasn't, but she'd wanted to hurt someone, had wanted to rip Mackenzie Cho into pieces for so long now that she ducked under a wild blow, drove her shoulder into a beer-stained stomach, straightened, and threw the woman onto a pair of di'Taykan, all three of them kicking and flailing as they hit the deck. Close, but not quite. She blocked a piece of broken kiosk being used as a club, then jabbed stiffened fingers into a solar plexus. Spun and smashed her heel into the side of a knee. Cracked a nose with her elbow. Narrowly missed having a piece bitten out of her forearm, drove it instead in under the chin and stepped over the Krai now gasping for breath to stand at Big Bill's side.

The Grr brothers ensured a relative circle of calm, but the brawl was a mindless beast reputation would not affect. If they fought their way to a hatch, and Torin had to assume they could or they were shit bodyguards, they'd leave Big Bill undefended. No one would go after him deliberately, but in the heat of the moment, *accidents* happened. The space around them suggested a couple of accidents had already tried to happen. Given the amount of blood on the deck, an orange-haired di'Taykan would not be getting up.

One of the brothers licked his fingers clean. The other swallowed and wiped his mouth with the back of his hand.

"Enjoying yourself, Gunnery Sergeant?"

Torin pulled her lips back over her teeth. "I was just heading out to find you. I've finished the designs for training facilities."

"So quickly?"

"Yes, well…" She swept a disdainful glance over the crowd, noted that Mashona had worked her way out of the fight and stood watching, drink in hand, with a group from one of the bars, Werst was happily dancing around a di'Taykan and two Humans directly in front of the decompression hatch leading toward the ore docks, and… Torin frowned as a vaguely familiar Human male caught her gaze. His expression lifted the hair off the back of her neck—it was recognition on a macro scale. Not of her personally, but of what he thought she was. What. Not who. When she turned toward him, he disappeared behind a clump of di'Taykan. Trained instincts said *follow him*, but the situation required her to remain where she was. "If this lot is any indication," she continued, the pause lost in the continuing chaos, "then the sooner they begin training the better."

"No argument," Big Bill sighed, arms folded. "Can you stop it?"

"It? This?" Good question. If they were Marines, or even Navy, then yes. She could stop the fight and temporarily stop a few hearts. No one made senior NCO without having learned to sound like a lifetime of authority figures all rolled into one—parents, teachers, *jernil*, bosses, *sheshan*. No problem being heard either as Torin would bet high that Big Bill could patch his slate into the Hub's screens. Unfortunately, this lot was not predominantly military.

However…

"Fights like this have a limited duration." Turning a gesture into a signal for Werst to break it off, Torin snorted. "With no actual goal…" She frowned. "I assume they're not fighting *for* something?"

One of the Grr brothers snorted.

The other one said, "Never are. Fighting for shits and giggles. Scoring points. An opportunity for cheap revenge. More assholes than usual, that's all."

Sounded like a definitive sitrep to Torin. "If that's the case, then it won't last much longer."

Areas of the Hub had already devolved to groaning and bleeding and, given the number of slates out among the spectators, payoffs had clearly begun. Without Werst's involvement, the Human and one of the di'Taykan had slumped down to the deck in front of the hatch, looking miserable. The second di'Taykan continued to yell something about family honor and, possibly, ducks, but no one paid any attention.

Torin could see two dead—besides the di'Taykan the Grr brothers had killed. There might be more among the sprawled bodies, but those three she was certain of. She'd given the order to start the fight they'd died in. Not the first time… but the first time she didn't give a H'san's ass.

"I think it's safe enough now for you to move on." She turned so that Big Bill got her full attention. In order to stop him from heading to the ore docks, she had to become his primary focus. "Do we go to your office or the smelter to discuss these plans?"

"I was on my way to the ore docks."

Past tense. She had him. "Success?"

He seemed amused by her oblique question. Not a problem. He could be amused by whatever the hell he wanted as long as he continued to focus on her. "No, not yet. But I thought it best, given the contents, to do what I could to remove foolish temptation."

"Because that kind of content changes things, and Cho might screw you over if you're not there when it opens?"

His brows rose. "I have every faith in Captain Cho to keep to our agreement."

Torin kept her tone matter-of-fact. "He's a thief and a murderer, and you assume he's not a liar?"

"Harsh words, Gunnery Sergeant. I begin to think you don't like Captain Cho."

"Thief and murderer," Torin repeated. "That's his business, but given his business, having you and the contents together in one isolated place might be more temptation than he could resist." Were she doing the job she signed on for, she'd be telling him exactly the same thing.

Big Bill indicated the two Krai, now looking speculatively at the closest body. "I won't be alone."

"You don't allow weapons on the station, but that's no guarantee Cho won't have weapons on his ship. If he takes out the three of you, who's left to go after him?"

"You?"

Torin shook her head. "I just got here. Cho won't assume I'm a sure thing."

"She's right, Boss."

Big Bill stared at the Grr brothers in surprise. "If you're taking her side because she owns your souls, remember who owns your asses."

"Not taking her side," said one.

"But she's right," said the other.

"All right, you two go down to the ore docks. The gunnery sergeant and I will go to my office and look over her designs. Happy?"

Torin wouldn't have called the expressions the Grr brothers exchanged *happy*.

Craig got slowly to his feet as the hatch from the station into the ore dock opened. With only a maximum of two hours and seven minutes remaining, he was expecting Torin. He got Doc.

"And the level of bugfuk crazy rises to code red," he muttered, watching the other man cross toward the ship. No way he could have been heard, but Doc paused, glanced over at the storage pod, then changed direction.

When he got close enough, Craig realized he looked weirdly peaceful.

"How's your foot?"

"The one you cut the toe off?" Craig couldn't stop himself from glancing down. "It hurts like fuk, thanks for asking."

"If fukking hurts, you're doing it wrong," Nadayki called from inside the pod.

"He sounds chipper." Doc dropped into a squat and gently angled Craig's foot so that he could see the wound.

"Yeah." Craig fought the urge to pull his foot free and plant it in Doc's face. "Apparently, the Marine Corps can kiss the kid's lime-green ass; he owns their code."

"Good for him," Doc said absently as he examined the place Craig's toe had been. "I don't approve of you removing the dressing, but the seal's holding. Edges look good." Strong thumbs barely skimmed along Craig's instep. "There's a lot of bruising…"

"It's not bruising, mate. My foot's always been purple." He frowned. "And green."

"Well, I apologize for the inadvertent damage caused by my grip."

"You what? You cut off my fukking toe and you're apologizing for inadvertent damage?"

"I intended to cut off your toe—Captain's orders. I didn't intend to bruise the rest of your foot." Setting Craig's foot carefully back on the deck, Doc straightened, tucking a strand of hair back behind his ear. "If there's time, I'll replace the sealant."

"If there's time? You going somewhere?" It had to be Doc leaving; there was no point in replacing the sealant if they intended to dump him out an air lock. Craig had *seen* the condition Rogelio Page had been left in.

"I don't know. Hope so." His mouth twisted into something that didn't exactly resemble a smile, and as he turned, he said quietly, "It's funny."

Craig couldn't stop himself. "What is?"

For a moment, it seemed Doc wasn't going to answer, then he

stopped and shrugged, the *why the fuk not* almost audible. "It's funny where you find the things you've lost. Always the last place you think to look."

"Well, yeah. Because then you stop looking."

Doc stiffened, pivoted on one heel, his pale-blue eyes flashing a more familiar, crazy-ass expression in Craig's direction. But all he said was, "Good point."

Craig watched until the air-lock door closed behind the other man and the telltales were red again, then he drew in a deep breath and let it out slowly. "Okay," he muttered. "That was weird."

"That was Doc. He'll lovingly heal you so that you're in good enough shape for him to beat to death."

Leaning around the edge of the hatch, Craig found Nadayki kneeling in front of the seal to give his back a break. "You don't even know what I was talking about."

"Doesn't matter." The young di'Taykan twisted just far enough to sneer at Craig, his eyes light. "It's Doc, so weird only ever means one thing; it's the point where medic and maniac overlap. Either/or, that's one thing, but both..." His hair flicked out. "Both at one time is too fukking weird. Too weird for fukking," Nadayki added with a snort. "I don't think he's gotten laid since me and my *thytrins* joined the crew. That explains a lot."

It would to a di'Taykan, that was for sure. "Don't you have work to do?"

Nadayki flipped him a very Human gesture and bent back over the seal.

The sound of the hatch opening pulled Craig out of the storage pod. He didn't recognize the two Krai swaggering across the ore dock toward him, but he'd definitely got the impression this area wasn't open to all and sundry, so they had to be down here for a reason. Something about them pinged, but they were almost to the pod before he realized what it was.

Doc moved like danger barely contained. Like he had nothing to prove.

These two moved like they were more than willing to prove how dangerous they were. Doc's movements blown large.

Craig grinned. Torin would say it was like the difference between an NCO and an officer.

When they stopped in front of him, he realized that not all the mottling on their faces was natural. He resisted the need to touch the purpling on his own face and waited. They looked at him. They looked around. One of them went around him and looked into the storage pod while the other seemed to be deciding how he'd taste with a nice red sauce.

Then Thing Two called Thing One away from the pod, pointed at Craig, and said something in Krai. Craig knew the same Krai most non-Krai did—the profanities—and recognized none of what had just been said.

Or any part of the reply. Although he knew better than to generalize with other species, it sounded like Thing One disagreed.

Thing Two reiterated.

Thing One stared at Craig for a long moment, nose ridges opening and closing slowly, and said something that sounded very much like a solid maybe.

And then they both gave him a look that involved red sauce.

Fuk it.

"Can I help you, mate?"

"Big Bill sent us," smirked one.

"To keep an eye on things," sneered the other.

And apparently, that was all they felt had to be said. Given the choke hold Big Bill had on the station, it probably was. Either the captain's paranoia was justified and Big Bill was up to something, or Big Bill suspected Cho was up to something. At first glance, the second option seemed more likely if only because Craig knew Cho *was* up to something. Upon reflection, the first was just as likely if less absolute.

Honor among thieves was a myth.

Apparently satisfied that Nadayki was doing what he was supposed to, they wandered off to examine the head and the storage lockers. They snapped the sink down out of the bulkhead then back up again. They opened every door, every drawer, stared at the HE suits, turned to stare at Craig.

Craig leaned back against the pod. He didn't have to explain. Captain Cho had ordered the suits out onto the dock. They could take it up with him if they didn't like it.

Then Thing One, looking right at him, lifted the sleeve of one of the suits, and bared his teeth. Thing Two laughed. *Wouldn't it be funny if I took a bite out of this?*

"Be funny if you fukking choked on it," Craig muttered, then nearly jumped out of his skin as Nadayki closed a hand around his arm and leaned in close.

"Shut up, you ass. You don't know who they are."

Barely audible in spite of proximity, he sounded truly freaked, the ends of his hair tracing short, jerky arcs against Craig's cheek. Craig bit back his initial reaction and said at the same volume, "So tell me."

"The Grr brothers."

"The Grr brothers? You're shitting me, right?"

"I wish. If Big Bill wants somebody eaten, and not in a fun way, they're the ones who do it."

"Eaten?"

"Yeah." Craig felt as much as heard Nadayki swallow. "And I heard they like it better if the food's still screaming."

"That's... unpleasant." And over the top. And, frankly, trying way too hard. Maybe they were scary to a station full of losers who couldn't live within the broad parameters of the law, but Craig had seen Torin's face when she'd learned the polynumerous plastic aliens were using war as a social laboratory, and these two, they didn't know shit about being scary.

"Big Bill's sent them down here to keep an eye on things. He must know I'm going to be done early."

"How?"

"What?"

"How would he know?" Craig brushed an agitated lime-green veil away from his face. "Who's going to tell him?"

"He could be listening in."

Craig thought about the captain voicing his suspicions about Big Bill's plans. "He'd have a bigger reaction than just those two if he's been listening in. Besides, no signal in the pod."

"Hardwired."

"It's a storage pod for explosives, kid. It's a big box with reinforced walls."

"Okay, you're so fukking smart, why are they here?"

Still messing about the storage cabinets, the Grr brothers—and Craig had trouble even thinking that with a straight face—had found the abandoned tools. One of them was swinging the broken pipe wrench in lazy circles while the other sorted through the screwdrivers and ignored him. "Best guess, Big Bill's a paranoid s.o.b. That, and there's fuk all honor among thieves."

"Honor and a credit will buy you a bowl of *seesu*," Nadayki snarled. "We're coming out on top of this, not Big Bill."

"Hadn't you better get back to work, then?"

"Har vena ser shetinan!"

"Not after what happened the last time, kid." Any other di'Taykan standing that close would have grabbed his ass before heading back into the storage pod. It would have been instinctive, expected even given their positions. Watching Thing One toss the wrench aside while Thing Two bitched about wasting time in the ass end of the station, Craig wondered if maybe this time it wasn't the di'Taykan but the situation. These two really had the kid freaked. His mouth went dry as he remembered Huirre crunching down on his toe. On the other hand, maybe the kid had reason to be freaked.

He should give the captain a heads-up.

His hand was actually on his slate before he realized what he was doing.

He wasn't really crew. He didn't owe Captain Cho shit.

"I have to admit, I was expecting something more complicated." Big Bill folded his arms and stared at the plans for the smelter up on the big screen. "This is… basic. Except for the range, it looks more like a classroom than a place to train warriors."

Warriors? Torin took a moment to temper her response. And then another moment, just to be on the safe side. "They won't be learning how to charge in, guns blazing. Any idiot can do that and get themselves trapped between decompression hatches breathing vacuum."

"HE suits…"

"Because multiple crews emerging from docking arms all

suited up won't look at all suspicious."

"I don't think I like your tone."

Torin tried to look like she cared. "If you want to take over a station, you have to realize that the weapons in the hands are incidental to the weapons between the ears."

He shook his head and blanked the screen. "We don't want them too well armed, Gunnery Sergeant. They'll point their weapons where they're told."

"You still don't understand. When I'm done with them, they'll *be* weapons—head and hand. You'll be pointing them. What they want won't matter."

He stared at her for a long moment. "You can do that?" he said at last.

"I can." She could. She wasn't going to, but she could.

"And they just let you wander around loose?" He started with a snicker, then his response evolved into a full-out laugh.

Torin fought down another urge to punch him in the throat. And then considered the implication. The Grr brothers were down in the ore docks about as far away from Big Bill as they could get and still be on the station. If she killed him, what would they do? Would they know? Could she show up and send them away, passing on Big Bill's orders because of a sudden glitch in his implant? No, the paranoid bastard would have put contingency plans in place if the Grr brothers couldn't reach him. Given the Grr brothers, that plan would likely be violent, and Craig was in the ore dock.

She couldn't risk making things more complicated than they already were.

"Gunnery Sergeant, I am very glad you found your way to my corner of known space." Big Bill wiped his eyes with one hand and activated his desk with the other. "But now, if you don't mind, I have work of my own to do. Why don't you wander around and get to know the place a little better."

"I'd like to go down to the ore dock and check the security."

"Why?"

"We have a perfectly good armory. During training, it can be used to secure the weapons."

"I think you forget, Gunnery Sergeant, these are not Marines.

They'll have bought their weapons from Captain Cho."

Torin frowned as she worked through the variables. William Ponner was too smart to let his free merchants loose on his station, armed. He had to have come up with a way to control them because his fifteen percent of the armory's contents wouldn't be enough to…

"They'll own their weapons," she told him. "But you'll own the ammunition."

She thought he was going to deny it for a moment, then he bared his teeth in what wasn't a smile. "You're right. The ammunition won't be remaining in the ore docks, but here, where I can personally keep an eye on it."

"You think Cho will agree to that particular fifteen percent?"

"Mackenzie Cho, Gunnery Sergeant, is ambitious. Too ambitious for the Navy. He wants to make the decisions. He wants to command and I can give him what he wants. He'll be at the forefront of big changes, or he'll be a sad remnant of a system that didn't work. I think he'll come to see things my way."

"What if he's too ambitious for you?"

"Then he can leave. The way he left the Navy. But if you're that set on not trusting him, go to the ore docks by all means. I'll tell the Grr brothers you're relieving them. They do have other work. Supporting social change is all very well, but accounts won't collect themselves."

For a change, there wasn't so much as an argument in the Hub as Torin crossed through on her way to the ore docks. The dead were gone. The injured from crews without their own medics were no doubt off paying through broken noses to use Big Bill's staff and facilities. A couple of the kiosk owners had their heads together, probably complaining about damages, and two of the smaller cleaners were working their way around the deck doing an inadequate job of dealing with blood splatter, but otherwise things were quiet.

As Torin moved into the first corridor past the decompression doors, she tongued her implant. "Report."

Werst and I are bruised but back on board, Gunny. Mashona

sounded tired. Given how little sleep she'd gotten, no surprise. *Ressk says he's nearly got control of the subroutines.*

"I'm on my way to the ore docks. I need a value for nearly."

Soon, Gunny. Ressk's teeth snapped together, the closest he could get to telling her to leave him the hell alone.

"Hour and forty-one minutes and they'll have the fukker open," Torin growled. "Make it *sooner*."

Craig was sitting on something low by the open storage pod. One of the Grr brothers sat beside him, slate out, the other she couldn't see, so he was either in the head or the pod. It was unlikely he'd go any farther away from what Big Bill had sent them to keep an eye on.

She could feel Craig's gaze on her as she crossed toward him, but she split her attention between noting the exact location of the HE suits, the distance from the storage pod to the exterior hatch, the red lights on the air-lock plate leading to the *Heart of Stone,* and the one Grr brother she could see.

The second emerged from the pod as she reached it. Craig stood, moving carefully—not so much in pain as in anticipation of pain. He'd been sitting on an overturned bucket.

"The great thing about low tech," she said, nodding toward the bucket. "Multiple uses."

"So I've discovered."

His eyes were still bloodshot, but they were bright and focused. With no chance for sleep, he had to have taken a stim. Good. His exhaustion was one less thing for her to deal with. Moving so she could see both Grr brothers put her well within Craig's personal space, but it was a minor thing and a minor comfort and fuk it.

"What?" she demanded as one of them stared up at her, nose ridges flared. "Big Bill told you I was coming down."

"Yeah." He blinked and turned to his brother, nose ridges closing. "You were right."

"Told you." The second Grr put his slate away. When he closed his nose ridges as well, Torin shifted her weight forward onto the balls of her feet. Things were not looking good.

"Apart, it's not so obvious."

"Together, though…"

"Yeah."

"He had hair then."

"True."

"What are the odds that Gunnery Sergeant Torin Kerr would show up on the station where the salvage operator who went outside of known space to find her has been taken?"

It was the longest statement Torin had heard from either of them.

That's a very good question, Gunnery Sergeant. Big Bill's voice boomed in her head. One or both of the Grr brothers must have pinged him. *Care to answer it?*

"Big *serley* coincidence," one Grr brother smirked, lips pulled back off his teeth.

"Is your name Gunnery Sergeant Kerr?" Torin snapped.

They blinked in unison and stepped back, squaring their shoulders. They'd been Corps, for however short a time, conditioned to respond to that tone.

I'm waiting. Big Bill had not.

"They're wrong." They were moving forward again, although looking more embarrassed by their response than particularly fierce. "I've never seen him before in my life."

Kill him.

She must have reacted because Craig started to reach for her. When she shook her head, he let his arm fall back down by his side. "I don't kill on your command."

You might not.

The Grr brothers jumped for Craig; one aiming high, one low. As they passed, Torin grabbed a handful of their tunics, shifted her weight to her left leg, and spun around it, throwing them across the ore dock. In spite of their previous interactions, they hadn't expected her to react so quickly, but with one in each hand, she couldn't get a lot of distance. They hit, rolled...

Get your souls back, boys.

...and charged.

Gunny! I've got control!

"Cut the gravity!" As the gravity cut out, she folded into a crouch, then snapped her legs down, pushing straight up from the deck as the Grr brothers' momentum kept them moving toward where she'd been. Big Bill's last order had made this personal, so she had no worries they'd go after Craig while she was still alive. "Ressk! Secure the *Heart's* air lock!" She didn't need any more players in the game, and the last thing she wanted right now was to have her speculation about the possibility of the *Heart* having weapons on board to prove prophetic.

Both Krai recovered quickly. Torin waited until they'd committed to a trajectory, then pushed off one of the overhead railings and shot past them.

Except there were two of them. Using his brother as a launch pad, the other one headed right for her...

The gravity came back on.

Torin heard Ressk swear just before impact. Big Bill had regained control.

"Ryder! What the fuk is going on out there?"

Craig watched Torin get her hands under her and push herself up onto her knees. Breath knocked out of her then, not hurt. He wanted to go to her, but she wouldn't thank him for getting into the middle of the fight. He yanked his borrowed slate off his belt. As long as Nadayki was in the pod, Cho had a potential weapon on the dock. Not a great one, but even useless shits could turn the tide. "It's the Grr brothers, Captain!"

"I know it's the fukking Grr brothers! Nadayki told me." Yeah, big surprise; the little shit squealed at the drop of a hat. *"What the hell are they doing!"*

"Fighting! With the gunnery sergeant."

"She knows you!"

Fuk Nadayki's fukking ears! Had Torin admitted... He ran over everything he could remember of Torin's conversation with Big Bill. No, she hadn't. "The Grr brothers are causing trouble. They don't like that she's in tight with Big Bill."

"Then why is she supposed to kill you?"

"Not me, them!"

"Nadayki said..."

"He misheard! I was standing right beside her." Craig aimed

for Cho's ego, not exactly a difficult target to hit even for a civilian. "You were right! Big Bill's up to something!"

I fukking knew it!

"Captain, I can't get the air lock open." Nose ridges flared, Huirre ran through the sequence again. "Outer doors are under station control!"

"That son of a bitch!" Big Bill was going after the weapons. Cho had known it all along. Known from the start that anyone who stole an entire station from the government wouldn't settle for fifteen percent. Turned out they did want the same thing. "Dysun!" Cho slapped a hand down on the intercom by the hatch. "Dysun, haul ass out of your rack and get this hatch open."

"What? Captain, I don't..."

"You will! You want to see your share for those weapons, you'll get your ass to your board now! Get the *tasiks*," Cho snarled at Huirre, pivoted on one heel, and headed for the control room. "I want Doc out there with you the moment the door is open. If Big Bill wants a fight, he's got one!"

"Ressk!"

Working on it, Gunny!

The Grr brothers had been farther from the deck when the gravity kicked in, but they were Krai and Krai bones bounced. Torin rolled up onto her feet, aimed a kick at the closer brother, missed his head, hit his shoulder, and twisted out of the way at the last second. She couldn't let them grapple. Once they got a hand or foothold, teeth would be next. Pain and physical damage aside, no one reacted well to being eaten alive. She had to use her greater reach and hope like hell she could use one of them to disable the other. Again.

Her odds went up if Ressk regained control. As a species, the Krai might be naturals in zero g but in specific, she'd had a lot more training.

* * *

When the gravity kicked out, Craig anchored himself on the edge of the storage pod. He could hear Nadayki flailing and cursing inside the pod, and he realized the kid would have no trouble knifing either him or Torin in the back should Cho command it. Nadayki had to be dealt with before Cho remembered he wasn't permanently attached to the armory.

Even injured, Craig could take the kid in a fight. He was bigger, stronger, and although he had little experience with the kind of up-close-and-personal violence Torin excelled at, Nadayki had even less. Craig could take him down, tie him up with his own overalls, and when Ressk opened the outer doors, the kid would die. Sure, Nadayki was low on the list for di'Taykan of the year, his blood sure as fuk not worth bottling, but he had to give him a fair go.

When the gravity came back in, a moment later, he took his weight on his good foot then hopped over the lip into the pod, grabbing Nadayki's upper arm. "Come on, kid, move!"

Eyes dark, the young di'Taykan struggled but couldn't break Craig's grip. "Let go of me, you *senak*!"

"No, like it or not, I'm pulling your head out of your ass!" Craig shook him hard, lime-green hair flicking back and forth against the motion. "They've already fukked with the zero g; what happens if they vent the atmosphere next? I've seen a di'Taykan sucking vacuum and it's not pretty."

Nadayki shoved his slate into Craig's face. "Fuk you! I'm almost done!"

"Is getting this thing open worth dying for?" Craig demanded. "You think Cho would die for you? He's locked himself in the *Heart*—all safe and warm—and he's locked us—you and me—out here!"

"No way!" Twisting free, Nadayki pushed Craig aside, surged out the hatch, and stared toward the ship. Even with Human vision, the lockdown was obvious from the storage pod. "That *ablin gon savit*!"

"That's what I'm trying to tell you!" Craig grabbed his arm again. "Come on, if we can't get onto the ship, we go out into the station."

Nadayki's gaze flicked over to where Torin and the Grr

brothers were fighting. "But they said you're with her!"

"Right now, in the interest of not dying, I'm with you! Move!" He tightened his grip and hauled Nadayki around until he faced in the right direction. "We need to get the hell out of here before the crazy bastards finish with her and start on us!" Ignoring the fight, trusting Torin to survive, he hustled Nadayki across the ore dock to the hatch, cutting him off every time he tried to speak, finally shoving him through and slamming the hatch behind him.

Entry from the station to the ore docks had to be cleared through the station sysop. Craig doubted Big Bill felt much like opening doors right now.

He glanced at the big doubles, hoped Big Bill wasn't willing to sacrifice the Grr brothers for the win, and headed at his top speed toward the storage lockers and the suits.

One of the Grr brothers couldn't see out of his right eye, and the other…

Torin stomped down hard.

…had at least two broken toes.

He screamed.

She ducked under an attack and came up off the deck, driving her stiffened fingers into his throat. Not a move the Krai were familiar with as opponents tended to stay the hell away from their mouths. Clearly, they hadn't been paying enough attention as she'd fought her way across the Hub. As his eyes widened and blood gushed out his mouth, he grabbed a handful of her hair.

Torin twisted under his grip, turned a little too slowly to meet the other Grr's charge, raised her arm to block…

…and got sprayed with blood as Craig slammed him in the back of the head.

His teeth snapped shut.

The impact took them both to the deck.

"Torin!"

"I'm okay." They heaved the limp body off her together, and then Craig held out a hand. Torin didn't need it, but she took it anyway and let him help her up to her feet.

"You're bleeding."

She was covered in blood. "This isn't mine."

"On your arm?" He gently bent her right arm up closer to her face, his fingers warm around her wrist.

Her sleeve flapped loose, about four square centimeters of cloth missing, a smaller piece bitten out of her forearm. Adrenaline still buzzing through her system, Torin could hardly feel the injury but, later, it was going to hurt. "Okay, this is mine. But it's minor." She could use the arm. Right now, that was all that mattered. "Your foot?"

"Old news." He looked worried, relieved. And there. Right there. Right in front of her. When the corners of his mouth curved up, slowly, as though he wasn't sure this was real, Torin felt as though one of the Grr brothers had chewed a piece out of her heart, not her arm. She could feel each beat, and it hurt. Craig released her wrist and laid his palm lightly against her chest, as though he knew. "I'd kiss you, but you're covered in blood."

"Something to look forward to, then." Her smile felt too wide, awkward, but she couldn't dial it back. "What did you hit him with?"

"Pipe wrench." Brows up, he lifted his other hand. Blood dripped from the heavy curved end of the tool. "Wasn't sure you'd want me to get involved."

"No, it's good." She took a deep breath and all of a sudden it was. It was very good. "I'm all for you participating in your own rescue."

He grinned and let the wrench drop to the deck. "Fuk it, what's a little mess."

Gunny!

Torin jerked back just before Craig's mouth touched hers. "It's Ressk."

Craig rolled his eyes. "Yeah, the little mood killer's patched me through."

I've got the hatch, but Big Bill's unlocked the Heart!*

"You need Nadayki for this, Captain." Dysun's eyes were nearly black as she worked both index fingers over the screen of her slate. "This is more his sort of shit."

"Well, I don't have Nadayki, do I?" Cho snarled. "Or his shit." He'd dragged Dysun down to the air-lock controls when she'd been unable to free up the system from her board. Not that it had helped. Useless! They were all fukking useless! "Nadayki is out there on the other side of the…"

The telltales turned green.

"Finally!"

Dysun lifted both hands, eyes lightening. "It wasn't me."

"I don't care who it was. Doc! Huirre!" They each held a *tasik,* and the fingers of Doc's free hand kept folding into a fist and unfolding again. Cho doubted he knew he was doing it. Huirre had been less than enthusiastic about joining the fight until Cho'd reminded him his share of the weapons' sale was at stake. He watched them step into the air lock. Watched the door close.

"Outer door opening… Closing again!" Huirre sounded freaked. *"Hey! What the fuk are you…"*

"Outer doors have closed and locked again, Captain." Dysun slapped her thumb repeatedly against the screen. "Looks like the signal's coming from the station sysop. No one can crack Big Bill's system."

"You can't," Cho sneered, tried of hearing excuses. "That doesn't mean no one can. Huirre, report!"

"Doc's out. Shoved me, threw away his tasik *and squeezed through at the last second. He looked weird. Even for Doc."*

"Captain," Dysun's eyes were dark again when she looked up, and her hair flicked back and forth in short jerky arcs. "A body in the path of the door, even a moving body, should have stopped the door from closing."

Vacuum being what it was, air locks had safeties built into their safeties; everyone knew that. Everyone also knew who'd programmed Vrijheid. William Fukking Ponner.

"What part of 'Big Bill's trying to screw us' did you miss?" Cho snarled, rubbing his hands together. "Get that air lock open!"

Hostiles incoming, Gunny! I don't have control of the inner hatches.
Torin pivoted around toward the exit to the station. Interior

decompression hatches had access panels on both sides. "We can jam it from here."

*It's complicated, you'll have to… *

"Smash the panel."

Yeah, that'll work.

"Good." Torin bent to pick up the wrench, but Craig's hand on her arm dragged her back upright, and turned her in time to see the *Heart's* air lock close behind a Human male. Not very tall, broad shoulders, long dark hair. Vaguely familiar.

"It's Doc," Craig said quietly. "He's crazy. And when I say crazy, I mean certifiable. He was a doctor, an actual Navy doctor. His ship got destroyed, and it broke him. Literally broke him in two. There's the medic side and the likes-to-see-you-bleed side. And the likes-to-see-you-bleed side, it doesn't lose."

"What ship?"

"What ship? I have no idea." Craig scooped up the wrench and held it two-handed, across his body. "Does it matter?"

Torin shrugged, then continued the movement, working the stiffness out of her shoulders. "It might have. Go jam the hatch. I've got this."

"Why? Because he was military, you think you have to face him alone?"

Maybe. He wasn't Corps, but still… he'd been broken by his service and that made him her responsibility. It was entirely possible Craig knew she believed that; not that it mattered.

"No." She met his gaze and held it. "Because if Big Bill sends more of his people in after us, we're fukked." After a long moment, a moment she wouldn't have granted anyone else, Craig nodded. Acknowledged her point. "Torin, Doc is… he's good at violence."

"So am I." She managed half a smile. "Your tax dollars at work."

He wanted to say more, but he nodded again and started toward the hatch, half hopping, half hobbling, most of his weight on his right foot.

Torin had almost forgotten his injury—pushed it to the back of her mind while she did what she had to. Injuries weren't unusual in her old job; dealt with and the job went on. She didn't much like that she kept forgetting Craig was a noncombatant.

As Doc came closer, Torin realized where she'd seen him before. Most recently, watching the fight in the Hub, but before that, heading into the bar, into the game, where Nat Forester had set them up.

No mistaking the tension that pleated the soft skin around his eyes. Ex-military—the tells were obvious to anyone who'd spent as much time in uniform as Torin had—with the look of someone who'd seen too much and not been able to let any of it go. He was the first person she'd met since getting out that she wasn't entirely positive she could beat if it came to a fight.

As much as Torin wanted to destroy anyone who had a part in Crag's abuse, she forced reason past reaction. Not fighting this man would be the smart thing to do.

"We don't have to get into this," she began.

"Yes, we do." For all the teeth showing, there was nothing Krai-like about Doc's smile. It was a very Human smile. The last time Torin had seen that particular expression, she'd been looking in a mirror. "I've been waiting for you."

"For me?"

He shrugged and continued closing the distance between them. "For someone like you."

His eyes were a flat emotionless blue, not gleaming in anticipation. He wasn't going into this fight for the fun of it; he was the deadly serious kind of bugfuk crazy. The kind that would methodically torture Rogelio Page. The kind who would cut off a man's toe when ordered to so that the pain would teach him his place.

"Everyone figures the military broke him…"

Torin shifted her weight. This would not be a long fight, and only one of them would survive it. She noted the minor damage she'd already suffered as potential weak points she'd have to guard. Her heart began to beat faster. In all honesty, she was just as glad he hadn't backed down.

Unfortunately, time was on his side. She couldn't wait for him to make the first move.

Doc blocked her kick, dropped, and slid under her leg. Torin twisted on the ball of her foot and the side of his fist slammed into the meaty part of her thigh instead of the joint. When she pushed off his shoulders in order to flip around and face him again, he dropped further. She used her weight to drive him into the deck, but he tucked his feet under his body and threw himself backward.

She kneed him in the kidneys. Rolled clear.

He rolled with her, crushing the fingers of her right hand against the deck.

Her kick knocked him back just far enough to free her hand, spraying the deck with blood from the split along a cracked cheekbone.

They scrambled back up onto their feet and Torin blocked a body blow. He lunged sideways and her stiffened left hand jabbed into his shoulder instead of his throat.

His arm spasmed. His other hand closed around her wrist.

Lubricated by the blood from the earlier bite, she twisted in his grip, negating most of the torque, and slammed her forehead into his nose.

His knee came up, hard. Torin felt a rib crack, but she moved with the blow and slammed the point of her other elbow into the thinner bone at his temple.

He staggered and released her but got an arm up in time to stop her from taking out his right eye—a blow actually intended to distract from the hard one, two, three jab to the solar plexus. His mouth opened, but no sound emerged and, fighting for breath, he fell to the deck.

Swiping at the blood dripping from her forehead, Torin gasped, "Stay down."

Doc didn't have breath enough to laugh, but he tried it anyway.

Teeth bloody, he surged forward, curve of his shoulders tucked under her knees, weight slamming her to the deck. Torin wrapped her legs around his neck, rolled up, and wrapped her right arm around, his chin nestled in the cup of her palm, her fingers curled uselessly against his cheek. She ignored the blow that broke the damaged rib and twisted.

The crack was loud.

Doc grunted. And exhaled.

And went limp.

* * *

"Okay, the atmosphere's a match so I'm slaving the outside hatch to the inside and seeing if working them in unison will…"

Both hatches opened.

Ignoring Dysun's self-congratulatory babbling, Cho pushed past Huirre and charged out into the ore dock.

Doc would…

Doc wouldn't.

Doc dropped to the deck like a useless piece of crap, body collapsing into the boneless sprawl of the newly dead. Big Bill's gunnery sergeant stood.

Cho rocked to a stop.

Wiping away the blood that continued dripping from her forehead, right arm pressed against her ribs, right hand cradled against her chest, Torin turned toward the sound of running footsteps.

Mackenzie Cho stood staring, eyes wide, mouth open, about five meters from his air lock.

Torin smiled and started toward him.

Doc had done the damage, but Cho had given the orders. Time to make Cho pay.

The look the gunnery sergeant had been shooting him earlier in the storage pod had been Doc's *crazy under control* look. This look, this matched Doc's crazy out of control on every point— only Cho had never seen it directed at him. This look didn't say, *I'm going to kill you.* It said, *You're a dead man.*

No doubt. No question.

Absolute certainty.

He needed to run. Run now.

He couldn't move, held in place by the awareness of his approaching death.

Where the hell was Huirre? Huirre had the *tasiks*. Huirre

should be here, beside him. He shouldn't be standing alone, that's why he had fukking crew!

"Torin!"

Ryder. Still closer to the hatch than the gunnery sergeant but quickly closing the distance between them. To Cho's surprise, the gunnery sergeant jerked to a reluctant stop.

Craig hadn't expected Torin to stop. He'd hoped. If he'd had time, he'd have prayed, but he hadn't expected it.

When she turned, he wished he was closer. Wished he was far enough away he couldn't see the look on her face.

"Don't." No need for him to elaborate. They both knew what he meant.

Torin spat a mouthful of blood out onto the deck. "He deserves…"

"Not arguing." Almost to her now, Craig cut her off. "But what he deserves and what you should do about it… Torin, it's not who you are. It's not what you are."

Her expression was pure Doc. Her mouth twisted into something that in no way resembled a smile. "I've killed before."

"I know." Here and now, there were three bodies on the deck. Although he'd killed one of them and wasn't going to think too hard about that until they'd come out the other side of a Susumi fold and were safely away. "But there's a difference between killing and…" Fuk! He sketched meanings in the air. "…*killing*."

Torin knew what Craig meant. Probably better than he did. The differences between *killing officers* and *murdering officers* had come with Humans into space. Had come with the Krai and with the di'Taykan. Professionals recognized the difference.

Cho was the latter.

He'd used Doc, used the broken pieces of the man as a weapon.

Cho had taken the chance Craig had offered, turned, run for the *Heart*. Torin could order Ressk to secure the air lock. Hell, she could probably use the rage still sizzling under her skin and catch the son of a bitch before he reached the air lock. Make him pay for… for everything. For Sirin and Jan. For Sergeant Rogelio Page. For the destruction of the *Promise*.

For Craig. For taking him. For everything that had happened to him.

For Doc, when it came down to it.

Gunny! Werst sounded like he'd been trying to get her attention for a while. *Ressk has control, but it won't last. What do you want him to do?*

That depended on what she was going to do, didn't it?

"…you give us…" *Mashona looked at Ressk. Ressk looked at Werst. Werst half shrugged, making the usual Krai cock-up of the movement.* "…grounding. Direction."

But Torin had heard, Something to believe in, *in the pause.*

All those years at war and she'd never hated the enemy. She'd done what she had to in order to complete the mission and get her people out alive. What she had to. Not what she wanted to. Not even what she thought she needed to.

This wasn't what she was. If she let rage make her into a weapon, however justified the rage, where would it stop? And, once over the line, how much easier the second time? And the time after that?

How many times could she cross the line and still be able to cross back?

How many times had Doc?

Craig had been freed, but the armory was still in enemy hands.

She had a mission to complete and people to get out alive.

When she let the rage go, her knees nearly buckled.

"Turn off the gravity." Another mouthful of blood spat away from the implant. "Open the doors."

Gunny, you're not suited up. Neither of you.

Craig had reached her side. Torin sagged against him, breathing shallowly. "Give us three minutes…"

"Five," Craig corrected. And she remembered that Ressk had patched both implants into the ship's signal.

"Five," she agreed. "If we can't get suited up in five minutes, we deserve to blow out with the armory."

Cho reached the air lock.

Torin's good hand closed into a fist around a handful of Craig's overalls. On their way to the lockers, she paused, reached down, and closed Doc's eyes.

In her experience, the dead did not look at peace. They looked dead.

TWELVE

"**O**ut of my way!" Cho pushed past Huirre and slammed both fists down against the air lock's inner hatch. Once. Twice. "Get this thing open! Now!"

"*I'm trying, Captain!*" He could hear the whine of excuses in Dysun's voice. He should never have brought her and her *thytrins* on board. "*But with it slaved to the outer hatch…*"

"I don't fukking care! Get. It. Open!" He couldn't hear anything from the ore docks. Not fighting. Not her boots against the deck coming closer.

"You okay, Captain?"

He turned on Huirre, pleased to see his nose ridges snap shut as he backed up. "Where the fuk were you?" he snarled.

"She killed Doc! I wasn't fukking facing her unarmed. I was going to bring you the *tasik* Doc dropped, but it wasn't working. I tried to get it working." Huirre glanced over his shoulder and pounded on the hatch, but Cho wasn't falling for that *we're in this shit together* crap.

"Liar! Coward!"

"You ran!" Huirre's lips drew back off his teeth. He glanced back toward the outer hatch. "Is she coming after you? The gunnery sergeant?"

"Shut up!" She wanted him dead. She was hurt, but that wouldn't matter. People like her, people like Doc, they just kept coming. "Dysun! Every second I'm in here, you lose ten percent of your share!"

The inner hatch opened.

Yeah, that lit a fire under her ass. "Close everything and get to your board. You, too!" Cho turned far enough to see Huirre slinking out of the air lock. "And later, when this is over…" He layered enough menace into the pause to keep Huirre's nose ridges closed, then he pivoted on one foot and ran for the control room. "Move, damn it!"

Behind him, he heard Dysun ask about Doc. "Dead," Huirre told her.

Dead. Big Bill thought he was winning, but he was wrong. There was an oldEarth saying, *the bigger they were, the harder they fell* and every species Humans had run into since hauling their asses into space had a variation on it. These sorts of sayings became universal for a reason, and Cho was going to fukking prove it.

Big Bill was going down!

"Marines, we are leaving." Arm pressed against the broken rib, Torin struggled to match Craig's stride. He was making good time using the heel of his left foot, but pain of impact was easier to ignore than a potentially punctured lung.

Not a competition, Torin reminded herself silently. It didn't matter if Craig ended up carrying her the rest of the way to the lockers as long as they both got there while breathing remained an option. "Werst, take the *Star* out; rendezvous by the ore docks!"

She's locked down, Gunny!

Of course she was. "Ressk, you said if you took her out of Vrijheid's operating system, the station would kick her clear?"

Yeah, but when we detach from the station, proximity protocols will have the docking computer try and take control whether it has a record of us or not.

And that would give Big Bill control of the *Star*. "Can you lock it out?"

Not without closing down communications.

"What does… never mind." Torin raised a hand Ressk couldn't see. Explanations she wouldn't understand were explanations she didn't need to hear. "All right, shut down the comm. Then the gravity. Open the loading doors. Blow the *Star* free, then get in as close to the ore dock as you can. Mashona, get the grapples on the armory…" Mashona had never used a grapple gun, but she could blow the eye out of the Queen of Spades with anything else, so Torin had no concerns about her being able to fake it. "…and shoot one our way. We'll use it to get back to the lock."

Roger, Gunny.

Gunny, Ressk broke in. *"The Heart is armed."*

"Mashona, you're cleared to return fire."

With the cutting tool, Gunny?

"No, open a window and throw empty beer pouches at them. Yes, with the cutting tool! It's a just a bennie with delusions of grandeur."

Roger, Gunny.

"All right, people, you know what you're supposed to do. Get your thumbs out of your asses and do it!"

Meet you outside, Gunny.

Torin lost the ping of the implants going off-line in her labored breathing. Civilian life had left her appallingly out of shape, but she managed to sound almost normal when she said, "Looks like we're on our own."

"About time," Craig snorted as they limped to a stop at the lockers. "Cramps my style when the kids listen in."

"You have a style?" Torin reached past him for the latch, but he stopped her, fingers closing around her jaw.

"Your head's still bleeding."

"It's a head wound. They do that."

"We need to…"

"Rip a piece off my sleeve."

"What?"

"We just need to stop it from dripping in my eye. Running out of time," she added when Craig opened his mouth to protest.

"Later," he muttered, grabbing the edge of damaged sleeve and tearing a strip free.

At this point, Torin figured *later* referred to enough that there was no time to expand on it. When Craig raised the fabric tentatively toward her face, she took it from him and pressed it down over the cut, the blood on the surrounding skin tacky enough to hold it in place.

He rolled his eyes and yanked the locker open. "This one was Nadayki's. This one... Doc's." His tone said he thought she'd have trouble wearing the latter suit.

She felt closer to Doc than she had to anyone since Craig had been taken.

"You're too tall for Doc's." Torin yanked the suit out of the fill niche and let it pool to the deck, the torso held more or less upright by the tanks. "Fuk. My boots..." Bending was pretty much out of the question.

Craig dropped to one knee and unfastened them. Torin resisted the urge to run her fingers through his hair.

She had hold of the locker, mostly to help her stay standing, when the gravity cut out. Anchored, she folded her legs up and shoved them into the rising suit. Teeth clenched, she started to twist, but Craig's hand crossed in front of hers, reached into the collar, and magged her boots to the deck. After that, it was as simple as getting into an HE suit with a cracked rib and four useless fingers.

At least no one was shooting at her, which made suiting up significantly more fun than on three previous attempts.

Just before she slid her good hand down the sleeve, she reached into the locker and touched the gray plastic suit mount. Her fingers brushed against Craig's as he did the exact same thing.

It felt like the first time she'd smiled in... several lifetimes.

Given the smile, their teeth cracked when Craig leaned forward and kissed her.

Emergency klaxons didn't so much shatter the silence as bludgeon it flat.

"Because I'm just that good," Craig murmured as he pulled away.

Torin bit her lip. Laughing now would shatter the tenuous grip she had on the gunnery sergeant, and her work wasn't done.

The crack of seals breaking, of atmosphere beginning to vent, caused a hindbrain response, but training kicked in before panic, and Torin had her helmet flipped up and sealed before the currents started pulling. Craig may have been born dirtside but he was station raised and had lived his life in space—odds were high he'd sealed his helmet even faster.

The inside of Doc's suit smelled like hartwood, a popular scent for men's toiletries back home on Paradise. At one time or another, both Torin's brothers had used it. She hadn't smelled it on Doc when she'd killed him.

The rush of escaping air had already begun to pull on the outside of the suit when Torin released one boot, twisted, bent her knee, and remagged it to the wall. It was a fight against the equalizing pressure to get the second up, but she managed. Body parallel to the deck, helmet pointed toward the opening doors, she turned her head to see Craig had assumed the same emergency position.

The boots were designed to hold even against an atmospheric pressure of 1.06 kilograms per square centimeter suddenly leaving the station.

Leg bones were not.

The decompression doors were about five centimeters apart, and there was still enough atmosphere in the ore docks that the slam of the wrench across the break rang out loud enough to be heard in spite of the rush of air and helmets. Eight centimeters apart when the first of the Grr brothers hit, nine for the second, ten by the time enough bones had broken to fit them both through the space. When Doc hit a moment later, there was almost no delay—Human bones being so much easier to break than Krai.

Torin felt the bulkhead shake as the armory slammed against the inside of the storage pod. Given that it was nearly as tall as the pod and taller than the door, it was, unfortunately, going nowhere without help.

"Should we be worried about that?"

It seemed Doc had been a little hard of hearing. Torin lowered the volume on his suit comm. "The ship it was on blew up around it. It should be able to survive this."

"Should?"

The doors were at the two-meter mark, and most of the atmosphere had vented. Torin released her boots, used her hands to push off gently, folded her feet under her as she came up on the vertical, and used her legs to shoot toward the ceiling and the cargo runners.

Craig was no more than a second behind her.

Unable to get to them from within, Big Bill would send ships. That was a given. He wouldn't let the armory go without a fight. What was also a given was that venting the volume of atmosphere in the ore dock was enough to force the station computers to make orbital corrections. While that was happening, the docking computer would lock down the clamps to minimize the variables. They didn't have *much* time; hopefully, they had enough.

Reaching the cluster of cables, Torin grabbed one and turned so her boots hit the ceiling. "Where the hell are the controls?"

"Here." Craig flipped the ten-centimeter disk on the end of a cable so Torin could see the controls on its top. *"There's a manual fail-safe on each cable in case something takes out the central controls."*

There was—had been—a war going on. Stations were prime targets.

"Flick the release," he continued, adding action to words, *"Then push off toward the pod. The cable will scroll out with you."*

"What happens if Big Bill cuts the power?" Torin asked as she followed him down.

"We're screwed, so let's hope he doesn't think of it."

"Captain!" Huirre had both hands and a foot working his board. "The docking clamps won't release!"

"The docking computer is in lockdown, Captain. We can't access it."

We, Cho growled silently. Spreading the blame. He wanted to scream at Dysun to keep her fukking hair still.

"There's no way to get free of the station," she added.

"There fukking well is!" Cho slapped his palm down on his board. "Krisk! How much explosives do we have?"

"Why?"

"Why? So I can stuff them up your ass and detonate! Do we have enough to unlock the docking clamps?"

"We do." The engineer sounded bored. When they got out of this, Cho'd give him bored! *"You could always use the emergency blow."*

When Cho looked up, Huirre shrugged. "Use the what?" he demanded.

"It's a last resort in case the station gets attacked and is—oh, I don't know—falling out of orbit. It blows the ship away. Of course, it blows a fukking hole in the station and the atmosphere plus anything lying around loose vents right at the ship, so, like I said, last resort."

"Doors are almost all the way open, Captain." He could see from where he was sitting that Dysun had called up a new screen. So she wasn't completely useless. "The dock has lost atmosphere."

"Well, fuk it, if that's the case, use the blow. I'll send the command to your board. Hang on... Should be showing now."

"How do you know this?" How did he not know this? The *Heart of Stone* was Cho's ship. His. Not Krisk's.

The engineer snorted. *"I helped design the fukking ship for the Navy, didn't I."*

After this was over, he was going to have a talk with Krisk. Pry him out of his engine room and find out why he'd been hiding...

"Captain!" The hatch slammed against the bulkhead, and Almon charged into the control room. "Nadayki's not on board! He's still on the ore docks."

"Then he's dead," Cho said bluntly.

Almon's eyes darkened. "You left him there to die!"

Cho ducked the first wild swing, and then Nat appeared, nose streaming blood, and jabbed a trank into Almon's neck. He staggered sideways and hit the deck hard.

"Bastard slammed a pointy elbow in my face when I tried to stop him." Nat rolled him over with the toe of her boot. "My best guess is he'll be out for a couple of hours. What do you want me to do with him, Cap?"

"Drag him to his quarters and lock him in." Cho stared past Nat at Dysun. If he'd thought her fukking hair had been annoying before, now it was so agitated it seemed every hair moved independently. Her eyes were so dark no orange showed. "Big Bill vented the docks," he said. "Not me. You want to get back at him, avenge Nadayki, you stay at your station and we grab that armory and we come back weaponed up and kick his ass!"

Her hair slowed and her eyes lightened. "Your word that we come back."

"William Ponner thought he could take what was mine. Thought he could tell me what to do. No one does that."

Dysun stared at him for a moment, then took a deep breath and slid back into her seat. "Ready to blow the clamps, Captain."

"We'll make a pirate of you yet," Huirre snorted.

"Fuk you."

"In three, two, one!" Cho sent the codes.

The *Heart of Stone* shuddered, jerked...

"What the hell?"

Torin dove behind the armory as bits of metal and plastic shot toward her. "The *Heart* just exploded the docking clamps and ripped away from the air lock."

"Last resort blow. So as not to go down with a damaged station."

Craig lived on his ship. He should know.

Torin ducked behind the armory, legs drawn up, as pieces of debris ricocheted back, and found herself shoulder to shoulder with Craig. "You okay?"

"So far."

Yeah. She fukking hated zero-g shrapnel in an enclosed space. "Question." They headed back to opposite sides as things cleared. "Is the *Heart* making a run for it, or lining up with the hatch to grab the armory?

"The Heart's *armed, Torin. And Cho's got to be pretty pissed."*

"So the odds are high he'll come back shooting. Let's get this thing clear!"

They'd had to tip the armory onto its side to get it out of the storage pod—the cables, fed around a rod lowered from the runners, were attached at the lower edge of the armory with magnetic pads, and then the cables retracted. It was bit like threading a needle with explosives. Once out, Craig began moving the rod, and the horizontal armory tucked up against it, toward the doors.

Torin would have been happy to just fling it toward open space, but neither the runners nor the cables were set up for that. *Nor for speed*, she growled silently, emerging from yet another duck and cover. Ressk might be able to remove the safety protocols that kept them at a sedate crawl—weightless or not, the usual loads through here had sufficient mass to crush mere flesh and bone—but without Ressk on call, they needed to come up with another solution. "Leave the cables attached so that we have something to hold, but let them run free."

"Let the cables run free? You want us to drag this thing out of here by hand?" Craig sounded incredulous. *"I know you hate to hear this kind of shit, babe, but we're neither of us in great shape."*

Torin no longer felt an urge to comment on the endearment. "Cables have got it moving. Overcoming inertia, that's the hard part. Right now, we could both be missing a leg and still be able to move faster."

"Yeah, but…"

"The *Heart*'s armed, Craig. And Cho's got to be pretty pissed."

"You're a hard person to argue with."

She could hear the smile in his voice, and her lips twitched in response. "You're not the first to say it."

It was going to hurt. Craig's foot. Her ribs. Not to mention assorted mutual bruising. But it was going to hurt a lot less than having either Cho or Big Bill reclaim the armory.

Hurt a lot less than being hit by one of the remaining chunks of blown docking clamp.

Running was an acquired skill in zero g, and the armory skewed slightly sideways as Craig struggled to keep up. Torin adjusted her rhythm, matched her pace to his, and noted silently that the exit was about three times wider than the height of the armory, so even if they went through spinning on the long axis, there'd be room. It'd be the next thing to a clusterfuk, but there'd be room.

"I'm not going to be happy if you puncture a lung."

"Me either."

Craig was panting. Or she was. The sound of labored

breathing filled her helmet, hard to separate into his or hers. Hers might have been a bit wetter. In a military suit, like the one that had saved her life, she'd have hit the foam the moment they cleared the dock and immobilized the broken rib. Unfortunately, without that option, all she could do was clamp her arm against her body and tell herself she'd survived worse. Her right hand, swollen to fill the glove, had immobilized itself.

"Release the clamps on three," she called as they approached the edge of the ore dock. "One. Two. Three!"

As the cables retracted, Torin, Craig, and the armory shot out into space.

"There's the Star*!"*

"And there's the *Heart*." Twisting to look back at the station, Torin could see the flares of half a dozen ships. "Looks like the docking clamps have unlocked."

"Captain! Seven—no nine—ships are launching!"

"ETA?" Cho snapped, hand clamped white-knuckled around the edge of his screen.

Huirre turned to stare. "ETA? They're right *there*!"

"Coat of Brown and *Thegris Tay* are powering weapons! No lock on us yet," Dysun added. "But it's a matter of minutes."

"Nat! Grapples out!"

"Almon was…"

"Almon's unconscious, thanks to you! Get the fukking grapples on that armory!"

Craig caught the line from the *Star* with one hand and Torin with the other as its movement whipped him past her. "Hang on! You can't do this with one hand!"

"Want to bet?" But he felt the tug as she grabbed his tanks and gave thanks she favored practical over posturing. *"We're in Mashona's shot! Move!"*

"Mashona's is not the shot I'm worried about!" What looked like a Navy shuttle retrofitted for Susumi had a line on the *Star*, the armory, and, more importantly, the two of them.

* * *

"Do not let that bastard get the armory!"

Confused, Huirre frowned. "What bastard?"

"Big Bill fukking William Ponner!" Cho snarled, on his feet. How the hell was he supposed to just sit there? He could slave the weapons screen to his board, but a good captain knew when to delegate to those who were more skilled. Who could blow those fukkers into their component atoms! "The ships out there are working for him, but right now, they're all yours!"

Huirre's nose ridges flared. He grinned and danced the fingers of both hands and the toes of his foot across the board.

Instinct had Torin duck her head down in her helmet as the first energy burst flashed by. "I hate being shot at when I can't shoot back!"

"Good thing they're crap shots!"

"They're trying too hard not to hit the station." Well, Big Bill's ships were, she amended as a shot from the *Heart* left an elderly cargo vessel floating dead in space and another sent a di'Taykan design tumbling sideways. Problem was, no matter how good the gunner on the *Heart* might be, more and more ships were pulling away from Vrijheid and, in the end, numbers would tell.

Now she had more points of reference, Torin could see that they were moving toward the *Star* too quickly to be depending on Craig's pulling them in hand over hand. "The line... ?"

"Is being rewound, yeah."

Unable to look back over her shoulder because of the suit, or twist because of her ribs, Torin searched for other lines coming from the ship, other lines that should be hauling in the armory, and couldn't see them.

"Brace for impact!"

"Holy fukking shit, Cap! I got it! I got the fukking armory! First try!"

Cho's lip curled. It was a little fukking big to miss. "Roll it into the cargo bay while we move! Dysun, take the helm and get us out of here! Huirre, keep firing!" he yelled over his helmsman's protests. "Do not let those sons of bitches line up to get a shot at us!"

"Because I was a little busy trying to keep this ship in one piece." Hands still working the board, Mashona glanced toward the air lock just long enough for Torin to see she wasn't going to apologize for not grappling the armory. "I could get you or the armory, Gunny. I chose you."

"Thank you." Craig already had his helmet down, lying against his tanks while Torin was still unsealing hers one-handed.

When it finally dropped, she shuffled toward the board, gravity making the suit one hell of a lot harder to drag around.

"There goes the *Heart of Stone.*" His suit abandoned on the deck, Craig slid into the pilot's chair as Werst slid out, his hands dropping automatically to the controls. "They've got the armory."

Torin had seen Craig pilot the *Promise* through a swarm of enemy vacuum jockeys with pens extended and full of Marines. Seeing him at the controls now made her believe they still had a chance. "Go after them."

"Captain! In another hundred meters, we'll be far enough out for them to target us with the station's gun!"

The station only had one gun, but it was a big one. Originally from a battleship, rumor was Firrg had taken it from a salvage operator in Krai territory and sold it to Big Bill for enough to rebuild her engines and supply her ship for a year. Cho didn't give a fuk about the rumor, but he'd seen a battleship's guns in action and a ship the size of the *Heart* would be vaporized by that kind of firepower. "Nat!"

"I'd like to not slam a big metal box full of weapons through the fukking ship, Cap!"

"Captain!" Dysun's voice had sharpened to near hysteria. "Fifty meters!"

"Speed it up, Nat. We can survive a few dents!" He dropped

back into his chair and pulled up the Susumi equations. "Get ready," he snarled at Dysun and Huirre. "You'll lock your boards on my signal. The moment the armory is on board, we'll fold."

And if the Susumi vortex pulled apart the nearer half of Big Bill's fleet, then that would teach the son of a bitch to try and bring down Mackenzie Cho.

"He's got his Susumi engines on-line!" Craig's fingers danced over the board and, under the touch of an experienced pilot, the *Star* responded by leaping forward and closing the distance to the *Heart*.

"Gunny!" Mashona shifted the aft screen up where everyone could see it. "We're in range of the station's guns... right... now!"

Torin stepped out of the HE suit, leaving it lying on the deck like another body. "Fortunately, in order to hit us, they'd have to shoot through a crowd of their own ships."

One of the ships directly between them and the station's guns flared and disappeared.

"I think they're good with that, Gunny," Ressk pointed out.

Star fields tipped as Craig took evasive action. "We need to get out of here."

"Not without the armory." Teeth clenched, Torin shouldered her way into the crowd around the board and pulled up the long-range scanners. "The *Heart's* grapples have pulled the armory to the cargo doors." She slid her thumb across the board, shifting programs between the dedicated stations. "I've slaved the scanners to the cutter. Mashona, can you hit it?" Mashona had been the best sniper Sh'quo Company had ever seen.

"Hit the armory with a cutter this size? Gunny, it'll..."

"I know." Torin met Mashona's eyes. "Can you hit it?"

"Yes, Gunny."

"Do it!" She snapped the order out with all the force of Gunnery Sergeant Kerr behind it. Her responsibility. Lower lip caught between her teeth, Mashona bent over the controls. Training had her draw in a deep breath and hold it, settling into a moment of perfect stillness before she fired.

* * *

"Cargo doors are closing, Cap!"

"Ha!" Cho entered the Susumi equation and sat back. "We—"

The front port polarized as the *Heart of Stone* exploded, but it wasn't quite fast enough to keep the sudden blast of light, white in the center and blue around the edges, from burning into Torin's retinas. Hand gripping the back of Craig's chair, she blinked away afterimages and tried to keep from feeling triumphant.

Because the feeling had very little to do with keeping the armory out of the hands of pirates and a great deal to do with the knowledge that Mackenzie Cho had just been reduced to his component parts.

"I'm not reading debris!"

"There is no debris!"

"What the fuk was in that thing?"

Mackenzie Cho had just been reduced to his component parts on a subatomic level.

Torin felt Craig's hand cover hers and squeeze. He thought he understood. Maybe he did. One more thing on the list of things they should probably talk about.

He snatched his hand away as the view suddenly went completely opaque. Before he could get his hand back on the board, the radiation wave hit.

And the board died.

"On the bright side," he muttered, hooking his thumbnails under the inert edging and popping it off. "There's no debris. Torin, my…"

"Tools." She nodded her thanks to Werst and passed them forward.

"What are the odds the blast took out the ships behind us?" Werst growled.

The *Star* bucked forward.

"Fuk!" Craig spat the word out. "Feels like we just lost one of the lateral port thrusters!"

"You can tell that from the feel?" Mashona had her hands in

322

place to turn the cutter and fire the moment the board came back.

Craig twisted far enough to grin up at Torin. "Not the first port thruster I've lost in a firefight."

"At least Werst and I are inside this time."

"View was better outside," Werst muttered.

"And you're insane. Move," Ressk added to Mashona. He shoved her out of her seat and slapped his slate down on the board.

"We can't fly with a slate!" Mashona protested, reaching over the chair to keep her hands by the cutter's dead controls.

"But when Ryder has the power back up, I can reroute past damaged parts of the board with it!" Ressk told her.

The *Star* shuddered. Inertial dampers went off.

"Helm's back. Ressk get the rest. I need eyes aft!" Craig dropped the ship straight down. "I can't avoid what I can't see."

Werst ducked under Torin's arm to hold Ressk in place as he worked his slate with his hands and the board with his feet.

Pieces of metal rang against the upper hull.

This time when Craig twisted to look up, Torin reached out and twisted him back toward the board. "What the hell… ?"

"Missile debris," she told him.

"Detonated early," Werst added. "Someone's mounted an XR779 externally."

"Sounded more like a 778," Torin said thoughtfully.

"Yeah, well, either way, Navy needs to keep better track of its toys."

"Not arguing."

"You two are fukking nuts," Craig muttered.

"Comm's back!" Ressk yelled, all four extremities still working.

"Screens or weapons, Ressk." Mashona bumped him with her shoulder. "Why the hell were you working on communications?"

"I wasn't. Came back on its own."

"Nav would be useful." Craig swept two fingers across the screen, fast to the right. "Hang on…"

Torin nearly landed in his lap as the *Star* swung hard to starboard and up on a forty-five-degree angle. The front port was still too dark for stars, but she thought she could see the streaks from an energy weapon move diagonally past. Past was good.

Wait...

"If nav isn't up, and you can't see forward, how are you steering this thing?"

Craig shrugged. "Space is big."

"Yeah, and remarkably full of shit. Ressk!"

"Working on it, Gunny! Nav is... shit!" He slammed his fist down on the board. "Life support is out!"

"What?"

"It's okay! It's back." The first two toes of his right foot tapped out a syncopated rhythm, and a screen popped up. "There's the aft view."

"Screen's got to be burnt!" Mashona protested as everyone stared at the clusters of lights. "Because if those are all ships..."

Torin snorted. "Big Bill offered a station discount to whoever takes us out."

"Fifteen percent off," Craig added, throwing an arm around her hips and pulling her against his side.

Mashona frowned at the scrolling data. "At least the station seems to have stopped shooting."

"Yeah, well, I imagine it's bad for business to blow up too many of your customers."

Nose ridges flared, Werst had a hand cupped around the back of Ressk's head, thumb scraping small circles through the bristles. "We are so screwed."

"This is the Confederation battleship *Berganitan*. Stand down!"

"Or not." Ressk scrambled for the volume.

Mashona expanded the aft screen. "They're scattering."

"But they are not going to be going far, so I am suggesting you are getting yourselves the hell out of here!"

"Presit!" Torin touched the camera still attached to her tunic with the heel of her injured hand.

Craig felt his brows rise pretty much free of any conscious involvement in the motion. "Presit?"

"You are thinking Torin are able to save you alone? Well, you are being wrong."

"Wait. You and Presit?"

Torin's smile looked almost fond. "Turns out we had something in common."

He was fond of the little furball himself, but Presit didn't... Right arm still holding Torin close, he reached across his body and wrapped his left hand around Torin's wrist, pulling her hand away from one of the fasteners on her tunic. "That's a camera? That's an illegal camera."

"So not the time to worry about that," Mashona murmured.

Craig ignored her. "You were filming for Presit? On the station?"

"Although I are not getting visuals when she are wearing the suit," Presit answered before Torin could.

Torin sighed, and Craig suddenly realized just how much of her weight she was resting against him. Her eyes, or at least the one eye not swelling shut, looked as tired as he'd ever seen them. "It's a long story."

"And there are being no time to tell it now. Merik are sending equations to station where Wardens are waiting!"

"Oh, I just bet they're still waiting," Torin growled. "God forbid they should actually do something."

"I are still recording."

"I are not giving a crap."

Smiling, although damned if he knew why because they were deep in crap whether Torin cared or not, Craig let his left hand fall back to the board. "Ressk... ?"

"Diagnostics are back. I've adjusted the parameter equations for damage taken."

Hoping Merik was Presit's pilot and not her PR flunky, Craig added the equation for the destination to Ressk's adjusted equation for the *Second Star* and brought the Susumi engines on-line.

"Merik are saying it are being a good idea to get your thumb out. Although everyone who are watching my vids are knowing that where Gunnery Sergeant Torin Kerr are being, the Berganitan *are being, too, we are not exactly looking like a battle cruiser if they are running long-range scans."*

Resisting the urge to cross his fingers, Craig punched it.

"Five-day fold," Ressk announced.

"Then I think you'd better sit down, Gunny."

Craig glared Werst away from Torin's other side. "I've got her, mate."

"You're not exactly in great shape yourself," the Krai snorted.

The reminder made everything ache as he stood. "I'm good for this."

"She's got herself," Torin muttered but Craig noticed she didn't fight him as he half carried her across the cabin. They needed this. Needed the contact. He eased her into the bunk—a temporary measure, he'd be commandeering the *Star*'s three-by cabin for the two of them as soon as he had looked at her injuries.

"Ow." She caught at his hand as he tried to pull the piece of fabric off her forehead.

"Fine. I'll get a damp cloth and soak it free, you big baby."

Ignoring their audience—Ressk, at least was trying to look like he wasn't watching them—Craig limped across the cabin and opened the hatch to the head.

The young di'Taykan sitting on the closed toilet blinked pale eyes, yawned widely, and muttered, "It's about fukking time. Who the *sanLi* are you?"

Backing up a step, Craig closed the hatch again. Took a deep breath and turned toward the bunk. "Torin, why do we have a di'Taykan in the head?"

"...and while it is true that you have gathered enough information that the *Law*..."

Years of practice allowed Torin to remain expressionless at the Warden's emphasis. If the *Law* hadn't been sitting on its furry ass, the pirates would have been dealt with and Craig would never have been taken.

"...has now moved forward and, working with the both branches of the military has all but eliminated this threat to peace and security in the sector of space shared by Vrijheid Station and, in point of fact, regained Vrijheid Station itself and prosecuted the one who created the false impression it had been destroyed..." One Who Examines the Facts and Draws

Conclusions frowned. Torin suspected he'd gotten lost in his own rhetoric. He shifted slightly, highlights rippling across red-brown fur, and continued before the Niln sitting to his left could interrupt. "It is, however, undeniable that you, in the process of rescuing Civilian Salvage Operator Craig Ryder and preventing a certain criminal element from gaining control of a Marine armory, broke a number of Confederation laws. While the deaths of ex-Private Reerir, ex-Private Tirrik, and ex-Lieutenant Commander Doctor Christopher Stephens could be considered self-defense…"

"And have been judged to be self-defense," Colonel di'Gui Salarji pointed out.

One Who Examines shifted his gaze off Torin and onto the lawyer the Commandant of the Corps had assigned her back before the judgment began. "Yes," he agreed ponderously although, in all honestly, Torin had to admit that *ponderously* was the Dornagain default so she shouldn't read anything into it. "These three instances have been judged to be self-defense, but there remains the assault of the civilian di'Carnibi Nia, abetting the illegal system tap…"

The colonel snorted. "An illegal tap in order to bring down an illegal system."

"Breaking the law to assist the law is still breaking the law, Colonel," Nawazinkah Huerzah pointed out, inner eyelid flicking across both eyes. "If the end is permitted to justify the means, chaos results."

Lanh Ng, the first Human Warden, appointed to ensure Torin's species rights were represented during judgment and clearly less than thrilled by One Who Examines' need to recap the entire proceedings, seemed revitalized by Nawazinkah Huerzah's interruption. He straightened and said, "Look, the decision of the Tribunal's been made, so can we stop arguing about the minutia and get this over with?"

One Who Examines turned and stared down at him. "Minutia makes up the Law."

Ng settled back in his chair and sighed. "Carry on, then."

"As we have not yet completed our business, I will." One Who Examines faced front, opened his mouth, and paused.

"Abetting the illegal system tap," Nawazinkah Huerzah prodded, perfectly deadpan.

"Yes. Also in the issuing of the order to fire on the armory that resulted in the destruction of the *Heart of Stone* and the deaths of ex-Lieutenant Mackenzie Cho, di'Berinango Dysun, di'Berinango Almon, Natalie Forester, Huirre…"

For a moment, it seemed he might continue with the Krai's full name. Krai family names were declarations of lineage and could go on for hours. Torin wasn't the only one relieved when he continued.

"…and the engineer, Krisk."

Colonel Salarji stepped forward, putting herself between Torin and the Tribunal. "The Confederation Marine Corps takes responsibility for those deaths as ex-Gunnery Sergeant Torin Kerr was acting on the Corps' behalf in keeping a sealed armory out of the hands of the criminally insane."

One Who Examines spread his hands, blunt claws clicking against the table. "And yet ex-Gunnery Sergeant Torin Kerr was not a member of the Confederation Marine Corps at the time."

"The Corps allows there is no such thing as an *ex*-Gunnery Sergeant."

Nawazinkah Huerzah's tongue flicked out, Ng covered his mouth, and One Who Examines sighed. "So I have heard. It is then the judgment of this Tribunal, particularly considering the extensive evidence presented by Presit a Tur durValintrisy, that all but the destruction of the *Heart of Stone* may be dismissed under the weight of extenuating circumstances. The destruction of the *Heart of Stone* is a matter for the Confederation Marine Corps to deal with as it, as a body, sees fit. This inquiry is complete."

Torin waited, standing at parade rest a pace behind the colonel's left shoulder as the Tribunal filed out. Then she waited a little longer as the colonel turned and stared, her eyes dark. Torin resisted the urge to reach out and touch the plastic stylus clipped to the side of the colonel's slate.

"Well, that's that," the colonel said at last. "I'd advise you not miss any of your sessions with the Corps' psychologists. And not just for legal reasons."

"Yes, sir."

"Say the word, and the Commandant of the Corps will put you back in uniform."

"My regards to High Tekamal Louden, sir, but my vest is full."

Deep-green hair flicked forward as Colonel Salarji frowned, but after a long moment, she merely said, "Take care of yourself, Gunny."

"Thank you, sir."

Torin waited until she heard the hatch close behind the colonel before relaxing her position. She touched the place a casualty cylinder would rest in a combat vest and closed her eyes. She'd carry Doc out, but the others could go to Hell on their own.

Craig and Presit were waiting for her in the corridor.

Presit made high-pitched clicks as Torin moved into the circle of Craig's arms. Approval, disapproval—Torin neither knew nor cared. She hadn't exactly been under arrest while the Tribunal made its judgment, but with Craig under a separate judgment—that took about fifteen minutes to clear him of any responsibility—the Wardens had insisted they be kept apart.

All things considered, Torin figured she was entitled to a moment, so she buried her face in the curve between Craig's neck and shoulder, breathed in his familiar scent, and hung on tight.

"You okay?" His mouth against her hair, his voice was a soft burr of vibration she felt as much as heard.

"Got offered my old job back. Didn't take it," she added when he stiffened. "And the colonel warned me not to skip out on any therapy."

His laugh held a touch of bittersweet. They'd actually crossed a number of things off the *we need to talk about this* list during the five-day Susumi fold to the MidSector station. "That's one smart colonel."

"Are you two being done with the touching?" Presit snorted, poking Torin in the hip with a claw. "There are still being more documentation to be signing, and I are having better things to be doing than waiting around here to be acting as your witness. I are having awards to be winning."

When Torin turned, Presit had her muzzle raised, teeth very white against the black of her lips. "You got the interview with Big Bill."

"I are having the exclusive," Presit bragged as the three of them started down the corridor. By the time the Navy had reached Vrijheid, most of the pirates had scattered. William Ponner had refused to leave the station, his station, and had been taken. "He are being most cooperative and are being willing to identify those who are been using his station."

"Fifteen percent of them, anyway," Craig said dryly.

"You are not being funny," she snapped. "Remember, I are having to be turning over to the Wardens everything Torin are having shot for me on the station..."

"It was an illegal camera."

"It are having been an illegal station!" Presit extended her protest all the way down to the station's financial office, covering the failures of media law, media ethics, and the personal failure of Sector Central News to defend genius.

"You sure about this?" Craig asked, thumb running along the inert plastic trim of the desk as the financial officer sent the final numbers to their slates.

Torin shook her head. She didn't know how Craig had got the idea she didn't want to be paid for risking her ass for the greater good. It was how she used to make a living after all. "I'm sure."

The mining cartels that had lost ore drones to the Vrijheid pirates had put together an obscenely large reward. Presit had skimmed a little off the top, but the rest was Torin and Craig's to divide as they saw fit.

"And you're sure that's all you want?" Torin asked the reporter, thumb over the screen.

"Any more," Presit sniffed, indicating that Torin should close the deal, "and I are being in danger of losing my status as being an objective observer."

"And you've already made close to this by licensing an interview you haven't shot yet," Craig pointed out.

"I are having to overpay staff," Presit told him, silvered claws glittering as she waved him off. "It are not like I are spending it all on manicures."

Craig added his thumbprint beside Torin's, then Presit added hers to the master file, and a sizable portion of the reward disappeared to cover bills already incurred.

"Easy come, easy go," Craig sighed as they stood.

"You think that was easy?" Torin snorted. Craig grinned, and they both let their fingers linger over the plastic switch cover as they left the office.

"You are letting me know the next time you are riding to the rescue," Presit said as they walked her to the first vertical. "I are being there."

Torin closed her hand around Craig's. "There won't be a next time."

Presit paused at the hatch, head cocked, Torin's reflection in her mirrored glasses. "Not like this, I are hoping for that, too. But..." She waited until a pair of Rakva exited, chattering about yeast cakes, then her ears flicked forward. "I are not doubting that there are being a next time of some kind. You two are not being destined for having a quiet life."

"You think Presit's right?"

"About us not being destined for a quiet life?" Torin shrugged. "I think precedent agrees with her. I'm not sure I do."

None of the verticals in Admin went all the way to the docking level, so they found one that descended as far as the atrium, shared one strap, and ignored the glances and giggles from rising office workers. Given that more rumors had been generated in verticals than in bars, they maintained a companionable silence until they flipped out into the three-story open area at the center of the station.

A few people might have recognized them, but the size of the station and the crowds granted a certain anonymity.

"If Presit is right," Craig said thoughtfully as they crossed to the vertical that would take them to the lower levels. "I don't want to be seen as the victim next time."

"You got grabbed and tortured by pirates," Torin pointed out.

"Sure, but I delayed the opening of the armory. You might not have gotten there in time if I hadn't."

"True."

"So let's not do that again."

"Deal."

They walked another couple of meters in silence, then Craig let out a breath Torin hadn't realized he'd been holding and said, "You know, I was thinking just before Presit showed up pretending to be the *Berganitan* that we needed a miracle, and I half thought that…"

When his voice trailed off, Torin had no difficulty finishing the sentence. "You half thought that Pedro and the rest would have realized they were wrong, that they should have listened to me and come after you, that at the last moment, a ragtag fleet of salvage ships would blast out of Susumi and wreck vengeance on the pirate fleet that dared to go after one of their people."

He half laughed as they detoured around a cart selling fake H'san ceramics. "Yeah."

"Me, too."

"I figured, given your reference to a ragtag fleet and all." After another half dozen steps, he added, "That's not who they are."

"They?"

Craig threw an arm around her shoulders. "Seems like it might be who I am. And don't worry, I'll get your pension back from Pedro when we return the *Second Star*."

Torin hadn't been worried. She looked forward to facing Pedro and the rest with Craig at her side.

As they reached the verticals, he turned to face her, mouth twisted. "I would have gone after him."

"I know."

Werst, Ressk, Mashona, and Alamber were waiting for them in the Legless Worm.

"Did they just randomly cram two words together to name this place or what?" Torin muttered, sliding into a seat. She picked up the six-centimeter plastic KC-7 that had clearly come out of Alamber's glass and had probably once skewered a piece of fruit. She thought about asking what the hell he was drinking, and decided she didn't want to know.

"*Promise* is almost ready to go." Torin's slate pinged as Ressk sent over the specs. "All the damage has been repaired, and the new quarters have been added where the pens were. Just the new converter to hook up, and we're good."

She scrolled through the schematics and turned to look at Craig in the chair beside her. "So we're really going to do this?"

It hadn't been that long ago that sharing the limited resources of a tiny one-man ship had given Craig panic attacks. Space was unforgiving, and he was used to being alone. But then, the *Promise* wasn't a tiny one-man ship anymore. And he wasn't alone.

He took a long swallow of the beer just set down in front of him, and nodded. "We're really going to do this."

The Wardens had brought the *Promise* to this MidSector station as evidence. It had been pure dumb luck that the station included the sector's second-largest dockyard. The Wardens had been convinced to pay to have the aft end of the *Promise* extended and a shuttle pad added because the Wardens had decided to put them to work.

"It appears to be obvious, ex-Gunnery Sergeant Kerr, that the end of the actual hostilities with the Primacy, regardless of how much fighting continues to occur, has created social voids that we as a government organization are not equipped to investigate. Speed of investigation appears to be becoming essential when gathering certain facts for later deliberation. When you are finished with this inquiry, we have an offer for you and your companions."

"And we're really going to do this," Craig continued, "because I got the impression it wasn't an offer any of us would be permitted to decline."

"Good point," Torin admitted, raising her glass.

"*Any* of us?" Alamber leaned back, all loose limbs and promises, but Torin could see the insecurity under the *more di'Taykan than thou* posture. He had no family, they'd destroyed the life he'd managed to find for himself, and he desperately needed somewhere to belong. Someone to tell him what to do.

For her own peace of mind, Torin planned to wean him off the latter need as soon as possible. "I'm not turning you loose, Alamber. So, yeah, any of us."

Craig's shoulder bumped hers. "Are we ready for children?" he sighed.

Alamber's eyes lightened even further. "I was thinking threesome."

"They're really not ready for that," Werst snorted.

Torin threw the plastic KC-7 at him.

He snatched it out of the air with a foot and threw it back. "Your round, Gunny."

Torin beckoned the server over but kept the little plastic gun when he cleared the glasses. Her assigned Corps therapist would probably have a field day about how much more comfortable she felt having even a pretend weapon close to hand.

"So…" Alamber took a long swallow of his new drink, the same pale blue as his hair. "I keep meaning to ask, back on Vrijheid, I know Big Bill had the docking clamps locked, so how did you really break your ship free of the station?"

"Easy." Ressk looked pleased with himself, but Torin figured he had the right. "First, I disabled the proximity alerts, then I removed her from the sysop, and the station kicked us free."

Alamber shook his head. "Uh-uh. I know that story, but you're totally talking through your ass if you expect me to believe it. Big Bill had sleeper programs in place to prevent that." Generally, it wasn't easy to spot a di'Taykan rolling his eyes, but Alamber made the motion obvious. "Come on, seriously, it's not like you were the only ones there with brains. Big Bill was an ass but a clever one."

"Yeah, but…"

"No, but." Alamber pulled out his slate. "Link up. I'll sketch out the defense programs, then you tell me how you got past them."

They all watched silently as Ressk stared down at his screen. "That isn't…"

"I'm not done," Alamber sighed. "Keep your boots on." He sketched with the back of a painted fingernail instead of a stylus. "There. You know, roughly."

Ressk's nose ridges actually fluttered as they opened and closed. "He's right."

"Of course I'm right."

"I didn't even see that code. The docking clamps shouldn't have released." Ressk didn't look pleased with himself anymore. If Torin had to name his expression, she'd say *freaked* covered all bases.

"Yeah, but they did," Werst reminded him.

"So the question becomes *how* did they release?" Mashona drained her glass and added, frowning, "Or maybe the question is why."

"Way I see it…" Alamber snapped his slate back onto his belt. "…the only way you…" He paused, his hair flicked forward. "…*we* could've gotten free was if there was what amounted to a physical failure of a part of the clamp at exactly the time you needed it to give way. Exactly. Bottom line, you guys… us guys…"

"We." Mashona held his gaze until he nodded.

"Okay. *We* were either a part of the biggest fukking coincidence ever or we have the kind of luck that says *we're* loved by the gods."

"What gods?" Werst wondered.

He shrugged. "Does it matter?"

Torin looked down at where the little plastic KC-7 had been. Then she checked the floor in case she'd knocked it off the table. "Alamber, what were those docking clamps made of?"

"What were they made of? Same thing every other docking clamp is made of. Metal. Ceramic. Plastic." He looked around the table, eyes darkening. "What?"

ACKNOWLEDGMENTS

Apparently, it takes a village to get the holder of a B.A.A. through high-school physics. I'd like to thank Bill Roper, Bill Sutton, Tom Wiegand, Paul Kwinn, Bruce Schneier, Peter Alway, Vicki Farmer, and a good chunk of my live journal friends list whose full names I don't actually know, for helping me bounce Torin through vacuum. Also, thanks to Sgt. S.K.S. Perry for adjusting Presit's signal so it couldn't be discovered.

Special thanks to Violette Malan who helped with Pedro's Spanish and warned me that I might have to defend my choices. Languages drift, people. That's my defense.

All help gratefully received. Any mistakes that made it into publication are my own.